The Mark of the Salamander

Also by Justin Newland

The Genes of Isis
The Old Dragon's Head
The Coronation
The Abdication

The Mark of the Salamander

BOOK 1 OF THE ISLAND OF ANGELS

Justin Newland

The Book Guild Ltd

First published in Great Britain in 2023 by
The Book Guild Ltd
Unit E2 Airfield Business Park,
Harrison Road, Market Harborough,
Leicestershire. LE16 7UL
Tel: 0116 2792299
www.bookguild.co.uk
Email: info@bookguild.co.uk
Twitter: @bookguild

Typeset in 10.75pt Adobe Garamond Pro

Printed and bound in the UK by TJ Books Limited, Padstow, Cornwall

ISBN 978 1915853 271

British Library Cataloguing in Publication Data.
A catalogue record for this book is available from the British Library.

To those brave men, all 164 of them, who set out to sail around the world, including:

Francis Drake, admiral and captain of the *Pelican* and the *Golden Hind*.

Little Nele, aka Nelan Michaels, ordinary seaman.
Great Nele, aka Great Nelan Andersen, master gunner.
Diego, Francis Drake's *cimarrón* manservant.
Thomas Drake, Francis Drake's brother.
Thomas Doughty, gentleman adventurer.
John Doughty, Thomas Doughty's brother.
Francis Fletcher, chaplain.
John Wynter, vice admiral and captain of the *Elizabeth*.
Thomas Moon, captain of the *Christopher*.
John Thomas, captain of the *Marigold*.
John Chester, captain of the *Swan*.
Thomas Blacollers, boatswain.
Robert Winterhay, surgeon.
Thomas Cuttill, shipmaster.
Oliver, master gunner.
John Brewer, bugler.
Luke Adden, able seaman.
William Horsewill, ordinary seaman.
Richard Minivy, ordinary seaman.

Now let the story begin.
And it has been said *Ex Insula Angelorum.*
From the Island of Angels, no less.
For always was it so and always thus to be.

The Wonder Story Group, *The Tales of the Men of the Sea*

There is a tide in the affairs of men,
Which, taken at the flood, leads on to fortune;
Omitted, all the voyage of their life,
Is bound in shallows and in miseries.

William Shakespeare, *Julius Caesar*

Sic Parvis Magna.
Out of small things, great things arise.

The motto on the arms of Sir Francis Drake

1

The Fire

The village of Mortlake, near London, England
31st March 1575

Nelan stepped carefully over the planks of the wooden jetty, moist from an early morning shower. He boarded the wherry bobbing in the flow of the spring tide. The wherry master grinned, showing a tranche of rotting black teeth behind a ragged salt-and-pepper beard. As far as Wenceslaus was concerned, this passed as a morning salutation.

Wenceslaus let go of the rope and kicked the jetty with the sole of his tattered boot, shoving the boat into the flow of the River Thames. As usual, the wherry master's breath stank of ale, and to enhance the delights of the morning, he let out a huge fart. As with everyone else in England, more vacant air than solid food filled the wherry master's guts. Well, it was Maundy Thursday, the last day of Lenten fasting. Wenceslaus eased out the oars and bent his back to the task, and with each pull he emitted a low grunt, like the wild boars that roamed the woods near Nelan's Mortlake home.

"Tide's on the full, little master," said Wenceslaus.

"'Tis that," Nelan said.

Reaching the middle of the flow, Nelan glanced back at his house. Next door and nestling on the bank was their neighbour's place – a large, rambling house just west of the church between it and the river. The natural philosopher and celebrated astrologer to the court of

Queen Elizabeth, Dr John Dee, lived there. Dr Dee was a great friend of Nelan's father Laurens, who had encouraged Nelan to visit Dee's house for private tuition in matters both sacred and secular. Just the other week, Dee had agreed to cast Nelan's horoscope, but before he could reveal his findings, Dee's second wife had died. And on the day of her funeral, the Queen herself had paid him a surprise visit. How Nelan mixed with such exalted company!

Today was a special day: the last school day before Easter. Nelan pulled out a crumpled broadsheet that Dee had recently given him. It was dated March 1575, and depicted an elegant city with tall spires protruding into the heavens. One more term at school, and Nelan would be off to university and strolling down Oxford's alleys. The time was ripe for him to make his own way in life.

They passed wherries tacking upriver, and avoided ferries crossing from bank to bank. Wisps of mist rose from the glassy swell. Wenceslaus stopped by the hamlet of Sneakenhall to pick up two other boys from Nelan's school. Dressed in doublets of fine Spanish cloth, leggings, and leather shoes, they stood behind their stepfather, St John of Southampton, or San Juan de Antón in Spanish. They sniggered and pointed their fingers at Nelan, but that wasn't unusual. The brothers climbed into the wherry. Nelan had been born in Sangatte, Picardy, Northern France, while Guillermo and Pedro harked from Seville, Spain. They attended the same school and were of a similar age. They had that in common. But Nelan couldn't stand the boys; nor they him. They had that in common too.

Wenceslaus disliked their rivalry. "Now, be civil to them both, young Nelan," he warned.

"I'll try," Nelan murmured.

"You do just that."

Nelan said, "Good morrow, Guillermo, Pedro. The Lord be with you both."

"I want nothing to do with your Lord!" Guillermo snarled. "Now move over, you stupid!" He pushed Nelan off the seat.

"Oi!" Wenceslaus intervened. "Stop it. Hell's teeth. Every mornin', every month, every year. Always the same. You two spar like a pair of fightin' cocks. An' old Wenceslaus gotta keep yous apart."

2

He was right, Nelan thought. But what could he do? In Queen Bess's England, the law compelled ordinary folks to follow the new Protestant religion and forgo the old Catholic one. Nelan was Protestant. The brothers were Catholic. He and they were like oil and water. They fought in words on the wherry, just as their respective armies warred in Europe and clashed all over the New World.

A pall of silence shrouded the rest of the trip around the Barnes–Chiswick oxbow. As Wenceslaus grunted and groaned, passing more air from his orifice, he rowed the wherry past Putney and then Battersea Fields. Nelan stretched his legs. He was a shorty, and they barely reached half the length of Guillermo's, who sat, arms folded, avoiding eye contact. Pedro mimicked his older brother, brooding beneath a dark, forbidding frown.

As the wherry moored by the Westminster jetty, Nelan and Guillermo stood up at the same time, rocking the boat. Wenceslaus scowled at them, which annoyed Guillermo, who took a leap. The jetty was still moist from the overnight rain, and he slipped and smashed his knee.

As Guillermo winced with pain, Wenceslaus passed comment and more air. "Silly boy. Serves you right; it does that."

Rubbing his knee, Guillermo snapped at the wherry master, "Me, I am Guillermo. You ferry me and my brother to school and back. You speak to me like that again, I tell my stepfather. You know he is very important man, ¿cierto?"

"Beggin' your pardon, young master," Wenceslaus said, doffing his cap and clutching it to his chest.

As far as Nelan was concerned, this was more respect than the boy deserved for his rudeness and arrogance. But Guillermo's stepfather was a senior figure with influence at Elizabeth's court. A word in the local constable's ear, and Wenceslaus could easily have spent the day battened down in the stocks at Putney market.

Pedro jumped out of the wherry and helped his brother hobble along the landing quay. Passing the woodshed, they headed towards an imposing brick building boasting tall, graceful spires and elegant stone etchings: Westminster Abbey. Next to the abbey lay the entrance to the newly formed Westminster School. There, the school's steward, a burly man with a black beard and black cap, stood by and greeted them one and all.

Nelan joined the rest of the school for the church assembly. Pastor Christopher, the school's minister, conducted the morning service, which concluded with the singing of Psalm 23, 'The Lord is My Shepherd'. Nelan mouthed a silent prayer to the Lord. If only He would shepherd him to the place where he could deal with Guillermo. Because of late, the Spanish boy had grown increasingly hostile towards Nelan, and it frightened him.

After Mass, Nelan attended lessons in Greek, Latin and French. Then came rhetoric, astronomy, and classical studies touching on the School of Athens and the philosophers Plato and Aristotle.

On another day of fast, Nelan's stomach rumbled like the eruption of Vesuvius. Dusk drew in its gentle wings. To celebrate the end of term, all the boys ran out of class and jumped in the air with elation. Nelan said a prayer of thanksgiving in the abbey, then headed towards the river to find a wherry to take him home. He spotted Guillermo talking to Pastor Christopher by the school entrance, and then the boy turned and headed Nelan's way. To avoid any confrontation, Nelan darted into the woodshed.

In the shed stood a solid oak table. Its numerous scratches and indents bore testament to a life of long and dedicated service. It was as old as King Henry VIII, the father of Elizabeth, the present Queen. In the middle of the table was a ceramic bowl, like the fruit bowl on the cedar table in Nelan's home, except that this one had no fruit in it. Twists of straw and a scattering of dead leaves bedecked the top of the table. The shed was crammed on both sides with logs, kindling and twigs, various tools, saws and axes.

Nelan's right palm itched. He scratched the source of the irritation: three wavy vertical lines beneath his middle finger. His father had scolded him when he was a child, saying that, because he never washed his hands, the lines were like three wisps of smoke rising from his smelly paws. Nelan was unconvinced. Either way, he scratched his palm. He'd always wondered how he'd got the lines. Were they a kind of birthmark? His father had never told him. And what did it mean when they itched at certain times, like now?

From outside the shed, he heard the distinctive sound of Guillermo's limp. His heart sank. The door squeaked open. Nelan ducked beneath the table.

Too late, because he heard a voice crow, "Come out, *muchacho*!"

Nelan crawled out from under the table. Guillermo lurked on the other side.

"I'm not a baby. I'm a man!"

"You not a man! A man, he stand up like a pole. He face the world. Insects, they creep along the ground!" Guillermo thundered, smashing his fist on the table with so much force that it shuddered under the impact.

"What's got into you? Are you possessed by a *diablo*?"

Guillermo put his palms on the table and leaned towards Nelan, his eyes glaring like fire. "My stepfather says all Protestants are heretics, and we must cleanse the world of their sin."

"You Spanish do that anyway. All around the world you spread torture and cruelty! Spain is pain."

"No! Spain is top, highest country in world. You, you're a low country boy. You're from the nether regions. Ha!" Guillermo laughed at his pun.

"Yes, I lived in the Netherlands… until you Spanish invaded, forcing my family to seek refuge here!"

"Bah!" Guillermo gritted his teeth, rubbing his forefinger and thumb together. "You are a flea, a tiny flea, and I, Guillermo de Antón, am going to squash you!"

"I may be small, but I'm not *that* small," Nelan said, trying to make light of the insult.

"You're – how you say? – seventeen years old. I meet you when you come here six years ago. But after that, you never grow. Not like me and Pedro. We big, strong Spanish boys. For King Felipe, we build a world empire."

The spite flowed thick and fast. As much as he wanted to fight, Nelan swallowed his bile and lurched around the table.

"Ha! You *cobarde*!" Guillermo sniped, blocking his way.

Nelan faced his nemesis. "Enough! I'm no coward!"

Quick as a flash, Guillermo pulled out a small canvas bag from the pouch hanging from his belt. He emptied its contents, a brownish powder, into the ceramic bowl. The powder whiffed of sulphur.

"What on earth are you doing?"

5

"You'll see, *amigo*," Guillermo scowled. With both hands he scooped up the twists of straw and dried leaves and dropped them on top of the brown powder.

"Wait. You're not going to…?"

Guillermo pulled two strike-a-light irons and a flint from his pouch and brandished them in front of Nelan's face. "*Sí, amigo*. I am," he said with a mischievous grin.

"Let me out!" Nelan cried, and tried to push past the Spanish boy again.

With a demonic expression on his face, Guillermo shoved him aside, and Nelan fell against the log pile, but got up as quickly as he could.

"It's gunpowder! You'll kill us both!"

"No! I run out the door. You heretic, you die! It's Easter. It's the time to cleanse the world of sin!" Guillermo crushed an iron against the flint. A solitary spark leapt from the flint, but didn't catch the strands of straw and leaves. He shoved one of the irons back into his pouch, then crunched the other against the flint, squeezing out another spark.

Thankfully, the gunpowder failed to ignite – or so Nelan thought. But he smelled burning. A spark had lit a piece of straw next to the ceramic bowl. Again, he rushed at the madman. Flint in hand, Guillermo raised his fist. Nelan ducked to avoid the blow. Guillermo lost his balance and fell, dropping the iron and flint. He winced with pain as he clutched his knee, then crawled along the floor.

The door was flung open. Two men stood there: the school's steward and Pastor Christopher. Nelan swept up the iron and flint. The gunpowder was going to ignite. The men blocked the exit. A small blue flame leapt from the straw across the open space and, as if drawn to the bowl of gunpowder, dropped into it. The shed was about to explode. *Think. Quick.* Nelan crawled across the floor and dived between the men's legs before scrambling through the open door.

The world ground to a shuddering halt. Everything slowed, like the actor he'd seen at one of those new theatres in the city who moved at a snail's pace. A burst of flame followed a massive explosion. The force of the blast threw him backwards. Winded and half blinded, he crawled away from the scorching heat. Hungry flames devoured the kindling, sending orange-yellow embers into the dusk. Had it not been so frightening, it would have been beautiful. The flames crackled and spat as the logs caught fire. Nelan's ears were ringing, but the sound was muted. His head spun like a top. The burning seared into his mind's eye.

As the flames engulfed the shed, it rained hot embers, covering the steward in soot. The pastor crouched on the ground, holding his head. The explosion must have thrown them clear. The blast had also ejected Guillermo, but only just. Smoke rose from his ruined clothes into the dry, early evening air. The Spaniard lay on the ground near the blazing shed, his mouth open as if he were shouting or crying. Nelan could hear no sound coming from his mouth. Pedro hared across the yard towards them.

Dazed and confused, Nelan hugged his knees, rocking back and forth. It eased the pain. Because in his imagination, he saw painful, destructive pictures from his past. In this vision, he was in an earlier time, another town, a different country altogether. It felt strange, unreal. It was as if he watched the scene unfold from a distance. He stood at the edge of a crowd. They yelled and shook their fists. They shouted, but not in English. He was young and small. Even on tiptoe, he couldn't see over the tops of the heads of those in front of him. He climbed on top of a barrel to get a better view. Before the heaving crowd, soldiers lashed two men and a woman to three wooden posts. They tied the woman to the middle one. She wore a black headscarf from which a loose strand of brown hair protruded. Nelan yearned to tuck it into her scarf, but he couldn't. Tears rolled down her cheeks. Her chin trembled. She glanced towards him and then turned away. She moved her shoulders, wrenched her arms, and twisted her legs, but then fell as still as a scarecrow. Had she accepted her fate? No. She must never do that. She must keep struggling to get free. Nelan desperately wanted her to escape and take him with her.

A wooden crucifix hung from the top of each post. Perhaps Jesus peered down from the cross at what was about to transpire. Did He know that this was being done in His name? Why didn't He stop it? A crow glided over the heads of the crowd – once, twice – and then squatted on top of the woman's post. Black wings, black beak, black squawk; an omen that the woman's soul was about to fly off into the beyond. She was going to surrender her soul. But was it to Jesus or to the black crow? No one answered that question. Nelan wished they would.

A military cohort appeared from behind him. Pikes pointing up and frowns pointing down, the soldiers pushed through the crowd. Following them came a man wearing a black cloak. A pair of narrow eyes looked out from two tiny slits in the hood. The cohort stopped by the woman tied to the pole. Nelan stared at the pole and the woman. It was no ordinary pole. She was no ordinary woman. Kindling, logs, bits of rags, and curved struts from broken barrels nestled at the base of the post. It was a fire in waiting. This was an *auto-da-fé* or an act of faith, though he doubted there was much faith involved.

The image of the woman and the pole shattered, and he was jolted out of his reverie.

"Nelan! Nelan Michaels!" someone called.

Nelan turned around.

"Hell's teeth," the steward said. "What are you doing sitting there like a stone?"

The huntsman accompanied him, along with a clutch of schoolmasters and a legion of boys drawn by the roar of the explosion and the spectacle of the fire. The huntsman's wife tended to Guillermo. Pastor Christopher got down on his knees and prayed for the boy. Pedro cradled his brother's head in his hands. Wisps of smoke rose from Guillermo's jerkin as he shrieked in agony.

"Quick. Move the boy to the infirmary. Get a hand cart," the steward said to the huntsman, and then added, "Boys, get in a line. We need water."

They passed buckets from hand to hand, scooping water from the river and dousing the fire, then sending the empty vessels back to be refilled. The woodshed resembled the burning bush; an eternal flame, a testament to the Lord's fury and His power to cleanse the furious and bring down the proud. From where he stood, at twelve paces, Nelan felt the heat of the fire. He didn't move as wave upon wave scorched his face and arms. The flames were a marriage of reds, yellows and golds. Deep within the inferno's inner sanctum, they were coloured a lithe violet blue.

Pedro confronted him, his face a picture of anguish. "You. You let my brother burn!"

8

"I did?" Nelan murmured.

"¡Sí! I saw it with my own eyes. My own brother. His clothes burn. And you. You did nothing to help him. You wanted to give pain to my brother!"

Guillermo screamed and writhed on the ground. The flames didn't care. They burned anything and everything. They were ravenous, with neither mercy nor pity.

Nelan shook himself and said, "I-I don't know. I-I would've done. I didn't mean it. I don't know what happened to me."

"You always hate him," Pedro said, jabbing a finger at him. "You want him to suffer. Happy now?"

The huntsman approached with a rickety handcart and said, "You boys, help me get the lad onto the cart."

Nelan went to help. Pedro blocked him.

"Let me help. I want to."

"Stay away from him!" Pedro said, staring him down.

Carefully, the men lifted Guillermo. He yelled as they loaded him onto the cart. Nelan had heard screams like that before – from a fox snared in a trap.

"You will pay for this!" Pedro growled.

Nelan shrank back. *I defended myself. And that dreadful vision... Why doesn't anyone understand that?*

The huntsman hauled the cart across the courtyard towards the infirmary, followed by his wife and Pedro.

"How could you ignore the boy's distress?" the steward said.

"It... It wasn't my fault," Nelan stammered. "Guillermo's mad. He wanted to blow me up. He lit the gunpowder and wanted to leave me in there."

"Is that what you saw, Pastor?" the steward asked. But before Pastor Christopher could answer, the steward added, "Because that's not what I saw."

"But... he started the fire. He wanted to kill me," Nelan murmured.

"No! When I arrived, you stood over Guillermo, who lay on the floor. You'd hit him!"

"I didn't. You must believe me."

"I saw you clutching the strike-a-light iron and flint. You must've started the fire."

Nelan bit his lip. A silent scream rose from the depths of his being. "No! It wasn't like that!"

"Go home, and don't come back!" The steward shooed him away like a fly.

"What d'you mean?"

"You're expelled."

"But I've only one more term before—"

"We don't want the likes of you at Westminster School."

Nelan slouched off towards the river, as low as he'd ever felt since arriving in England. He found Wenceslaus and slumped down on the wherry seat. Plunging his hands into his purse, he fingered the iron and the flint – a lot of good they'd do him now.

By the time they pulled into the jetty at home, the cloak of sadness and misfortune weighed heavily on his shoulders. He hauled himself out of the wherry. He felt like a creature dredged up from the ocean's depths, thick with sludge and bound with seaweed. Now he had to gird himself to tell his father. With hard steps on grassy soil, he trudged along the path from the jetty to his house.

The maidservant told him that his father had gone to the city on business and would return early the next day. Nelan waited in his room. His clothes stank of fire and smoke, evoking memories of the explosion. Images of the woman tied to the stake flashed through his mind. Her screams beat against his ears… or were they Guillermo's yells of pain? From his north-facing room, he could hear the swishing, gurgling sounds of Old Father Thames as it raced towards its destiny in the estuary. The river had ferried him to Westminster School and back for nigh on seven years. And in this, his last school year, his dream to attend university in the autumn had gone up in flames. His head sank low. The Lord was pitted against him. For this to happen to him, he must have committed some awful sin. Either way, he needed justice and a pardon, and quick. Damn Guillermo. And once and for all, he needed to know the identity of the woman tied to the Inquisition's stake, lest her image haunt him for the rest of his days.

He must have dropped off to sleep, because when he awoke, the first slithers of dawn slanted across the river, and he heard his father's booming voice echo around the rafters of the house and the front door slam shut.

Nelan knocked on the door of his father's study. Laurens Michaels was a bulk of a man; as tall as an oak tree and just as thickset. His bald head showed his years. Dressed in his favourite dark green velvet doublet, he dominated his desk.

When Nelan had explained what had happened, his father got up and adjusted his flat, black Anglican hat. Pacing the floor, he asked, "Nelan, what's happened is terrible. But why did Guillermo threaten your life? Tell the truth, as God is our witness."

"He said his father wanted him to cleanse the world of heretics."

"So, it concerned religion. I might have known," Laurens said with a sigh. "I've always tried to be neighbourly to the St John family, but to no avail. By coming to England, I hoped we'd escape Spanish persecution. I was wrong."

"We left the Netherlands… what about…?" For a moment, Nelan's head spun. He turned away from his father's gaze and instead stared at the painting behind his father's head: the hamlet of Sangatte with its white, sandy coastal dunes. It brought back memories of his mother; her smell and her touch. He felt her staring at him from one of the cottages in the painting. He jerked his head away and looked through the study's solitary window. On this cloudless day, he could see all the way to the bank on the other side of the river.

"What about what, Nelan?" his father repeated.

Once and for all. Nelan's voice broke in his throat. "Mother."

"What about your mother?"

"What happened to her?"

"I told you already. She was English. Her maiden name was Pickford. She fell into the arms of Our Lord before we left the Netherlands."

"Yes, I know, Father. But you've never told me *how* she died."

This time, his father averted his gaze and studied the wainscoting.

"I'm seventeen; you don't need to protect me anymore."

"I'm going to tell you—"

There was a loud rapping on the front door. The door opened, squeaking on its hinges. Footsteps marched up to the study door. The footman hauled it open.

"Sir."

"Yes? Who is it?" Laurens asked.

"Dr Dee."

"Dr John Dee?"

"Yes, sir, the same. He's on the porch."

"It must be important for him to call at this time of the morning. Well, don't stand there, man. Show him in."

"Sir."

Dr Dee had a milk-white beard and was a tall, wiry man with the stare of a lighthouse. He wore a black cap and a long black gown with hanging sleeves, crisp in the morning's rays. "Good morrow to you both," he said in a husky voice. "May the Lord be with you."

"And with you, Dr Dee," Laurens replied.

"I cannot stay long; I must return to my experiments," Dee said. He appeared to drift around the room, touching the spines of the books on the shelves and then examining a portrait of Laurens attending a Low Church Calvinist meeting.

"Our condolences over the demise of your dear wife," Nelan's father said.

"Thank you. I've been in mourning these last days."

"She's resting in the arms of Our Lord," Laurens said.

"Have you been able to cast my horoscope, m'lord?" Nelan asked. "I'm so excited to hear your interpretation of it."

"Yes, I've just finished it, and that's why I come bearing urgent news," Dee said. Every word he spoke sounded like a Sunday sermon. "I'm here to warn you that over these two days – yesterday and today – the planets Mars and Saturn figure prominently in your chart. Has anyone in the family recently died violently?"

"That's extraordinary! No, not in our family," Nelan said, "but yesterday evening an explosion badly hurt one of the St John boys."

"I see." Dee nodded. "There's also an unfortunate opposition in Libra, the scales of justice."

"What does that mean?" Nelan asked.

"I suspect it means that the law is now involved in this case, and that there's a warrant out for your arrest."

"What? That's not justice; that's injustice," Nelan yelled.

"So, we'll wait for the constables, then," Laurens said.

"Father, they can't arrest me. Only the pastor and the steward witnessed the incident. On their evidence, they'll hang me. I'm sorry, but with the news Dr Dee has brought, I must leave."

"If you've not sinned, the Lord will protect you."

"The Lord might, Father, but the law might not. I must clear my name."

There was a loud knock at the front door. A cry rang out: "The Queen's constables here. Open up in the name of the law."

"Well, that was prescient, Dr Dee," Laurens said. "They're here already."

There were voices at the front door, and then a knock at the study door. It was the footman.

"What is it?" Laurens asked him.

"The constables are here with a warrant to arrest Master Nelan for murder."

"Let them in," Laurens said.

"No, don't!" Nelan cried.

"Let. Them. In," Laurens snapped.

The footman left the study.

"Then I must go," Nelan said.

"No," his father replied. "We are visitors here. Refugees. England is renowned for its adherence to the law. You must surrender to the constables."

"Quickly, Dr Dee, what do I do?" Nelan asked.

"There are other significant elements in your horoscope that suggest you have a part to play in the future of this country. That's why I'm here to help you escape: because you can't do that while confined within a prison. So, you must run away and avoid capture for as long as possible. Then you can absolve yourself of this unjust accusation. Now, you must go," Dee said, pointing to the window.

Nelan opened it.

"Do not go," his father said. "You must defend yourself, and my honour."

"Father, I must. The constables—"

Laurens squeezed himself between Nelan and the window. There he stood, legs astride, arms folded, glaring at him. At times, he had a fearsome presence. This was one of them. "You are staying here," he said through gritted teeth.

"But, Dr Dee, even if I run, they'll catch me," Nelan said. "It's broad daylight outside."

"Not anymore," Dee murmured, nodding his head. "Look out the window."

Outside, a mist as thick as pea soup hung over the river. *Where's that come from? Did it arise naturally, or did Dr Dee conjure it out of the ether?*

"Where is he?" an unfamiliar voice boomed from the corridor.

"Nelan, be a man," his father said, "and account for your actions. If you flee, you will dishonour the Michaels' family name."

Nelan clenched his fists. "Father, I have to find another way to clear my name. I'll not end my days in Newgate or Marshalsea for a crime I didn't commit. Besides, if anyone's guilty, it's Guillermo. Now, move, please!"

"I will not!"

"This time, I'll not bow to your wishes. I'm innocent and disappointed that you don't believe me. I beg you, get out of my way."

"No."

The study door burst open, and Laurens glanced towards the intruder. In one swift, agile movement Nelan darted between his father's legs and came out the other side. He scrambled onto the windowsill and jumped down to the ground outside before his father had time to stop him. Finally, he'd found an advantage to being small. The ground was moist and soft from the mist. A light breeze swirled vapour around him, adding a ghostly effect to the scene. From the study he heard muffled voices: those of the constables, his father, and Dr Dee.

He knew the paths leading to and from the house like he knew the course of the river. He felt invisible to the world, and in a way, he was. Leaving one life behind and taking the first frightened, tentative steps into a new one, he concentrated on every footstep. He could barely see the path, but he knew that the river flowed by some fifty paces in front of his house.

There he met an extraordinary sight. He stepped out of the swirling mist and into broad daylight. Apart from his house, everywhere was clear: the north bank of the river in Chiswick, the monastery of Syon Abbey to the west, and to the east the city of London, where filaments of woodsmoke snaked into the dawn skies on the horizon. The mist had settled around his house, but nowhere else. He'd never witnessed such a strange phenomenon in all the years he'd lived there.

He still didn't know the identity of the woman in his vision. During the fire, she had made him freeze at the crucial moment. Providence had spoken. So had Dr Dee, and so had Nelan's horoscope. Dee had told him that he had a part to play in England's future. What on earth did that entail? If only he could have had more time with Dr Dee. But time was the one thing he didn't have, so, after one last Parthian glance at his old home, he set off along the riverbank away from the mysterious cloud of mist and into a new life.

2

The Smithy

1st April 1575

Nelan agonised over the events of the previous day and night. Why
had the Queen's constables been summoned to his father's house?
Perhaps Guillermo had died in the infirmary, in which case, it must
have been either the steward at Westminster School or Guillermo's
stepfather, St John of Southampton. After all, the St John family lived
in Sneakenhall, only a brief ride away from Nelan's house in Mortlake.
But how had Dr Dee divined the issuing of the warrant and the arrival
of the constables *from his horoscope*? The question circled his mind
like a conspiracy of ravens. Had Dee used only astrology to make his
predictions and calculations? Or had he also deployed other arcane
skills, like the subtle art of scrying; the practice of gazing into reflective
objects like crystals to predict the future? Nelan found it fascinating
that the future could be divined, but, for the moment, he felt weighed
down by his ignorance.

He stopped in his tracks, his senses pitching. He heard the snap
of a twig and glanced behind him. Was someone following him? A
fox darted into the undergrowth. The mist and the morning dew had
soaked Nelan's feet. Panting hard, he trudged along the riverbank until
he reached a fork in the path. The way heading north hugged the river,
and the other headed east across the fields. If he followed the riverbank,
he'd pass Dee's house and then Guillermo's – an unnecessary risk, and
a longer route around the oxbow. Heading towards the rising sun was

16

the quickest way to Putney. From there, God willing, he'd board the ferry.

Up ahead, in a muddy field, a flock of black birds stalked a scarecrow. All stork and no belly, the poor thing looked as if it had barely survived the recent famine. The birds had blue-black beaks – a murder of crows. A lot of good that scarecrow was, then. Murder, murder, everywhere. Nelan stumbled across the field, passing the scarecrow. The murder flew off in disgust and harangued a couple of innocent wood pigeons which had trespassed into their territory. Good Friday morning had that brisk early April chill to it, but with the promise of light and sunshine to come. The birds sang and danced amongst the willows. There was a spring growth in the grasses of the fields. The flower heads bobbed in the gentle breeze. Though none of this eased Nelan's fevered mind. His stubborn father had forced him to go on the run. While Guillermo was the victim of a tragedy of his own making, now Nelan was a victim too. He'd never be able to prove his innocence, and so had resolved to evade the charges by becoming a runaway. With his whole life turned upside down, he'd survive on his wits, plus the few pence in his purse.

He trudged along the old church road, passed St Mary's, Barnes, skirted the small ponds, and soon found himself in the wetlands by Barn Elms. If he wasn't careful, he'd be spotted by the occupants of the manor house there. Perhaps the constable with the warrant had warned them to apprehend him. He recognised the place by the distinctive weathervane on its rooftop: a black metal fox. Foxes made him suspicious; they were cunning, hostile creatures. Many scuttled around the meadows and hedgerows. They'd rip chickens to shreds. Francis Walsingham owned the manor house. He sat on the Privy Council, although Nelan wasn't sure what that involved.

Being small and agile, he hid in the long grasses and ducked in and out of the bushes along the riverbank. He got his feet wet crossing the Beverley Brook near where it joined the Thames, then reached The River Ran Inn near the village of Putney. A derelict cottage sat beside a deep trench of muddy water and a broken fence. A clutch of sheep grazed at one end of the common land. At the other end, a round straw target sat ready for the traditional Lord's Day archery practice.

He found the jetty. *Damn.* Not only was the ferry coming back from the northern bank, but worse still, a constable stood near the other passengers. Nelan panicked. Maybe the officer had got here from Nelan's house before him. But that wasn't possible, was it? The constable turned and stared at him. Nelan failed to act naturally because his palms were as moist as the dew dripping off the grass. He edged forward and stopped. He didn't know whether to run or stand still. The constable was tied at the wrist, by a length of frayed rope, to another man; a prisoner. So, this constable couldn't have been one of those who'd been called to his house. Nelan sighed with relief. The constable had the charm of a hobgoblin – scrunching his face, picking his nose, and prodding his ear. Then he adjusted his codpiece and scratched his crown jewels, oblivious to the two women waiting for the ferry. Nelan wondered if he was a simpleton. There were plenty of those about the place. The prisoner looked anything but simple or content – he had a bruised chin and wore a look of disdain that bordered on arrogance. His breeches and jerkin were made of fine wool, and he had an air of an educated man.

The prisoner pulled on the rope, which annoyed the constable, who rebuked him, saying, "Listen, Master Henry Peter, or whatever your name is—"

"It's Henrik Pieters, fool!" The man spoke with a Dutch accent.

"Don't matter to me," the constable continued. "I got me a job to do, and I done it. See, your lot got arrested in Aldgate yesterday, an' somehow – Gaud knows how – you escaped. Well, not for long. The long arm of Constable Mussell got 'twixt you and your freedom, didn't it? It's back to Newgate for you, m'lad, to join your mates. You can't escape the Queen's justice, y'know."

Pieters jerked the rope again, further irritating the constable.

"If you don't behave yourself and stop pullin' on this 'ere rope, I'll drop you in the Thames. You'd like that. You Baptist fellas is always goin' on 'bout gettin' dumped in water!"

"Yes, I'm a Baptist and proud of it!"

"That may be, but we got your leaders. They're locked up good 'n' proper."

"Masters Weelmaker and Toorwoort are God's men," Pieters barked, and yanked on the rope again, pulling the constable towards him, who stumbled and nearly fell over.

"That's enough!" Constable Mussell said, and heaved on the rope, forcing Pieters to grovel on the ground. "What's the matter with you Dutchies? You all here-tics or whatever them's called?"

The surname had a familiar ring; this fellow Pieters was a Dutchman. The constable's words both shocked and confused Nelan. Since Queen Bess had ascended the throne and taken the country back to the Protestant religion, the Catholics were the heretics. These Baptists weren't Catholics – they were Protestants – so why was the constable calling Pieters a heretic? Nelan assumed the Baptists held extreme beliefs. The accusation of heresy was terrible and punishable by the most painful execution. He wanted to ask the constable about it but felt conscious of his Dutch twang and being on the run, so he kept quiet for fear that it would draw unnecessary attention to him.

Despite the constable's preoccupations, Nelan's stomach churned with indecision. If he boarded the ferry, he'd be unable to escape. And he swam poorly. He'd probably end up with the bottom swimmers before he reached the riverbank. And in this section, the river ran deep and the current was fast. He could wait for the ferry to cross and then return, but that would take several hours, and he might get caught loitering on the jetty. He didn't want to walk any further along the south bank because, like everyone else, he'd heard rumours that the bandits and thugs of Wandsworth and Kennington would pounce on anyone without mercy. This made him think – perhaps he should sell his well-tailored woollen doublet and tight-fitting hose? He noticed that his attire drew admiring glances from the younger of the two women; a lass a year or two older than him.

The ferry arrived at the jetty and its master lashed it to its mooring, and the passengers disembarked.

"Quick on you, me hearties," the ferryman barked at them. "The Lord waits for no man. Neither do I, and neither do the Thames tides."

Nelan had no choice. He put one foot in front of the other and shuffled aboard the ferry.

As the master shunted the ferry away from the jetty and into the river flow, the lass sniggered and whispered a few words behind a secretive hand to the older woman – perhaps her mother. A tuft of red hair protruded from her French hood. Realising that he stared at her, Nelan averted his eyes from her pretty Irish face. It didn't help.

Being a shorty, his experience with women often bordered on the embarrassing. Most were taller than he by a head or more, meaning his eyeline took in their bodice, which only emphasised the charms concealed within it.

"Like what you see, mister?" the girl said, thrusting her considerable assets towards him.

Nelan took an involuntary step back and flushed from ear to ear. His tongue got stuck in a vice. While he tried to prise some words out of it, the lass had more to say.

"Are you little *everywhere*, me wonders?" she asked, tilting her head suggestively.

He had a good idea to what she referred. At seventeen, he'd discovered that parts of his anatomy had, in recent years, radically changed their composition. They'd declare their growing virility, and sometimes quite vigorously, whether he had a mind to it or not. His beetroot-red face did not get any paler. And then the girl's mother saved his blushes and, with a fierce gesture, ordered her daughter to turn her back on him.

While he swallowed his embarrassment, he passed an empty gaze over the flowing waters of the river. In his dire situation, he couldn't enjoy the ride. He was a wanted man on the run. He had little experience of life, hardly any money, no skills and nowhere to rest his head, and he faced an uncertain future. What was he going to do with the rest of his life? What had happened to him was so unjust. His cloth purse hung from his belt. He checked it for money and felt the rough edges of a few coins. His bodkin was also tucked in his belt; the small dagger helped with self-defence as well as cutting and eating meat. The sun had risen, and the distant bells of St Mary's, Barnes, announced midday. He paid the ferry master and watched with mild envy as the two women stepped into a waiting carriage. The lass winked at him suggestively, turning his cheeks as red as the poppies by the roadside.

He wandered past All Saints' Church in Fulham. Thinking he'd be safer in a crowd, he headed north towards the Bath Road, which ran east to west from London to Bath. Along the way, vagabonds, drunks and errant children accosted him. A few more loose women seemed strangely drawn to his diminutive stature. As the afternoon wore on, he met a clutch of farmers returning from the market accompanied by garrulous geese, compliant cows, and some crazed canines. A half-mile down the road, he met their various excretions, which added a sulphurous odour to this part of his journey. A horde of flies buzzed around his head like demons until he swatted them away.

Late in the afternoon, he reached the Bath Road and turned his back to the setting sun. Finally, he headed towards the city. His feet were sore and his ankles chapped, and hunger gnawed at his rumbling stomach. His throat was parched. As he sat nursing his grievances with his back against a gnarled oak, a burly vagabond stumbled towards him. He had a stick slung over his shoulder on which a piece of cloth was tied, probably carrying a morsel of bread and a slice of cheese. The man stank of piss, stale ale and cold sweat.

"What you doing 'ere, lad? Lost your way?"

"No, I haven't," Nelan said. "What's your name, sirrah?"

"I'm Foibles – Mr Foibles to you."

"I'm Nelan. But I've got enough foibles of my own," Nelan said with a sprig of rue.

"Oh, you bein' funny now? You laughin' at old Foibles?" Foibles clenched his fists and scowled. The pockmarked skin on his face and his ragged appearance spoke of a hard life of vagrancy on the open road. And at five-and-thirty, the man wasn't old; he was ancient.

Laurens had warned Nelan about these roadside thieves; highwaymen who'd rob a man blind and relieve him of his doublet, his shoes and even his breeches.

The vagrant moved towards him with menace aforethought. "Ha! Don't be scared of an old Foible. It be 'armless," he added with a grizzly smile.

Nelan didn't believe him, and slowly backed himself up against the tree and into a standing position.

"Ah! A little lad, eh?" Foibles complained.

"And what of it?"

The vagabond removed the stick from his shoulder and waved it in front of Nelan's nose. "Give 'em me right now," he growled.

"I got nothing on me."

"Bah! Hand over your angels."

"I'm telling you; I got no gold angels."

"Then give me your doublet. It smells o' smoke an' that, but it's still gotta be worth a shillin'. Come on, get it orf, an' be quick 'bout it."

Nelan felt inside the purse hanging from his belt. In it were Guillermo's flint and strike-a-light iron. He grabbed them. With one in each fist, he confronted his Foibles.

"What you gonna do, you pillock? Punch me in the sacks?"

"The Devil take your sacks. But you're not going to take my doublet. Now, be gone, you brigand, before I..."

With hands all a-tremble in front of him, Foibles closed in on Nelan. The vagrant brandished his stick, ready to smash it on Nelan's head. With nowhere to run and nowhere to hide, Nelan covered his head with his hands and winced before the expected blow, ready to meet his Maker.

Then a voice yelled, "Oi! What's goin' on 'ere? Put that boy down. Declare yourself!"

To Nelan's surprise, he recognised the constable from the ferry. He still had Pieters, the Dutch prisoner, in tow. But he'd come to Nelan's rescue. Foibles turned to the constable, spat prodigiously on the ground and slouched off towards the city, doing a spit-poor impersonation of one of the Queen's runners.

Hobbling up to Nelan, the constable asked, "He snatch anything from ya?"

Nelan heaved a sigh of relief. He was out of the frying pan, but now... what did this blessed constable want with him? Hopefully, not his liberty. "No, sirrah, he did not," he said, lightly thumping his heart with his fist.

"What's you got in them there hands? Open up; let Mussell see for hisself."

"Thank you. Is it Constable Mouse Hole?"

"Nah. Not Mouse Hole; Mussell be me name. Constable Mussell to the likes o' you. An' you gonna tell me what you hidin' in there or not?" Mussell said, pointing to Nelan's fists.

"Oh, these," Nelan said, opening his palms.

"An iron an' a flint," Mussell exclaimed with the simple joy of a child identifying a toy. "You a fire-maker, then?"

"A fire-maker?" Nelan asked.

"Yeah, it's a fella what makes fire."

"Oh, you mean like Prometheus?"

"Pro-them-sus?" Mussell scrunched up his face.

"No, *Pro-meth-e-us*. A Greek hero – he brought the gift of fire to a fledgling human race."

"Well, only Greek fella I knows is old Christos. He's a stevedore on the docks at Queenhithe."

"Nah. Don't know him."

"But you got an iron an' a flint. You got a char cloth too?"

Nelan patted his purse and nodded.

"Then you can make fire," Mussell said with an admiring glance.

"Yeah, maybe I can; what of it?" Nelan asked, shoving the iron and flint back into his purse.

"Me brother's a smith, he is that."

"And?"

"And… well, it's a sad old story. 'Is lad went an' got his 'and chopped."

"Chopped?"

"Yeah – he stole a loaf of bread from a baker and paid for it with 'is 'and. Chopped it orf at St Paul's Cross, just outside the cathedral. Poor lad's only got one now. He may be 'andy, but he ain't no good no more as a smith. Me brother needs another 'prentice. Said I'd look out for one for 'im. I like me brother, I do. You interested, lad?"

For once today, the Lord had smiled on Nelan. Well, maybe the second time after he'd enjoyed the view of that redhead's bulging assets. "Yes, I'm interested. Where will I find your brother?"

"Ah! He's at Queenhithe docks. You know 'em?"

Nelan shook his head.

"They're on the north side o' the river."

"Give me the directions."

"Head for the city and Thames Street. Then you come to one o' them crossy roads."

"Crossroads?"

"Yeah. One o' them. You got Bread Street on the… what's that called? This side 'ere," Mussell said, waving his left hand.

"The left?"

"Yeah, well, don't turn down that one. Turn down the other one."

"The right?"

"Yeah, that one. It's a woody street – no, it's… ah, I know: High Timber Street."

"And your brother's smithy is there?"

"Well, yeah, it's on the corner with Stew Lane. An' if you get to All-Hallows-the-Great…"

"What happens then?"

"Oh! It mean you gone too far."

"Constable Mussell, thank you for saving me from that wretch Foibles, and for telling me about your brother."

"You tell him I sent you. Don't forget now, will ya?"

"No, I won't. What's his name?"

"Same as mine, master. It's Mussell."

"Mmm, yes, I know that," Nelan said, stifling a mocking laugh. "What's his *Christian* name?"

"Oh, yeah, 'course," Mussell said, smacking himself on the forehead. "Ask for Edmund – Master Edmund Mussell. He'll see you right, he will that."

With the night drawing in, Nelan had to get to the city before the watchmen closed the gates. This could be his chance to make amends and end this awful day on a rising note. He set off into the shadows of London's underbelly. He edged around a raucous crowd of drunks singing and yelling outside a coaching inn. The vapours of sulphur mixed with those of stale, warm ale made his eyes water. There were few advantages to being a shorty, but this was one of them. It allowed him to merge into the shadows and avoid the cutpurses, vagrants and prostitutes. He headed into the dull gloom of the lanterns along Thames Street. All was quiet except for the occasional scurry of rats and the curt, low barks of the foxes scavenging amongst the debris strewn along the road. He found High Timber Street and the corner with Stew Lane. Several ladies of the night frolicked with clients up against a wall in a darkened alley. Stew Lane lived up to its name.

With a sigh of relief, Nelan glanced above him and noticed the sign of the anvil, hammer and pincers. At last! What a journey! He'd found the home of a modern-day Hephaestus, the ancient Greek god of blacksmiths. Now he'd forge a new beginning to his life. He tried the door knocker; a vast, moulded metal roundel.

A burly man with arms like tree trunks and holding a candle peered around the door and said, "Forge is closed till the mornin'. Come back then."

"I'm sorry to bother you at this late hour, but—"

From inside the house came a woman's shrill voice. "Who's that? And at this time of the night? Can't a woman sleep in peace no more?"

"Go back to bed, Matilda, will ya?" the man shouted.

"Please, Master Edmund—" Nelan said.

"How you know me name, eh? Did old Christos tell you 'bout me?" Edmund asked, lifting the candle to see Nelan's face.

"No, it was your brother, Constable Mussell."

"Did he now? Well, state your business, an' make it quick, else you'll 'ave more than me to answer to," Edmund said, tilting his head in the direction of his wife's voice.

"I'm Nelan. Your brother told me you need an apprentice and here I am."

"'Tis true, I do needs one. Show me them hands."

Nelan held out his hands.

Edmund pressed his thumb into the flashy part of Nelan's palm. After a derisory grunt, he scoffed, "They're as soft as a baby's bum. You never done no hard work in your short life. You won't last the time it takes for the tide to go out. Now, git."

"No, wait. I can do it, Master Edmund. I have a way with flame. Your brother said so."

"And what's he know?"

Nelan heard voices at the far end of the street. Only the shadows of cut-throats, vagrants and watchmen moved in dark alleys at this time of the night, and he didn't want to meet any of those right now. A dog yapped. A man raised his lantern. *Damn! Must be a watchman.*

"Close the blessed door; it's freezin'," Matilda cried from inside the house.

Edmund moved to shut it, but Nelan shoved his foot in the gap.

"Take your foot out of my door!" Edmund stepped into the alley and called out, "Oi! Alexander! Over 'ere!"

"You're in no danger from me," Nelan hissed. "How can I convince you to take me on?"

25

"Listen, Nellie, or whatever your name is. I need brawn an' guts. Most of all, I need a man of fire."

"I got all that."

"I don't know 'bout that."

A sudden gust of wind blew out the candle flame, plunging them into darkness. The watchmen edged closer. Their hound barked at invisible ghosts.

Quick. Seize the opportunity. Nelan delved into his purse and pulled out the char cloth, iron, and flint. A tiny, deep blue spark emerged from the ether and kissed the char cloth. He blew on it to conjure a flame, which he held to the candle's wick. "*Fiat lux!*" he said with an air of satisfaction.

"What's that?"

"It's Latin for 'Let there be light.'"

Alexander the watchman arrived; lantern in one hand, pike in the other. He wore a long, scraggy beard. His hound pulled on its tether and frothed at the mouth, barking loudly. "Shut it!" Alexander said. It obeyed. Then he said, "Praise the Lord. Need any help here, Big Ed? If this fella's givin' you grief, I can throw 'im in the Clink."

Edmund held up the candle, its flame shedding light into the darkness. He paused and glanced at Nelan, and then back at the watchman. Nelan held his breath. The culmination of the day; this was his moment of reckoning.

Edmund slapped the man on the shoulder and said, "Nah, Alexander. We's all good 'ere. See this lad? He's my new 'prentice."

"Ah! Easy. Heat him up an' then bash 'im into shape," Alexander said.

"With God's will, I'll do just that!"

Nelan breathed out. What a relief. The same strike-a-light iron and flint that had made him a runaway had now come to his rescue.

For the first time in his life, he slept with a forge.

Early the next day, Edmund explained his duties. "You're gonna clean the forge an' keep the fire ablaze. And no funny business, or I'll have your guts for garters. Or the fire will."

Nelan replied, "Yes, master."

On that first day, he kept accidentally burning himself; nothing was sacred, not his fingers, nor his thumbs, nor his forearms. He kept underestimating the sheer power of the heat of the forge. When towards the end of the day he grew tired, it was worse. He felt aggrieved about his father; about Guillermo and the injustice of it all. Then he singed his eyebrows!

He sweated until the perspiration fell off his forehead. Edmund gave him a leather apron, gloves and boots, and a hat to protect his hair, but he had to pay for them out of his wages. His duties began with sweeping the floor clean of straw, charcoal dust, metal fragments, and other debris.

Edmund scowled at him. "Put your back into your work, you knavish lout."

So, he did.

Then came the cleaning of the forge. Nelan wanted to start, but Edmund kept telling him, "Wait, will you? That furnace is like Satan. It's as hot as Hell."

It cooled, and Nelan found his diminutive size helped him reach into all the nooks and crannies.

Edmund asked him, "Listen, little man, how comes you knows how to do this writin' an' readin' an' countin'? How comes you workin' for the likes of me, a master smith and member of the Worshipful Company of Blacksmiths? Why ain't you out and about in a college or university?"

Nelan had expected this question. "I want to learn a trade," he replied. "And, as your brother found out, fire is a constant source of fascination to me. The way it flares up with these many-coloured flames – red and crimson, yellow and gold, blue and azure…" He lifted his hands and made a whooshing sound, and then added, "Then it dies down, and then there's the black smoke and the white fumes. And the flame, it's ancient, older than we are, and in another way it's young, fresh and vibrant every time."

"Guess I never thought about it like that. But mind you pay attention to your work. I don't want you going off spouting poesy or treadin' the boards with the King's Men."

"I won't do that, Master Edmund."

"Then tell me, lad: what happened to your ma and pa?"

"No, and no siblings either." Nelan choked at this point. "I was born in Sangatte near Calais. But we moved to Leiden in the Netherlands. Then my father brought me to England."

"Immigrant from the canals, eh? Well, you ain't alone. There's a few of your sort about the city these days. And some of them Frenchies – them Huggnots."

"Huguenots," Nelan corrected him.

"Yeah, them. There was that mass-a-care a few year ago."

"Massacre, yes, in Paris on St Bartholomew's Day," Nelan said, biting his lip. Talk of the massacre rekindled his hatred of Catholics. "That treachery was nearly three years ago. The Papists murdered our Protestant brethren in cold blood – women and children too. Like my father and I, they came here to escape persecution."

"Well, you're safe here in England under the protection of Queen Bess, God bless 'er," Edmund said, mouthing a valediction.

The next day was Easter Sunday. Accompanied by those of St Paul's, the bells of the city's churches rang out in unison, calling the congregation to worship. Edmund washed his face, ran his fingers through his locks, and smoothed his doublet. Matilda dressed up in her best. Nelan got ready too. The Queen's recent statutes concerning religion meant that attendance at a Protestant liturgy was compulsory, even for declared Catholics. Still, he had to decide which church to attend.

As Edmund left with Matilda, he asked Nelan, "You goin' to worship at the Dutch Church? There's one at Austin Friars."

Though he wore different dress, Nelan remained reluctant to go there for fear of being recognised. Mortlake was only ten miles away, so he could easily bump into a Dutch friend or acquaintance of his father's. So he said, "Oh, no, I think not. If I may, I'd like to join you."

"You're welcome. We're to St Michael's. It's round the corner."

The church bells stopped pealing, and their echoes washed over the rooftops of London, lifting the heavy atmosphere. Once in the church, Nelan, Edmund and Matilda stood near the front, hands pressed together in prayer. The minister wore the hues of Protestant England: Anglican black and white. His sermon proved a tad more colourful.

"We must repel the rude intrusion of these Spanish," he said, thumping the eagle lectern. "I warn you: be wary of their endurance and fanaticism. They've built an empire from the Spice Isles in the Far East to the silver and gold mines in South America. Despite these riches, they're grasping for more. They're spurred on by the motto of their King, Philip the Prudent: *Non Sufficit Orbis*. It means 'the world is not enough'. If the world isn't enough, what is? The sun, the stars, the universe? That's not prudence; that's hubris. The Dons are full of that all-consuming greed. They've built an empire across the great oceans of the globe. We're different. We must shun the Papists' pride. We must not sin. In days of yore, England was a mystical land and a land of mystery. It still is. The angels of England wait for us to rise again; to find those who are kin to their spirit. They will help us, but only if we are on their side and want the same as they do. To gain their trust, we must be true to the English nature: strong but fair, stubborn but tenacious, disciplined and ingenious. That's how they can recognise us."

The minister's words shocked Nelan into reflecting on his mundane life. For the first time, it made sense. Up to now, his life had been a mishmash of wrong turns and missed opportunities, starting in Sangatte, then moving to the Netherlands, and then making a fresh start in England. Then had come the searing injustice of the fire at Westminster School, followed by another new chapter at the smithy. But in the light of the preacher's sermon, he saw a pattern and a meaning he hadn't hitherto perceived. Dr Dee had sparked his interest in astrology, in the movement of the stars, and in how to read a destiny from their subtle interchange and progression. Perhaps the stars were pointing him towards a different kind of apprenticeship; more than that of a smith. He had an uncanny feeling that he walked on the path of a momentous quest. These days of apparent toil and drudgery were not only significant, but written in the stars. The feeling was akin to the end of winter when a gentle warmth in the wind heralded a fresh start; a new beginning. Yes, he'd set his feet on the path of becoming an accomplished smith. But there was much more to it than that, because it allowed him to indulge his burgeoning fascination with the element of fire.

In the days and weeks that followed, he learned to treat the forge and its intense heat with humility, care, and a massive dose of respect. Fire was merciless. It would ensnare him time and again. It was a feral beast that could never be tamed. He learned to give the flame space and time and protect himself from it by confining it with physical guards. By the end of each day, despite his thick, long gloves, his forearms bore a score of dagger-like cuts; scalding marks that criss-crossed his skin where the flames had spurted out of the fire and the forge had bitten him. The work was arduous. Sometimes, he felt like he was married to the forge. With God's will, he learned to scrub the furnace, clean out the ashes, and then build a fire once more. Fire after fire. As Alexander the watchman had predicted, he gradually softened, just as the heat of the furnace moulded metal. Edmund showed him how to use a pair of bellows to aerate the forge, and handle pincers and tongs to grasp the heated metal. And eventually, he learned how to use the hammers to shape it.

Often, the fire was a brutal mistress. Constant in her inconstancy, she ranged from the spark when the flint struck the iron, to the warm glow of the charcoal embers in the hearth, to the fierce, searing heat of the forge.

The smithy was always busy. The local ironmonger often stocked up on nails and small tools like hammers and knives. Other times, the yard bustled with shipwrights, coopers and carpenters from the Queenhithe docks. Old Christos was a regular visitor along with the other stevedores. On occasion, Edmund did business with merchants across the Narrow Seas in Calais and Antwerp.

For safety's sake, Nelan never strayed far from the smithy. His beard grew a tad. Hard work and heavy toil made him fit and lean. In his blacksmith's apron, cap and gloves, no one would recognise the tentative, innocent little Dutch schoolboy of old. He got to know the Pead family, who ran a bakery on the corner of Bread Street and Thames Street. Whenever the pangs of hunger gnawed at his belly, he nipped across there and picked up a morsel of bread from Charles Pead and his wife, Imogen. At their bakery, he met their fifteen-year-old daughter, Eleanor.

Summer days worked him hard, but they satisfied him, especially as he grew closer to understanding the nature of fire. She was his mistress: lithe and alive, light and alight, as severe as she was helpful, as unforgiving as she was kind. With each day that passed after the minister's Easter Sunday sermon, Nelan's relationship with the element grew ever more mysterious. It encouraged him to understand its ways and meanings. He wondered why, of all the four elements – earth, water, air and fire – only fire seemed to have no permanent existence. We could all walk on earth; we could all breathe air and drink water. But fire came and went. Unlike the other three elements, it demanded extreme caution and respect. It needed to be summoned with care. Used for wrongful purposes, it could easily overwhelm and destroy. Ask Icarus. He flew too close to the greatest fire in the heavens – the sun – and suffered accordingly. Fire was a gift from the gods. Or did Prometheus steal it from them?

Everything prepared him for an unknown task. As before, he felt like he was on the right path, and for the moment, that remained good enough for him. He thought he could hear the sweet voices of those angels of England beckoning him to join that special enterprise. What greater destiny was there than to participate in the unfolding future of one's chosen land and its role in world affairs? Wasn't that what Dr Dee had intimated?

He settled down on his straw mattress next to his bedmate, the forge, and went to sleep enshrouded in subtle, numinous dreams.

3

The Cordwainer

22nd July 1575

Nelan worked from dawn to dusk, ate from a table near the forge, and slept on a mattress of twisted straw. Even Matilda left him in peace, except when she berated him for some minor indiscretion, or he spied a glint in her eye. She'd stare at him. That unnerved him because he couldn't challenge the boss's wife, but he guessed what throbbed in her heart – or, should he say, between her legs. Whenever this happened, he'd creep off and leave her to her desires. Even though he had ended up married to a smelly, sooty forge, when he'd desperately needed sanctuary, Edmund had supplied it. However tempting the offer, Nelan would never stray with Matilda; nor, for that matter, with any man's wife.

During the rare quiet periods, he'd sit on the riverbank and watch the river's ebb and flow and the swell rise and fall along its banks. Sometimes Eleanor, the baker's daughter, would join him. She'd play with her auburn hair, twiddling and twisting it into strands and then loosening it again. Together through the warm summer days, they'd sit revelling in the quiet scene of the boats coming and going along the waterfront. Wherries travelled up to Putney and the palace at Hampton Court. Ferries criss-crossed the river, carrying merchants and townsmen to Southwark and back. Larger boats carried passengers and goods upstream as far as Windsor, Maidenhead and Reading. Nelan and Eleanor enjoyed watching the young ladies and their gentlemen board and disembark on the jetty on the opposite side of the river at St Mary Overie. On special days, they'd catch sight of an important personage: a wealthy merchant, or a member of the Privy Council heading down the river to the Tower of London or Greenwich Palace. A dozen rowers heaved on their oars, driving their boat forward so that their lord and master could attend a meeting with the French Ambassador or a German Prince.

Once, they enjoyed the treat of all treats. Sitting there one glorious afternoon, with the sun glistening on the water and their legs dangling over the bricked riverbank, they heard excited cries from downriver.

Eleanor stood up. She turned to Nelan with an expression of joy and wonder. "The Queen!" she cried.

Nelan stood on tiptoe to catch sight of Queen Elizabeth. Sure enough, a large barge, bunting fluttering in the stiff breeze, punted under London Bridge. Uniformed rowers pulled the oars, obeying the call of the stroke with perfect discipline. The royal barge passed so close he felt he could reach out and touch Her Majesty. She headed upriver to her palace at Kew or Richmond. Regal and serene, she sat under a parasol, her pearls glittering in the sunlight, a white ruff soothing her torrid emotions. It seemed as if the whole world was at her fingertips. Subtle, discerning and all-seeing, she appeared an elegant woman, a fine Queen, and a noble personage in her own right. Her flag fluttered in the breeze at the stern of the barge. On it was her royal coat of arms: the three red lions of England quartered with the fleur-de-lys of France, emblazoned with her motto, *Semper Eadem*; 'Always the Same'. Those three words spoke of a constant lady, loyal and true to her word. The royal coat of arms had two supporters: the golden lion of England and the red dragon of Wales. Nelan wondered why the dragon was in profile and looking to the side, but the lion stared straight at you. Perhaps it meant that, to live in this land, one had to face the lion in one's heart and be one's own courageous leader. This event marked the pinnacle of their riverside sojourns.

On other days, Nelan would sit with his friend enjoying the river and the boats, the bunting and the musicians, and most of all, her pleasant company. Once, on a day with barely a breath of wind, he sat on the bank and watched in awe as a light gust kissed the surface of the river, creating a patch of larger ripples like cats' paws. Eleanor came to join him. Sitting beside him, she rubbed her shoulder briefly against his, sending a frisson of excitement through his whole being. He dared himself to glance at the lustre in her green eyes. He didn't need to dare himself to enjoy her enticing smile. With such a heady and intoxicating mix, she seemed to hark from another world. He loved her vibrant laugh and her long auburn hair. She was a girl and yet a young woman. With no sisters, and no mother present for his more recent formative years, Nelan had missed the opportunity to engage with the opposite gender. Secretly, he breathed in Eleanor's aroma, soft like a rose, and loved feeling the closeness of her presence.

On another day, they were sitting shoulder to shoulder when a gust of wind blew off her headscarf, which floated high into the air. When the breeze died down, her scarf did a pirouette and landed on a ledge on the top of a stone wall. Nelan jumped up and went to retrieve it, but the ridge remained just beyond his reach.

"Oh, let me try," she said.

"But you're no taller than I am," he said, a mischievous smile playing on his lips. In truth, she was, but not by much.

"Oh, but I am," she complained, throwing him a look of mock hurt. Standing on tiptoe, she stretched up. "I can touch it with my fingertips!" she said. "But it's just out of my reach."

"There, told you so!" he said with an air of triumph.

"I still want my scarf back," she said, tousling her auburn locks.

"I know what we'll do," he said. "If you let me lift you, you can reach it."

She nodded. He put his hands around her waist and lifted her. She felt so light, so lithe. She grabbed the scarf, and gently, he put her back down. She turned, kissed him on the cheek, and ducked out of his attempted embrace.

That day, she caught him.

One day, around high summer, he arose before sunrise. It was still dark. He poked his nose outside into Stew Lane. On most days, he got a whiff of the stench coming off the Thames, coupled with the stale, overpowering perfumes of the whores who frequented the lane. These mingled with the noxious smells emanating from High Timber Lane, piled up as it was with rotting debris. Horses, donkeys and mules were convenient to move goods or ride, but God's animals had an annoying tendency to leave a smelly, messy trace of their passage. The rich aroma of freshly baked bread wafted across from the bakers beyond Thames Street.

Glancing up at the eastern sky, there it was, along the line indicated by the three stars in the belt of the constellation of Orion: the brightest star in the heavens, the Dog Star, Sirius. It was the first sighting of the year. The ancients believed the Dog Days heralded sultry weather, social upheaval, and riots. Today, the 22nd July 1575, marked the start of the time of the astrological sign of Leo.

The Queen regarded Nelan's old tutor and astrologer, Dr Dee, in such high esteem that she had asked him to advise her on the date of her coronation. Dee had taught Nelan the rudiments of astrology. He knew his birth sign: having been born in Sangatte, Picardy, on the 12th December 1557 brought him under the influence of Sagittarius, symbolised by the archer. He often wondered how the positions of the moon, the planets, the sun and the stars above that place and on that date could shape his life. Perhaps they inclined rather than compelled a person to behave in a particular way. Maybe they prompted certain lines of action and thought more than others. A person had to rise to their best to reap that stellar influence. Aries, Leo and Sagittarius represented the three aspects of the element of fire: the lighting of the furnace, its roar, and its warm embers; the ignition, the heat, and the residual glow.

The lion was the astrological animal of Leo. The king of the beasts was rampant on the royal heraldic arms of England. It was both the emblem of Richard the Lionheart and the natural occult protector of the Island of Angels. Nelan remembered the nursery rhyme:

As fire brings the light,
The lion gives the fight.
As flame dispels the night,
The lion champions the right.

Even an archer bestriding the heavens had to earn his keep. Nelan lugged tinder and charcoal into the smithy from the docks. In the crisp, dry air, the forge fired easily and quickly. Within minutes, a subtle blue flame became a massive conflagration. He could hear the flames beat against the thick metal door of the forge, yearning to escape their terrible confinement and devour and destroy; such a mercurial substance, this fire. The flames inside the forge sounded like a constant, vociferous roar. He wiped the sweat from his brow with his forearm.

"Forge is ready, master," he said.

"Mmm," Edmund grunted. "Let's see. It'd better be good." The terse reply was nothing new. He prodded a digit near the forge and, jerking his finger away, licked it. "For once, lad, you're right. Stoke it some more, will you?"

A man Nelan had seen before came to the front of the yard. Richard, the cordwainer, donned a rough-hewn cloth and a thick apron. Beneath his flat cap was a strong forehead, like a cliff face that overhung his eyes. Clinging to his chin was a scraggy beard resembling the heel of a shoe; the emblem of his trade.

When Edmund saw Richard, he said, "Nelan, grab me four of those," and pointed to the row of horseshoes hanging over the lintel.

Nelan climbed on a stool to reach them and hung them one by one over his forearm. The horseshoes weighed him down as he made his way to the front of the yard.

Richard moaned, "By the Lord, I swear to you, Edmund, what with the price of meat and ale, the plague and the ague, the stench of the sewers, and the cutpurses, we've enough trouble earning a living in our blessed city."

"Hell's teeth, I'm with you on that. We've struggled too," Edmund admitted. "And you know why, don't you?"

"Big Tom?" Richard suggested with an assured nod of his head.

"You know it."

"Who's Big Tom?" Nelan asked.

Edmund grunted. "The master o' London Bridge. He's almost as old as the bridge itself. Trouble is, he's as slow as a snail in opening the damn drawbridge. And trade has suffered 'cause of 'im. Nowadays, grain and other foodstuffs are offloaded upriver. Trade at St Michael Queenhithe has dwindled from a torrent to a stream. An' it's all his fault, it is."

"Cordwaining ain't much better, I tell ye, Edmund. I'm sure folks is getting lazy and not walkin' as far as they used to."

"Maybe they all got 'orses?"

"Nah." Richard shook his head. "You got one? Didn't think so. And what about all them vagrants on the Bath Road? They fight amongst 'emselves over a scrap of food like a murder o' yappin' crows. Then there's Papists everywhere. They've infected us like an illness. Oh, I tell ya, it brings out the rheum in me."

Edmund grunted. "But it's not gonna stop you payin' for these horseshoes, is it?"

"How much, then?"

"Usual price: twopence. Come on, hand it over."

"Thing is, I'm spent out," Richard said, emptying the contents of his cloth purse onto the table. It contained a knife with a broken blade, a few old pieces of leather, and a coil of string. Notably absent were coins of the realm. "But I have it at my workshop. Come with me and I'll pay you, promise."

"I can't leave the smithy. Nelan, go with Master Richard. Carry the horseshoes for him, and he'll pay you for them when you get there. And come straight back – no drinkin' or whorin', y'hear? Now git to it, lad."

Nelan followed Richard past St Paul's, the cathedral's spires glistening in the July sunshine, and then past Newgate prison. At St Sepulchre's, south of Smithfield, they joined hordes of people heading in the same direction. Wagons and coaches, horses and donkeys, men selling pastries and savouries, women and their daughters in their finery and lace ruffs, lords in their wigs, constables complete with pikes and staffs; the entire city headed there. Nelan felt a strange tightness around his throat, and it wasn't the early afternoon heat. It was all over, like an ominous cloud hanging over the area. It pressed down on him. His shoulders felt like they carried the weight of the world, and his limbs felt like the lead from the forge. The houses on either side of the narrow alley loomed over him and constricted his throat. He stopped and coughed a dry cough.

"What's the matter, lad?" Richard asked.

"Nothing," Nelan rasped. "Tell me – what on earth's happening today? Is there someone in the stocks?"

"No, no stocks today. But it could be a market, or a fair, but I don't see no flags or bunting. When there's so many heading for the Elms, it can only be one thing."

"What's that?"

"An execution."

Nelan grunted an acknowledgement. Perhaps that explained why he felt so awful. Anyhow, he plodded on alongside Richard.

As a string of carts trundled by, their headman called for folks to clear the way ahead. The carts at the front carried kindling and twigs. The ones behind transported faggots: twigs tied together in hundreds of bundles; kindling for a day of fire and brimstone.

"There, I'm right," Richard said excitedly. "It ain't no ordinary execution. It's a burning. He's got to be a Papist. May his heretic soul rot in Hell. Come on, let's stop and enjoy the spectacle."

"I-I…" Nelan said. "Do you mind if we pass on by? I need to get back to the smithy."

"Fine," Richard replied. "But you're gonna miss a great show."

Drunks, farmers, shopkeepers, innkeepers, carpenters, and mothers with suckling babes at their breasts clearly intended to do otherwise. Nelan felt relieved when Richard changed course away from the Elms at Smithfield. He did not want to feast his eyes on excruciating suffering. To avoid the swarm, they doubled back. The roundabout route took them by Chick Lane, but with the raucous crowds, it took much longer than Nelan had anticipated. Edmund would be wondering where he'd got to.

It was late in the afternoon when they approached Richard's premises. Nelan knew that they edged near because of the smell, which was even more odious than usual for a city street. Not only was the cordwainer situated next door to a tanning yard ponging of old leather, but Smithfield's sheep pens were further up the lane. Richard's apprentice opened the yard gates. Between the smears of mud and grime, all Nelan could see of his boyish face were a pair of brown eyes flitting from left to right like those of a frightened mutt. The yard was a cornucopia of cobbler's tools: knives, hammers, cutters, piles of spare leather, a couple of forlorn-looking shoe stands, and several pairs of rickety old boots awaiting their appointment with destiny. A low table sat in one corner of the cobbled yard. Next to it was a pile of freshly deposited horse shit.

Richard said, "Nelan, put the horseshoes there," and pointed to the base of the table.

"And the twopence?" Nelan asked.

But before Richard could pay him, a man rode through the gates. The intricacy of his doublet, with flashes of silk and wool, spoke of his high standing in society. His equerry dismounted and helped his master to do the same.

Richard greeted him. "Master Digges, my pleasure."

The man gave a cursory nod.

Richard turned to his apprentice. "Fetch the master's shoes from the shop. And jump to it, you lowly knave!"

The boy scuttled off, relieved to escape Richard's attention. While they waited for him to return, Nelan examined the uneven cobbles and glanced at the new arrival. He'd heard the name Digges before. He searched his memory but couldn't for the life of him place the man.

Digges asked Richard, "How long before the shoes wear out this time?"

"They'll last as long as the Lord wills it, Master Digges," Richard piped up. He sounded like he echoed a morsel of wisdom from a Sunday sermon. It worked as well as an ill-fitting shoe. "I warrant you that my shoes are the best this side of Eastcheap."

"Eastcheap's only round the corner, so that's not saying much," the equerry observed with a wry smile.

"You've never complained before," Richard muttered as his apprentice scurried back.

"Well, we have now," Digges replied. "What I'd like is some of those special shoes. You got any of those?"

"Which ones would they be, Master Digges?"

"The ones that don't wear out!" Digges said, with a mischievous glint in his eye.

"Dunno what you mean, Master," Richard replied, pulling an earlobe for good measure. "My boots an' shoes is good an' tough, but even they wear out walkin' the Queen's highways and byways."

"Bah, never mind," Digges said, waving away a flotilla of flies swarming around the horse dung.

"Here they are, Master," Richard added, showing Digges the uppers and soles of his shoes. "As you can see, these are prim 'n' proper, the best you'll get in the city."

The equerry helped Digges onto his horse and led it out of the yard.

Digges' comment about the shoes fascinated Nelan. What shoes never wore out? And the man had hinted that he knew more than he'd said. Nelan wanted to hail him and ask him about these strange shoes, but then Richard called out to Digges, "May God bless you and Dr Dee."

Nelan froze. He recalled now that his father and Dr Dee had spoken of Digges. The man followed Nicolaus Copernicus's new, controversial theory that placed the sun, rather than the earth, at the centre of the solar system. It was a slice of good fortune that Nelan and Digges had never met at Dee's house. Even so, he needed to be careful. Richard could never find out about his association with Dee, lest it reveal his true identity. All the same, he felt a curious yearning to know more. *The shoes that don't wear out! And that look in his eyes as he said it…*

He hurriedly squeezed the twopence out of Richard and set off after Digges. He resolved to follow the man and, at the first opportunity, ask him about those strange shoes.

As he made his way through the city, a watchman, accompanied by a trusty hound, called the hours: "The hour is seven of the evening, and all's well."

Up ahead, another watchman kicked a pile of stinking rubbish, scattering the debris into the middle of the alley to prevent fire taking hold and spreading to the houses on either side. Fire in a city of wooden houses was worse than the plague.

The crowded and narrow streets prevented Nelan from getting closer to Digges and his equerry. Approaching Smithfield from the west, they met scores of people heading the other way. Having witnessed the cruelty of the burning, the throng was more excited than they had been when Nelan had last seen them going to the execution. He pushed through the crowds and wondered about the shoes that never wore out. If they existed, he'd find a pair and learn how to make them. Buy one pair of shoes and have them last your whole life – now, that would be a feat. He'd make a fortune overnight.

He lost sight of Digges and found himself squeezed into an alley with rickety terraced houses along either side. A rowdy mob pushed against him. Folks stood gaping outside their front doors, cheering the passers-by, who yelled back at them with raw, demonic glee. The men in the crowd made obscene gestures at the women standing on the thresholds of their houses. A scuffle broke out amongst lads intoxicated by ale and wine. The group wore a callous, empty look in their eyes, dulled by witnessing the horror of the execution. The heretic had been burned at the stake. The barbarism exceeded Dante's vision of Hell. Nelan felt disgusted. Punish a person for a grievous crime, but then apply the balm of mercy.

He pushed through the maelstrom, trying to catch up with Digges. Shoved by a young man, he tumbled to the ground, grazing his hands on the cobblestones. On occasion, people had failed to notice him, but this was different. This time, the act was deliberate and callous.

"Oi, little fella. What you doin' down there? Wanna kiss my boots?" the young man taunted him. His eyes were aflame with a poisonous mix of liquor and righteous indignation.

Nelan felt a pang of fear grip his stomach. "No, I don't, and you pushed me," he said, heaving himself up.

"What did you say?"

"You heard me."

The young man glared at him like he was the village idiot, and pushed him again, but this time Nelan stood his ground. "You ain't from around here, are ya? You a Johnny foreigner?" he asked.

"I'm a smith's apprentice; that's who I am," Nelan replied.

"Hey! You got the accent like the two what got burnt in Smithfield. You're all from the Nether Lands," another young man said.

"Yeah, that's right. What was their names?" the first man asked.

"Jan Weelmaker and Henrik Toorwoort. Weird names, eh? Yeah, that's them," the second man said in an eerie, heartless monotone, as if his soul, along with mercy and forgiveness, had temporarily departed his body.

Nelan remembered Henrik Pieters, the man on the Putney ferry with Constable Mussell. So, Pieters was another one of those heretical Dutch Baptists.

The second man said, "In April, a constable discovered a congregation of Dutch Baptists worshippin' in Aldgate. Those heretics was condemned to be burnt. They was taken to St Paul's Cross. Them that recanted was sent back to them Nether Lands. Good riddance, too. Two of 'em refused. That's Weelmaker and Toorwoort. Them's the ones that's got all burned up today."

"What's so special about these Dutch Baptists, then?" the first man asked.

"They only get baptised when they've grown old enough and acquired enough understanding to request it for themselves. And those two was mad to boot, 'cause they could've recanted and gone 'ome like the others, but they chose to die. That make 'em brave or foolish?" Then the second man turned to Nelan and said, "You got their accent, anyway, so you're a heretic too", and smashed his fist into his face.

It took Nelan by surprise, and spun him around like a whistling top before he hit the ground. Kick after kick rained down as the men laid into him. He curled up into a tight ball, but the blows kept coming – to his head, his back, his legs.

"Dutchie, go home!" the first man yelled.

"We don't want you 'ere," railed the second.

After that, Nelan heard only the hue and the cry, and shouts and raised voices full of ridicule. They pummelled him. Spat on him. A groan oozed from his mouth. He drifted in and out of consciousness. The ground beneath his face was warm, wet, and sticky with blood. His blood. He was in agony.

He eased out of his body, then floated upwards and peered down at his wretched, twisted carcass and the men abusing it. Looking down and seeing his own body made him feel afraid but comforted at the same time. Because outside of his body, he felt no pain. He got a feel for how to control the movements of this new, light body, and willed himself to drift higher above the crowd. Below him, his view of the men, the houses and the street was blurred, like that time during the late evening when, in the hazy light, the birds sing their last songs. Shadows moved by and around him like wraiths. Perhaps he was dreaming it all. Maybe he'd died and was going to Heaven. Or to Hell? Perhaps he'd float outside of his body like this forever, held in this weird, suspended state.

After a while, his assailants must have grown bored with beating him to a pulp, and he must have drifted back to consciousness, because he saw them slap each other on the back in malicious celebration and walk off down the alley. Again he drifted above the roofs of the houses, looking down at his body. If he re-entered it, would he feel the pain again? But how long could he safely remain outside of it? Was there a limit beyond which re-entry was forbidden or prevented? Everything in this mysterious realm frightened him.

A cloud of dark fumes appeared before him. Slowly they grew into a thick black fog, which sent waves of fear through him. He tried to move away from it, but it followed him. Then a thought hit him. This ominous presence could well be another person outside of their body, just as he floated outside of his. Was he being haunted? If so, by whom or by what? A second cloud appeared next to the first. Slowly, their shapes changed, and Nelan recognised a head, a torso, and then arms and legs. The familiar form of a human emerged from the cloud. There were two of them. He could see more detail: their bodies and their twisted faces. Their eyes, empty of life, were devoid of light. Their open mouths were fixed in an eternal scream.

"Who are you?" he asked.

In the caverns of his soul, they whispered two names. "Jan and Henrik."

Nelan re-entered his body with a jerk, and his world went as black as forge soot.

4

The Council of Blood

23rd July 1575

It was dark when Nelan awoke. Very dark. He was a coil of pain. His head was spinning. His bones hurt. His lungs gasped for breath. Perhaps the men had placed heavy weights on his chest, as they did in *peine forte et dure*, the cruel punishment applied to those who refused to enter a plea in a law court. Frantically, he felt his chest with his hands. It bore no weight. He still felt riven with guilt – why, he didn't know. It suffocated him. His spirit had shrunk back.

He pressed his palms to his temples, praying that the vision of the two wraiths and the sound of their screams would go away and never return. A cold wind chilled the embers of his soul. A solitary lantern at the end of the alley cast a gloomy light on the detritus left by the Smithfield mob. A vagrant, curled up in a corner, cuddled his tankard like a baby. His snores were loud, but not loud enough to rouse Jan and Henrik.

Nelan groaned and wiped away a smear of blood from his face. He tried to sit up. That was excruciating. At least he lived. An inner voice urged him to get out of the alley. Despite his guilt, pain and grief, he had to stand up. He had to put one foot in front of the other and return to the smithy. He still had the twopence. Wait, did he? He felt inside his purse and… nothing. God's teeth! The boys had nicked it. Edmund would think he'd stolen it. He'd be furious and Matilda apoplectic.

Apart from the theft, Nelan felt better physically; his head spun a little slower than before, and he didn't feel like vomiting after every breath; just after every other breath. He tried to stand up, but felt dizzy and sat down in a dishevelled heap.

He heard raised voices at the end of the alley. Under the dim light of a lantern, some folks prodded the sleeping vagrant.

"There's another one down 'ere," the voice proclaimed.

It sounded familiar, but Nelan couldn't place it. Like the rest of his faculties, his memory resembled a cart in motion with a missing wheel.

The lantern holder walked up to him.

"Do it! Do it!" Nelan snarled, thinking his assailants had returned to finish him off.

"No, no, you're safe. I'm not gonna hurt you." This voice was soft and kind.

"Who are you?" Nelan glanced up to see a young woman. Was she part of his dream, or had that ended?

"I'm Agnes."

"Mother?" he murmured.

"No, I'm not your mother. I'm with my pa, the local constable. Can you sit up?" Agnes asked. "There, that's it. Your face is smeared with blood."

She took a cloth and wiped it away. *If only she could remove the guilt and the shame.* Slowly, painfully, his feelings returned like rain on a land blighted by drought.

"Thank you, Agnes."

"You're strugglin' to draw breath. What happened?"

"Some ruffians. Lads. Wild boys, they beat me."

"They were cruel. Why'd they pick on a little fella like you? What you do to deserve this?"

He met her pale blue eyes. A wisp of brown hair crept out from beneath her headscarf. He wanted to tell her the truth. But what was the truth? Why had they done it? The words squeezed out of his mouth. "I... I was raised in the Netherlands. You can hear my accent. The men in Smithfield... they wore the sackcloth of... a heretic."

"Oh, what? So, those ruffians reckoned you was one of them Baptists?"

He nodded.

"Can you get up?" she asked, helping him.

Her gentle presence imbued his aching muscles with the strength and resolve to stand. She wasn't much taller than him, nor much older.

"Why are you helping me?"

"'Cause you need it," Agnes said, as if it were that simple. Her dulcet tones and subtle touch soothed his fractured mind. And her round, smiling face was as fresh as a spring flower, and just as pretty.

"Come on, little Aggie," a voice boomed out further down the alley. "We gotta finish our rounds."

"That's my pa. I gotta go." Agnes turned to leave, and then added, "At least tell me your name."

"It's Nelan." Then he whispered, "And I saw them." *There, I've said it now.*

Agnes didn't seem to hear his confession, because she raised a crooked finger, pointed at him and said, "Well, my pa, he's a constable, see. In April, a tad before Easter, he discovered the Baptist congregation in Aldgate. They all got arrested. One escaped but got recaptured; Pieters, I think his name was. Them two what died today was their leaders."

"That so?"

"'Tis that," Agnes said. "My pa said that John Foxe wrote to our Queen about them an' said they posed a threat to the safety of the realm. So the Queen sentenced them to death. Good enough for Queen Bess, good enough for me and my pa."

"I heard of them and their sect, but I've only seen them once, and that was just now."

Agnes scrunched up her face. "What did you say?"

"I said I saw them just now."

"Who? The... the two heretics?"

He nodded.

"Yeah, everyone saw them at the burning at the Elms at Smithfield. Wait, you got a strange look in your eye. That's not what you mean. Just *when* did you see them two Dutchies?"

"After the boys gave me a beating and a little before you came along."

"Did they want you to take revenge for their deaths?" Agnes said excitedly.

"No, they only told me their names. And by the grace of God, I'm glad. I couldn't stand to see them. It was awful. Their faces were frozen, their mouths wide open; they yelled in agony. Strange, I can still hear the echoes of their screams in my head. They weren't human anymore. That had been burned out of them. They floated like empty shells. I saw them... their spirits... on their way to Hell."

"How could you see them? They were executed before the men beat you up."

"I... I don't know."

"I do. You saw their ghosts."

"I suppose I must have," he said with a sigh.

"Were you related to them?"

The question stopped Nelan in his tracks. Something turned deep inside him; a hidden cavern. An underground door creaked open. He'd known it existed, but had always run away from it and avoided ever going near it. This time, he had to be brave. He had to face the past; not let it make him cower in its shadow. He brushed away the cobwebs and entered the cellar of his mind. There lurked a memory of a woman; of Agnes. Not this Agnes; another one.

"No – now I remember. The fire. The burning. The pain. I was there. I-I witnessed... the burning."

"What burning? What are you talking about?" Agnes asked.

The forgotten memory flashed through his mind. He was ten years old. His father had told him it had happened during the Council of Blood. At that age, Nelan hadn't known what a council was, let alone a Council of Blood. He did now. The Spanish had invaded the Netherlands, and the Dutch mounted an insurrection which the Spanish instituted the Council of Blood to suppress. It was a cruel, dark enterprise; a thing of evil that pitted man against man for no other reason than how they worshipped God.

In the memory, he stood in the central square of the Dutch town of Leiden. At one end, three wooden stakes were planted in the ground. They were like trees uprooted from the soil, stripped of their branches, and then speared back into the earth. A procession led by a priest and a cohort of Spanish soldiers appeared from one side of the square. They hauled three people into the execution yard: two men and a woman. Scores of people, young and old, rich and poor, merchants and peasants, witnessed the tragedy unfolding before their eyes. More soldiers held the crowd at bay, allowing the procession to pass.

Laurens Michaels pressed a white lily into the woman's bound hands. Her face was fraught with anguish mixed with a strange, uplifting pride, and her eyes were filled with tears. She smiled at Nelan with pain and joy, grief and succour. Then she brushed her fingers against his cheek with such tenderness. He smelled the fragrance of the white lily. He touched his cheek, rekindling the feeling. The woman's hand was as cold as ice. His father tried to cover Nelan's eyes with his hands, but Nelan pushed them away. He wanted to bear witness.

The condemned were bound to the stakes and blindfolded. Then men scurried around them like rats, loading faggots, twigs and brushwood at their feet as if to build them temporary wooden thrones. But this was no coronation. This was no adoration. This was murder perpetrated in the name of religion. That couldn't be right. Religion had nothing to do with murder. Religion represented a supreme endeavour to improve oneself in every aspect of one's life, to acquire as many skills as possible, and to understand as much as possible about living, helping others and assisting the great works of the Creator. The way of religion was simple and natural; the same as life itself. It had three principles: abide by the rules, don't be perverse, and do no harm.

Yet there Nelan was, ten years old, witnessing the execution of three of his countryfolk. The priest blessed the fire. The flames needed blessing. Nelan didn't know why. Perhaps they'd inflict more pain if they were blessed. A soldier with black hair stepped onto a platform. He brushed down his uniform. Perhaps an execution merited cleanliness. Nelan didn't know. The man addressed the crowd. Nelan didn't hear his words because he was choking with emotion.

Another man, dressed in a long black robe and a black cap, strode into the arena. He brandished a lighted torch. The crowd hurled insults and obscenities at him. He lifted the torch and thrust it at the base of the first stake. Then, with exaggerated effect, he moved around the bonfire, shoving the torch gleefully into the faggots. As the flames licked his flesh, the male prisoner yelled in agony. The mob shouted. The bonfire roared.

The man in the black cap turned to the woman tied to the middle stake. He stalked his victim, snarling at her, saying words Nelan couldn't hear. The crowd surged forward. The Spanish guards drew their pikes to force them back.

A man in the crowd called out, "By the Lord our God, have mercy. Free the woman!"

The people took up the refrain. "Free her! Free her!"

As the crowd's angst reached a noisy, turbulent crescendo, the black-capped man lifted his torch into the air, then thrust it again and again into the kindling at the base of the woman's stake. As the flames kissed the faggots, she screamed, filling the air, the town and the whole world with her cries of anguish. Nelan pressed his palms against his ears to blot out the sound. He wanted her to die now. With all his being, he wanted her to be released from pain and to depart this earth. He didn't want her to bear this suffering. But he was a little boy, and she... well, he didn't want her to die. Of course he didn't. How could he?

Because he knew her name. It was Agnes.

He knew her. She of the white lily was his mother.

On that day, she died. And on that day, he stopped growing.

5

The Fire Breaker

23rd July 1575

Struggling back to the smithy, he kept hearing his mother's cries of agony in his head. Leiden; what a memory. The name of the town derived from the German '*liden*', which meant 'to suffer'. Yes, he had to right the wrong of his mother's execution.

The sun rose over the houses, casting long shadows across the cramped alleys and byways. Even the street dogs raised a racket. Servants buying for their masters and people shopping for their daily fare packed into the narrow confines of Bread Street. As he reached the junction with Thames Street, Eleanor bounded out of the baker's shop and wrapped her arms around him.

"Oh, my Nelan, welcome home. They said you'd run away. I told them you'd be back, and here you are, in front of my own eyes. Oh, I worried about you. I missed you," she said coyly. Then she asked, "You're limping, and... what happened to your face?"

"It's a long story, but I'm all the better for seeing you," he said, holding her hands in his and gazing into her green eyes. Her warm and genuine welcome lifted his spirits. Edmund wouldn't greet him in the same way.

Crossing into High Timber Lane, he saw his master with his back to him, remonstrating with his wife.

Matilda spotted Nelan. "There he is!" she yelled, thrusting an accusatory finger at him.

Edmund turned and shouted, "Hell's teeth! The varlet's dared to show 'is face. Where the 'ell you been since yesterday, eh? Fightin' in the streets? I'll give you fightin'!"

"They attacked me, Master Edmund," Nelan said, bowing with due deference.

"Attacked, eh? That's more like sound and fury, I'll warrant." Edmund grabbed him by the scruff of his neck and lifted him off his feet, so that his legs dangled in thin air. "Give me my money!"

"M-money?" Nelan stuttered.

"Yes, you jackanapes! My twopence," Edmund hissed.

"Oh, yes, that."

"You ain't got it, have you? You've spent it on warm ale and loose women, haven't you? You drunkard! Whoreson! You should've been back 'ere yesterday afternoon. But now you got the gumption to come back without it? God's blood, Nelan! You'll pay me for this."

Edmund dropped him, and he fell on the floor in a crumpled heap.

"But, Master Edmund," he said, struggling to get up and rubbing his throat, "the gang beat me up and stole the money. It couldn't help it. I'll pay it all back, though. My word is my bond." He heard himself utter these words as if in a dream. Again, injustice. Again, false accusation. Was it a curse on his life? If it was a test, it was a hard one.

"You will that, lad. Now, get to work. I want that forge shining like the sun! Get her fired up, and be quick about it! And don't give me any of your damn moanings an' groanings."

Nelan heaved a sigh of relief, scuttled over to the forge and shovelled the cold ashes out of its base. He coughed as the dust billowed into his eyes and down his throat. 'Ashes to ashes, dust to dust'; that was his lot, but not in the biblical sense.

As he got on with his work, he overheard Matilda saying, "Edmund, that boy's a thief and a lazy braggart. I'd hand him over to the constable, but not you. Send for your brother. He'll take him to Newgate. I don't understand you. Why in God's name have you taken him back?"

"Oh, I promise you, my sweet Matilda, that I'll dock the twopence from his wages, plus the earnings we've lost because of his absence. He owes us good an' proper, he does. And 'cause of the war with the Dons, we got to pay more taxes than ever. And I don't have the time to train another apprentice."

Saved by providence, Nelan thought gleefully.

But Edmund hadn't finished. "I'm not as stupid as I look. Can't you see? It's obvious. He's a well-educated boy, ain't he? Can't he read an' write? He talks all posh and uses them long, flummoxin' words. He even speaks Latinus. But he's working for me, Edmund Mussell, a lowly smith from Queenhithe. Why d'you think that is? Well, I'll tell ya. It's 'cause he's on the run. He's done some awful crime; he must 'ave. So, yes, I might call on me bro, but that's the last thing young Nelan wants me to do. From now on, he's gonna be as good as gold. You watch."

"Husband, I think you're right." Matilda nodded, her lips twitching in mock satisfaction. "For once," she added with a wry smile.

Nelan awoke. The predawn shadows wrapped the world in a gentle, maternal embrace. The four days since he had returned to the smithy had been a hard graft. That made it the twenty-seventh day of July in the year 1575. Amidst the street sounds outside, he could hear the dawn chorus, a natural celebration of the birds in response to the wash of the incoming dawn. He closed his eyes.

In his mind's eye, he saw a strange shape: three curved lines crawling up the wall like lithe, silvery flames, throbbing, flashing alternately light and dark. He opened his eyes and the lines remained there, vibrating on the opposite wall. Perhaps lizards had infested the place. He stood up to confront them. The apparition dissolved into the wall and disappeared. He'd heard the biblical story of the Feast of Belshazzar, in which writing appeared on the wall out of the ether, but it hadn't mentioned lizards or silvery flames. If he ambled towards the wall, perhaps they'd return and speak to him, or show him a sign? That would be a mark of progress. What about scrying, the art of looking into objects like crystals for the purposes of divination? Perhaps spirits were appearing to him, using the wall as a mirror. Maybe this was how these curious creatures could impart wisdom and tell him about the future. He edged towards the wall, stared at it, and hesitantly placed his hand on it. Nothing happened. Well, what did he expect? He was Nelan, a runaway, an apprentice, but an apprentice of what? A smith, a fireman, a man of fire, a fire lover, the new Prometheus? Perhaps he suffered this vision because he was exhausted or deluded. Or was he actually seeing strange shapes crawling up the forge wall?

The vapours of the new day crept under the workshop gates. He shoved them open. The three wavy lines hovered in the middle of the alley. Now they seemed like an apparition that beckoned him. He followed them as far as the corner of Bread Street and watched, mesmerised, as they hovered, unaffected by the gusts of wind, outside the bakery door. Hell's teeth! Why had they led him here?

A donkey cart rumbled by, and he darted to one side to avoid a collision. He was turning to return to the smithy when he saw it in the dim dawn light: a thin sliver of smoke. His nose twitched. In the air, he caught a warm, earthy odour that soothed his nostrils as if he'd smelled it many times before while sitting in front of... yes, in front of a roaring bonfire. He smelled woodsmoke. *God's breath! Fire!*

At the top of his voice, he called, "Fire! In the bakery! Wake up!"

Clouds of white-grey smoke billowed from beneath the lintel of the baker's door and through the seams of the tiny windows. Some neighbours rushed out, still in their nightgowns and nightcaps, and ran around on stockinged feet on the warm cobblestones.

Nelan smashed his fist against the baker's door. "Eleanor! Charles! Imogen! Wake up! Fire!"

Doors and windows were flung open. More neighbours raced out of their houses.

Edmund joined the throng, shouting, "Open the damn door!"

"Door's bolted," Nelan said. He fought to keep the panic from rising.

A lean, flea-bitten dog ran up to him, barking and yelping. Its master, the inimitable Alexander, followed close behind. The watchman pulled his bell from his belt and gave it a resounding peal. The loud clang drew the attention of all the locals, including some ladies of the night still working in Stew Lane. They joined a score of men frantically battling the gusts of wind to enter the bakery.

Nelan screamed at them, "What are you waiting for? Grab the buckets! Form a line to the river! We need water! Now!"

They needed no more telling. Fire was an ever-present danger in this city of packed wood-framed houses. For most folks, losing their home and job would mean only one thing: a life of vagrancy followed not long after by premature death.

Nelan grabbed Alexander's pike and smashed it against the bakery door. As it gave way, a gust of searing smoke and flame threw him backwards onto his arse. In a flash he got up and ran into the burning house. The smoke and flames swirled around, driven by the draughts of wind. He could barely see his hand in front of his face but, knowing the layout of the house, he headed for where he thought he'd find Eleanor's bedchamber.

Then he tripped over an object on the floor. It was soft on the outside and hard on the inside. A body. He stooped, feeling for an arm, a head or a leg. He grabbed both arms and pulled for all his worth, dragging the body along the floor. Coughing and spluttering, his eyes stinging like Hell, he burst out of the house and hauled the body into the street. It was Imogen. Eleanor remained in the inferno.

Imogen burst into a fit of coughing. Matilda sat her up and smacked her on the back. People gathered buckets of water from the river, passed them along the line to Nelan, and he poured them onto the flames. Black smoke billowed from the door, driven by the stiff breeze. More people joined the line, bringing buckets. The bell clanged. People gaped. Smoke wafted. The dog barked. Nelan moved to go back inside.

Alexander grabbed his shoulder and said, "Stop there, fella. By the Lord, I seen fires in my time. This one's as hot as Hell. Go back in there, an' we'll be pullin' out your charred remains."

"I don't care." Nelan shouted to make himself heard. "I have to save her."

"Then take this," Alexander said. He doused his scarf in a bucket of ripe Thames water and handed it to Nelan. "Use it to cover your mouth and nose."

Nelan shot back into the blaze. With his mouth closed and his eyes narrowed, he stumbled towards Eleanor's tiny room. Fumbling around in the smoke, he found her lying on her bed. He lifted her in his arms and staggered back through the narrow corridor. As he approached the front door, the fire surged and pushed him back into the house. He dived into an alcove and the flames shot by him, then died back momentarily. In the middle of the corridor the fire blazed, smoke spinning like a top around it. Nelan turned back the other way. More flames and smoke barred his way. Eleanor stirred in his arms. His throat hot and dry, he spluttered into the wet scarf. His eyes were scorched, like when the forge taught him a harsh lesson. This fire was his nemesis.

In that moment, his right hand throbbed as if a brand was burning into his skin. At first he thought a fragment of hot wood had scorched him; then he realised it was his palm, in the exact location of the three wavy lines beneath his middle finger. Wait. That was the symbol – the three vertical silvery lines – which had mysteriously led him to this fire.

An idea formed in his mind. He shifted his whole being and all of his senses onto the fire. Hovering above and amidst the red tips of the flames, he saw the three lines. Whatever they were, they added sheer elemental power to the fire. It was incessant. A living Hell, it licked his feet, burning and scorching his legs, the wind blowing it in all directions. But because he'd grown accustomed to the heat of the forge, he could endure it. Tensing every sinew, his jaw squared and his eyes blazing, he willed the silvery lines to disappear.

At first, nothing happened... or so he thought. But when he narrowed his eyes and looked again, one of the lines had dissolved into the ether. By the Lord, were the flames a little less ferocious, or was he imagining that too? Now there were two lines. If he could send them back from whence they came, the fire's strength would wilt, and he could save Eleanor. With all his might, he willed the second line to disappear. It did. Inside, he jumped for joy. The gust of wind died down and, with it, the flames. What remained were hot coals and searing debris. He willed the third wavy line to disappear. It did, and so did the fire. Now it was nothing more than lukewarm embers, like the ashes he cleaned out of the forge.

Eleanor stirred in his arms, and he almost dropped her. "What's happening?" she murmured.

"It's me, Nelan," he said, steadying his grip on her. "You're safe. I've got you."

He squeezed through the corridor. Stepping out of the burnt-out bakery, he was coated in soot and grime. A crowd waited anxiously outside.

"Charles is still in there. Save him!" he cried.

Alexander dashed into the smoke-filled house and soon emerged with the baker. Imogen's face was a portrait of pain and happiness. She opened her arms and smiled a sad, winsome smile of victory and defeat. Charles embraced her. With Eleanor ensconced within her family, Nelan collapsed in a heap on the cobblestones.

When he awoke, he lay on the ground, covered by a rough-hewn, smelly blanket.

"He's awake," Edmund said. This time, he roared like that larger-than-life gentleman of yesteryear, Sir John Oldcastle, though Sir John was not amongst the circle of smiling faces surrounding Nelan.

Nelan couldn't for the life of him remember what had happened. So many faces looked down at him, laughing, happy. His stomach rumbled. Had he farted?

"Sirrah, how you feelin'?" Matilda had never asked him that before; much less addressed him as 'sirrah'. What had brought on her sudden concern?

Still on the ground, he glanced between the legs of the assembled company and saw the burned-out shell of the bakery. He reached out a hand.

"They're all safe," Edmund cried. "Thanks to you."

"And so are all of us," a neighbour chimed in.

This roused a cheer from the crowd, joy and relief etched on their faces.

"Your bravery saved the family and the houses," Alexander added.

Gradually, the crowd drifted back to their homes. Nelan stood up alongside Edmund, Matilda, Alexander and his scraggy mutt.

"You done good 'ere today, lad," Alexander said. "I want you t' join our force."

"You do?" Nelan said.

"Sirrah, we got lots to do to make our city safe. Guardin' the streets, catchin' them prowlers, and – most of all, Master Nelan – sniffin' out them there fires. Me an' Billy here," he said, stroking the mutt, "is real good at that."

"I'm glad for you both."

"Thing is, we need good men."

"Alexander, it's kind of you to ask, but I can't join the watchmen."

"Nah, you got me wrong, fella. It ain't to join the watchmen. It's for some special group only to deal with fires. I mean, how did you put that one out? You knows you got a gift. Come and join us."

"For fires, well, that's different. Yes, I'd be interested," Nelan said.

"What say you, Master Edmund?" Alexander asked. "Can you lend us your brave apprentice?"

"I hear you good," Edmund said. "You wanna take my 'prentice from me? If he's gone, who's gonna do all the hammerin', bendin' and cuttin'?"

"You ain't no slouch," Alexander said.

"True enough. Well, he saved the neighbourhood. If he wants to help, he can," Edmund said, wiping his nose on his sleeve. "And you'll pay him, won't you? Yeah, that's good; Nelan can pay back his debt to me even earlier."

"Then that's agreed," Alexander said.

As Edmund patted the watchman on the back, Charles the baker staggered towards them. The poor man was coated in debris and coughed into his sleeve. "Nelan," he wheezed.

"Charles. How are you?"

"By the grace of God, and with your help, I'm alive," Charles replied. "Listen, you saved our daughter from a terrible ordeal. She's resting with her mother. But you rescued her. She's our little angel, our future."

"I could do nothing less than save her and you."

As Nelan left the scene and returned to the smithy, he had much to ponder. He had certainly earned his laurels with Eleanor, he was reinstated in Edmund's good books and the hero of Queenhithe, and now he'd joined a new bunch of guardians – fire men, no less. And he'd witnessed how real fire could strike fear into people's hearts.

He stared at the three wavy lines beneath his middle finger. They looked the same as the other lines on his palm. They weren't a birthmark, so where had they come from, and why did they itch sometimes? Now he saw them outside of himself; in the air, in the ether. They seemed to give him some control over the elemental power of fire. At first, the thought thrilled him to the core. It meant he could wave a gratuitous hand and extinguish fire. He'd be rich in reward and thanks. Then again, did it also suggest that he could *cause* fires;

bring the tiny spark to life and unleash horror and devastation? This marvellous ability was both a gift and a responsibility, and he'd better find out the rules of the game. Otherwise, it might turn and rend him.

6

Eleanor, Eleanor

2nd December 1577

Over the next two and a half years, Nelan continued his apprenticeship as a smith and a fire breaker.

He attended many fires. Some burned themselves out, starved of wood. The fire brigade doused others with a thousand and one buckets of water. One time, a house of three storeys burned down on Jacanapes Row near St Paul's. When the debris had cooled, Nelan and the rest of the firefighting team swept up the fragments, searching for any items of value, such as metal objects, that had survived the inferno. When they'd finished, they poured the ashes into a drinking horn. The evidence of the destructive power of fire was right there in that horn. In less than an hour, the planks, rafters and floors of a large house had been reduced to a cupful of ashes. It had been a family home; a sanctuary for a man and his wife, a haven for their two sons, and a place of rest. Now it was a small pile of ashes and dust. And so was the family. It was a tragedy. The fire had no heart, no soul and no mercy.

When they buried the family's ashes at the funeral, the pastor mouthed the biblical verse:

In the sweat of thy face shalt thou eat bread,
Till thou return unto the ground;
For out of it wast thou taken:
For dust thou art, and unto dust shalt thou return.

Nelan wondered about mortality. What did it mean that, at death, the physical body could be condensed into a paltry handful of dust and ashes, which returned to the ground? Did anything endure after that? He thought it did. He believed that a fiery spirit animated the body and spawned all of life's love and passion. If so, the body was a precious thing; a temporary temple and a sacred host to that spiritual fire. Also in that Bible quote was the idea that things returned to their origins. Separated from its master, a dog would eventually find its way home. A homing pigeon would do the same. The body returning to the earth suggested that it was only borrowed or given in trust during the time a person lived and breathed. As for the fiery spirit, to where did that return – the stars?

During the halcyon days of Nelan's youth, Dr Dee had taught him the rudiments of astrology, and how the constellations influenced events and people on earth. In his travels around London, he confirmed that there were more fires – and more riots and social upheaval – during the time of Leo and the Dog Days of July and August. During the reigns of the other fire signs, Aries in March and April and Sagittarius in November and December, the fires were less fierce but had greater endurance and longevity.

Nelan wanted desperately to discover how to control the three silvery lines. But he rarely saw them at the fires he attended. When he did, no matter how hard he tried or how much willpower he exerted, they would not disappear. He must have misunderstood them, but how? It frustrated him because he wanted to find the link between the three lines in the fire and those beneath his middle finger.

He never stopped thinking of the home he had left behind. He still rankled at the injustice of his exile. He racked his brains seeking ways to convince his father, the St John family and Westminster School, that Guillermo had unintentionally brought about his own downfall. The school steward and Pastor Christopher had only partially witnessed the event, but the steward had nonetheless judged Nelan guilty of the crime. Nelan kept Guillermo's iron and flint, hoping that they would one day prove his innocence. The best he could hope for was to avoid capture for as long as possible and to discover what part he had to play in England's unfolding future. And he'd make good his promise to right the wrong of his mother's awful death. With God's will, he'd succeed.

And so he walked alone, a runaway accompanied by his own shadow and the fear of capture. Forever looking over his shoulder, he lost himself in the forge and the fire-breaking. He explored the enigma of fire and the miracle of the flame. He admired the strength and skill of the smith and his work at the anvil, for that was where a true artisan could be appreciated. Edmund showed him how to work with the hammers and which ones to employ for which metals. Developing the arts and abilities of the blacksmith, Nelan learned how to make nails, use punches, keep tools sharp, work the hammer, and respect the anvil. The simple but profound process of heating metal to make it soft and malleable fascinated him. He could make pikes and bells for the constables, swords and armour for the gentry, and nails and furniture for householders.

On that December day, Edmund asked him to make some door handles and latches and deliver them to the minister of St Martin-in-the-Fields. Nelan had once feared straying too far from Queenhithe to where he might be recognised, but over the years he'd grown heavier and bulkier, and his beard had thickened. He'd even shed some of his Dutch twang, making him more confident to venture away from the smithy. He found the little chapel with its neat, well-kept graveyard and its view of the fields stretching out west beyond the city walls. At the top of White Hall was a lovely stone statue. It resembled a giant, elongated pin, much taller than Nelan, with a broad circle of stone at its base that narrowed to a pinnacle at the top, with elaborate carvings of religious symbols and a coat of arms. He asked a passer-by, who told him all about its fascinating history. He immediately thought of Eleanor and couldn't wait to show it to her.

A few days later, he invited her to accompany him to St Martin-in-the-Fields to attend a service. After the Baker Street fire, she and her family had moved in with her auntie in nearby Cheapside. Nelan went to collect her, and together they headed off to the chapel. A hoar frost, the first of the winter, crept over the roofs of the city's houses. The ice glistened and shone; it was as if an angel had fluttered its wings and sprinkled stardust on the land. Shivering with cold, they walked together along Fleet Street, avoiding the carriages rushing important people to church. Fox droppings and horse manure littered the streets, but the frost had laid a carpet over it all, enabling Nelan to enjoy the simple pleasure of Eleanor's company.

By the time they breached the west end of the Strand, they had merged with a small crowd heading up St Martin's Lane to the church. Inside, Nelan and Eleanor found a place to stand near the back. As they waited for the service to begin, the congregation continued to shuffle in through the door, bringing with them a chilling blast from outside. Folks spoke in hushed tones, their breath steaming in the frigid air, and rubbed their hands to keep warm.

Someone next to them said, "Wonder what the sermon will be about today?"

"I'll wager it'll be more fire and brimstone," came the reply.

When the time came for the sermon, the minister stepped up to the brass lectern, its eagle head frowning upon them all. "Parishioners, welcome to St Martin-in-the-Fields," he said. "First, I bring you good tidings from Plymouth Hoe. Our great privateer, Francis Drake, set sail from there nearly three weeks ago. The Dons – the Spanish to you – call him *El Draque*, The Dragon, because he breathes fire over their ships and their settlements. For many a year, he's harassed them in the Isthmus of Panama and the Caribbean, bringing back wealth and glory to lay at the feet of our noble Queen. We wish him God's speed, and may he lay a heavy glove on them.

"But today, in our realm, we face yet another crisis. No, not the Papists this time, though they are always trying to disrupt the peace of our land. And no, not just because Pope Pius V excommunicated our beloved Queen. Seven years ago, he issued the papal bull – and a lot of bull it is too. What has a bull to do with human life? Nothing.

"Let me tell you about the rite of excommunication. It has three parts, commonly referred to as Bell, Book and Candle. The bell is the ringing of the church bells, the book denotes the reciting of the Mass of the Anathema, and the candle is the lighting and then the extinguishing of the candles. The purpose of the rite is to cut off the person from receiving the holy sacrament and sever their connection to the Catholic faith. And not only has our Queen been excommunicated, but you have too – all of you."

The preacher pointed at the congregation. A silence fell on the little chapel.

"The truth is," the minister continued, "that the Pope not only excommunicated the Queen, but he also excluded all the members of her Privy Council, as well as all the earls and lords of our land, and all of us. That's you and me. Why? Because, since Her Majesty's excommunication, you have obeyed her orders, her statutes and her laws. By the terms of the papal bull, you and I have joined our gracious Queen in the odious state of excommunication. That's why."

He thumped the lectern with such a blow that the eagle seemed to shudder. In a low growl, he said, "Excommunicated! The sheer gall of the Pope! He called our Queen a pretender. He said she no longer rules in her own land. The Pope has no authority to govern here, nor to tell us how to govern ourselves. The Papists do not rule here. Elizabeth Regina is the Supreme Governor of the Church of England. *She* rules here. The Pope is the pretender, and his bull is treasonous. These Papists are the Devil incarnate!

"Satan is roaring like a lion. The world is going mad. The Antichrist is resorting to every extreme. Soon, he'll come like a wolf and devour us, the sheep of Christ. And these signs indicate one thing, that we face the end of the world as we know it."

Then the preacher paused, as if waiting for the power of his words to find a home in the hearts of the little congregation. Wise in the ways of the world, he spoke not only to them but, through them, to the world at large. The words he had just spoken still rang like pistol shots around the rafters of the little church. He sucked his teeth and said, "Not content with excommunication and burning heretics in the Netherlands; now they foment a terrible revolution. And as their excommunication failed, so this new crisis will too.

"From the ancients, we know that the only change in the universe happens in the sublunar realm; that is, between the earth and the moon. The moon waxes and wanes. It changes. The earth has her four seasons. She changes too. But everything beyond the realm of the stars is fixed and cannot move outside of its orbit. Now, you may have heard that the astronomers have reported movement beyond the sublunar realm. They call it a comet. I say it's impossible. There can be no movement in that realm. The ancients told us so, and they don't lie. It's another Papist plot. With news of this comet, they're trying to undermine our view of the order of things. Stand firm; we must. And stop them, at whatever cost."

The congregation of chandlers and weavers, bakers and fletchers, farriers and smiths shuffled uncomfortably in the aisles. There was scratching of heads and chewing of the cud as most of the sermon seemed to waft over their heads. Not Nelan. He found it fascinating. A comet – nothing like this had happened before. The news was unprecedented and portentous.

Once the liturgy had finished, he left the church with Eleanor. The weather was dry but bitterly cold as they walked down St Martin's Lane to the Strand. Eleanor wanted to go home, but Nelan took her gently by the hand and led her towards the top of White Hall.

"Here, come this way," he said. "Let me show you something."

The stone cross was ahead; the one he'd seen a few days before. Needle-like, the frost made it shimmer in the winter sun. Together they watched the other couples leave the church. As they passed the cross, each one paused for a moment's silent remembrance. The men pressed their caps to their hearts. The women bowed their heads. Some shed a solitary tear. Others walked on, lost in thought.

"This is poignant," Eleanor said. "What's so special about this cross?"

"Edward I accompanied his wife of many years when she died near Lincoln," Nelan said. "The King brought her body back to London on a bier. At each of the twelve stops along the way, he erected a memorial to her: a cross; a charing cross."

"I didn't know that," Eleanor said, holding back a tear. "And these ordinary folk, they show her such deep respect. On a freezing day, it warms the cockles of your heart."

"People behaved the same the other day when I came here. I wanted to share this special place, and what it means, with you."

"What was the name of his Queen?"

Nelan looked her softly in the eye and whispered, "Eleanor."

"Oh, but that's… my name," she said, choking on the emotion.

"It's also called Eleanor's Cross."

"Nelan, you brought me here… you thought of me. That's kind. Thank you. It's a wonderful story of a love that lasts beyond death and into the afterlife."

The moist sparkle in her eyes warmed him inside.

"I wonder," she mused, pressing his hand into hers, "is the fire of love between a man and a woman immortal?"

"Perhaps one day we'll find out," he murmured.

Impervious to the cold, Nelan glowed inside with the subtle fire of love and the living of it; each moment quickening the next. Love resided in the way a precious flower returned each spring with gentle petals and an exquisite aroma, ever-present and never to be forgotten. The presence of the Eleanor Cross embraced them both. It represented an ideal larger than life itself. He was filled with the glory of life, of living and of sharing that instant, which was like an enduring string of milk-white pearls joined one to the next; always there, never-ending. For would there not be love tomorrow and the next day? Would a Chinaman not love a woman with the same passion as an Englishman would love his? Would the same reverence for living and for life itself not course through their veins? The timeless moment held them in its sway; a spirit clamp watched by more than just the two of them. It seemed as if other eyes looked through theirs to see what they saw; to witness what they witnessed. A sublime moment of beauty and belonging was the nearest to a religious experience that Nelan had ever had.

When they finally moved on, they headed along the river. Even there, Nelan felt the cross's presence and its vital awareness remain with them. The moment had been etched indelibly into their lives.

On returning to Queenhithe, Nelan knew the time was right. He led Eleanor to their special place by the docks. They had sat there in the summer, watching the world go by, waiting for their time to take their place in it. There was a tide in his affairs; a tide to be taken at the flood. And this was it. Inside his purse, he found a metal ring he had made in the workshop. He rubbed it against his sleeve until it sparkled with his love; then he stood before Eleanor with a huge smile as if he'd found the crown jewels.

"Eleanor, I want to ask you something."

"Yes, Nelan?" she said, a twinkle in her eye. "Anything."

"Will you…?"

"What do you want of me?" And then she guessed his next words. "Are you…? Oh, my Lord, you are."

"Will you marry me?"

"Yes, yes, I will marry you," she cried, and she flung her arms around his neck and kissed him on the lips.

Once they'd disentangled, he nervously placed the ring on her finger and said, "Let this be a proof of our engagement. From now on, we are one. We are joined together."

As they walked to her auntie's home in Cheapside, they talked of nothing but the wedding. Allowing for the banns, they set the 28th December as the date for the ceremony. It would be a union of their two lives and bind them together for the rest of their days on earth.

Nelan felt his conscience prick him. To be fair to her, he had to tell her of his troubled past. "Eleanor?"

"Yes, my dear husband-to-be?" Her smile was broader than the river.

"I have a secret to share with you from my earlier years. It's important you know everything about me."

"Oh, how exciting! But can we keep it until next time?"

"If you wish. Until tomorrow, then," he said. Then, skipping home, he sang:

I can't ask for more,
Dear Eleanor, Eleanor.
It's you I adore,
Eleanor, Eleanor.

7

The Burning Bush

5th December 1577

The following day, long, cold shadows crept across the forge workshop like an old cripple. Nelan opened his eyes. In seven days, he'd turn twenty – an achievement in itself.

Then there was a loud banging on the outer gates of the smithy, and a dog yapped. "Ne-lan! Ne-lan!" came the cry.

Nelan recognised the voice of the man and that of the hound. Alexander and Billy had never called this early in the morning. There must be a fire. He pulled on his hose, jerkin and cap, and grabbed a pair of gloves and a kerchief for a mask. The cold forge would have to wait. "I'm ready!" he shouted. Buoyed by the high emotion of the day before, he bounded out of the door. Now he thought of himself as a married man, committed to honouring his bride-to-be and cherishing her, and loving her as only he could.

Alexander was halfway down the jetty when Nelan emerged into Stew Lane. "Come on, lad. No time to lose!" he urged him.

Nelan ran to the river, dived into the wherry and got hold of an oar. Holding the tiller, Alexander called the time. (Billy barked the time too.) Nelan sat in the middle of the line of five pairs of rowers and faced the river's south bank. Stored at the front of the wherry was fire-breaking equipment: buckets, axes, hammers, gloves, and leather gowns. The sun rose on another clear, frosty day with high, thin, wispy clouds and a pale turquoise sky. With the tide on the flow, they sped through the water. Usually, they would go no farther west than Chelsea to extinguish a fire, but they had already glided past the hamlet. Soon, the chapel of All Saints at Fulham drifted into view. After half an hour's strenuous rowing, the sweat poured off Nelan and his short arms ached from having to lift the oar higher to gain the proper purchase.

"Hold up!" Alexander cried. "Ferry passing!"

What a relief. Panting with exhaustion, Nelan slumped over his oar. The man next to him sat quietly, his oar resting in his lap. He had narrow eyes and a strong, square chin. For all the emotion he ever showed, which wasn't much, his face resembled a flat piece of granite. He wore a Chinaman's hat, a habit which, unsurprisingly, earned him the nickname of China.

"China, where did you say we're heading?" Nelan asked.

"Where d'you think? Open your eyes, and you'll see where." China was not known for his conversational arts.

Nelan looked around and, sure enough, a large plume of black smoke billowed into the early morning air. "Where's that coming from?" he asked.

"Far side of the oxbow."

"The Barnes–Chiswick one?"

"You know another?"

A frisson of anguish knotted Nelan's stomach. It couldn't be his father's house, could it?

The ferry was close to docking, clearing the way ahead. Alexander called the rowers back into action. Nelan grew anxious about their final destination. He was still a runaway; a fugitive from justice. From their route, it looked increasingly like the fire raged in Mortlake. Nelan had not grown an inch since arriving in England, making him as recognisable as a rampant lion in a marketplace. But so far, his beard had worked as a good disguise. Still, despite his new-found confidence, he pulled his cap down over his forehead.

As they rowed north up the curve of the oxbow, passing Fulham, he recognised Walsingham's manor house at Barn Elms by its fox weathervane. Across the other side of the oxbow, the plume of black smoke grew ever thicker. There were few prominent houses in that area; at least none so large as to burn with such ferocity and for so long. What other possibility was there? It could be Dr Dee's house, or the nearby Church of St Mary the Virgin, Mortlake. Oddly, he couldn't shake the feeling that it was his old house. His father couldn't die in the same terrible manner as his mother, could he? Surely, Laurens had survived. And what had happened to the maidservant, the footman and the other servants? Nelan had seen the awful effects of fire: the burns, the scabs, the scalding, the scorched skin that fell off the bone like leprosy, and the terrible scarring. Some families never recovered from losing their home. After a life on the road dodging cut-throats, cutpurses and other highwaymen, they stumbled into an early grave. If life wasn't bad enough, there was always famine, war and the plague.

A light westerly breeze blew up, and the smoke plume spiralled and twisted towards them. The wherry rounded the top of the oxbow and glided towards the St John house in Sneakenhall. Keeping his head down, Nelan concentrated on rowing in time to Alexander's rasping cries. As they approached the St John residence, he peeped out from under his cap and, to his horror, saw two men directing a dozen others, who loaded trunks and cases into several wherries tied to the jetty. The two were St John and his stepson Pedro. Nelan's stomach cramped, and he ducked his head down between his knees.

Alexander hailed them. "You's all in a hurry. What's going on 'ere, then?"

"Moving house," St John replied.

"Where to?" Alexander asked.

"Far away from here." St John's voice was tinged with bitterness. "And you? Where are you going?"

"Attending the fire upriver, m'lord," Alexander explained.

"That's the Michaels' house," St John replied. "They're finally getting what they deserve."

"Why's that, then? What they done to you?" Alexander asked.

"I could tell you the story, but the Lord knows the truth," St John said.

"It's the house of the damned," Pedro added gruffly. "We're praying it burns to the ground."

That confirmed Nelan's worst fears: his father's house was aflame.

Alexander hurried the rowers, and they pressed on down the western curve of the oxbow. John Dee's house sat in front of a cloud of black smoke. As they rowed by Dee's jetty, Nelan spotted a man outside the house. It was Digges, the man who'd set him off trying to get a pair of shoes that never wore out. Fortunately, he appeared more interested in monitoring the spread of the fire than in talking to them. Either way, Nelan did not want to be recognised, so he crouched down until his face thumped against the oar.

They breached the jetty by his old house, and Alexander attached the boat's ropes. Nelan had walked down that rickety jetty and jumped into a wherry almost every day for nigh on seven years, and here he was, returning to Mortlake, this time as a runaway and a fire breaker. He scanned the scene for his father. No sign of him. A terrified group of women and children from the village huddled together on one side of the jetty, transfixed by the fire's relentless power. A clutch of feral boys ran around the blazing inferno like demented rats. The fire burned with derisory fury, its flames licking the morning sky like a starved lover. Red-yellow flames married with black-grey smoke, which billowed from the house. A chain of men hauled buckets of water from the river to the house and sent them back empty to be refilled. The line was fifty paces long, though the fire seemed distinctly unimpressed with their efforts.

Alexander leapt onto the jetty. The fire men removed the equipment from the wherry. Nelan could feel the heat of the fire on his face from where he stood. Now, what was he to do? Would the servants recognise him? It was with mixed emotions that he saw no one he knew. Frantic, he grabbed the first person he came across by the shoulder.

The man turned like a whirlwind, raising his stick at Nelan, and with a snarl said, "Get your hands off me!"

Nelan stepped back from the man, who had a long, pointed face and a wrinkled forehead. He wore a scraggy beard and had deep-set blue eyes that danced like a galliard, never resting in one place for an instant. His face was ashen, and he smelled of smoke.

"Who are you?"

"I be Parsons."

"From Parsons Green?"

"Nah, not me."

"Did you see anyone leave the house?"

"Yeah. A gaggle of servants. Oh, an' two men come from that neighbour's house to 'ave a look-see at the fire, but they gone now."

"Did you see a tall, fair-haired man?" Nelan asked.

"Nah, didn't see no one like that," Parsons said.

"You been staying here?"

"What's it to you? This your 'ouse?"

Nelan couldn't answer that question truthfully without giving himself away.

Fortunately, Alexander butted in. "For Christ's sake, tell us: d'you know if there's anyone inside that inferno?"

"Listen, I told yous already. I seen the servants an' the men; that be all."

"What you doin' 'ere, then?" Alexander asked.

"Fighting the flames. Me, I'm the local fire breaker."

"Why didn't you say?"

"Bah. You didn't ask, did ya?"

"What'll we do?" Nelan asked.

"We'll have to wait till the fire dies down," Alexander said. "Then we'll check through the remains."

The news was uncertain. Nelan's father could be away on business – or had he been trapped inside the house, or moved away altogether? The flames leapt towards them, right into their faces, forcing them to retreat to a safe distance.

"I don't get this fire," said Parsons, taking off his cap and scratching his head.

"What don't you get? House is made o' wood. Wood burns like Hell; always has, always will," Alexander said.

"I been to fires like this since before you was suckin' at your mother's breast," Parsons grumbled. "This fire burns like no other I ever seen. I mean, why's them flames so fierce?"

"What you sayin'?" Alexander asked.

"I'm not saying nothin'. I'm only askin' a question," Parsons replied. "See, this fire's young an' 'ungry. We been fightin' it for hours. If it be a normal fire, it be tamed b' now, but it ain't."

"And...?"

"And this fire's attracted stuff: spirits; more than flames. It's attracted them devils; you know... from the pits of Hell."

Nelan's mouth dropped open. So did Alexander's. In all the fires he'd attended, there had been a few strange ones – people saved by the skin of their teeth – but never any talk of spirits or devils. In Parsons,

71

Nelan had found a kindred spirit. They both loved fire. He interrupted. "God save us all, but how can you be sure?"

Parsons spat on the Lord's earth. "I knows it in me bones. Fire comes out of thin air, but you can't see it. It's either restin' or active. When it's restin', it's everywhere: all around us, hiding in the air in tiny pockets, so small we can't see it. But it's there all right, ready and waitin' to be called. When it comes, it comes with a vengeance. It don't belong here, see. But it shows itself through flame, smoke, heat an' all that. It ravishes everything it can. It's a lithe spirit that gotta be controlled, but none of us knows how to do that. There's the Devil in the fire; that's why it can't be tethered. The Devil's breathin' fire on this one, an' that's what keeps them flames a-burnin'."

"Maybe you're right. Perhaps it's not the burning bush, but the burning house. Both burn everlasting," Nelan said.

"I learned me Bible lines good an' proper. The burnin' bush was where Moses got appointed to lead them Israelites out of Egypt and into the Promised Land," Parsons said with unconcealed pride.

"Now, what are *you* saying?" Nelan asked.

The question hung in the air. A snaking line of men and boys carried buckets of river water but failed to extinguish the fire. Nelan noticed the women, like a coven of witches, intoxicated by the eternal power of the fire; and the children, running around like little savages, their cries and shouts brimming with fire and brimstone. The fire crackled, and a plume spurted high into the air, reaching towards Heaven. At the crest of the plume, Nelan saw a strange shape against the searing blue-violet flames. He had to wipe his eyes because he couldn't believe it. He looked again, and there they were: three wavy, silvery lines, like thin lizards crawling up and inside the tongues of the flames, their legs moving all the time but holding their position in the air. In a flash, the wildness of the fire subsided, the flames receded into the house, and the three wavy lines disappeared. There followed a deathly silence, as if all the noise and hubbub in the world had been sucked into the earth. The quiet resembled the one after the trumpet had played the funeral sentences by a graveside; it gripped Nelan like an invisible ring, tight around his neck.

Parsons bequeathed another globule of spit to God's earth and broke the hollow silence. "If this be the burnin' bush, who's the Moses; the man to be appointed? And what's the Promised Land?"

These were poignant questions to which no one had the answer.

The fire seemed to lose its vigour, as if the spirit animating its brightened flames and stifling heat had moved away to occupy some other bonfire. As Alexander, China and the rest of the crew dampened the last embers, Nelan went round to the back of the house. He tried desperately to avoid looking at it because every time he did, he welled up and a tear leaked from his eye. He was distraught that his old house had burned down. And what had happened to his father? He felt truly alone, afraid and vulnerable.

A short distance along the river was Dr Dee's house. All Nelan's memories of his tutor came flooding back. Dee had helped him to escape from the constable and given him the vision of a bright future. Perhaps he could do so again. Maybe he knew his father's whereabouts.

Nelan left the burned-out shell of his house and walked along the path to Dee's house. With no sign of Digges, Nelan entered through the front door and peered into the study. Absorbed in an experiment, Dee was fiddling about with an unlit candle and an egg-shaped glass crystal in a cradle. He pressed the fingers and thumb of his right hand into a cone shape and pointed it at the crystal. Then he moved his hand slowly towards and then away from the crystal. Breathing in the rays of light emanating from Dee's hand, the crystal began to glow. As if by magic, it throbbed in a dance of blues and whites. Dee picked it up and aimed its pointed end at the unlit candle wick. As the wick flickered and then caught fire, Nelan sucked in his cheeks.

Dee turned and said, "Greetings, Master Michaels. Please join me. Though it's a shame that you return to Mortlake to find your house aflame."

"I'm searching for my father, Dr Dee. Have you seen him or any of the servants?"

"When the fire broke out," Dee said in his kindly, avuncular sort of way, "I went to see if I could assist, but it was already raging. I didn't see Laurens; nor do I know where he is."

"Do you know how the fire started?" Nelan asked.

"I don't, but it burns with a strange vengeance. But ask Digges; he might know more. You'll find him in the church. That's where the servants are sheltering."

"I will, m'lord. And by coincidence, some years ago I saw Digges in Smithfield, where I overheard him speak of shoes that don't wear out. Ever since then, I've grown intrigued by the idea of these strange shoes. Please, is there anything you can tell me about them?"

"Why do you want to know?"

The atmosphere in the room, so charged with mystery, lent Nelan an unusual eloquence. "Since you told me I have a part to play in England's future, I've been fascinated by fire. And what about these shoes? How does a person wear them?"

Dee coughed into his sleeve and said, "I'll help you. Get hold of a Geneva Bible. Read the Book of Job, Chapter 10, Verse 1, where you'll find a clue to help you find the answer."

"I'm grateful," Nelan said.

"Now, watch this," Dee said. With the crystal in his left hand, he pointed it at the candle flame. The air in the room was as still as death. But the flame flickered and then went out.

Nelan shook his head in disbelief. "Is that conjuring?"

"Yes, it is," Dee said, with a mischievous glint in his eye. He opened a box on the table and took out a rough-hewn, dark-coloured stone and some metal filings, then sprinkled filings on the table.

"What are you going to do?" Nelan asked.

"Look and learn," Dee said. He moved the stone towards the filings, which miraculously jumped in the air and stuck to it like glue.

"That's magic!"

"It's not; it's quite natural. This is lodestone; the filings are magnetised iron ore. Sailors use it to locate where they are at sea."

"How does it do that?"

"Every object emits rays which, like the crystal and the lodestone, affect other objects nearby. These forces exist at all levels of creation. Just as the lodestone and the iron filings work in the smaller sphere, so the influence of the moon, sun and stars on our thoughts and beliefs works in the greater sphere. Understand the forces of nature, and you can conjure them."

"How do you use them?"

"I employ them to help England take her rightful place on the world stage."

"That's what I want to do. You've spoken about the very thing that has sat inside me all these years. I don't want to be a spectator of life. I want to be a participant in the unfolding greatness of this land and, in so doing, find myself therein."

"I feel your passion," Dee murmured. "As a reward, I'll give you a writing of mine. Here, it's recently returned from the press." He handed Nelan two printed pages.

Nelan handled them like he'd received the keys to the heavenly vault. "What is it?"

"It's entitled *The Limits of the British Empire*."

"The British Empire? What's that?"

"Read the document, and you'll find out."

"I will, sir, thank you," Nelan said, folding the paper and placing it inside his doublet. "I've never known the name of this calling; the one that prompts and urges me to discover fire and all things natural. What's natural to me are the three wavy lines on my palm. And just now, framed in the flames of the house fire, I saw three wavy lines, like lithe serpents, crawling around."

Dee raised an eyebrow beneath his black cap. "They're salamanders. They are the spirits of fire."

"So, that's what they are! Fascinating." Nelan pressed his hands together three times in prayer, one for each of the gifts he'd received: a clue as to how to wear the shoes that never wore out, the knowledge that he had seen salamanders, and the document about the British Empire. The moment was uncanny. Amid the grace of this new knowledge, he had an unshakeable feeling that he was in the right place at the right time. Everything in his past and his future had been written in the stars. By his acceptance of them, he obliged those secret, hidden influences. He knew that he belonged to these times; that he lived in a way that was right for them. He had come home. "M'lord, the wisdom you have imparted is a great blessing to my life."

From outside the house came the noise and clamour of voices raised in anger.

"He's in the study!" It was St John.

"Nelan, run!" Dee shouted.

Too late. Nowhere to go. St John burst into the room. Another fellow trundled along behind him. Of all people, it was Constable Mussell.

"This is the killer," St John said to Mussell.

"I knows him already," Mussell said through gritted teeth. "And so does my bro."

"He murdered my stepson, Guillermo," St John cried. "Arrest him!"

Mussell grabbed Nelan by the hands and said, "You come quietly now, y'hear?"

"I thought I saw you on the wherry! You scurrilous piece of *caca*!" St John vented his fury.

"Leave 'im be, sirrah," Mussell said, holding back St John. "He be mine now."

As Mussell led Nelan away, Dee said to him, "May God be with you."

"Thank you, m'lord," Nelan replied. He could kick himself for getting caught.

His feet crunched on the frozen ground. Constable Mussell led him past his burned-out house. A few wooden struts remained alongside a tangled cascade of blackened charcoal. A filament of grey-white smoke snaked into the chilled air like a last, desperate message of surrender to the gods. With his hands tied, Nelan couldn't even wipe a tear from his face. Alexander, Parsons and China poured bucket after bucket of water onto the dying embers.

"He arrested?" Alexander asked the constable.

"Yup. I got him," Mussell replied.

"What he do?"

"Killed a boy at school a year or two ago," the constable replied, "then ran away and deceived Edmund, me own brother."

Alexander spat ignominiously onto the ground, then asked Nelan, "That so, lad?"

"It's not. The boy tried to kill me. I was defending myself."

"The court'll decide that," Mussell said, and pulled Nelan towards him.

Nelan lowered his head. Waves of shame pulsed through his body. His life as a fire man and apprentice smith was burned to a crisp. And Eleanor? He was to marry her after Christ Mass. She'd think he'd abandoned her. She'd believe his love for her had been a whim; a plaything to be cast aside like a child's toy. She'd never forgive him.

As the men watched him shuffle by, Billy sniffed and pawed the ground amid the remnants of the house. Alexander strode over to examine what the dog had found, then walked up to Nelan, took off his hat and pressed it to his heart. Nelan knew what had happened. He felt like he'd been kicked in the belly. His legs buckled, but he forced himself to stand.

"Billy sniffed out some charred remains," Alexander said. "They were of a tall man."

"Could you make out what he was wearing?"

"It looked like a velvet doublet, dark green, I think."

"My father's favourite colour," Nelan said, his chin trembling with emotion.

"So sorry, lad," Alexander said.

Nelan felt hollowed out inside, as if the subtle filaments of his soul had been sucked out of him. Laurens Michaels was no more. After his mother's death, his father had cared for Nelan and brought him to safety in England. He'd worked hard to afford to send him to Westminster School so that he could benefit from an excellent education. Even though Laurens hadn't supported him after Guillermo's death, Nelan had, over time, come to forgive him. Perhaps the corpse wasn't him. He wanted to believe it, but Alexander's solemn face cast a long shadow over his hopes. Laurens had gone to meet his Maker thinking that his son was a murderer. In the coming days Nelan would have to live with that awful thought.

The Fates had deprived him of the opportunity to lay his father to rest and to recite a prayer of thanksgiving for his life at his graveside – loss upon loss, grief upon grief. With no family, he was an orphan. And now the court was going to condemn him to die for a crime he hadn't committed. This marked a low ebb in his life.

8

Marshalsea

5th December 1577

Towards the end of the day, a thick mist rose from the sluggish river. Mussell shoved Nelan towards the jetty. He knew every creak on every plank and every knot in the wood on that old jetty. And there was the wherry and its grumpy master Wenceslaus, who'd taken him to school for seven years. As Nelan climbed into the wherry, Wenceslaus threw him a visceral grunt. With Mussell on the other end of the rope, he and Nelan did a macabre dance as the boat jigged and jagged from side to side. They rowed downriver, first by Dr Dee's house and then by St John's. Both times, Nelan bent his head in shame. To add a sting to his misfortune, St John and Pedro were back outside organising their move. They spotted him.

"Pull the wherry in over here," St John's voice thundered through the gloom. "I want to give him a piece of my mind!"

"Can't do that, sir," Mussell said. "Rest 'sured, he'll get his comeuppance."

"Where are you taking him?"

"Nearest prison. That be Marshalsea, sirrah," Mussell said. "They'll give 'im a right romping good welcome there."

Pedro stood at the end of the jetty and flung a stone at the wherry. Nelan ducked, and it clattered against the boat's wooden struts. The young Spaniard followed them along the riverbank, hurling insults. "*Asesino!* Murderer!"

St John walked up to Pedro and restrained him.

But Pedro still got off a parting shot: "May you burn in Hell! Soon you'll join your father!"

St John hauled his stepson back to their house.

While Mussell argued with Wenceslaus about the latter's pay for this trip, Nelan examined his assets. In his purse, he could feel twopence, his char cloth, his iron and flint, a piece of scrap metal from the forge, a chunk of leather, some metal scrapings, and a bunch of fluff. When they rowed past Westminster School, he felt more pangs of disgrace. In his purse, he found a folded broadsheet about Oxford University. He'd dreamed of studying divinity and philosophy there. Now he examined the hairs around his navel (not that he had many), while on the way to London's most notorious prison. Oxford was near the top of the ladder, but he was heading for the bottom rung. He tried to read the broadsheet, but his mind refused to focus. In a pique of anger and frustration, he tore it in half and threw it into the river. Wenceslaus gave him his best frown. Tucked away in his doublet, Nelan found Dee's paper on the British Empire. At least he could look forward to reading that.

London Bridge loomed in the distance, a pile of old stones slung precariously over the river, and filaments of smoke streamed from chimneys into the fractious air. London at dusk was as noisy, smelly and disgusting as it was at dawn. On the river's northern bank were the steps leading to the docks at St Michael Queenhithe.

The sight must have pricked Mussell's conscience, because he got right in Nelan's ear. "Yeah, look over there – recognise that little harbour? You should do, you jackanape. When you was in trouble, I come an' saved your skin, didn't I? Foibles was gonna give you a beatin', but I stopped him. Me. Constable Mussell. Then, like a king's fool, I trusted you to 'elp me bro, but you let me an' 'im down. As soon as I deliver you to Marshalsea, I gotta go and tell 'im why you ain't comin' back to the forge and he gotta do it all 'imself. What you got to say for yourself, eh? Yeah, nothin' at all, huh? Happy now?"

No, Nelan was far from content. Though this was neither the time nor the place for squalid apologies. Besides, Mussell was right: he had let everyone down, but in his defence, he'd only been trying to keep out of reach of the law. And how was he to know that the Lord would have him witness a fire that destroyed his cherished home and killed his father? *May his soul rest in peace.* Both his parents had perished by fire, the very element to which he was drawn. Was that a curse or a blessing? Would he end his days like that too? Please God, he would not perish in that terrible way. And something Pedro had said irked him: that he would join his father in Hell. How did the Spaniard know that Laurens was dead?

As they approached the southern dock, a boat drew up alongside theirs. It was rowed by a bunch of men, all with their hair tarred black. They wore woollen jerkins, knee-length trousers and long stockings.

Wenceslaus had a moan. "Oi! Bloody sailors! Anyone would think they own the seven seas." He shook a fist at them, which disturbed the air but little else.

"Old sea horse, we've navy business 'ere. So, outta the way!" their officer replied in a haughty tone. "Right, all hands up them steps. At the double."

Barefoot and bare-faced, the navy men secured the boat and raced onto the quay.

Wenceslaus moored his wherry on the jetty next to the navy boat. "Here we are, at the steps of St Mary Overie. Not far to go now, my boy."

They disembarked onto the stairs in the pale late afternoon light. Mussell grabbed Nelan's rope and pulled him along behind him. Halfway down Stoney Street, outside a printer's yard, a couple of locals drunk on ale voiced their anger.

"Get on with ya, scum!" a man shouted, and deposited a large globule of spittle on Nelan's shoulder.

The other lad was equally eloquent. "Seen a few of your kind swanning down 'ere, we 'ave. Had enough of it, ain't we? Us, we're good, law-'bidin' citizens. And all yous do is rob us of our hard-earned pennies. Shame on ya."

Mussell led Nelan down a narrow alley into a muddy court, with leaves piled in the corners like it was God's waste bin. A prison warden, who smelled worse than a London street, came and challenged them. Mussell hastily explained their business.

A pair of sturdy wooden gates, held fast by an iron bar and an enormous padlock, surrounded the courtyard. This was Marshalsea. Its high stone wall and infamous double-arched gates were lit by torches set in cradles. A spiked barricade sat atop the wall; ample persuasion for the inmates to remain inside. Its terrible reputation had struck terror into generations of London's debtors, even those owing as little as an angel or ten shillings. Nelan had grown accustomed to the rancid smell of London's streets and the miasma of the river, but the stench emanating from the building was putrid. Even from outside the gates, Marshalsea reeked more of sulphurous fumes than he imagined the pits of Hell would. He wouldn't be surprised if the wardens had horns and tails.

Inside was so badly lit that Nelan couldn't see the poor sods, though he could hear them grunting like pigs and scuffling around in this den of iniquity. Rats of the four- and two-legged varieties scampered around in the shadows.

The warden led them to the turnkey's office; a filthy room lit by a single candle shedding its paltry light onto the grimy walls. "Wait 'ere," he grunted, and shuffled off into the gloom.

Nelan heard a man whistling 'Greensleeves'; in this setting, an incongruous tune if ever there was one.

The door squeaked open with evident reluctance. The whistler stood there, a bunch of keys jangling in his hand. He wore a long cape, a black cap, a greying beard, and a dark, forbidding look. "Bliss," he said. "Thomas Bliss at your service. What can I do for you?"

Bliss – now that's a name to be conjured with.

"Mussell, sir, Constable Mussell. Got an inmate for ya who goes by the name of Nelan of Queenhithe."

"Nelan, eh? What's he in for? Debt? We got plenty o' those 'ere."

"Nah – killed a boy at his school, then ran away."

Bliss puffed out his cheeks and said, "A murderer and a runaway, eh? They're two a penny. But, Muscle, or whatever your name is, we're full to the gills. Can't you take 'im to Newgate?"

"Nah. It's full of them Baptists, so I brung 'im 'ere," Mussell said, doffing his cap. "Oh, an' he's Dutch."

"No, I'm Flemish," Nelan protested.

"Bah. Same thing," Bliss said. "And a murderer too?"

"Let's see at the trial," Nelan said.

"You're guilty as Hell. Me, I can tell it a mile off. You all think you can get away with your despicable crimes. Well, you can't. Not with the likes of me – and you – on the job, eh, Muscle?"

A prison warden stepped outside the office and rang a large bronze bell, the sound of which echoed around the sombre walls. The warden tugged on his beard and started his rounds, now and again shouting, "Strangers out! Women and children out!"

"Now, Dutchie, you better listen to Master Bliss. I'm tellin' ya, this place ain't like no other, 'cause many come 'ere, but few leave. Them that do's the lucky ones."

A couple of crows circled the court like creatures who'd escaped from the underworld. Their raucous cries darkened the glowering shadows. In this sombre ambience, there followed an exodus across the courtyard. Mostly, they were women. Tousling their hair, and adjusting their rumpled clothing, made it appear that some had been there on business. A few carried suckling babes, while others pulled young children by the hand, sobbing and yelling in distress at leaving behind their fathers. Nelan felt a pang of envy for them. If only he could turn around and follow them out of the gates.

"Visitors allowed only in the day," Bliss went on. "But woe betide you – and them – if they're not out by nightfall. I've brought together the best persuasions in the land to keep yous on the right side of the law. Let me introduce you to my babies: there's the shears, the thumbscrews, and my favourite, the skullcap. See, little fella, this is the best-run inn in town. We got two rules 'ere; one for them what can pay, an' one for them what can't. If you can pay the garnish – the prison fee – there's oblivion over there," he jerked a thumb towards the alehouse in one corner, "and if you wanna see the world at night, there's a chandlery nearby to buy yourself a candle. And when your time comes – and it'll come – you can confess your sins over there." He pointed at the chapel. "You gets what you pays for. You pays for your bed and everything else. If you can't pay, you owe. I got the tally."

"Is there work? I can work," Nelan said.

"We'll see 'bout that," Bliss said.

The warden who'd been ringing the bell returned. He smelled so rank that Nelan pulled away in disgust.

Bliss, who seemed more accustomed to the man's condition, asked, "Turnip, any room for this new fella?"

"Nah. It's near Christ Mass. There's no room at the inn," Turnip sniggered.

"Where shall we put 'im, then?" Bliss asked.

"How's about the strongroom?" Turnip suggested with a casual air, but the undertones of rancour struck the fear of God into Nelan.

"Share it with the toads, he could. A big green fella just moved in," Bliss said, every word dripping with malice.

The prison resembled Satan's inn – and smelled like it too. A thick heaviness crept out of the ground like a miasma, snaking up Nelan's legs before winding into his heart. Solid like lead, it weighed him down, pulling him into the nether regions of the earth. No matter where he slept, he doubted his fevered mind would allow him any rest.

Bliss and Turnip revelled in his discomfort. After they shared another joke, Bliss said with a dismissive air, "You decide where to take 'im", and then went back to whistling his favourite tune.

"Where's that going to be?" Nelan asked.

"You'll see," Turnip said, and grabbed his wrist tie and led him off into the dark.

"Can't wait," Nelan said. He was already fed up with the warden taunting him.

When Turnip left him in a dark, dank corridor, Nelan felt cold, alone and frightened. Not even Eleanor knew of his whereabouts, though Queenhithe was only a short punt across the river. And he was betrothed to the poor girl. He'd fallen in love with her and now look where he'd ended up: imprisoned for a crime he hadn't committed. Was he cursed? For being Flemish? For being a shorty? For being alive?

The following day, he woke up feeling hollowed out, as if his soul had departed his body and was guiding his life as best it could from somewhere nearby; where it was sweeter to reside and the bile and the pain were less – the bitterness, too. His soul was no doubt as disgusted by his surroundings as he was. The acrid taste in his mouth was as awful as the place. He wedged himself into the corner of a corridor outside the infirmary. His back was stiff. His eyes were glued together with sleep. His toes were cold. So were his ears, and the tip of his nose. His breath was steamy. In the cold light of the morning, he witnessed his own hardship.

He hadn't slept the sleep of the dead; far from it. The prison was full of errant souls. It reminded him of that terrible place the Papists called

Purgatory, that netherworld for tortured souls perched precariously outside the gates of Heaven. And there were plenty of ghosts to testify to the fact. They'd invaded his fractious dreams from the moment he fell asleep to the moment he awoke; a procession of wraiths, from a woman heavy with child to a man heavy with grief and, in the finale, a child heavy with choler. The howls of pain emanating from the infirmary added to his sense of desolation.

He shivered so much he could barely stand. He didn't know if it was from the cold, the fear, the exhaustion, or all three. He rested his palm flat against the opposing wall. A curious oily film covered its surface. How many scores of dead souls had passed through these walls? He wondered if this thin, glutinous veneer was the accumulated deposit of their astral departure. His mind was haunted by a vision of the extreme suffering that had passed for healing in the infirmary. Men with severed limbs. Men recovering from the tortures liberally applied by Bliss and his officers. Children with more than just broken hearts. Nelan had to get out of this place, and fast. No matter what. He heard a deep rumbling. It was his belly. The previous day, he'd barely eaten a morsel. Fodder – he needed fodder.

Turnip and another warden had other ideas. The two of them burst out of the infirmary, grabbed Nelan by an arm each, and hauled him along the corridor.

"I'm coming, I'm coming," Nelan moaned.

"You're late," Turnip muttered under his breath. Nelan could smell stale ale.

"They've already started," growled the other warden.

"Late for what?" Nelan asked.

"You'll see," Turnip said.

Were they taking him to the notorious strongroom? His mind frayed and split into fragments until, in the distance, from across the yard, there came the sound of singing. It sounded more like a dirge than a hymn; desperate voices thick with fear and suffering the throes of retribution. The wardens led – or rather dragged – Nelan into the chapel through the Devil's Door and let him go, so that he dropped to the floor like a man struck down by the sweating sickness. Nelan witnessed the parlous state of the inmates: most had bare feet, few wore winter clothing, some had sores and bruises, while others had scabs and rotten teeth.

The chaplain brought the inmates' choir to an abrupt halt. Any more singing like that, and the Lord Himself would have begged them to stop. During the short sermon, the chaplain pleaded with the inmates to pray for forgiveness for their many and various transgressions. Then he drew the service to a close. The inmates shuffled out of the chapel with downcast eyes and hunched shoulders. Some walked slower than the snails that had left a generous trace of their slime on the flagstones.

While the chaplain cleared the silver from the altar, Nelan grabbed a copy of the Bible from the pulpit. Thankfully, it was the Geneva Bible, the same version Dr Dee had mentioned. He leafed through the pages until he found the Book of Job, Chapter 10. He read Verse 1 repeatedly until he'd committed it to memory, then returned the Bible and wandered into the yard.

Most inmates were returning to their cells, while others greeted their wives and children arriving for their daily visits. Nelan spotted a small gap in a wall. There might be a way to escape. With no wardens in sight, he squeezed through the opening and found himself in another courtyard, enticingly empty of another living soul. He walked around, enjoying the feeling of space and solitude.

A door opened from the main building, and a man in a Chinaman's hat shuffled into the yard. Dressed in a long black robe and with his sleeves rolled up to reveal a selection of tattoos, he resembled a cross between a Benedictine monk and a criminal exile from Canton. "My name, sir, Lao Long. You name?" he said, bowing low.

"Me Nelan."

"Hi-lo, Mr Ne-lan," he said, and went off on a tirade about his dislike of waste and dirt and how he wished he was wrapped in his lover's arms in his bed in Limehouse.

Nelan wasn't listening. He simply wanted to escape and find Eleanor. To stop Lao Long talking, he held up his right hand with his palm facing him.

Lao Long's eyes lit up, and he grabbed Nelan's hand. "This one. This one here is part of your higher soul," he said, pointing to the three wavy lines beneath his middle finger.

"Higher soul?" Nelan said, suddenly interested.

"You, me, all people, we have not one but two soul."

"We have two souls?"

"Yes, yes," Lao Long said excitedly. "Two soul, one lower, one higher. See. Lower one standard. Normal. Everyone got. Make heart tick, legs move, eyes see. Understand? Other soul higher. This one has to be grown like plant in garden."

"This is fascinating. How is it grown, this higher soul?"

"Make qualities, you know, like honour, service, care, respect, patience and humility. These here long before Lao Long, before Ne-lan, before everyone. Left here by the spirits. Here after Lao Long and Ne-lan pass on from this earth. Qualities, they last very long time, see. Live forever. Get qualities, become immortal, see. Heaven give gift to you and me," Lao Long added, chuckling at his own bardery.

"Very good," Nelan said. But before he could ask another question, the Chinaman shuffled back into the prison building.

Emerging from the other side of the courtyard were two men wearing grubby, tattered sailor's gear. They sauntered up to Nelan as if they were on board a ship at sea.

One snarled, "Lad, get ye gone, will ya? This yard's for us."

"Who's 'us'?" Nelan asked.

"Mariners only."

"Oh, I didn't know. I only arrived last night."

"Well, ya know now, don't ya? The Chinaman knew; that's why he scarpered. Now git."

"Please, have you got anything to eat?" Nelan asked, rubbing his stomach.

The man frowned and stomped off in a huff.

The other man said, "Don't mind him. What you in for?" He had more crags on his forehead than the ocean had waves.

"I'm accused of killing a boy. But I swear by the Almighty that he attacked me. I wanted to live, so I defended myself. I'm allowed to do that, aren't I? How about you, sir?"

"I'm on trial at the Bailey. Disobeyin' orders," the man said, his voice rasping like a piece of grit. "Never mind me; what's your name, son?"

"Nelan. I worked as a smith in Queenhithe."

"I'm Robert of Hull," the man said, shaking Nelan's hand.

His grip was as firm as a vice. His palms were calloused, as were the tips of the fingers of his right hand. Nelan guessed he'd got the calouses by plucking that lute slung across his back.

"I'm a navy man," Robert went on. "Let me warn ya, you'll never know how cruel the navy is."

"So, why did you stay?"

The old soak leaned on the wall and gazed at the clouds scudding by above the courtyard. With a dreamy look in his eye, he said, "You don't understand. You can't; not till you've been there, not till ya been t' sea. The waves, the swirling currents, the fresh winds, the white foam – ah, it's almost too much for a man to bear."

"When I was young, I crossed the Channel from the Netherlands to England. It made me seasick even then."

"Mmm," Robert murmured. His eyes glazed over, and his lips moved as if he were having an inner conversation with himself. Then he said, in a soft, whimsical voice, "The sea, she's like a lady: sometimes silent, other times raucous. Like any true lady, she seeks the company of those of kind, those equal to her, and she calls those men to her. Like they say of true love, you chase a lady until she catches you. Same with the sea, lad. She seeks the courageous, the fearless and the bold to serve her. And the hardships are eased by the many wonderful, mysterious things that happen at sea."

"Like what? Tell me more."

"Can't do that," Robert replied. "I'm not one for words. I could play it for ya tonight?" He pointed a thumb at his lute.

"Yes, please," Nelan said.

"Listen out for it," Robert murmured. "Caressin' those strings is like lovin' a good woman. You gotta feel she wants you. 'Sides, you never know; one day, you might find out for yourself."

Suddenly Turnip burst into the yard, shouting and jabbing a finger at Nelan. "You can't be 'ere. Git out now, or else. Sailors only in 'ere."

"I'm going now," Nelan muttered.

As Turnip bundled him out of the yard, Robert shoved something into Nelan's pocket and whispered, "For you."

Turnip led him back to the main yard. "Now, stay 'ere, will ya? For Gaud's sake, wait until we find a space for ya. Come dusk, you head for the infirmary. You 'ear me?"

"Yes, sir."

"You'd betta. Else I'll be getting Bliss to sort ya out," Turnip said, and scuttled off towards the main gates.

The yard resembled a crowded marketplace. As a newcomer, Nelan was met with narrowed eyes and furrowed brows. Even the rats and insects seemed wary of him. He found a private nook and quickly, before anyone could see him, delved into his pocket. What had Robert given him? It was soft and pliable. Bread. Oh, it was bread. He stuffed it in his mouth, chewing slowly, savouring each bite. What a difference! A natural vigour coursed through his body, and he felt alive again.

Feeling for Robert's gift, Nelan's hand brushed against a crumpled piece of paper. He pulled it out of his doublet and examined it. It was print on paper. It read, 'This is a summary of my tract, *The Limits of the British Empire*'. Dee had given him this priceless gem. Nelan dared not read it in the courtyard lest the inmates see him with it and tear it up or steal it. Besides, it would alert them to the fact that he could read, and he didn't want to stand out, so he carefully secreted it away and spent a farthing on a candle stub at the chandlery. To slake his rabid thirst, he then spent another farthing on a beaker of weak ale at the inn.

As the embers of the day spread like soot across the sky, he spotted Robert of Hull as the guards hustled him out of a prison wagon and into the sailors' yard. Nelan guessed that he was returning from the Old Bailey after another day's trial. One day, Nelan too would defend himself at trial. But how long before that happened? A month? A year? Forever? The bell rang, heralding the exodus of visitors he'd seen on his arrival. As the yard emptied, he headed for the infirmary and slumped down on the floor, wedged in a corner in the same place as before.

During the night, he heard shouts that chilled the soul. Haunting screams circled the infirmary. In the other prison buildings, cries of alarm and pleas for help filled the loathsome air. But the chimes of another purpose drove him forwards. Nelan worked the strike-a-light iron and the flint to conjure a flame on the char cloth and light his candle, bringing light to the darkness. Dr Dee's document was manna from Heaven. At the very least, it would transport him away from the stench and brutality of Marshalsea.

The inmates in the other buildings went quiet. All of them were listening to a noise in the background. No – it was music. At first it was quiet and distant, but as it grew louder, Nelan recognised the strumming of a lute. The solemn playing suggested the depths of the sea and its dark, unseen undercurrents. Then it changed, and a lilting melody suggested rolling waves rising and falling to the tune of the milk-white goddess of the sea. Then the rhythm broke into fast, silvery salvos of satisfaction. In the end, it evoked the majestic melancholy of a man's inner dialogue with his own soul. When it finished, a stillness descended on the prison. Robert of Hull. What kind of life had he experienced to conjure a song of such heartbreaking tenderness? His notes had quelled the rabid beasts of Marshalsea, who had drifted off into their dreams – or was it their nightmares? A strange hiatus settled on the prison, in which Nelan wondered how one man's chords could soothe the dangerous, squalid souls of hundreds of his fellows.

He smiled and picked up Dee's *The Limits of the British Empire*. What an intriguing title! Sovereignty or authority to rule defined an empire. In ancient times, there had been a Roman Empire. Today, it was the Holy Roman Empire. Before now, no one had spoken of a British Empire. This was a new idea. What exactly was Dee proposing? Nelan's mind spun around the opening clauses.

It is written in the annals of divine providence that the ancient and noble land of Britain will achieve imperial status. It will do so by acquiring dominions in the New World and ousting Spain from her overseas possessions, all by means of a mighty Royal Navy.

What Dee proposed was already happening, in that privateers like Drake harassed the Dons and brought home riches of silver and gold. But Britain had yet to acquire dominion.

Nelan read on.

I exhort our royal majesty Elizabeth to recover the ancient rights and special privileges. I refer to the land called America, recently named after the explorer Amerigo Vespucci. This great tract of land was previously colonised in 530 by Arthur, King of the Britons, and later in 1170 by the Welsh Prince Madoc ab Owain Gwynedd. Oh, Albion; Oh, England; Oh, Britain, let us come together, retake this distant land, and thereby restore the ancient empire of Arthur Pendragon, the once and future King.

Dee's idea of empire was more than wishful thinking – it was founded on a moral imperative and a restoration of old rights. The basis for the authority of sovereignty stretched back a thousand years to the court of King Arthur.

> *In defence of our realm, it must be said that we are islanders, and that if we become great masters of the sea, with a valiant and glorious Royal Navy, then our great British Islands will be impregnable.*

The best form of defence was attack; a clause that supported the need for a competent navy.

And what were the boundaries of this empire?

> *The lawful entitlement of our sovereign lady, Queen Elizabeth, is to acquire vast foreign dominions.*

The limits of the empire stretched to the edges of the known world and beyond. The thought excited Nelan. He wanted to help spread England's noble virtues and great values across the world. Now, *that* was a future worth pursuing.

What if other kingdoms opposed the expansion of the empire?

> *If these foreign powers dislike hereof, then, seeing as our right is grounded upon Christian equity and warranted by law, we may, by the vigour of the same right, use might sufficient to guard and enjoy the same, as occasion shall require.*

This was the finale; a potent vision of Britain's imperial future and the extent to which she might rightfully defend it. Britain wasn't Nelan's home nation, yet he felt the echoes of its destiny reverberate throughout his being. The pathway to glory was through the formation of a Royal Navy, and lay across the broad expanse of the sapphire-blue seas. The mandate for the vision was divine providence. The stars in the heavens were so aligned that the ancient lands of Albion, England and Britain would play a leading role on the world stage. Spain's esoteric traditions, founded in the walled city of Toledo and the sprawling hilltop fortress of Grenada, would no longer hold sway over the deeper consciousness of the world. Tomorrow was blue, the blue of the natural emanation of the land of England and its shades of light and dark; its Cambridge and its Oxford.

Nelan glanced at the second of the two pages. At first, he assumed it was a continuation of *The Limits*, but on closer inspection it was a different tract. He eagerly unfolded it and read.

Your Majesty may know of Johannes Müller von Königsberg, also known as Regiomontanus, who made this famous prophecy:

A thousand years after the Virgin Birth,
And after five hundred more allowed the globe,
The wonderful eighty-eighth year begins and brings with it woe enough.
If in the year of 1588, total catastrophe does not befall;
If land and sea do not collapse in total ruin,
Yet will the entire world suffer upheavals, empires will dwindle,
And from everywhere there will be great lamentation.

It was not a matter of if, but when. That question was answered: the year would be 1588, eleven years hence.

But first, Nelan had to escape.

The next day, Bliss told him that he could earn some garnish at the local chandlery, situated outside the prison gates next to a small chapel. "You'll be under strict supervision," he said, "so no runnin' away, y'hear? You can earn a crust to pay me for ya bedding, food an' ale. Turnip's your escort, got it? Oh, and there's some folks waitin' for ya on the outside."

"Folks? For *me*?"

"You 'eard me. Now git goin', will ya?"

"Yes, Master Bliss," Nelan said.

In that moment, he felt more alive than he had in days. Because outside the gates was none other than his beloved. Alexander and his mutt Billy kept her company.

"Oh, my dearest Eleanor," Nelan whispered as they embraced.

"I've found you," she murmured. "And you're still alive."

"I didn't do what they say I've done. I wanted to tell you, but—"

"I know," she said, putting her finger over his lips. "Alexander told me what happened at your house in Mortlake. I'm so sorry about your father."

A tear welled up in his eye, and she held his hand.

"What d'you need?"

"Food... and some money."

"That's enough talk," Turnip said. "This lad's goin' t' work."

"I have to go," Nelan said, kissing Eleanor.

"I'll see you same time tomorrow," she said with a smile.

The chandler showed him how to craft a wick with thin pieces of linen. Next, he had to dip it into simmering tallow until the candle was the correct size. At the end of his first day's work, Nelan smelled as evil as a sulphur mine because of the obnoxious odour of the grease. Even Marshalsea's most hardened criminals kept away from him.

But he'd seen his Eleanor. She hadn't abandoned him. And now she could bring him clothing, food and ale. Just seeing her was enough. He'd endure anything if he knew that she'd wait for him. Maybe she and Alexander could help him to escape.

That night, Nelan had both light from the candles and some valuable space. With no room in the cramped cells, some prisoners slept in the wardens' shed, and the new arrivals slept in the freezing yard. Marshalsea was a hard taskmaster; many fell by the wayside who could not afford the garnish. Squeezed into the corridor outside the infirmary, he got out his char cloth, iron, and flint, and lit the candle. Again, he read the two papers Dee had given him, but his mind prodded him about shoes. Not those in the cordwainers' and cobblers' shops, but the ones that never wore out. Dee had given him a clue in the Geneva Bible. Recalling the lines from the Book of Job, Nelan spoke Chapter 10, Verse 1 out loud:

My soul is cut off though I live.
I will... speak in the bitterness of my soul.

What did that mean? What were the connections between cutting off and living, and bitterness and the soul? And what had they to do with the shoes that didn't wear out? Dr Dee had said it was a clue, so Nelan resolved to muse on the biblical passage until it revealed its inner meaning. He recalled the fear he'd felt on waking during his first night in Marshalsea, and then he wondered about sweetness and bitterness. Was the soul averse to certain flavours? Perhaps it was more sensitive to some emotions than to others. Maybe the soul was like a little child who enjoys comfort and warmth, and cries and runs away if deprived of these basics for living. Dr Dee had set him a conundrum; one he wasn't going to solve while his bones ached and his clothes stank of fat. After an exhausting day in the chandlery, he could barely think, let alone concentrate on biblical quotations.

He cut off from the present and drifted into a restless sleep.

Bliss woke him at the crack of dawn to go to the chandlery.

"But it's too early," Nelan protested. "Eleanor will miss me at the gates."

"What do I care?" Bliss said, and gave him a whack over the head for his troubles before tying his hands together. "Stay 'ere till Turnip comes, got it?"

While Nelan waited, the other inmates marched out of the gates with their escorts, heading to their various day jobs. Nelan was no criminal, but these men were hard as nails and would give a bear a good fight for its money. How on earth had he ended up here?

Eleanor still hadn't appeared when Turnip staggered across the yard towards Nelan, barely able to place one foot in front of the other. It was a drunken dance, not a walk. "Right, you, let's go!" he slurred. Grabbing Nelan's wrist tie, he pulled him through the gates into the narrow confines of the Borough.

Halfway to the chandlery, Turnip stumbled, crossing his legs and clutching his codpiece in discomfort. Nelan kept a desperate eye out for Eleanor, but there was no sign of her; only the market traders setting out their stalls.

They were passing a cemetery next to a small chapel when Turnip stammered, "Wait 'ere, fella. I gotta go piss."

"Hey, Master Turnip," Nelan replied, "I want to go too."

Turnip spat prodigiously onto the ground, then threw him a look of withering disdain. "Well, I'm not going to get it out for ya, am I?" he muttered as he fumbled around until he pulled the rope tie apart.

Nelan rubbed his sore, rope-burned wrists.

"You be back 'ere, or there'll be Hell to pay, m'lad," Turnip warned, and ducked behind a yew tree nestling in the corner of the cemetery.

Nelan sighed. He hated the wrist tie and was glad to be free of it, at least for a short while. It epitomised his dire predicament and the injustice of it all.

He'd just finished his own business when he heard a cry for help from the other side of the cemetery. The warden pissed for England, so Nelan scampered off, thinking he could help and still return before Turnip did. He crossed the cemetery and, in the corner of a small pasture, spotted about ten men and a donkey cart; the navy men on the boat that had nearly rammed them at St Mary Overie.

The navy men surrounded another man, and their officer shouted at them, "By Satan's rotten teeth, get a bloody move on! We gotta make the tide."

The navy men grabbed the man and dragged him towards the donkey cart.

"Get your dirty hands off me!" he yelled.

Nelan thought he recognised the man they were abducting. He was tall and thickset with very little hair. This older man had his back to Nelan, who couldn't see his face. But his loud voice sounded familiar. By the grace of the Lord, it was his father! His father had survived the fire and come to rescue him. Nelan swelled with emotion and pressed his hands together in thanksgiving. God and the angels had looked favourably on him after all. His troubles were over. His father would get him out of this awful mess and save him from Turnip, Bliss, and the Marshalsea reprobates. He'd be free. They'd build a new home in Mortlake. Come what may, Nelan would go to Oxford! The Lord had saved Laurens to save him. Laurens Michaels lived. Nelan was not alone in the world. He had a family again.

Tears welled in his eyes as he raced towards him, shouting, "Father! It's me!" Then he growled at the navy men, "Let my father go!"

"What's it got to do with the likes of you?" The officer wore a deep scar from ear to shoulder and seemed to regard Nelan as little better than a piece of street soil. Whenever he moved his mouth, the scar echoed the movement with hideous accuracy.

"But he's my father," Nelan murmured.

As the older man turned, Nelan saw his stern, angular face and realised his mistake. It was not his father. He was dumbstruck. With every fibre of his being, he had willed this man to be his father. Yet he had deceived himself. He wasn't. He couldn't be. Laurens was dead and never coming back. A feeling of intense emptiness swept over Nelan. The uncanny thing was that he still felt ensconced in his father's presence. He felt sure that this was his father's way of saying farewell.

A navy man with shoulders as thick as a yoke bar smashed the older man with a broadside across his chin, and he fell to the ground like a sack of apples at harvest time. It took three men to grab his limbs, lift him, and throw him into the back of the donkey cart. Nelan still felt drawn to help him. He stumbled forward and tried to push the officer over, but the experience had sapped all of his strength.

The officer stood there like one of the Pillars of Hercules and laughed. "That the best you got?" he sneered.

"You bullies!" Nelan screamed as frustration and disappointment oozed out of him.

"Hear that, lads?" the officer shouted. "The runt thinks we're bullies. I'll give 'im bullies. Grab 'im."

The group turned on Nelan. Before he could make a run for it, they grabbed him, tied his hands, and hauled him, kicking and screaming, into the back of the donkey cart.

9

The Mary and John

8th December 1577

The donkey cart trundled over the cobblestones of the Borough and halted by the steps at St Mary Overie. Barely three days before, Nelan had arrived there from Mortlake. From one prison to the next. The navy men dumped him in the wherry with the other man; the one he wished had been his father. The man had arms like tree trunks. Tall in stature and with blue eyes, he resembled a Viking god of old. The wherry cast off, the crew pulling against the tide. Was Nelan ever going to ride with the flow?

"Where are you taking me?" Nelan said with an air of defiance.

"You talkin' to me, you cur?" the officer said.

"I am, yes."

"You'll find out soon enough. The plague be on you."

They headed under the arches of London Bridge, which bustled with houses, shops, and all manner of tradesmen. The wherry picked up speed with the swish of the oars and the grunts and groans of the navy men. The officer guided the tiller, grinning like a cat who'd unexpectedly found a morsel of cheese. A pall of drizzle hung over the oppressive spires of the Tower of London. As the bow cut through the waves, Nelan glanced longingly at the river. Should he chance it? He could swim, but poorly, and not with his hands tied. The officer must have sensed his intention because he drew his bodkin and brandished it at Nelan.

The waves were cold in the winter sun; the spray seemed to freeze in the chill air. In an hour or so, the rigging and tall masts of some ships came into view. This must be the port of Deptford. They pulled up alongside a larger seagoing vessel, the *Mary and John*. Nelan followed the Viking as he climbed aboard. One of the ship's crew, a giant with a cauliflower ear, sneered at him as he passed. The officer looked at Nelan as if he were an alien from the new lands of the Americas or the Indies. An able seaman opened a hatch. A vile stench wafted from it, turning Nelan's stomach.

"Git," the man growled, and pointed his dagger down the hatch.

Lantern in hand, an able seaman led the way. As they broached the first step on the ladder, a low murmur rose from the ship's bowels. It sounded like a lot of whispers and people talking. They trudged along the gun deck, and in the dark Nelan tripped over some rope coils before clambering down another hatch into the hold. In the dim light, he could see a score of faces peering up at him with desperation in their eyes. Many were only boys; some even smaller than him, others as young as six or seven. Straw covered the deck. Here and there, Nelan could make out a bucket of slops. The smell was rank, and he swallowed down vomit. It was a cold day, but the airless heat was stifling.

The able seaman slammed the hatch shut over their heads, plunging them into darkness. It took a while for Nelan's eyes to adjust. He and the Viking edged across the hold towards a corner, where they slumped down, backs against the wall. The wind filled the sails, and the boat got under way. They rocked from side to side, making Nelan queasy. The sea was in his ear. The ship creaked like his bones, and bucked like a feral mare from side to side. Perhaps Marshalsea had been a better 'sea' to be on because at least he'd been in London Town, and the earth hadn't moved beneath his feet with monotonous regularity. He shook his head, hoping that the drumming noises inside it would evaporate. They didn't.

Instead, a hoarse, gruff voice broke out of the darkness. "How are you?"

Nelan groaned. "Well, I think. How's your chin?"

"*Ja*, it's nothing. A scratch, brother."

"Brother? But I'm not your brother."

"*Ja*, I say we are brothers."

"Why's that?"

"We got pressed at the same time. And, like me, you're not from these parts. You're a visitor here," the man said.

"True enough; I was born in Sangatte in Picardy. My family moved to Leiden in the Netherlands, then fled Spanish persecution and sailed to England. Where'd you get that Nordic twang?"

"I am coming from the seas of the north. *Ja*, I'm Nelan Andersen of the great Kingdom of Denmark."

"Well, there's a coincidence. I've got the same name: I'm Nelan of Queenhithe," Nelan said.

"Pleased I am to meet you, Master Nelan. Folk call me Great Nelan. I shall call you Little Nelan."

"So be it," Nelan said. He heaved a sigh of relief. Although the navy press had been an unforeseen event, it presented him with a priceless opportunity to start a new life, and might act as a buffer or shield between him and his old life. No one here needed to know his surname.

Great Nelan glanced around the hold and said, "And thank you for trying to come to my rescue."

"For a moment, I thought you were Laurens, my father."

"I look like him?"

Nelan nodded. "Yes, you do. But he died recently, in a fire."

"Oh! That's eerie! You thought I resembled his ghost?"

"Oh no, it wasn't like that."

"What was it like, then?"

"I'm grieving for him. And, when I was imprisoned in Marshalsea, I was afraid I'd never get to tend his grave or mourn him properly."

"Well, don't mistake me for him again, eh? It'll cast the kiss of death on me, so don't ever call me by his name, understand?"

"Yes, I do," Nelan said, and then asked, "Do you know what this ship is?"

"It's got twin masts and a small retinue of guns. It's an armed merchantman."

"What'll happen to us?"

"They'll sell me on to a merchant ship. Not sure about you."

"Why's that?"

"I'm a seafarer. You're not."

"Oh, I see."

"Can you at least swim?"

"It's more like floating than swimming."

"Well, that's something. You won't believe how few mariners can swim."

"Why've they taken me, then?"

"You must have a special quality."

"I don't know what that might be. How come you know about all this?"

"*Ja*, I'm a master gunner. And I've sailed with the best of 'em around the Baltic from here to Copenhagen, Königsberg and the Bay of Biscay."

"Any idea where they are taking us?"

"We're heading into the Thames Estuary. When we reach the North Sea, there's a chance we'll tack across the Channel to Picardy or the Netherlands, but I doubt it. Too many Spanish boats patrol that coast."

"Where to, then?"

Great Nelan sniffed the air as if taking soundings in the Channel. "Ah, that's good. I like the feel of the sea currents coursing through my veins. Where to, you ask? If we sail north, it'll be to Great Yarmouth or maybe Newcastle. Head south, and we'll dock at Margate or Dover. Either way, this barque's got a long voyage ahead."

"How do you know that?"

"The *Mary and John*'s at full sail and moving as swiftly as Odin, Viking god of the wind," Great Nelan replied. "So, her hold is empty. But she's a merchantman, which means she lives and breathes cargo. She must be going to pick up some. You'll see I'm right, Little Nelan."

The wind billowed against the sails, waves smashed against the timbers, and the boards creaked, making it impossible thereafter for the two Nelans to hear one another. The others in the hold made a constant moaning and murmuring; the children's voices shrill and high-pitched.

Later that day, the officer ventured down the ladder with the able seaman. The stench must have been bad because the officer held his nostrils while checking his merchandise. The able seaman held a lantern; its flame casting eerie shadows over the cramped hold. In one corner, Nelan could see a dozen young boys huddled together like wheat sheaves in a barn.

One of the older boys dared to confront the officer. "Give us food. Give us water," he pleaded.

"You want food and water? I'll give you food and water," the officer snarled, and smashed the boy in the face with his elbow.

The boy hit the deck with a heavy thud. The able seaman moved to help him, but hesitated when the officer scowled at him.

Great Nelan got up and said to the officer, "You're a pathetic bully. Why don't ya pick on someone your own size?"

The Dane towered above the officer, who whipped out a dagger and brandished it before him, the blade flashing in the light of the lantern. With incredible speed, Great Nelan knocked the knife out of the officer's hand and squared up to him.

The officer scrambled to pick up the knife, brushed himself down, and hissed, "Well, for such a big man, you're agile and strong; that's good." Then he added, with a smug grin, "You'll fetch a gold angel if I ain't mistaken."

If they believed the Dane would fetch ten shillings, perhaps Nelan would be worth half that. Either way, it was clear that they, like the boys, were to be sold on as slaves. The question was: to whom?

Everyone else took a breather on the top deck, but Nelan and Great Nelan stayed cooped up in the hold, sweating profusely and cursing their luck.

In what seemed like the middle of the night, Nelan woke up. In the sweltering heat, he jumped back against the wall. Someone was moving around. Then he saw the flickering light of a lantern across the other side of the hold. The able seaman was handing ship's biscuits and water to the boys. Then he approached the two Nelans and planted his finger over his lips. In the depths of the night, and quiet as a church mouse, he led Nelan and the Viking up the ladder onto the forecastle. After the confinement of the hold, the freezing night air was like a refreshing bath. A gibbous moon hung high in the sky like a blazing lantern. The chill of the wind smacked against Nelan's face; the smell of sea salt revived his flagging spirits. He drank some chilled water; bitter as it ran down his gullet. He stretched his legs up and down the main deck. Never had the simple act of walking been so pleasurable, so meaningful, so profound. Dawn broke to the east, splintering the bleak December night. Like a glittering jewel, a diamond sparkling in the darkness, the first silver rays cast light over the dark clouds. That first sight of dawn at sea was a glorious, sublime feeling.

With the land to starboard, it didn't take long for Great Nelan to point out, "We're tacking south, following the coast. If I'm right, they're the lantern lights from the town of Deal."

Not long after, with dawn in full flow, the steep White Cliffs of Dover hove into view; a bulwark against the waves, white and blue. Docking by the harbour, the crew laid down a gangway. The purser organised everyone and everything, including the stevedores who swarmed up and down the gangway like bluebottles. By mid-morning, they sweated like the pigs they'd brought on board. Even the crew laid to, rolling barrels from the quay, up the gangplank and onto the deck. Great Nelan nodded approvingly like he'd seen it all before. The shipmaster had everyone chasing their tails in a frantic rush to load the cargo and sail out of the harbour. Then a storm blew in, forcing them to lower sails and wait for it to subside.

The next day, they tacked out of Dover harbour, the famous White Cliffs looming behind them, iconic in their presence. With all sails unfurled and a favourable wind, they headed west along the south coast of England, passing Beachy Head and the Seven Sisters, which boasted more white cliffs than Dover itself. They sailed throughout that day and the next. The waning gibbous moon gave a glimmer of light to the dark December night as they passed the narrow seas by Portsmouth and the Isle of Wight. The ship strained at the leash, with full sails at every opportunity.

Nelan felt low. He'd taken Eleanor to Charing Cross and asked her to be his bride only seven days ago. That week felt like a lifetime. He was meant to be getting married in a fortnight or so. He couldn't wait to stand next to her by the altar at St Martin-in-the-Fields. The thought broke his heart. Although his beloved had come to see him at the prison gates, it was a piss-poor substitute for the sheer joy of matrimony. Now he was marooned on a hostile vessel with thugs, children and strangers, and he'd missed her again. If he felt sorry for himself, he felt pangs of shame for his Eleanor. Hopefully, she'd learn about his fate from Bliss or Turnip.

He lumbered onto the deck with Great Nelan to attend the day's service. When it ended, they were privy to an argument between the shipmaster and the captain concerning the need for such speed and the reckless dangers that might ensue. In the end, the boat made sure and speedy progress along the south coast, passing the Isle of Portland and crossing the bay before rounding Start Point. As Nelan learned to roll with the waves, the feelings of nausea and sickness faded. He grew accustomed to the ship's continuous rocking, and enjoyed the sense of freedom and the sapphire majesty of the open seas.

The following day, Nelan and Great Nelan scaled the ladder to the top deck. It was a momentous day; not only because they had arrived at their destination – the famous Plymouth Hoe – but because it was Nelan's birthday.

When they docked at the harbour, every member of the crew, the rats, and each timber of the old *Mary and John* breathed a sigh of relief.

The ship's purser instructed an unruly bunch of stevedores. "Unload the decks: the pigs, the hens, the swords, the braziers, the meal, and all the barrels. The lot. Get to it, lads!"

They lugged it down the gangplank, across the quay, and onto a flotilla of ships moored nearby.

More cargo handlers swarmed over the vessels, which looked like they were being victualled for an imminent departure. A crowd of wives, relatives and friends of the crew keenly observed all the comings and goings from the harbourside. One of the five vessels, larger in mast and sail than the others, boasted eighteen demi-culverins. With that cannon power, Nelan guessed she was the flagship. On her stern, he spotted the emblem of a female deer; a golden hind.

The purser noticed his interest in the ship. "That be the *Pelican*, Master Francis Drake's carrack," he said with a nod and a wink.

"I thought he'd already set sail?" Nelan said, scratching his beard.

"Likely they had, sirrah," the purser said. "They left Plymouth a month ago when the moon be the same as it be today. But the weather gods were agin them, see. And the storms, well, they was terrible: the winds and the rains drove the flotilla back 'ere, where they been laid up ever since for repairs to the leaks, the masts, the sail an' the riggin'. Then, when they got the ships fixed up good an' proper, they waited."

"For what?" Nelan asked.

"For us: for the good ship *Mary and John*," the purser said with pride. "We got 'ere with all the cargo: flour, salt pork, beer, vinegar. Oh, an' biscuits, especially ship's biscuits. And ale. Plenty of barrels of ale. Now Master Drake's mighty fleet can go harry them Dons to the ends of the earth. Aye, they'll be off as quick as a twinkle in them stars, you'll see."

So, the *Mary and John* had sailed from Greenwich with such haste in order to supply Drake's latest expedition. Nelan sensed an opportunity, and so did Great Nelan.

"That Francis Drake is hell-bent on smashing the Dons," the Viking said.

"He's out for revenge," Nelan said.

"He is that, lad," Great Nelan said. "He sailed with his cousin, John Hawkins, to the Spanish Main along the Gulf of Mexico, where they traded with the agreement of the local Spanish authorities. A storm hit the English flotilla, so they sought refuge in Veracruz harbour. But when the newly appointed Viceroy of New Spain arrived, he treacherously reneged on the agreement and attacked the English without warning. The Spanish murdered hundreds of English sailors and sank several of Hawkins' ships. That's why Drake's bent on revenge."

"Because the Spanish broke their word?"

"*Ja*. So if you ever get to meet Drake, whatever you do, don't break your word to him."

"I'll remember that," Nelan said. "But what'll happen to us now?"

The officer strode towards them and barked an answer. "You'll find out soon enough." Then he shouted to the able seaman, "Tie 'em up and take 'em below decks."

"The pox on you," Great Nelan said, and spat a large globule of phlegm onto the deck.

The able seaman led them back into the primordial dark of the hold. They had barely eaten or drunk anything that day. Nelan felt as sick as a dog. A diet of mouldy ship's biscuits and stale ale was poor fare for any man.

"What'll they do with us?" he asked.

"What do you think, lad?" Great Nelan asked. "It's business. As sure as night follows day, they'll sell us to the highest bidder."

Well, maybe Drake would bid high for Nelan. Comforted by that thought, he dozed off in a fitful sleep until Great Nelan elbowed him in the ribs.

"They're comin' for us," he said.

The able seaman took them up on deck, where the purser was speaking with a man recently piped aboard.

"Good day, Master Thomas," the purser said.

"Who are these two?" Thomas asked.

"The two Nelans," the purser replied. "They're good men; the best we've got."

"Let me decide that for myself."

"Please proceed," the purser said.

"I'm Master Thomas Drake, Francis's younger brother," the man said.

"An honour to meet any member of the Drake family," Great Nelan said, his voice like the thunder of a cannon. "They call me Great Nelan."

"The admiral needs brave men – sailors with a heart of oak – to join our expedition," Thomas said. "But no jackanapes! We've seen plenty of them these past days. Every Englishman in sight of Plymouth Hoe has tried to join the flotilla. We've got no time for them. Understand?"

"I'm ready to fight for old England," Great Nelan chimed in.

"Good; glad to hear it," Thomas said, and scratched his beard. "What else you got?"

"Trained in the Danish Navy," said Great Nelan. "I'm a master gunner with the might of Thor."

"Good man," Thomas said. "And you?"

"I'm Nelan of Queenhithe. To the Viking, I'm Little Nelan. For nigh on two years, I was an apprentice to a smith in London Town. And I'd love to come aboard and join the fray."

"We can take Great Nelan," Thomas said. "But we got more smiths than smithereens."

After haggling with the purser, Thomas handed over a bag of coins and turned to leave with the Dane. Nelan had to think, and quick. The tide in his affairs was at the flood and could lead on to fortune. Francis Drake was renowned as a great English privateer; a man of rank and growing influence. Alongside him, Nelan could avenge his mother's death. And a man like the admiral could help him to overcome the injustice that hung over his head.

"Wait!" he yelled. "I have to get aboard the *Pelican*. I must fight the Spanish. You have to take me."

Thomas Drake turned to him. "Why's that, then?"

"I can count. And read. And write."

"A pretty trinity," Thomas said. "Any languages?"

"Fluent in English and Dutch. Oh, and I know a bit of Spanish and Latin."

"Spanish, eh? I'm not sure the admiral will take you as well."

"At least ask him."

"I will, but don't hold your breath. We've plenty of hands, and the gentlemen adventurers can read and write," Thomas murmured, and disappeared down the gangplank.

During the rest of the day, the crew hauled out the boys from the hold. Never to return, they were sold into slavery to other bidders. Nelan felt weighed down with disappointment. His friendship with the Dane hung in the balance, as did his dream of exploring the new oceans with a skilled navigator.

As dusk settled around him, Nelan sat alone, listening to the creaks of the planks and the water lapping against the bow, waiting for a reply from the admiral, if one would ever come. He contemplated his birthday and took a tally. The 12th December 1577 marked the start of his twentieth year. And where had those years got him? He'd disappointed his father, and Eleanor. He'd been imprisoned, and now no one wanted him. What use was a Sagittarian anyway? Or astrology? Or all that education? Would philosophy and rhetoric get him aboard the *Pelican*? In the shadows of the hold, dark thoughts hovered over him. He sat alone in the bowels of a slave ship, surrounded by brutes and haunted by the pall of injustice. Were all his dreams of conjuring fire elementals and helping England to end here? The world was so unfair. In this moment of doubt, tumult, and overriding confinement, he had a bitter, galling taste in his mouth.

Then, within this womb of dark foreboding, a flicker of light appeared before him in the middle of the hold. He thought he imagined it, and closed his eyes, expecting it to have disappeared when he opened them again. But it remained there, and glowed brighter. It was soft like a candle flame and white in hue. With it came a well-being that flushed his cheeks and quickened his spirit. Perhaps the Holy Spirit had come to endow him with knowledge, power and wisdom for the journey ahead?

He lifted himself from the deck and stood to meet it with all the dignity and humanity he could muster. The white light grew so bright that he had to look away, but it remained as small as the head of a nail or a pin: so small, he could hardly see it; yet so bright, it filled the hold. It hung in the air, suspended in the middle of the hold above. It brought illumination to his life. It energised his being. It filled him with the truth of what had happened and what was to come. From out of the darkness had come this pinprick of white light that flickered, alternating in brightness like a beacon, at once hidden and then visible. From out of the ether, it had come in his hour of greatest need.

A voice whispered the words from the Book of Job in his ear:

My soul is cut off though I live.
I will... speak in the bitterness of my soul.

He realised its meaning. Now, he knew what bitterness did to his soul. Also, he knew that tomorrow, his life would change.

At dawn the next day, Nelan awoke and waited. He knew what was coming, just as adulthood followed childhood and spring followed winter.

Later that day, the able seaman clambered down the ladder and, twitching his middle finger indiscriminately, ushered Nelan to the quarterdeck, where he found Thomas Drake waiting for him.

"I've come back for you. You fit and able?"

"Yes, I am, m'lord," Nelan said. "Where are we going?"

"To the *Pelican*."

"Can I ask, what changed the admiral's mind?"

"With the spectre of poverty haunting town and village, every villein in the country wanted to join us, enticed by the prospect of riches beyond their wildest dreams. But as the Bible says, many are called, but few are chosen. You, Little Nelan, are one of those few. You be young, and you have an education. The admiral can use that on the voyage. But you have to follow the rules. So, no loitering. The seeds of time are already running out."

As they rowed across the choppy waters to the quay, Nelan mouthed a silent prayer of thanksgiving to the gods of opportunity. He didn't know what he was letting himself in for, but he didn't care. It lifted his spirits, if only because he could quit the *Mary and John*. How curious that the sense of imminent change he'd felt the night before had come to pass. Above all, he wanted to join Drake. If anyone could help him to right the wrong of his mother's execution, Admiral Francis Drake could. The admiral had a record of smashing the Dons, profiting from their treasure, destroying their settlements, and sinking their ships. Nelan would help him to become the best privateer on the seven seas.

They weaved their way across the quay, avoiding the barrels, equipment and cargo being loaded at breakneck speed onto the five ships.

"Look, young Nelan," Thomas Drake said. "These are barrels of water. They get loaded at the last moment. That keeps them fresh for longer. You, you're like one of them barrels. You come aboard at the eighth chime o' the bell – that's the last one, if you don't know it. Maybe it's an omen that you'll stay fresh the longest. We'll see. Do as you're told, or you'll be in trouble, m'lad. Now get loading those barrels."

Nelan had seen how fate twisted a noose around the neck of a man who disobeyed naval orders. By now, poor Robert of Hull had probably gone to join his shipmates in Heaven. "Yes, sir," he said.

When he'd finished, Great Nelan waited for him at the top of the gangplank. "Welcome aboard the *Pelican*," the Dane said, and shook Nelan's hand with such vigour that he feared he'd pull it off.

For the first time in a long time, Nelan felt the warm glow of belonging.

10

The Shearwater

13th December 1577

On the next day, as the gentle, rolling hills beyond Plymouth Hoe disappeared below the horizon, disagreement sullied morale amongst the ranks. Great Nelan strode into the thick of it. The men argued over the sleeping arrangements in the forecastle. There was not enough room to pull an arrow into a bow, let alone to swing a cat. It was where the men slept, ate, gambled, drank, snored, farted, sang, told tales of the sea, and dreamed of their loved ones. They also moaned about everything else with irritating regularity. Unsurprisingly, the smell was odious. Then again, Nelan had grown accustomed to that.

He met some of the crew; notably little Oliver, who had stirred up the great debate about sleeping arrangements.

"I'll be sleepin' there," Great Nelan thundered, holding back the unfortunate seamen with one of his withering glares.

"That's my hammock! That one there." Oliver dared to disagree.

"*Nej.*" Great Nelan shook his head.

"What's that mean, eh? Can't you speaken in Een-glish?"

"You insulting Great Nelan?"

"You don't get the best hammock; I do!" Oliver insisted, pushing Great Nelan in the chest.

That was not a good idea. Even Nelan could have told him that. Then, to confound everyone, Great Nelan grabbed a crossbow from the balustrade. Deftly, he pulled back the string, shoved in the arrowhead, and levelled it at Oliver's chest. The atmosphere grew thick with tension.

"Whoa, now hold on a mo," Oliver protested, holding up his hands in a gesture of surrender. The lad wasn't much taller than Nelan.

"Put that thing down, now! And on the day of sailing!" a voice cried. Just in time, too. It was Master Thomas Drake, and another lad clad in a flat cap, a neck scarf, a rough linen shirt, and tight breeches. "You're coming with us to see the admiral. He'll sort out this mess," Thomas insisted.

"Leave that thing 'ere, will ya?" the other lad added, pointing to the crossbow.

"Why? Who the Devil are you?" Great Nelan wanted to know.

"I'm Thomas Blacollers, the bosun. On a good day, you can call me Tom. This ain't one of 'em," the man snarled. "Now, look lively, able seamen."

Nelan, Oliver and Great Nelan were hauled up on deck, with Thomas Drake and Tom the bosun in attendance. Squeezed in one corner of the quarterdeck, a navy man talked to a preacher and a black man. The navy man was exquisitely dressed and sported a well-trimmed beard and 'tache. He was neither tall nor short, yet he held himself high with a natural bearing and dignity. Even with the vessel pitching from side to side, he kept an even keel. He had a glint in his eye, somewhere west of mischief but east of daring. Nelan didn't know whether to be excited or fearful, because this was none other than the privateer and gentleman adventurer Admiral Francis Drake. Nelan guessed that he was in his late thirties. Even in that time, the man's exploits had acquired legendary status amongst English folk: the brilliant seamanship, the daring raids on Spanish settlements, the enterprising sea battles, the buccaneering, and the pursuit of a haul of Spanish treasure.

"Have the four masters of our fleet joined us?" Drake asked the black man.

"Yes, Admiral. Thomas Moon, John Chester and John Thomas are all aboard and await your orders." The black man spoke with a conspicuous Spanish accent.

"And the fourth master; my vice admiral?"

"Master John Wynter is being piped aboard as we speak."

"And is Thomas Doughty with them?"

"Yes, Admiral."

"Thank you, Diego. Please bring them all to me."

The five men, each with a seaman's distinctive swagger, approached Drake, who greeted them and said, "Captains, welcome aboard the *Pelican*."

One of them scrunched up his face, spat on the deck, and twisted his boot into the spittle. In a raised voice he said, "Admiral, with the fleet fully victualled, and two supply ships and a raft of guns, we're embarking on a long and dangerous voyage. Yet we, the shipmasters and crew, have no idea of our destination. Please will you see kindly to release us from our misery?"

"Master Chester," Drake said, "patience produces character, and character produces hope."

"A wise sayin', Admiral. Please let us all partake of that hope," Chester said.

"Then listen, and listen good," Drake said, raising his voice above the swell. "If you lose us or get separated from the rest, we meet at Mogador. Be there on the 25th, when we'll celebrate the birthday of Our Lord together."

"Mogador, is it?" Chester asked with a trace of sarcasm.

"Yes – it's a port on the Atlantic coast in far-off Barbaria. That's Morocco."

"I know full well where it is, Admiral. Mogador is well south of the Straits of Gibraltar."

"So what if it is?"

"I was thinkin' we was sailin' for the Levant, though I had me suspicions we followed a different current."

"Oh, and why was that?"

"What about all these 'ere demi-culverins on the *Pelican* and the other ships? What do you need all them guns for if we're only on a trading voyage to Egypt?"

"A man can't be overprotected," Drake said. "The Dons can be treacherous."

"We know of your travails at the Battle of Veracruz, m'lord," Chester said. "You're not the only one to suffer at the hands of the Papists."

"Like I said, Master Chester, we'll celebrate the Lord's birthday at Mogador."

Chester cleared his throat, and then said, "Well, long ago, at least Mary and Joseph knew where they were staying that night."

"You will hear this," Drake said to them all, taking a deep breath and heaving his stout frame up to its maximum standing. "The reason this ship is called the *Pelican* is that it's the emblem of Queen Bess herself. The bird symbolises strong discipline. A pelican will draw blood from its own breast to feed its young. Our Queen is a paragon of virtue and noble self-sacrifice for her people. And that's what we must be to those who serve beneath us. As the Queen inspires us, we must inspire our crews to do great deeds. Now, to your carracks, and God's speed to you all."

With this endorsement ringing in their ears, the captains departed for their vessels, grumbling amongst themselves. When they were out of earshot, Nelan whispered to Great Nelan, "What just happened?"

Great Nelan cupped his hands around his mouth and replied, "*Ja*, the destination of this voyage has been a source of great speculation. Like Master Chester, the crew guessed we aimed our bows at the land of the Sphinx and the Pyramids. Instead, it's Mogador. But the question that hangs in the air like the Sword of Damocles is this: where are we headed after that? Will we follow the slave route down the west coast of Africa, or…?"

Before Nelan could answer, Thomas Drake beckoned them to attend the admiral.

Francis Drake asked, "What spirit of manhood do we have here, good brother?"

"In truth, m'lord, they're too much of a fighting spirit," Thomas said.

"Troublemakers, eh?" The admiral sounded them out.

"Just a difference of opinion, Admiral," Great Nelan said.

"As I said, troublemakers," Drake said with a wink and a smile. "I know Oliver and Great Nelan, but not you, little fella."

"I'm Nelan, sir. They call me Little Nelan," Nelan said with a brisk bow.

"Ah, you're the counter, the reader 'n' writer. Welcome aboard my ship," Drake said. "Now, what's all this about?"

Oliver was in his ear. "Gotta say, Admiral, I's worried as Hell, I am that, as are the crew." The lad bit his bottom lip.

"Oliver, you're the barrel man," Drake replied. "You're perched in that barrel in the crow's nest. You see everything before any of us on deck. So, why are you so worried, little man?" He stroked his beard with an air of nonchalance. "You're on the *Pelican*; the best ship with the best provisions and the best sea captain the world's ever known. We're about the Queen's business (and not just any Queen – the Queen of England), and that's to aggressively and persistently hound and hinder the Dons and get back what they've taken from us. We go forth with her warrant, so what's there to be worried about, lad?"

"Admiral, that may be," Oliver said, "but we've already set out once, and here we are again. And today's a mighty bad day to sail."

"And why would that be?" Drake said, twiddling his 'tache as if he knew the answer.

"'Tis Judas's day."

"Aye, it may be the thirteenth of the month, but it's a great day because we're finally setting out on this glorious expedition. And, lad, I'd not worry about such odious superstitions," Drake said. "As the proverb says, time and tide wait for no man. Sail we shall, and sail we have."

"'Tis so, Admiral," the preacher said in a haughty tone, looking down on everyone from his pre-assigned perch in Heaven. "There's clear blue sky above, and we'll not be wasting God's fine weather. That's a holy sign that He's looking after us."

"Well said, Francis Fletcher," Drake said. "Now, for your troubles, you three can all be captains for the day."

"We can?" Nelan said excitedly, although he didn't know what was implied.

Great Nelan and Oliver frowned at one another, and seemed to share a secret.

"Yes: captains of the head. Now get to it," Drake added with a wry grin.

The bosun pulled them across the deck, saying, "Follow me."

"Now you've done it," Great Nelan said to Nelan in a tone of disgust.

"Why? We're captains, aren't we?" Nelan scrunched up his face. What did they know that he didn't?

"*Ja*. We're captains of the head. The 'head' is the latrine." Great Nelan scowled. "Today, we're to clean the bilges."

"Oh," Nelan said.

Those first days at sea dragged like a lead weight. The fleet tacked west along the Channel of old England, reaching the low hills and gentle coves of Bryher Island in the Scilly Isles, then headed south to Ushant off the French coast. Each one of those thirty-five leagues was a great relief to Nelan's soul, which had been so constricted by his brief stay on the *Mary and John* and in Marshalsea. Whatever its destination, this voyage gave him a much-needed fresh start. He left behind that terrible confinement, both physical and mental, and he felt nearer to an abiding sense of freedom, opportunity and destiny. For a simple boy from Sangatte, the idea of personal destiny was a ladder of complication on which he stood on the bottom rung. Yet today, he felt it sat within his reach, if not his grasp, to marry his fascination with the element of fire, his curiosity for the salamander, and his knowledge about the soul with a new love of the sea. He coined a little rhyme:

The fresh winds blew.
The white surf flew.
On the wing, the curlew.

As well as his sea legs, he discovered the rhythm and poetry of the sea. But at least he had met the admiral.

There were as many questions as the moods of the ocean. Where had all the water come from? Had it always been there? And why salt water and fresh water? And the way it behaved was another mystery. It seemed to act in union with itself, in a vast conglomerate and mobile mass. It was alluring yet dangerous at the same time, and in that regard a neat foil to his favourite element of fire. As salamanders occupied that element, so sleek undines swam and bathed in the element of water.

Today, he scrubbed the decks. He gazed up through the flapping sails and oak masts into the azure skies, there to behold the wild antics of the creatures of the feather. A flock of migrating birds were harassed by a large predator; a majestic raptor with a broad wingspan ending in a single feather at each tip. As the raptor approached, the flock dispersed; some flying in one direction, others heading in another. The spontaneous action suggested that they knew how to separate to escape danger. Then, without ever colliding with one another, the flock would reform and fly on towards land. As Nelan returned to scrubbing the timbers, a bolt of guano splashed onto the deck.

"Gadzooks, you must be as blind as love. Here, you missed a bit," Tom chuckled as he pointed to each morsel of bird shit. "Get to it, m'lad, or we'll hang you from the yardarm and worse. After a good keelhaulin', a man's never the same."

"Yes, Bosun," Nelan said.

Once, Dr Dee had shown him a strange mechanical bird in his study. Wound up with a key, its imitation songs could easily be mistaken for the actual song of a warbler, a tit or a thrush. The metal bird never shat. Some comfort that was to Nelan now.

On the *Pelican*, he learned the ropes and discovered the differences between port and starboard, the mizzen and the foremast. That was his lot: work, learn and watch. On the small ship with its crew upwards of seventy souls, the decks were always crowded. The crew included Francis Drake, the gentlemen adventurers with their posh language, the preacher with his Bible, a bugler, artists, master gunners, carpenters, cooks, and a clutch of mariners. The musician caressed the strings of his lute. The sounds were sweet; they'd melt a man with a granite heart. And when the men gathered in the forecastle, they each had a story to tell.

Great Nelan introduced Nelan and the other new hands to the gun decks. With huge pride, he said, "Here's the powder keg."

The brown powder brought back painful memories to Nelan, so he shuffled to the back of the clutch of recruits.

Great Nelan went on, "And here's the cannonballs. Black balls. You don't want to be on the end of one of these. Blow you to smithereens." Then he led them to the lower deck. "Here we got twelve cannon – demi-culverins. On the upper deck, we've six smaller guns. These have thick metal barrels. And see how these guns are set on two wheels? We can point them in different directions."

"Is that important?" Nelan asked.

"Yes, it is," Great Nelan said. "I've seen the guns on the Dons' galleasses and galleons. The big difference is that they are fixed to the deck."

"So you can only point them in one direction?"

"Lot like the Dons themselves, if you ask me." Great Nelan chuckled at his own joke.

On reaching the south-western edge of the Iberian Peninsula, a great seabird, a shearwater, appeared above the *Pelican* and circled it with menace for an afternoon. Unconcerned by superstition, Nelan wanted desperately to learn all the ropes and the intricacies of the cannons and the demi-culverins. Not so Great Nelan. Pointing up at the seabird, he grew restless. Its wings were spread across its long, thin body, making it appear like a flying cross. Shaking his head, Great Nelan paced the boards, grumbling to himself in Danish, occasionally stopping at the gunwale and shouting abuse at the bird.

That night, on the eve of Christ Mass, below decks saw japes, merriment and song. Several fingers of grog amplified the crew's raucous singing. Even Nelan joined in with 'A-Rovin', A-Rovin'".

In Portsmouth town, there lived a maid,
Bless you, young woman.
In Portsmouth town, there lived a maid,
Do mind what I do say!
In Portsmouth town, there lived a maid,
The British Navy was her trade,
I'll go no more a-rovin' with you, fair maid.
A-rovin', a-rovin', since rovin's been my ru-i-in,
I'll go no more a-rovin' with you, fair maid.

As the night drew on, the men's singing grew shot with rue as they sang of their wives and lovers, far away in the ports and towns of old England. Slowly, they drifted off to their hammocks and straw mattresses to conjure their dreams. Nelan climbed into his hammock and slept the sleep of Siloam.

Dawn broke, and its subtle rays of light peered into the forecastle. Nelan woke to find Great Nelan sitting with his back to the boards, hands hugging his knees like a babe in arms, his chin cupped on the tops of his knees, staring into space and rocking gently back and forth, almost as if in a dance with the ship herself.

"What are you doing?" Nelan asked him.

"Can't you hear it?" Great Nelan's eyes were wide in terror.

"What? You seen a ghost?"

"*Nej*, but it's been haunting me all night."

"What has?"

Then Nelan heard a shrill yell.

"*Ja*, you got it now, haven't you? I can see it in your eyes."

"What is it?"

"The bird," Great Nelan whispered, as if it were a secret between them. "It's coming for me. I got to fight it. I tell you, Little Nelan, it's it or me." He grabbed the crossbow.

"Where are you going with that?"

Great Nelan reared up to his full height, stared at Nelan momentarily and then, without uttering a word, stormed out of the forecastle and was quickly swallowed by the early dawn shadows. His mind racing with possibilities, Nelan chased after him. Did his friend imagine the bird? Was he going mad? If it was a spectre, a crossbow was useless. But Nelan had heard the infernal noise; a rapid squawking. Perhaps it was an errant spirit. Was it a bird, a ghost, or the ghost of a bird? One of many superstitions prevalent amongst men of the sea was that seabirds carried the disturbed spirits of shipwrecked sailors, and that their desperate, screeching cries were an omen of an even greater danger to life at sea: a raging tempest. To kill a seabird at sea was tantamount to killing a member of one's own family.

By the time Nelan made it up on deck, Great Nelan was nowhere to be seen. A gentle sou'wester rippled the surface of the sea. The sun's upper rim rose to the east, bringing light to the darkness and bathing the scudding clouds in rays of gold and red. The only men on deck were the watch, the barrel man, the tiller, and a couple of hands.

A cry came from the crow's nest. Oliver was in the barrel. "Land ho!" His voice sped across the deck, waking sleepy mariners and gentlemen alike.

Nelan peered eastwards. Barbaria's hazy mountains and golden sands appeared on the distant horizon. Another yell of anguish whipped through the sails; this time from aft. Nelan rushed to the mizzenmast.

There, a tall man stood with his back to him. In the dim morning light, he looked like a titan; a colossus. He examined something on the deck.

"What is it? What've you done?" Nelan cried.

"I got it," Great Nelan said. The crossbow sat on the deck next to him.

"What happened here?" Nelan asked again.

"*Ja.* I done it. I saved us."

The bell rang, calling the men to morning prayer.

Great Nelan stared with almost childlike innocence at the dead bird, which lay with one great wing twisted underneath its black-and-white body. Carrying a single white feather, a pool of blood spilt onto the deck. "*Ja.* I saved us all," he repeated.

The preacher stumbled onto the scene, followed by the pilot, his assistant, the purser and, last but not least, Tom the bosun and his mate.

"What ya done now?" Tom said, quickly taking stock of the situation. "Great Nelan, ya gone and killed a bloody shearwater! Now we're for it. Storms like you never seen before. The Devil's own weather's comin' our way, and nothing'll stop it. Pierced that bird with ya arrow; that's bad. And it's landed on the deck; that's the worst. You bloody brute, you ain't got no idea what evil you done brought down on us. Gawd 'elp us all."

Great Nelan stared open-mouthed at the creature spreadeagled on the deck.

"Well? What you gotta say for yeself?"

Great Nelan hung his head.

"We're gonna tie the bird round his neck and keelhaul 'im. That'll teach 'im good an' proper. Now, go! Git some rope!" Tom said.

The bosun's mate went off for some. Nelan felt petrified for his friend. Amongst the catalogue of harsh sentences perpetrated by the navy upon its rank and file, keelhauling was an accursed punishment. The victim was dragged under the keel from one side of the ship to the other. Few survived, and those who did became demented. Great Nelan said nothing. He seemed oblivious to what was happening around him. It was just as well he ignored the men's spite, because otherwise a humongous fight could have broken out. Thomas Drake and the other gentlemen joined the boisterous crowd.

"Wait! You're not doing this," Nelan spoke up for his friend.

"You!" Tom got right in his face. "Little Nelan, stay outta this. It ain't got nothin' to do with the likes o' you."

"Oh, but it has," Nelan said. "It's got everything to do with me."

Admiral Francis Drake marched onto the deck, followed by Diego, his manservant.

"So, what 'as this gotta do with you?" Tom asked.

What Nelan had to say next would bring down the wrath of God upon him. He swallowed hard and said, "Because I was the one who shot the shearwater. I did it."

"What? You kiddin' me, lad? You couldn't hit a barn door at ten paces," Tom said.

Nelan snatched the crossbow, notched the arrow, and launched it right into the middle of the mizzenmast, some twenty paces away.

"Bah! That don't prove nothin'." Tom remained decidedly unimpressed.

"He's right," Francis Drake said, injecting some order into the rabble. "But a man has to pay for the bird; that's the lore of the sea. The death has to be appeased."

"An eye for an eye – that's the spirit of the Law of Moses," Fletcher chimed in.

The bosun's mate returned with a coil of rope.

"Get the bird," Tom said, bossing them around. "Yeah, that's it. Tie it round his neck, good 'n' proper. Let it 'ang there, all bloody an' squishy with its innards fallin' out. See how he feels about it then."

The bosun's mate and two deckhands grabbed Nelan and lifted him like a sack of parsnips, his feet dangling in the air.

Great Nelan shook his head with such intensity that Nelan thought it would work itself loose from its moorings. "Let him go," he thundered.

"Ain't nothin' you can do to stop this now, Great Nelan," Tom said. "Little Nelan's owned up to it all. He's gonna pay, so get back."

"You listen to me, Tom."

"Why should I, you great lump of Danish lard?"

"Because Little One is lying. I did it," Great Nelan said, as terse as ever.

"What?" Drake interrupted. "What are you saying?"

"No, don't listen to him," Nelan said. "He's befuddled, can't you see? Listen – *I* shot the bird."

"*Nej*, he didn't. By the Lord, I will tell the truth. Bird was preying on me. So I killed it. Stone dead. With the crossbow."

A rose-pink ray of dawn lit the deck as the sun shone from behind the mountains. The men ranted and raved like good English sailors, chasing the anger across the deck until it wedged inside their hearts and minds.

"This kind of disagreement washes away our chances of success on the voyage," Drake said. "I'll not have anyone bear false witness against his neighbour, y'hear?"

"And on the Lord's birthday, too," Fletcher reminded everyone.

"I don't think so," came a voice from the top of the mast.

"Who's there? Who said that?" the admiral asked, looking up into the sails.

"Oliver," came the reply. With the agility of a lithe monkey, the little lad eased his way down the shrouds from the crow's nest.

"Tell us then, little barrel man: what did you see?" Drake asked.

"I saw it all. He done it," Oliver said, pointing at Great Nelan.

"You're telling the truth, little fella? God help you if you're not." Drake stood firm.

Oliver nodded.

"*Fiat, fiat*; let it be done, let it be done," Drake said with an air of finality. "This is what's going to happen: Great Nelan, you're free to go. You killed the shearwater, but you made amends. You couldn't let your friend take the blame for your action. Good man – I admire that. I won't tolerate those who bear false witness. Walk away before I change my mind. But you, Little Nelan, are a liar, and God hates lying lips. I wish I could make it easier on you, but I've set the punishment. Keelhauling it's gonna be. Bosun, get to it."

"Along the whole of the keel, from bow to stern, Admiral?" Tom wanted to know.

"I'll be merciful. Drag him under from starboard to port," Drake said.

"So ordered, Admiral," Tom replied.

As they gathered around the mainmast, a vicious roar of approval rose from the deck. He almost fainted at the putrid smell of the dead

119

creature tied around his neck. Then Tom pushed him hard in the back. He stumbled and fell head first onto the deck, squashing the seabird into his midriff. Blood and guts oozed onto his chest and onto the deck. All the hands guffawed. Whoops of laughter rose into the yard on currents of scorn. But this wasn't funny; not for Nelan. He had a vision of conjuring salamanders to combat the Dons, of righting the wrong of his mother's death, of helping Drake to destroy Spanish ships and settlements, and finally of convincing the admiral to quash the erroneous charges against him. But his dreams evaporated into the early morning sea mists. He stared death in the eye and turned white with fear. But he had no regrets. He'd done what he thought was right. The tide of history had washed up on his shore and, even if he could, he wouldn't have changed a word. "Account for your actions," his father had said. Yes, he'd do just that.

"Get ready now, lads. Run the rope under the keel, bring it up the other side, and tie it to his feet. Jump to it; Admiral's orders," Tom said.

Francis Fletcher stood clutching his prayer book to his chest in a gesture of piety. At least he brought an air of dignity to Nelan's last moments on God's earth. "Quiet," he said.

The men raised such a clamour that they barely heard him.

A roar cut through the air. "*Hold kæft!* Shut up!" Great Nelan brought the men to attention.

They stared at the Dane, who, with a subtle flick of his head, reminded them that the preacher had words to impart. Was this reprieve meant to prolong Nelan's agony and impending death? Either way, it gave him precious moments in which to attempt to dissuade the admiral from this course of action. Fletcher pressed his hands together in prayer. One after another, starting with the admiral, the gentlemen and mariners followed suit until all seventy men were solemn in piety.

"Make this quick, Fletcher," Drake whispered. "We got a boy to keelhaul."

"Admiral, I have words to say about that," Fletcher began. "I want to remind you that today is the birthday of Our Lord."

Nelan had come close to death near Smithfield, but this was terrifying. A rank smell of fear arose from his clothes and mingled with the disgusting odour of the dead shearwater; its innards now plastered on the front of his doublet. It stultified him. His breathing was laboured. A heavy weight weighed down his chest like in *peine forte et dure*, the punishment meted out to those who refused to take the oath of allegiance to the Queen. A pall of silence hung over the ship, and the gentle words of the preacher swirled around Nelan like a cocoon of solemnity.

"By the Lord Jesus, Our Saviour," Fletcher said, "and our hope for the future, the Lord is for the children and the young people of this world. He protects the innocent; those who are new to the world's travails. He who died for our sins preached forgiveness and redemption."

"What you sayin', Preacher?" Tom wanted to know. "Give 'im a blessing – them Last Rites, is that what you call 'em? – then do it, and let's drag this dead 'un under the keel."

Fletcher ignored him. "Therefore, Admiral, I pray that you hear my words. Look you. This Little Nelan has barely taken on the mantle of manhood. He first trod these boards some twelve days ago, so he's innocent of the ways of the sea. He's young and still wet behind the ears, so deserves a second chance. I say forgive his misdeed; especially because today is the day of the birth of Our Lord. Pardon this boy, just as you showed mercy to Great Nelan."

The preacher's words struck a chord in the men's hearts.

The admiral thought otherwise. "Fine words, Fletcher. But the man broke the code of the sea. We have to make obeisance to the Lord. You know that."

Nelan could not allow himself to succumb to this terrible punishment. He had to find a way to get Drake to see sense and pardon him. "Let me speak," he said.

"What have you to say for yourself?" Drake asked.

Nelan got to his feet. Holding himself as erect as he could, he said, "Admiral, I won't apologise for my actions. I'd do the same again. But don't do this to me. You mustn't risk my life."

"Hah! Hear that, me hearties? Not risk his life! Why's that, then?" Drake taunted.

"Because doing so will risk the future of your country."

"Will it? And how is that?" Drake chuckled.

"I have a part to play in it."

"In the future of our country? How do you know that, then?"

"It's in my horoscope."

"And why should I believe you?" Drake's tone was no longer condescending.

"Dr Dee cast it and told me so."

"*The* Dr John Dee?"

"The very same, m'lord."

Drake asked, "How do you know him?"

"He assisted in my education."

"I see," Drake said. "I attended seminars by the good doctor, who, with Sir Christopher Hatton, encouraged me to sail into unknown waters and test his navigational theories."

"Dr Dee was my private tutor." Nelan took a deep breath. His heart beat like a drum. His ears were ringing. His head was spinning from the odious smell of blood and guts. He hoped this last morsel of information would mitigate his sentence.

"In that case, I'll take counsel," Drake said.

While he consulted with his brother and the other captains, a row of seagulls landed on the yardarm. Nelan watched and waited. So did the gulls.

After lengthy deliberations, Drake said, "On this special day, I am inclined to offer clemency to the young man."

A chorus of cheers greeted the decision.

"Bosun, relieve him of his burdens," Drake ordered.

Tom and his mate removed the ropes. Nelan felt utterly exhausted, and his legs gave way. He hung on to the gunwale for dear life, but refused to let the crew see him faint. He glanced at Great Nelan for help, but the Viking folded his arms and drew his lips into a Nordic snarl.

The Dane had finished with Nelan, but Drake hadn't. "Little Nelan," he said, "though you're free to go, I'll keep a wary eye on you. Mark my words, if you bear false witness again, you *will* be keelhauled. Understand?"

"Aye, Admiral," Nelan said.

"Listen to me, all you hands," Drake said, his voice scouring the men. "This expedition is bigger than any of us. It's for our Queen, for England and for God. So, I'll have no more lies, no more transgressions, and no more bloody shearwaters!"

11

The Dog Watch

7th January 1578

The waves crashed against the bow of the *Pelican* as it ploughed through the deep blue sea off the North African coast. Recovered from his ordeal, Nelan scrubbed one section of the quarterdeck. Great Nelan cleaned the part in front of him. Since the shearwater incident, silence had drawn a curtain between them like an invisible pall. For a reason Nelan had yet to fathom, Great Nelan's lips were tighter than the shell of a clam. Nelan resolved to prise them open.

Nelan stood up and glanced to port at the distant coastline. The contours of the hills were as unfamiliar as their straw-coloured slopes, which were pitted with the occasional splash of translucent green. The sun rose high in the azure sky. At midday, the watch turned over the thirty-minute sandglass and rang eight bells to mark the end of the forenoon watch. The pilot arrived with his apprentice to take readings. The man used a curious instrument, pointing it upwards and trying to hold it level with his eye. Next to him, his apprentice scribbled the readings on a paper with a squeaky quill pen. Nelan guessed that the three-sided instrument was an astrolabe. The pilot always used it at this time of the day. It resembled a flat metal disc with a scale or series of notches around the outer edge, and a pointer or needle which stretched across the face of the astrolabe and pivoted in the middle. Mounted at either end were brass plates with small holes in the centre.

"I've shown you how to do this several times already, and yet you still haven't got the hang of it," the pilot said with an air of frustration. "So, watch me closely now."

"Oh, yes, sir."

The pilot held up the astrolabe by a piece of cord threaded through a hole in the top, and watched as the pointer turned until the sun shone through the holes at either end. He noted where the pointer rested on the scale on the outer edge.

"What coastline is that?" the apprentice asked.

"You tell me," the pilot replied.

"Err, it's..." the apprentice murmured.

"You've no idea, have you?" The pilot shook his head. "It's Cape Rhir." He pointed to the chart in front of them.

"Is that so?"

"It is, and today the Lord is assistin' us with this stiff nor'easter."

"We're headin' south into strange climes," the apprentice said. "The days are warm, yet we're in the clutches of winter."

"You know it's early January."

"At home with my missus right now, I'd be freezin' me bits orf, I would, or out and about scratchin' around the henge an' the hedgerow for kindle an' firewood."

The pilot seemed less impressed with this new information, and gazed at his instruments.

The apprentice said, "I mean, I like lookin' up at them twinklers, I do. In England, I'd be admiring old Orion, striding across them night skies like the governor of all them stars. I was lookin' for 'im last night, but could I see 'im up there?"

"You won't see the constellation of Orion this far south."

"You're tellin' me, Master Pilot. All I see was this strange mix of winklers 'n' twinklers, staring at me all night long, for sure they was."

"What did they look like?"

"A cross that had fallen over on its side."

"Ah, that would be the Southern Cross, the Crux."

"Well, the crux of the matter is that I wish I knew where we was headed. It's a mystery to me and everyone else. Captains and mariners, masters and gentlemen, we's all in the dark. You know, like you get at the bottom of a well. No place to go. An' for all I knows, we's headin' for the Spice Isles. Listen – I left my missus, me ma and pa, and a little plot of land so that I could sign up for this voyage. I come aboard to make me fortune and learn some goodly sea skills, but I ain't doin' much of either."

The pilot scowled. "Listen, you cur. You've not sailed with the admiral before, but I have. So curb that wagging tongue of yours. Loose talk is like a black cloud on the horizon: it ain't nothing to begin with, but when clouds fill the sky with darkness, and the storm beats against the ship with the force of Neptune's trident, then you'll know about it."

"I hear you, master."

"I don't know if you have. Let me tell you about our admiral. The son of a preacher, he's an honest, God-fearin' man, an' the finest sailor alive. And he's a West Country man to boot. He'll tell us our destination when he's good and ready and not a moment before. Meantime, so long as we do our daily taskings, we'll all be Jack-a-dandy."

"Only wanted to know our bearing."

"Don't we all? But you don't hear me doing a song and dance about it," the pilot said. "Besides, this is your first long sea voyage. By my reckoning, you'll all be in for a big surprise in a few days."

"What's that, then?" the apprentice asked. It was exactly the question on Nelan's mind; he hated surprises as much as the next man did.

"Ah, you'll see… it's for all you new hands to look forward to," the pilot said with a knowing chuckle. "Now, let's report our findings to the admiral."

The two men trudged off to Drake's cabin, leaving Nelan wondering what surprise lay in store. He'd ask Great Nelan, assuming the man would talk to him.

The big Dane scrubbed the deck with a scary ferocity. "What are you lookin' at?" he growled.

"I was looking at you," Nelan replied.

"Why? Never seen a man put his back into his work before?"

"Enough of your rough justice," Nelan said. "It's about time you forgave me. The preacher has. The admiral has. All the crew have. Only you persist in continuing to punish me. I was trying to take a burden off your shoulders."

Great Nelan towered above him. "*Nej.* You know nothing. Take a burden off my shoulders? Who do you think you are, the strong man holding up the Pillars of Hercules? Well, you're not. You make me look a fool in front of the whole crew."

"So, it's your pride that's hurting?" Nelan asked.

"All a man has got is his reputation. And you took that away from me. Now, I've got nothing."

"They tied that bloody bird to *my* chest, not yours!"

"Doesn't matter. That's what happened. And nothing you can say or do can change that."

"You want me to say I'm sorry," Nelan said. "But if the circumstances arose again, I'd do the same thing."

"You would, eh?"

"And for what it's worth, I'd still respect you."

"Mmm, I suppose it's worth a jot." Great Nelan said the words like they were being dragged out of him along with one of his rotten teeth.

"Friends again?" Nelan pleaded.

Great Nelan grunted like one of the brown bears Nelan had seen fighting mastiff dogs in the London bear pits. Nelan took that as a yes and went back to scrubbing the quarterdeck, knowing that his friend would stop treating him like a horned devil from the pits of Hell.

A few days later, Nelan reached a milestone, albeit a nautical one: he'd survived a month aboard the *Pelican*. Slowly but surely, he'd gained his sea legs and settled into the varied but predictable daily routine of a mariner's life. A life of foam, fish and the fantastical; of gulls, gall and gumption; of Heaven, Hell and hard work. He even enjoyed singing the various sea shanties and work songs the crew had for each task.

With Tom the bosun, Nelan was on the first dog watch; the two-hour stint from late afternoon to early evening. While no one knew precisely how it had acquired that name, the marine experts in the forecastle, including the pilot and his apprentice, were convinced it celebrated the appearance in the evening sky of Sirius, the Dog Star. The astronomer in Nelan could live with that explanation. With the rest of the crew and the gentlemen at supper, all was quiet on deck. Tom rang three bells to mark the passage of the third half-hour. In another half-hour, they'd finish their watch and it would be their turn to grab some food. Nelan was salivating because he knew it would be fish again – a welcome change from the bland daily fare of stale ship's biscuits. The previous week, on the 7th January, they'd snatched their first prizes of the voyage: three Spanish fishing vessels and (equally important) the contents of their holds – fresh fish aplenty.

That evening, Diego strode onto the quarterdeck. Light and nimble on his feet, the man sported a fluffy black beard. Dressed in a red shirt, a tan overshirt and black leggings, he stood by the rail on the port side and gazed at the African coast, his brown eyes full of yearning. Drake emerged from his cabin, followed by an artist.

"Greetings, Admiral," Diego said to him.

"Diego," Drake replied, and instructed the painter to draw the coastline.

Drake leaned over the gunwale, and they watched the sun sink slowly into the western horizon. Nelan had never witnessed such a view while on land. With each passing day, he felt more at home at sea.

Drake asked Diego, "Homesick?"

"Yes, m'lord. That is Africa, the land of my birth. I have not seen it since…" Diego choked on his words.

"Diego, I want the crew to know who and what you are so that there's no misunderstanding," Drake said. He turned to Nelan, Tom, and the artist and said, "Diego is a man of courage. He endured the terror of Spanish transportation across the Atlantic. The Dons took him to Nombre de Dios in Panama. I led an attack on the port in 1572, during which Diego ran through a hail of gunshots to join me. He's a runaway, or a *cimarrón* in Spanish. He has many skills and speaks the language fluently. As my manservant and friend, I warrant you treat him with respect."

"Thank you, Admiral," Diego said. Then, to the others, "I can say that Admiral Drake is my saviour. He helped me and many of my countrymen to escape the yoke of Spanish enslavement. He is the first Englishman I've met to give back our lives to people of my colour."

"With your help, Diego," Drake said, "my Queen enjoyed the bounty of the treasure we intercepted in the following year. She, I, and all of England, owe you a debt of honour."

Diego acknowledged Drake with a respectful nod of his head.

As the upper rim of the sun's orb sank into the horizon, the sky turned amber, the sun appeared to expand, and an orange glow spread out from the globe of fire. Its lower rim touched the line of the horizon, the golden orb sank a quarter, then a half, and finally the last segment disappeared below the horizon. Abruptly, its light was gone. A light green cloud appeared above the place where the sun had set, and an emerald-green ray pierced the evening sky.

"D'you see that?" Nelan said to Tom. "Look… oh, it's gone. It was there; I saw it. A flash of green light."

"A green flash, eh?" Tom said. "Some folks insist it's as real as the hand in front of their face. Me? I reckon it's a trick of the eye. Gotta watch what you see out on the ocean, y'know. Many's a time when sailors have been convinced o' summat when it ain't even been there; just an illusion, a ghostly apparition. Drive you crazy if you ain't careful. I mean, look what 'appened to Great Nelan with that shearwater. And you better watch out, lad. If you're seein' the green flash, you're heading that way too."

"Why do you say that?"

"Reckon those who see it got the gift."

"The gift?"

Tom shook his head with an air of rue. "Of seein' into the other world."

"What… other world?"

"You know, *that* other world: nebulous, like clouds in the sky an' flashes of colour in the foam; the livid flames of St Elmo's fire, an' all that," Tom said in hushed tones.

Nelan stood in wonder. For a fleeting moment, the veil was drawn away and he glimpsed this other, mysterious world. Perhaps it was the world of wraiths and ghosts he'd temporarily inhabited after his terrible beating at Smithfield, or the world of spirits and salamanders, or the realm in which to wear the shoes that never wore out.

The barrel man hailed Tom, who climbed up the shrouds to see what he wanted.

Diego turned to Nelan and said, as if listing the ingredients of a stew, "*Pequeño* Nelan, the sun is green."

"What do you mean? The sun's yellow. Everyone knows that."

"My people believe the sun is a green planet," Diego said. "In the green flash, you glimpsed it for a moment."

"I don't understand. The sun is a planet?" Nelan asked.

"Yes. And like our planet, it's surrounded by water. Here it's blue waters, blue sky and blue planet. The waters mostly nestle in the oceans, while some water floats in the sky as clouds. But on the sun, it's the other way around. Most of the water there circulates above the surface as sky waters. There it's green waters, green sky and green planet. Hence the green flash."

"Where do the sun's heat and light come from, then?" Nelan asked.

Diego continued, "That happens when the outer edge of those sky waters meets the awesome power of the universe. That coming together causes a fierce burning. That's what we see – the sun's sky waters incandescing. That's the yellow charisma."

Nelan stood with his mouth open. Green sun, yellow charisma – this was extraordinary. "I've never heard of this before," he said.

"Now you have. And there's more to this mystery. After many thousands of years, the roles of the sun and the earth reverse: our planet's waters rise into the sky, and the opposite happens on the sun. With barely any water on its surface, earth shrinks in size like a dried prune."

Nelan asked, "Is there any proof of this theory?"

Then Drake butted in. "Have you heard of the Yorkshire prophetess, old Mother Shipton? I see you're nodding. One of her sayings is 'Men beneath water shall walk, shall ride, shall sleep, shall talk'."

"You mean…?" Nelan asked.

"I do. That's what she was referring to," Drake said. "And in the Book of Genesis, we're told that it rained for forty days and forty nights. That was when the sky waters on our planet came down, causing the earth to swell and shifting the land masses to where they are today."

Nelan was amazed. But by now the sun had set, dousing the ship in darkness. Duty called, and he joined Tom and Great Nelan to light the ship's lanterns. Drake headed for his cabin, and Diego followed.

That night, Nelan settled into his hammock; so cramped he almost slept on top of Great Nelan to one side and Oliver to the other. Dear Lord, how the Dane could snore!

The sun was a green planet orbiting behind a yellow charisma; an incredible idea. But he'd witnessed the green flash, and Tom had suggested that it was only seen by those with the gift to peer through the veil into the other world. In which case, Nelan sailed the right course, leading him to where he could fulfil his and England's destiny.

That night, he dreamed he was high up in the barrel of a vessel sailing through a wine-dark sea. To the east, a lime-green sun rose, bathing the sea in a gentle glow of jade. Off to the west was a funnel of spiralling water, from the surface of the sea right up into the sky, in which a vast ocean circulated like sky waters. Nearby, from out of the heaving waves, a numinous figure arose: human in aspect, female in form. Nelan feared that she was one of those tricks of the mind that Tom had speculated about, or a legendary sea creature like a mermaid or a siren. Her long auburn hair maintained her modesty by covering her breasts. Below that, the rest of her slim, naked body glistened and sparkled with seawater. She drifted across the waters, but in an odd way. He looked again; she glided on the surface of the waves. Striding from one to the next, she approached the vessel.

He floated back to his hammock, and the young woman eased into the forecastle, hovered over him, and then settled herself on top of him. He groaned with pleasure as his manhood rose to greet her. Her body was so light that he couldn't feel her weight; yet her smell was deliciously familiar and intoxicating. It stiffened his resolve. She slid his mainmast into her blocks, moist with desire. Slowly, rhythmically, she moved her hips. Her hair brushed his cheeks, her breasts pushed against his chest, and her eyes glowed like emeralds.

Erupting with pure pleasure, Nelan gasped, and grunted her name. "Eleanor."

And she was gone.

Two days later, Nelan stood on watch with Tom and Great Nelan. Shoals of silver-backed fish drifted alongside the fleet. Full of bloated pride, Tom announced that the pilot had told him that the coastline was Cape Barbas.

As the first slither of dawn broke over the low hills of the African coast, Diego appeared on the quarterdeck. The *cimarrón* approached slowly like he followed the coffin of a dear friend. His face wore a look of absolute awe. He peered at the rising sun with such reverence it seemed as if he witnessed it for the first time in his life. He stood there, small in person but large in stature, watchful and alert. He glanced towards the rising sun and, on occasion, nodded his head like he was secretly conversing with a mysterious, invisible being. Planting his feet astride, he adopted an odd posture. He stepped forward with his right foot and reached his left hand into the sky with his fingers in a cone shape. Then he held his right hand by his side and pointed his coned fingers down at the deck. His eyes seemed fixed on the dawn. The more he stood there, transfixed, the more Tom danced around him like a phantom.

"Bah, don't like the look o' these shenanigans," he moaned. "What's this fella up to now, eh?"

Diego's body shimmered with its own luminescence, and his face shone with the brilliance of the sun. His eyes emitted a piercing ray of light. Then, with no warning, he collapsed in a heap on the deck.

As Nelan went to help him, Tom said, "Stop! Leave 'im be."

"Why? He's in trouble and can barely breathe," Nelan replied.

But Diego's face was lit by a broad smile, and his eyes sparkled as if he'd found a hidden hoard of gold.

"This ain't the antics of no Christian, is it?"

"What's it to you, anyway, Tom?" Nelan wanted to know.

"Matters to me. Matters to me a lot, 'cause I cares about the success of this 'ere voyage. Like it matters to Fletch. He's a man o' God. Reckon it matters to all us good Christian folk aboard the *Pelican*."

"What are you saying?"

"If Diego ain't no Christian, he'll bring down bad luck on us like a black thunderstorm."

Nelan puffed out his cheeks. "Well, that's sailors' lore. But it won't stop me from helping the man, whatever he is or isn't."

"So, is he a Christian, or isn't he? With all this statue nonsense he's performin' in front of us, then he's a-collapsin' on the deck like a sack o' turnips. Who knows what's gonna happen next?"

"He's the admiral's manservant," Nelan said. "He told us to respect Diego, and that's what I'll do."

Tom threw up his arms in disgust and stomped off to aft.

"What happened?" Nelan asked Diego.

Diego sat up, looked out to sea with a misty gaze and murmured, "I felt it. Did you feel the wonder? We passed through it."

"Passed through what?" Nelan said, glancing around. There were barrels and ropes, gulls and clouds, waves and foam, but nothing out of the ordinary, at least as far as he could see.

"We crossed it," Diego whispered and, with his hands pressed together, he traced a line in front of him from left to right.

"Crossed what?"

"The line – the sacred line."

"I'm confused. The only line I know is the one that skirts the middle of the earth. The equator."

"No, not that one. We've just crossed a different one. We just crossed into the Torrid Zone."

"Oh, you mean the Tropic of Cancer?"

"Is that what you call it? Did you feel its sacred power?"

Nelan shook his head. Perhaps if he could walk in Diego's shoes, he would feel whatever had lifted the man off his feet. Maybe he wore the shoes that never wore out.

"In my tribe, we worship this power," Diego said, his eyes misty with emotion. "It's special; it's high; it's holy. It's our religion. I feel the glory of life and living. We revere what lives on this line. *Señor*, think: the great religions of the world have appeared on it."

"Sorry, but I didn't feel anything," Nelan admitted. "But clearly it's affected you deeply. What is this sacred line?"

Diego smiled and got up. Before he could answer, the admiral strode onto the deck with the rest of the crew for the morning service. Nelan attended the service and left Diego talking with Drake.

To Nelan, the *cimarrón* was a pillar of wisdom. First he had spoken of the sky waters and the green sun, and now he talked of the Tropic of Cancer. It seemed an astonishing assertion, but what Diego had said was true. The major religions of Christianity, Judaism and Islam *had* all appeared on and around the line of the northern tropic. What would Diego say when they crossed the southern Tropic of Capricorn?

Nelan pondered the broader implications of this revelation. If he had misunderstood or underestimated the significance of the tropics and their place in the greater sphere of human affairs, what other matters had he left unquestioned? What else had he assumed was true because someone older and wiser had told him so? He needed to verify these things for himself, or he'd adopt other people's unchecked facts.

The next day, at the start of the forenoon watch, the bulk of the crew of the *Pelican* cast their nets into the water to catch fish while the rest mended the sails. They moored off Cape Blanc, the White Headland. Diego had told them that the Dons regularly fished the area for whales, whale calves and monk seals. With dawn shadows chasing them across the open sea, two pinnaces rowed towards the *Pelican*. The crew all stopped to gawp because the four captains of the rest of the fleet were in the small boats, again accompanied by Master Thomas Doughty. He passed for one of the gentlemen adventurers, although Nelan hadn't witnessed the spirit of adventure in any of them.

An old soak with tarred hair in a ponytail, breeches, and shoeless feet rolled onto the deck carrying a brass bugle. But the odd thing about him was that he'd tied a small, shiny whistle to the end of his straggly beard. For the ship's bugler, the passage of air and wind was clearly important.

"John Brewer," Drake said to him. "You know what to do!"

The bugler piped the men aboard. They were joined by the preacher and Thomas Drake, who said to them, "Welcome, good captains and gentlemen. The admiral awaits you on the quarterdeck. And if only Captain Wynter and Master Doughty could attend him first."

Wynter and Doughty spoke briefly with Francis Drake, but in such whispers that everyone, including Nelan, instinctively believed that they shared some secret collaboration. The other three captains – the cantankerous Master Chester, Thomas Moon, and John Thomas – strolled onto the poop deck, and the two trios faced each other. Francis Fletcher sat alongside Drake. While they exchanged suspicious glances, Diego rushed around, trying in vain to lighten the turgid atmosphere. He brought trays of dried fruit and dainty bites, which none accepted. They even refused a drink of Spanish sack. Nelan guessed that they wanted to keep clear heads for this important navy business.

"Officers and gentlemen," Drake said, "we have reached a crucial point in our voyage. I will reveal to you the true purpose of our mission."

"We look forward to hearing about that," grumbled Chester. "The other day, we crossed the northern tropic into the Torrid Zone. Trouble is, most of my men never sailed this far south. They're twitchy like fish outta water, an' anxious for their futures. They wanna know—"

"And I will tell you, so that you can tell them, Master Chester," Drake interrupted. "Masters Wynter and Doughty are by my side because they are privy to our commission from the Queen."

"Then where are we headed?" Chester asked.

Drake cleared his throat and said, with a confident grin, "To South America via the South Atlantic Ocean."

"A straight answer! I had prayed for as much!" Chester said with joy and relief. "I feared we were going a-slavin' down the African coast."

"No. I don't do that. I want to work with the Africans, which is why Diego is my manservant."

"What's our course?" Chester asked.

"First, to the Cape Verde Isles. Then we'll set sail for the Strait."

"In that case, we'll cross the equator; a new experience for the men."

"And we'll make a ceremony of it; I'll warrant you," Drake said.

"You'll want the crews to brave the Atlantic storms as well as the notorious doldrums," Chester said. "To do that, you'll have to promise them more than the derisory catch from a few fishing vessels, which is all they've savoured so far."

"There'll be plenty of booty to come," Drake said. "You captains and gentlemen adventurers, as well as the lords who generously sponsored this mission – all of you have a vested interest in making such conquests."

"Then, we can pray for another success like the one at Nombre de Dios," Chester suggested.

"'Tis true, that was a glorious day!" Drake replied, a look of excitement glistening in his eyes. "After Diego joined me, I stayed in and around the port waiting for the Dons' annual treasure shipment. When it came, we jumped them and attacked the mule train. You should have seen the amazement and surprise on those men's faces! It was like they'd encountered the Medusa. They were stung to silence. We praised the Lord for our success and made off with gold and silver beyond a man's telling. And I promise you, that's exactly what we're doing in this voyage. Now, go sing about it to all hands."

"I will, m'lord," Chester said, scratching his full-length beard. "But this ocean is uncharted waters. Look, even the pale blue of the waters here differs from our northern climes. The Portuguese navigator, Ferdinand Magellan, sailed here before us, but can you show us your copies of his South Atlantic rutters, or his navigation and coastal charts? Or confirm that you have studied them yourself?"

Drake shook his head.

"As I thought," Chester said. "Then how will we find our way?"

"We're men of Devon, men of valour, and men of the Island of Angels. And what we undertake here today, we do with our wits, our seafaring experience, and trusting in God's guidance to see us safely home."

"With all due respect, Admiral," Chester said, spitting on the deck with evident disdain, "what does that mean?"

"It means," Drake said, staring Chester in the eye, "that if a Portuguese can do it, so can an Englishman, and an Englishman with a heart of oak too. My navigation skills are second to none because I am divinely assisted."

"Can you see into the glass darkly and peer into the future or summat?" Chester scoffed. The other captains and gentlemen smirked along with him.

Drake shook his head. "Listen to me, ye of little faith. The Almighty is on our side. Master Chester, do you doubt that He is our guide in this and all things? Is that what girds your loins and fills you with rank insubordination?"

Chester said, "So, I assume that we shall *all* be under His good grace?"

"What do you mean?" Drake said with a growl.

"We need all of us – and I mean *all* of us – to receive His grace."

"Are you…?"

"Yes, I am. We must baptise every crew member. Including him," Chester said, flashing a scowl at Diego.

"Leave him be," Drake snapped. "He's helping me, which means he's helping all of us. That's good enough for me, and it should be good enough for you. Now, get to your ships and make ready. We still have a long voyage ahead."

Nelan drew a breath. They headed for South America. It had been one of the strongest rumours. Some had bet for it; some agin it. But whatever the crew had thought before, they now knew that they were going where no other English ship had sailed. Nelan was excited. The possibility of seizing a Spanish treasure ship drew closer, as did the avenging of his mother's death. He was awestruck. He would see places no other Flemish man had ever laid eyes on before, let alone any Englishman. He was honoured. No longer a spectator in life, he was now a participant. One of his profound dreams was about to come true.

John Brewer blasted his bugle. As the sound rolled out across the waves to the men on board the other vessels, everyone knew that they were going to cross the line of the equator.

12

Crossing the Line

24th February 1578

The barrel man cupped his hands to his mouth and yelled, "Black rain!"

A thundercloud haunted the north-eastern horizon. The wind was to the south-west and heading their way. Since leaving La Brava, the most southerly of the Cape Verde Isles, these sudden, ferocious storms had become all too frequent. That was at the end of January. This storm rolled in at dusk, menacing the fleet. But it brought a strange phenomenon that both absorbed and fascinated the hands: a translucent blue light that, like a flame, seemed to glow on the ends of the ships' masts. In spectacular fashion, the lithe blue flames came and went, lighting up the vessels, the men, the sails and the sea, before disappearing almost as quickly as they'd arrived, casting all back into darkness. Nelan was awestruck. His hands were moist with fear and excitement.

Great Nelan grunted, "Uh! Don't worry." A blithe grin hid amidst his fair beard.

"Why? It's… it's a terrible storm."

"Bah! Nonsense. It's fire. And this time, it's good fire. It's the saint's fire."

"What saint?" Nelan asked.

"St Elmo, of course. He looks after us sailors. Our patron saint and our guardian at sea. When nearly struck by lightning, the man carried on preaching. He'll see that we're safe."

"Glad to hear it," Nelan replied.

Following the spectacle of St Elmo's fire, the rains came, cooling their brows, which were fevered from the work of heaving to and hauling sail. They also brought much-needed fresh water, not only to drink, but to clean the cannons. Food supplies had also run low – except the ubiquitous ship's biscuits. The purser insisted on reduced rations. The quartermaster doled out the warm beer only twice a day instead of the usual four times. Almost as thick as a rope strand, the rain slanted into the ship's bow. It beat in waves against the fleet and splattered into the sails, pots and pans they laid out on the decks to capture what they could. The lightning forked against the sombre skies, lighting up the gloom like the end of days. Grown men, hardy sailors to the bone, cowered below decks, fearful that this heralded the Devil's Sea. By the time the chill and the dark clouds passed, the men wore black looks. Anxiously, they stared into the haze and the mists that rolled over their precious fleet and disappeared into the ether. Tom murmured that it would suck them all into a watery grave.

It wasn't only the biblical rains that worried everyone. It was the eerie calm that followed. Some called it the doldrums. Others, the calms. It didn't matter because, in the hot, sultry weather, their shirts stuck to their skin, and sweat poured off them with the slightest movement. Men slouched in corners, seeking shade wherever they could – anything to escape the stultifying heat of the day. And the nights were no better. At one point, little Oliver took bets on whether he could fry an egg on the quarterdeck. Motionless for days, the crew moaned about the sea monsters that lay in wait. Tom remained convinced that he'd seen one off the starboard bow. The crew raced on deck and Tom pointed into the mists which hung from the sky in thick curtains. There was a soft rustling noise, like the wind through the leaves of a tree. Some claimed it was mermaids; beguiling women with bare breasts, pointed nipples, hair that flowed like locks of gold, and a giant tail fin instead of a pair of legs. Others told of a vast sea serpent that would rise from the depths and devour the ship. Tom said it was the legendary sirens, and plugged his ears with his fingers to shut out the eerie singing of those awful temptresses. At first, Nelan did the same, but then he decided to test the veracity of Tom's tall tale. Releasing his fingers, he heard nothing.

Drake pounded the decks, stern-faced, gazing anxiously at the sails in full and eager anticipation that they would soon be swollen with a gust of wind. Even a breath would have been welcome. He and Diego held animated discussions on the poop deck. The pair stared into the ocean void and pointed at the cats' paws where invisible air currents ruffled the surface of the implacably calm sea. They pointed excitedly at a shoal of fish that broke the surface. If they read the signs, they would be like a scout in the desert who, with nothing to see for miles, knew instinctively which route to follow. When a light wind blew up and ruffled the sails, the crew raised a muted cheer, and Fletcher celebrated with a thanksgiving prayer.

They sailed on, surrounded by an unfamiliar ocean, until one day Drake entered the poop deck and instructed the pilot to change course. On deck that day was Nuño da Silva, the English-speaking pilot captured from a Portuguese vessel off Santiago in the Cape Verde Isles.

"*Señor*, you have my charts – my rutters," Nuño da Silva insisted. "I know the course I plotted on them. I have sailed these seas before. This is not the way to take."

"You may be familiar with these waters, but we," Drake gestured at Diego, "or rather I, believe that there is a better route from West Africa to the coast of South America."

"*Señor*, I did not take you for a fool. Please, you change course to the one I showed you," Nuño said, waving his arms around in a frenzy.

"I'm a mariner; the best there is," Drake replied. "I read the signs: the winds, the clouds, the texture of the light, the currents, the shade of blue of the water, the shape of the cats' paws, the movement of the birds and the fish. That's how I decide on the course."

"I see it in your eyes, *Señor*," Nuño went on. "You trust the *cimarrón* more than you trust me. So be it. You don't want to take the advice of a Christian man; a man of God. You prefer to listen to a heathen stranger from some faraway place."

Drake let out a long, slow hiss. Hands on hips, he stared the Portuguese down. "Never question my decision again," he snarled. "And never disrespect my friend and manservant."

"*Almirante*," Nuño replied, and beat a hasty retreat.

Soon after they changed course, the light wind subsided. Everything was eerily still. The dreaded calms had returned. The older mariners slouched around the deck, grumbling about "the breath of death". It sometimes smelled like it too, because the bilges were noxious in the stifling heat.

Nelan had risen before dawn for the morning watch, starting at the fourth hour of the night. He beheld the sunrise like a great golden orb on the horizon, and again witnessed the green flash. It brought on a wave of feelings. He stood in awe of this moment, his life and everything that supported it – the ship, the ocean, the sun, the stars, the constellations. Touched by a reverence for life, he felt he belonged in the universe, or uni-verse; namely, a single wholeness. He was part of it just as it was part of him; in the same way that a rose was part of the earth and the earth was part of the rose. His spirit glowed with living fire, and he felt the purpose of the Creator pulse through his soul. Now his existence was dignified by its authority for living, as was everyone and everything else's.

In the glow of these fine emotions, he reflected on his childhood. He thought of home and the belonging of home; of the feeling on the Sabbath afternoon of resting bones weary from a week's work in the fields on the edge of which his mother and father's house had stood. There, the corn had stood high, wisps of grain mingling with the sunshine. Butterflies danced in the sun's rays, guided with gentle kindness towards the flower heads. A cloudless sky hung over them like a dreaming canopy of blue, gracing them with silence and bathing them in summer's awe. From the white cliffs of Sangatte, Nelan had admired the ebb and flow of the sea as it coursed up and down the English Channel. On a clear day, he could see the White Cliffs on the other side, and wondered if he would ever get to stand on their summit and look back the other way.

Then he returned to the *Pelican*, listening acutely to the groaning of the bulkhead, the creaking of the ropes, the occasional raucous squawk of seabirds overhead, the swish of the water as a porpoise broke the surface, and the half-hourly sounding of the bell by the watch. All creatures worshipped at the altar of the great rising sun in the east. The expanse of the sea all around, from horizon to far horizon, was a sight to behold. If only the wind would return. The calms gripped them in their clutches. The doldrums drummed silence into their ears. Nelan grew apprehensive. Instead of enjoying the ocean's great expanse, he now dreaded its oppressive stillness. His palms were moist and his throat dry. At every noise, he feared that a sea monster would lurch out of the water, tower over their little fleet, and send them all to Jonah's Locker.

With remarkable aerial displays, the flying fish distracted the crews from their daily chores and anxieties. These spectacular creatures emerged from the silent sea into the sullen air, not for the men's amusement but more to escape the deathly clutches of the schools of dolphins and shoals of ray-finned bonitos that fed on them. The extended fins of the flying fish lent them grace and elegance in flight. When they thudded onto the deck, the mariners rushed them to the galley. The creatures fascinated Nelan, as they seemed equally at home in the air and in the water. The artists on board filled pages of their notebooks with lively pencil sketches of these airborne fish.

As the sun bestowed its rays upon those in its thrall, Nelan made ready to change watches and grab a few moments' respite before the duties of the day caught up with him and the daily routine began again. Heading towards the forecastle, he nearly slipped on the dewy surface of the deck. He grabbed the rope with both hands and swung around, keeping his momentum rather than falling into an ignominious heap. He ended up with his legs in front of him and his ankles on the deck as he clung to the rope. Gently, he let himself down and sat there, chuckling merrily at his clumsiness and wondering if he'd ever get his sea legs.

Laying his hand flat on the deck to lift himself, he noticed a serpent-like marking in the dew. It was a curved line about the width of a man's forefinger and the length of his arm. He guessed the dew had settled around a rope and, when one of the crew had moved it, the strange imprint had remained on the deck. Yet more often than not, a rope was connected to a longer piece – a coil – so it was doubly curious that the curved mark in the dew was so short. And during Nelan's watch, not another soul had come on deck.

He heard footsteps behind him, and Tom snarled, "With this swell, it's no wonder your legs gave way, eh, lad?"

There was no swell, and Nelan knew he had no excuse, so he chuckled and ignored Tom's sarcasm.

As Nelan got up and walked away, Tom said, "You'll see. Yeah, you got it comin', you 'ave."

Early on, Nelan joined the morning watch. In this morning of beauty, the sky was a uniform powder blue. He was going to ring the bell and turn the hourglass when he glanced at the patterns of dew settling like a blanket of stars on the deck. It was the same place where he'd seen the wavy line the day before, except this time there were three lines; one next to the other. Finally, he'd witnessed the mark of the salamander; the mysterious, lithe creature of fire. They spoke to him in rhyme, their words dancing in his mind like fairies:

In the day,
They'll be fay.
Pluck the lute,
And blow the flute.
They'll be kind,
And never bind.

He glanced around, expecting to see them nearby, but his only companions were the vast expanse of the ocean and, beyond that, the mysterious horizon. Why had these strange creatures left their mark for him to see? What did they want of him?

A sultry breeze blew up. Heat signified the passing of the salamanders, so the wind was no surprise. It almost scalded Nelan's skin, and the dew evaporated into the void. But the sails billowed and the flags fluttered. John Brewer blew his whistle and then his bugle. Finally, they made headway. More than that, it gave the hands, the gentlemen adventurers and the mariners, relief from the oppressive burden of the calms.

Moments before midday, the pilot strode onto the deck, his apprentice close on his heels. In the sticky air, a few hands swabbed the deck; others played cards and drank their daily tot of ale; and a few rolled the dice. Some sat with their backs to the masts in a vain attempt to escape the scorching heat. An artist sketched the play of light on the waves. The musician caressed the strings of his lute, teasing out a gentle melody.

By eight bells, the pilot had taken his astrolabe readings. "We're getting very near," he said as he and his apprentice made their way aft to the admiral's cabin.

"To what? I don't see any land." The apprentice's voice had all the subtlety of a trumpet blare.

"Bah! You are gormless. Did you learn nothing in these past days and weeks? Don't you know where we are?" the pilot chastised him.

"Err, at sea. And out of sight of land," the apprentice added hurriedly.

The pilot hissed and said, "Yeah, but we're closing in on the equator. If this light wind persists, we'll cross the line tomorrow."

"The equator. Mmm, is that so, Master Pilot? Tell me, what does it equate?"

"I'll equate you if you don't pay more attention," the pilot grumbled, and then muttered to himself, "Better tell Fletcher we're close."

John Brewer gave three mighty blasts on the bugle, calling the men to assemble. Two pinnaces set off with messages to the rest of the flotilla. The light vessels soon returned with the shipmasters and gentlemen adventurers, who gathered with the crew on the deck of the *Pelican*.

"What's happenin'?" Oliver asked.

Tom knew it all. "Must be summat to do with the pilot. See 'im up there on the poop deck, discussin' marine matters with the admiral an' the preacher?"

The pilot unfolded a chart in front of Drake and stabbed his finger at it. Drake asked him a question, and the pilot nodded with feverish intent. Nuño stood to one side, frowning and shaking his head, apparently consumed by the fires of doubt.

"Now, men," Drake said, holding his hands in the air, "listen to your admiral. We've reached a significant moment in our great journey. We're soon to cross the line. By this time tomorrow, our sails will be filled with the winds of the South Atlantic."

A muted cheer greeted the news. The men were as hot as their emotions, and this represented a further imposition on their already exhausted minds and bodies.

Fletcher adjusted his black cap and said, "Men, if this wind keeps up—"

"Mmm, wind? What wind? I can flap my shirt harder than this little breeze," Tom snorted, prompting derisory laughter from the crew.

Undaunted, Fletcher continued, "If this wind keeps up, we shall be conducting an important ceremony tomorrow. We'll be crossing the equator; a moment in the voyage that needs to be marked with the gravity it deserves."

A couple of flying fish skirted Nelan's line of vision. One landed on the deck, and the bosun's mate scampered off with a net to snare it. They made good bait for the larger fish, the dolphins and the bonitos.

"What's all this 'crossing the line' about, then?" Oliver cried out.

"It's a ceremony for sailors who've never before crossed the equator. Which accounts for most of you," Fletcher said.

"From what I 'eard, it's another bloody baptism!" Tom interjected.

"We are talking about a holy ceremony, so mind your tongue," Fletcher said. "Its purpose is to induct all you novices into the fraternity of God's mariners, to guard us all against bad spirits, and to keep away the tempests. In the end, good brother, it's to strengthen your resolve and help us return home safely."

"I'm all for the baptismal font," Tom shouted, bringing howls of approval from the collective. Then he added, "How's it all gonna work? We all gonna get dunked in the briny?"

"You will all be called tomorrow, one at a time. And I must prepare you for it, hence this gathering," Fletcher said. "As it says in the Good Book, the first shall be last, and the last shall be first."

"What's that mean?" Tom again.

"It means the last man on board will be called first. And that's—"

"Nelan! Little Nelan hisself!" Tom shouted, before the preacher could finish his sentence.

"The other names are Robert Winterhay, William Horsewill, Thomas Cuttill, Great Nelan, Richard Minivy, John Gallaway…"

By the time he'd finished, the preacher had named almost all of the 164 hands. The exceptions were Admiral Drake himself, who had sailed down the southern coast of West Africa, and John Fry, who'd been kidnapped at Mogador. Everyone had a smile on his face, if only because talk of sea monsters and sirens was an amusing and welcome distraction.

The shipmasters were ready to return to their vessels when a familiar voice broke the sense of achievement. "There's one name missin'!" Tom proclaimed.

"No, I don't think so," Fletcher said, checking his list. "Who's that, then?"

"Diego."

Diego shifted uncomfortably on his feet. Fletcher looked at Drake, who shook his head.

The preacher got the message, and said, "It's not important for him to be a part of this."

"Why's that then, Admiral?" Tom asked.

First Captain Chester, then Nuño da Silva, and now Bosun Tom – this itch about Diego was becoming an open wound.

Drake stepped into the breach. "We're Christian folk. It's our religion, not his. I believe God is like a splendid, many-crusted jewel. One man will focus on the jewel's shining girdle. Another will delight in the play of light on its pavilion. A third witnesses a glint of brilliance from its crown. It's the same jewel, the same light, and the same wonderful grace of God. Diego is a God's man, but his path to the Almighty is different to ours. So, show him respect and leave him be."

"Bah, dunno 'bout that," Tom grumbled. "Methinks Our God's gonna be mightily displeased and He'll send us tempests aplenty. You'll see."

"We'll not fall as low as the Dons and enquire into the hearts of other men, so long as they believe in the Creator," Drake told him. Then he turned to Fletcher and added, "Now, lead the men to a place of compassion and kindness in their hearts."

Fletcher nodded and began, "The Lord is my shepherd…"

The following day, close to the eleventh hour, the crew gathered on the afterdeck, standing like a bunch of pelicans, the heat of the sun bearing down upon them like during the Dog Days. The pilot levelled the astrolabe, took readings and then retook them. He cupped his hands and whispered a few words to Fletcher.

A broad smile emerged on the face of the preacher, who announced, "We are here. We have done it. Let us pray."

They all bowed their heads and knelt on the deck. Nelan had never understood this kneeling business. He did it every morning and evening, as directed by either the admiral or Fletcher. But for a start, it hurt his knees. Further, he remained convinced that the Creator needed fully fledged participants in His great universal plan, not a load of supplicants bowing down like snivelling cockroaches. That served no good purpose at all. Each era seemed blinded by its customs and conformities, and this was one of them.

Above them on the poop deck, the preacher stood behind a table adorned with a white cloth, on which were two copper bowls. Next to the table was a barrel, from which protruded an assortment of thin sticks, wicker brooms, and yard-long poles of wood. "Little Nelan, you're to go first. Don't look so anxious. It's a great privilege, lad."

The potential menace of those brooms suffocated Nelan's sense of honour.

Fletcher said, "The rest of you, grab a stick from the barrel. That's it. Take only one, Tom. You've got two; put one back! Good. And, Great Nelan, that's broken; fetch another. What are they for? Well, I'll tell you when you've all got one in your filthy paws. You're either the quick or the dead, so don't be tardy."

All the able seamen – even little Oliver – collected a stick or a broom. Nelan noticed that Tom the bosun practised swipes with a long, stiff broom.

"Now," Fletcher said. "Line up all around the gunwale."

"That's it; do as he asks," the admiral said.

"This is a rite of passage," Fletcher said. "In it, you all chastise the initiate, and the first of the crew to go is Little Nelan. That's what the sticks are for. He's going to run around the deck three times, and as he passes, you're to give him a stinging wallop. The greater the pain he suffers, the more of a sailor he'll make. So, no slacking. Got it? Good. We'll start each lap by ringing the bell."

The heavy, sombre tones of the bell resounded around the little ship. Nelan hared around the deck. Despite his speed and agility, in his first run of the gauntlet he was soundly thwacked, mainly in the back and upper arms. With one circuit completed, he returned panting and sweating, bent double, hands on hips.

"Twice more, come on – no shirking. Get to it," the preacher said. Nelan didn't know whether these words of encouragement were intended for him or the beaters.

The ship's bell rang a second time, and off he sprinted. The crew heckled and snarled like he was Judas for the day. Oliver spat at him, and the spittle landed on Nelan's face. Another hand tripped him up, and he fell, face down, onto the burned-raw wooden decking. He got up and stumbled to the end. By the time the bell rang for the last lap, his body resembled one large bruise. With the men cheering and jeering in equal measure, he skipped over the obstacles thrown to trip him up and suffered blow after blow to his arms and back. He staggered towards the end. Tom raised his broomstick. Nelan ducked out of the way, but the wood thudded against his temple. Dizzy, and with his head spinning, he crashed onto the deck.

In his mind's eye he saw strange, airy, fleeting visions, like those he'd witnessed in the alley near Smithfield on that awful day. A young woman, uncannily like his Eleanor, drifted into his blurred vision. Dressed in white robes that flowed like the surf, she caressed his fevered brow and made him feel as sweet as honey.

Water splashed onto his face. The men were cajoling and guffawing. Nelan touched the wound on his temple and felt blood spouting from it. The bell rang to denote the end of the trial. A helping hand appeared in front of him, and he grabbed it like a thirsty man would a flagon of ale. It was a giant hand, warm, and fierce in strength yet gentle in disposition. He looked up. He could barely manage a smile, but his eyes shone with relief and gratitude. It was Great Nelan. The Dane wrapped a kerchief around the wound on Nelan's temple, then jutted out his chin. For the Viking, that was equivalent to an acknowledgement of bravery and prowess. Nelan felt a wave of immense pride swell his heart.

"How about doing that one more time for us?" Tom mocked.

The crew fell on the deck laughing, except for Nelan, and Great Nelan, who offered them his best Danish scowl.

After more collective hilarity, Fletcher raised his hands and said, "That's enough, you rabble. This is a serious matter. I'm going to make holy water, so you'd better be as righteous as cherubs, else I'll unleash the fury of the Lord upon you."

Except for the occasional squawk of the birds and a creaking of the boards, a pall of silence fell on the ship.

Fletcher announced, "Well done, Little Nelan. Now stand up and be counted. This ritual has three parts, and you're ready for the second. The good thing for you is that you only have to witness this part. On this table in front of me are two bowls. One contains sweet water; the other a pile of salt. I'll begin by exorcising the salt." He glanced longingly at the Heavens before intoning, "In the name of the living God, I cast out the demon from this salt. May you be purified; a means of health for those who believe; a medicine for body and soul for all who make use of you. May all evil fancies of the Foul Fiend, his malice and cunning, be driven far from the place where you are sprinkled. And let every unclean spirit be repulsed by He who is coming to judge both the living and the dead and the world by fire."

Using the same words, he then exorcised the Devil from the bowl of water, purifying it for ritual use. He grabbed a handful of salt and, forming it into a cross on the surface of the water, poured it into the bowl, saying, "May this salt and water be mixed together, in the name of the Father and of the Son and of the Holy Spirit." Then he made a strange action. The preacher fisted his left hand and brought together the fingers and thumb of his right to form the shape of a cone, in precisely the same way Nelan had seen Dr Dee make while working his magic with the crystal. Fletcher pointed his coned fingers at the surface of the salt water and moved them up and away, and then back towards it. Repeating the movement, he muttered a prayer: "May the presence of the Father, the Son and the Holy Spirit act through me and imbue this purified water."

Nelan glanced at the faces of the crew, who looked every bit as mystified as he felt, gawping in wonder at the preacher's machinations. Even Drake seemed mightily impressed. Only Diego, who had sneaked onto the poop deck to catch the end of the ceremony, nodded approvingly. Fresh water mixed with salt and charged by human astral power; were these the ingredients that made holy water?

When Fletcher stepped back, Nelan's ordeal approached its third and final part. A few deckhands clambered up the Devil's shrouds and prepared a rope high on the yardarm. Nelan looked up and saw how the rope reached beyond the gunwale and danced over the water. Its end dangled below the surface of the waves. He knew what would come next.

The mariners ushered him onto the yardarm, hauled up the rope from the ocean, and tied the end, now soaked in seawater, tight around his ankles. Inch by inch, they hauled him up until he hung from the top of the yardarm, feet first. He had a bird's-eye view of the deck and the rest of the ceremony. Fletcher picked up the bowl of holy water and carried it as if it contained the blood of Christ Himself. He walked solemnly across the deck, his feet gliding over the beams, until he stopped at the gunwale directly below the yardarm from which Nelan was dangling. Everything took on an ethereal, magical quality. The waves were as lethargic as the preacher's movements; like putty, thick and resinous rather than thin and watery. The air seemed charged with a holy essence, as befitted the occasion.

With a slow, ponderous movement, Fletcher tipped the bowl and poured the holy water into the sea, yelling, "The voice of the Lord is over the waters; the voice of the Lord is majestic. By this act, we marry the salt waters of the earth with the holy waters of the Lord, and thereby sanctify the greater waters in His name."

He pointed up at Nelan, and then down to the water. The mariners pushed Nelan off the yardarm and he plunged through the air like a majestic bird, and in that fleeting instant, he knew what was happening and why. Just before he hit the surface of the ocean, he braced himself. The waters divided, bending to his purpose, in the same way as the waters of his mother had once nourished him. *May she rest in peace.* He sank into the womb of the holy waters of the earth, and was cleansed by them. When he rose to the surface, he gulped in the refined air of the equator. He felt buoyant, renewed and full of joy.

The preacher's words echoed across the waves and resounded in the caverns beneath the oceans: "Verily, I say unto thee, except that a man be born of water and of the Spirit, he cannot enter into the kingdom of God."

The mariners hauled Nelan back aboard the ship. He rose from the waters, dripping like a fish, gasping for breath and taking gulps of fresh air. They lowered him onto the deck and untied the rope from around his feet. He stood up, facing them; facing himself. He wondered what their silence portended. Had he failed? Had he erred?

Great Nelan lifted his hands above his head and gave a gutsy roar that roused the spirits of the sea and called them to witness a newcomer to their ranks. The other men joined him, lifting the vault of Heaven with a great cry and then bursting into a raucous sea shanty. Nelan felt like Odysseus returning home after a long and dangerous journey. The mariners slapped him on the back. With japes and smiles aplenty, Great Nelan lifted him onto his broad shoulders and carried him in triumph around the deck. John Brewer blasted the news to all hands and the great expanse of the Atlantic Ocean.

The equator joined north and south; those two vast hemispheres of planetary power which, like the numinous times of dawn and dusk and the mystical union of man and woman, could only commune for a fleeting moment before they were forced apart and resumed their separate identities. Soaked in the waters of the earth, Nelan had merged with the holy waters of Our Lord. His clothes stuck to his body like a leech. He could taste salt on his lips. His eyes stung with it. They called the next man, Robert Winterhay, to undergo the rite, and as he watched the surgeon running the gauntlet, Nelan tried to absorb his achievement.

Diego sidled up to him. With a mischievous look, he asked, "How do you feel?"

"I'm twice uplifted," Nelan said. "I'm accepted on board by the men, and I'm graced by a mighty presence. I feel it, though I couldn't name it."

"One day, perhaps you'll be able to do that. At least now you know the origins of the ceremony of baptism."

"I do?" Nelan asked, raising his eyebrows. "What do you mean?"

"Remember the sky waters, the yellow charisma and the green sun? The sun and the earth are joined by a gigantic, invisible spring, in which the moon is the pendulum. After many thousands of years, the sun and the earth swap roles. The sky waters on the sun fall onto its surface, and the waters on the earth's surface rise into the sky."

"So, when they are up, they are up, and when they are down, they are down," Nelan chuckled. "But what's that got to do with baptism?"

"When the waters are up in the sky," Diego said, "they're imbued with the latest presence from the universe, which you call the Holy Spirit. When the waters fall from the sky, that's the deluge spoken of in your Bible."

"Let me see if I've got this," Nelan said. "I saw Fletcher drop salt into the water and bless it to make it holy. Only a saline solution can hold the high, pristine content of the Holy Spirit. Then, after the flood, people want to bathe in the sacred waters and absorb the Holy Ghost into themselves."

"*Sí*, Little Nelan. This is the origin of the rite of baptism."

Nelan swallowed hard on this golden nugget of wisdom. He didn't know what to say. He felt blessed with an understanding of a mystery from humanity's rich heritage. On this day, towards the end of February 1578, he had crossed two lines: one was the equator, and the other was in his life. No longer a boy, he had emerged on the other side of that narrow, ephemeral line as a man, ready to undertake his duties and responsibilities and enjoy the greater opportunities therein.

13

The Rite of Baptism

5th April 1578

"Land ho!" The cry rang out from the crow's nest, across the deck, and down into the forecastle, upsetting the legions of mosquitoes and rousing all hands from their hammocks and straw mattresses.

Nelan followed them as they scampered up the steps into the oppressive heat of the mid-afternoon sun to witness this long-awaited sight. It was so dark in the forecastle that climbing the ladder usually felt like an escape from the thick confines of the underworld – but not this time. As he reached the deck, he noticed that the sea was a lighter blue and the smell of salt more acute than in the Narrow Seas of the English Channel and the southern North Sea. This was another sign that they were far from Ushant and the Bay of Biscay. This was the South Atlantic, and the land was South America. On this day at the beginning of April, a slender strip of green land edged with silver sand stood off the starboard horizon. What a sight! The first land they'd seen since heading out of the Cape Verde Isles at the end of January.

They knelt on the deck, heads bowed, hands pressed together, as Fletcher led a prayer of thanksgiving. After that, old salts like Tom, Oliver and even the pilot burst into song. The men danced a spontaneous jig around the deck. It felt like Christ Mass and Easter combined. Drake folded his arms and nodded. Striking land represented a huge achievement and the first success in this incredibly ambitious voyage. It marked not the end, nor even the beginning of the end, but the end of the beginning. A great roar of acclaim greeted his order to the quartermaster to break open a barrel of Spanish sack. Their voices loosened by the fortified wine, the crew's singing got steadily more raucous, and their jests more salacious. Nelan suspected that the admiral needed to keep morale amongst the men as high as possible because, without a doubt, there would be more hardships to come.

While on board, Nelan had seen the moon wax and wane four or five times, but that didn't mean he knew all the words to the men's most popular sea shanties, or understood the lore of the sea, or even what motivated these old hands to leave their home shores and their loved ones for such long periods. How odd that many of them couldn't wait to sail out of Plymouth and heave out to sea, only for, after the months had passed, that sentiment to be replaced by a longing for dry land. A mere glimpse of it would suffice to know that it was still there, waiting for them like a mother for her child, faithful to the last.

In the extreme heat, the sweat rolled off the men. Tentacles of sea fog settled on the ocean, obscuring the distant coastline. The mist had a wispy, light, even ethereal nature. As Nelan wondered if this shrouding of the land represented a portent, Diego sidled up to him and leaned over the gunwale.

"'Tis a welcome sight," Nelan said.

"*Sí*," came the reply. Diego played with a piece of loose cloth on his sleeve as they watched the mist move over the surface of the water.

"You must feel vindicated."

"Why?"

"We all heard Nuño the Portuguese suggesting a different route to cross the ocean. And despite a fractious argument, the admiral followed your advice and, well, here we are, safe and sound and within sight of the land of Amerigo Vespucci."

"*Sí, Señor*, but I am not vindicated. I do not understand charts and rutters. I read the signs. I am a scout; that is all."

"You make it sound so simple. I'd love to know what signs you look for."

"The traces that nature shows us. They are the fish and the birds – the shearwater and the dolphin, the seabird and the flying fish – all creatures of the Great Mother. So, like any mother, you expect Her to care for Her children. That's why She provides them with food, and with safe places to breed. She helps them find their destination when they migrate by giving them an instinct. That way, they are guided by hidden paths on land, in the air and in the sea. These lines are mostly invisible to us, but not to the fish and the birds."

"And that's how you advised the admiral?"

"Our ship, she follow the route of migrating birds and fish. And when we are on those paths, is like a great wind fills our sails. That's how we know we are on the right path. *¿Comprende?*"

"I shall watch for these signs. Talking of which…" Nelan gazed at the head of water off the starboard bow. "Look, can you see them?"

"Where?" Diego asked.

Nelan pointed above the surface of the water, midway between the *Pelican* and the lee shore. The water rippled as if wind blew across its surface. The heat was intoxicating. "Look – see those three silvery lines, like serpents next to one another, vibrating?"

"Mmm, now I see them."

"Salamanders."

"My tribe calls them Djinn; spirits of the air and fire," Diego said.

"You know of them?"

"*Sí.* The Djinn of fire are helpers of humanity. Like an angel, they offer guidance."

"Fascinating. Tell me – what are they like?"

Diego replied:

"They're oh so bright,
When they ignite,
An' give us light,
Into the night."

"Why couch this knowledge in rhyme?" Nelan asked.

"We live in dangerous times," Diego said. "The courtiers of Spain, France and England are all wary of alchemists, conjurors and occultists. For now, they're interested in those arts and want masters of them to tell them of the fruits of their knowledge. But should the tide of opinion change – and one day it will – they'll just as soon turn around and accuse them of heresy. That's why folk wisdom is often clothed in rhyme: so its author has an alternative explanation."

"Thank you, Diego," Nelan said.

"The Djinn only appear to men of honour. It's like the desert. Some men can read the desert. Others know that the desert reads those who pass through it. Those men are special. I see you are one of them. I shall be pleased to call you brother," Diego said, shaking Nelan's hand warmly.

Nelan felt as tall as a shire horse. This represented a step forward in his understanding of salamanders. A guiding angel, Diego had said. He wanted to ask more about them, but at that moment he and Diego were transfixed by more threads of mist spiralling out of the water nearby. Slowly, the threads fanned out from where Nelan had spotted the salamander. They stretched and grew into tentacles, bringing a chill to the air and banishing the salamanders. Something was afoot.

Alert to the danger, the leadsman rushed past Nelan.

"Sandbank!" the barrel man shouted.

Great Nelan and others dashed onto the deck.

Coating his lead with beeswax, the leadsman threw the line over the side. Within moments, he had hauled it back in. "By the mark five. And the bottom's full o' sand!" he shouted.

John Brewer let out three long blasts on the bugle. The warning of imminent peril brought everyone up on deck, including Drake, Nuño and Diego. Nuño said a few words. Nelan couldn't hear what he'd said, but Drake waved him away and conversed with Diego.

"Five fathoms and headin' into a sandbank!" the leadsman thundered.

The ethereal tentacles expanded into small, thick, hazy clumps, like a miasma on a marsh. The coast was obscured. The cold and the damp reached through the crew's skins and into their souls; their inner sanctum.

The leadsman threw the lead and hauled it in again before calling out, "By the mark four! An' more sand!" Then with a furrowed brow, he added, "Four fathoms. That's only twenty-four feet. That isn't good. We're shoaling in the mists and driftin' towards an invisible lee shore."

The ship slowed. From the helm there came an ominous scraping noise. Barrels toppled over and rolled across the deck. Men tripped and fell.

"Bejesus, we're scraping the arse of the ocean," Tom said through gritted teeth.

The leadsman called, "Ready there?"

Nelan shouted, "Heave!" The lead arced forwards and hit the bottom. When the line went slack, he called the depth. "By the mark three!"

Still in the shallows, the mist swirled around them, thick like a London fog. They needed a miracle. Fletcher sank to his knees to pray for one.

"Again!" Drake yelled.

The leadsman threw out the line, and Nelan hauled it in. As he examined the line and the lead, anxious bearded faces, tanned with the southern sun, turned towards him. What he said next could decide the fate of the voyage and all that rested upon it, including the future of England.

"By the mark three!" Nelan shouted.

No change. The crew grew as silent as the night, and their fear just as thick. If they drifted onto the sandbank, that could spell disaster and the end of the voyage. The tide might never lift them off. Marooned on a strange coastline, they'd ponder what might have been, homeless, bound to an awful fate in a far-off land of strange people. They'd miss the tide on the flood, and the rest of their lives would be bound in shallows and in miseries. They could barely see the ends of their noses in the swirling fog. Some hands climbed up the shrouds and onto the yardarm to get a better view. Everyone else hung over the gunwale. Drake barked orders to the helmsman. He sailed blind. These were excruciating moments.

The leadsman threw out the lead again.

Nelan hauled it in and called out, "By the mark three!" The same as before. Which way were they heading? Would they ease off the sandbank, or head back onto it? The next call would be crucial.

"We're heading out of the shallows." Drake's voice was charged with uncanny certainty. He seemed to be the only one in touch with his vessel.

The boat steadied. The grinding of the helm quietened. The leadsman threw out the line.

Nelan yelled, "By the mark five!"

"Steady as she goes!" Drake called.

The relief was palpable. There were gaps in the swirling mist. They

156

could see. They were free. The hands roused a muted cheer. Safe now, they headed into open seas.

"All's well!" cried the barrel man.

Choosing this moment, Nuño swaggered up to Drake. Pointing at the swathes of mist, he said, "I see them before. This a *pampero*. Is a cold, thick fog. It come sudden. It come often on this coast, *¿sabe?* But I am here. I am Nuño. I can tell you, warn you. But you don't want hear Nuño before. So Nuño seal his lips. What you say now, eh, *Señor Draque?*"

"Master Nuño, we're safe; no thanks to you. But you can tell me all you know. I'm listening."

"It's them," Nuño said, making a strange twisting motion with his hand as if loosening the cork from a bottle.

"It's who? What are you talking about?"

"Bah!" Nuño said, his small dark eyes gazing imperiously at Drake like he and his people owned half of the world. And perhaps they did.

Drake raised his hands in mock desperation. "This is no time for enigmas. We've narrowly escaped a shipwreck. Tell us what you know!"

As the *Pelican* hove into sunlit waters, Nuño said, "*Sí, Señor*. The locals are a people to fear. They have very clever arts. They practise strange crafts."

"I know a few myself," Drake admitted.

"When I bring our ships to this coast," Nuño said, "the local people, they no want us. They no want Portuguese. They no want Spanish. They magicians. They conjure rain. They make mist. They can create fog in the air! Is true!"

Drake nodded. Everyone listened. Had the natives here summoned the sea fog out of clear air? Nuño had suggested as much. Nelan wondered if this skill was an ancient art common amongst native peoples. But Dee had conjured just such a mist to help him escape the constable. If he had rediscovered the art, how had he done it?

Nuño went on, "So, our galleons sail long way away from shore. We no come near to coast. You want know Portuguese name for this region?"

"*Sí.*"

"Tierra de Demônios – or, in your tongue, the Land of Demons." Nuño glanced over his shoulder, perhaps expecting these demonic creatures to manifest behind him.

"Mmm, I see." Drake scratched his beard. Then he said in a loud voice, "But we do not cower in the face of this magic because we have our own skills: those of the true-born English sailor. God and His angels watch over us; that is our protection from these arcane arts. How else have we survived the rigours of the South Atlantic and arrived safely in this Land of Demons?"

"Amen to that!" Fletcher chimed in.

While everyone seemed satisfied with the outcome of this conversation, in that Nuño and Drake were at least talking to one another again, Nelan glowed as bright as a brazier. The prospect of conjuring a hurricane fired him up. How was that even possible? Was Nuño's story suspect or true? He wondered long and hard how a human being could affect the weather. To conjure clouds from the ether, to draw the doldrums from the air, to summon a squall from the sky – these were uncanny arts. But then again, so was the origin of the rite of baptism.

14

Isle of Justice

21st June 1578

The fleet sailed down the coast through April and May, passing the Bay of Montevideo and the estuary of the River Plate. As the storms battered them, so speculation was provoked amongst the crew. Were they natural tempests or those conjured by the natives? They even asked Diego, who wisely kept his own counsel.

Above the keel, a storm of the human kind brewed between the mariners and the gentlemen adventurers. Everyone had heard the whispers. At the centre of the web of intrigue were Master Thomas Doughty and his brother John. Below decks, dark rumours circulated that held both of them accountable for raising the storms and the mists. The reason: to undermine Drake's command.

The Doughty brothers were not Drake's only problem. Once again, the men whined about their destination. The fleet had reached South America. They sailed in the aquamarine waters of the South Atlantic Ocean. Yet the farther south they got, the more likely they were to be heading for the manifold dangers of the Strait of Magellan and, beyond that, the uncharted South Seas. Whenever he was asked about the matter, the admiral remained tight-lipped. After the fleet moored off Nodales Bay on the Patagonian coast, Drake broke up and burned one of the two supply ships, reducing the fleet from five to four vessels.

As they sailed further south, the nearer they got to Puerto San Julián, or St Julian's Bay, the more the men grew apprehensive.

This time, it wasn't fear of the Strait; it was simply the prospect of mooring in the bay. Nelan overheard them muttering about it amongst themselves.

"Though we're in dire need of water and fresh food," Tom moaned, "I'd rather give up a pot of the Dons' gold than drop anchor in St Julian's Bay."

"But you ain't got a pot of gold," Oliver pointed out.

Tom took a swig of ale and sallied forth, "Not yet, I ain't, but that's why we're all on this 'ere boat, innit? If I was 'ome in Lulworth right now, me belly'd be grumblin', me kids too, me wife'd be saying, 'Get you a-labourin'.' But there'd be no work on the lordship's land, an' if there was, he'd pay me a Queen's farthing; not enough for a loaf o' bread. So that's why I'm 'ere: to grab some o' the Dons' gold. But I'm tellin' ya, Oliver, lad, this place is wicked. Don't care what you say; I got a tight feelin' in me guts."

They looked out on a bland coastline with low-lying hills, brown-yellow dunes and a stony beach. A small, featureless island guarded the bay, in the middle of which stood a solitary wooden pole. Beyond the island, they saw a natural harbour, where the ships laid anchor. On arrival, Drake broke up and burned the second supply ship, the *Christopher*, trimming down the fleet to three before attempting the Strait.

Curious about St Julian's Bay, Nelan sought out his namesake, who got to work cleaning the gun barrels with a pot of clean water.

"I don't understand," Nelan said with a sigh. "This isle is an ideal place to rest, plug the leaks and take on victuals. Why are the men so wary?"

"I can feel it; can't you?" Great Nelan said. "Read the signs. Look at the waters of the bay. They're choppy and a dark, murky blue. See the way the birds skirt around the isle like they're afraid to roost on it. This isle's soaked in bad blood. It's got a history that smells of the bilges, especially to sailors."

"Why's that, then?"

"*Ja.* This be the Isle of Justice. So named nearly sixty years ago by Ferdinand Magellan hisself. Then, the men of Portugal sailed down the west coast of Africa, around the Cape of Good Hope, and headed east across the Ocean of India before plundering the Spice Isles. The Dons were greedy for the rich spice trade, but the Pope forbade them to sail that way around the globe. Magellan, on his voyage, demanded that his crew sail where no one had ever sailed before: west around the world via the South Seas. Voyaging into the unknown tests a man's tolerance to the limit. A few can handle it, some even thrive on it, and others baulk and wither in the face of it. Four of Magellan's captains lost their nerve and sparked a mutiny, which he quashed with customary vigour. He had two of them beheaded, drawn and quartered, and then hung their bloody body parts on a gibbet, right here in the middle of this isle."

It was Midsummer's Day 1578, but it was the middle of winter in the southern hemisphere. The seasons weren't the only things upside down in this place.

Drake chose the watering party to accompany him ashore. Alongside his brother Thomas, he took Fletcher the preacher; Oliver, his master gunner; and Robert Winterhay, the surgeon. Nelan went too, along with Diego. Drake instructed Oliver to bring his arquebus, while Winterhay brought his longbow. They carried gifts and trinkets for the natives, a score or more of whom had already gathered on the beach to greet them.

As they boarded the boat, Drake said, "Remember, the Dons have occupied this land for decades, and in that time they've cruelly mistreated the natives. Ask Diego; he'll tell you. The natives are more suspicious of us than we are of them. When we land, approach them as if they are quick to anger. Treat them as you would a feral beast. Be very careful and make no sudden movement."

With this warning ringing in their ears, they cast off into the chilly waters. Nelan felt his muscles warm as he pulled the oars in time with the other rowers. Like the sky, the sea wore a cloak of grey. They dragged the boat onto the beach, all the while keeping an eagle eye on the natives, who started whooping and yelling in childlike excitement. Drake led the landing party up the long, flat, stony beach towards where the natives had assembled.

For Nelan, this was the first time he'd set eyes on an indigenous people of the southern continent. Perhaps he had expected men similar in stature to his own tribe: the people of the Belgic tribe, or the Low Dutch. He hadn't expected these tall natives of Patagonia, with their high cheekbones; rounded, moonlike faces; and arms and legs adorned with florid tattoos. Instead of doublets, jerkins and breeches, the twenty Patagonians wore the skins of animals. They had no guns; only bows and arrows. And where were their horses and carriages; their towns and villages? Perhaps they lived in caves or wooden shacks. Nelan was a Christian. His English comrades, all God-fearing Protestants, believed in the Holy Trinity. However benign the natives' intentions, their dress and behaviour was rudimentary. When Nelan looked around for guidance from the Preacher, he saw Fletcher standing at the rear of the landing party fingering his crucifix while mouthing some holy utterance.

Standing twenty paces apart, the two groups stared at one another with caution and curiosity. In this meeting of worlds, there was wary suspicion, coupled with a strong desire to make allowance wherever possible. The natives' world was primitive and tardy in development, while the Europeans' was, comparably at least, expansive and sophisticated. The natives' society appeared not to have changed in centuries, but the Europeans' had evolved and grown. There were differences, but thankfully no conflict. No one yet knew if the two would mix or not.

Brandishing their bows, the young warriors yelled and stamped their feet as if daring the landing party to respond in kind. Winterhay stepped into the breach, raised his longbow, notched an arrow, aimed well away from the native band, and launched it down the length of the beach. It clattered to the ground some distance away, near a tamarisk bush. A young native with a winsome smile took up the challenge. He cocked his bow and dispatched an arrow high into the air towards the same bush. When it skidded past Winterhay's, the natives cheered loudly and jumped into the air with joyous innocence.

A group of older natives emerged from a nearby path. Dressed in animal skin and a feathered headdress, their leader was as tall and well built as a stallion. A clutch of fifty of his companions thumped their chests with warlike aggression and pointed accusatory fingers at the youngsters. Winterhay cocked another arrow and prepared to launch it into the air. Perhaps he was intimidated by the sudden appearance of the older natives. Whatever the cause, his aim went awry. His fingers slipped on the nock of the arrow and the bowstring snapped, sending the arrow spiralling towards the chieftain and wounding him in the leg.

There followed a moment's awkward silence. Then all Hell broke loose. The natives unleashed a volley of arrows, which thudded into Winterhay's chest and neck. With a final, pitiful groan, he sank to his knees and fell flat onto the beach. Oliver lifted his arquebus and pulled the serpentine, but the gun failed to discharge and emitted only an embarrassing puff of smoke. The natives let go another hail of arrows, hitting Oliver in the head and legs until he too slumped head first onto the stony beach. His body twitched and writhed in the last throes of agony before giving up the ghost.

Far from home, Drake and his crew were confronted by marauding natives, defiant in their protection of their land and homesteads. Their wounded chieftain led the revolt. Screaming like a banshee, he charged toward them. Everyone turned to stone. But not Nelan. Heeding Drake's advice, he kept his head. Winterhay had not, and had paid the ultimate price. Nelan swooped over to where Oliver lay in a pool of blood and grabbed the arquebus from the boy's hand. Quick as lightning, he handed it to Drake. The chieftain's angry cries filled the bay. With the man bearing down on him, Drake took aim and pulled the serpentine. At point-blank range, the withering array of shot smashed into the chieftain's torso, shredding it to pieces. The chieftain stood like a statue; then his body quivered until he fell backwards onto the beach, landing near Winterhay and Oliver. Three corpses on a sad morning. So much justice and so much blood, on a single isle!

The native band scattered like chaff in the wind. With Nelan close behind, Drake led the chase. They soon found a compound of mud huts, each with a single oval-shaped entrance. Nelan ventured inside one. Clay bowls and cups, pans and cooking utensils, and foods like grasses, berries and root vegetables lay strewn over the ground. Alongside were pots of coloured paint, and thin leaves tied into a brush. The natives had run away.

When they returned to the beach, Fletcher intoned a soulful prayer. They mourned for their two deceased friends before transporting their bodies back to the ships to prepare them for burial.

The next day, the boat carried the two corpses back across the stretch of water between the *Pelican* and the small island. The hands were nervous and curious about the natives. Nelan joined the other mariners stalking the beach and guarding the boats. Except for skeleton crews, the entire fleet's complement gathered at the graves. Fletcher presided over the burials, extolling the virtues of the surgeon and the young barrel man.

With the service over, Thomas Doughty was in Tom's ear, saying, "Shame they had to be buried so far from home."

"Yeah, but you know mariners prefer to be laid to rest in God's earth." Tom was inconsolable.

"We should not have ventured this far south," Doughty said. "Our official commission only gives us a warrant to trade in the Levant."

John Doughty helped twist the knife. "And think, Tom: your friend Oliver would still be with us if we had not ventured into this godforsaken land!"

Tom frowned and pressed his fists to his temples.

"And our master surgeon," Thomas Doughty added. "What'll we do without Winterhay? Our wounds will fester. Scurvy will take us down, one by one. Driven by lies and falsehoods, this expedition is turning into a farce. Next, the admiral will be convincing us to sail through the Strait – and that's not the route to the South Seas and the Spice Isles!"

Everyone heard his derogatory remarks. Drake certainly did. "Methinks m'lord has no grace," he said, biting his lip. "Thomas, I'll not have you fomenting discord amongst the hands. Haven't you upset them enough already, what with your japes and your bribes? Oh yes, I know you offered angels and crowns to the quartermaster in exchange for food. And now you loosen your poisonous tongue at a solemn funeral, of all places. It's difficult enough sailing into uncharted waters without you undermining my authority at every turn. I'll have no more of it. I believe the rumours that you've cast a grotesque spell on this voyage. From now on, Master Doughty, keep your mutinous thoughts to yourself."

"You rewarded me with the command of that Portuguese vessel we captured," Doughty replied, "and then you humiliated me by giving it to another. What will you strip me of next?"

"This expedition will succeed! The Almighty will have it so. Don't push me, or I'll deal with you in a way you'll never forget!"

"You wouldn't dare! I'm the private secretary of Sir Christopher Hatton, who sponsored this voyage and paid for the *Pelican*!"

Drake planted his hands on his hips and snarled, "We know. You told us already – many times. You may have friends in high places, but what have you done yourself? How has the Queen, our gracious Majesty, rewarded your achievements? Oh, but she hasn't, has she? Because you don't have any, do you?"

"I-I'll head back to my vessel," Doughty said, hesitating before moving away from Drake towards the launch.

"You will not!" Drake thundered, sticking his face in front of Doughty's. "You'll leave when I so order it, and not a moment before. In the meantime, m'lord, wait here until all hands are safe aboard their ships. Then, and only then, may you return to yours. Is that understood?"

Thomas Doughty smirked, folded his arms, and thrust his bearded chin at the admiral. Unbowed, the man refused to be intimidated. John Doughty stood next to him, the two brothers like a couple of snarling bloodhounds.

As the funeral congregation broke up, the men waited to return to their respective vessels. Tom and two other able seamen strode into the middle of the island to investigate the solitary ten-foot pole. When they started whooping with excitement, the Doughty brothers joined them, no doubt to see what the fuss was about. Nelan went along too.

Tom ran his palm down the thick pole. "It's made of spruce," he said.

The constant wind and rain coming from the South Atlantic had bent the pole at an angle. A stub of rotting wood protruded from the top of it. At the base, they saw fragments of what appeared to be more wood debris.

"Is this what I think it is?" Thomas Doughty said, staring at the pole.

"Ah, sir. I think it is." Tom pawed at it like a prized asset.

"It's the gibbet, isn't it?" Doughty said. "It's Magellan's gibbet. It must be."

Tom nodded and smiled, displaying teeth as rotten as his mind.

"Let's make sure," Doughty said. "John, go fetch us a spade."

John Doughty returned with a couple of spades from the gravedigging. They dug around the base of the pole and unearthed various items which had survived nearly sixty years of Patagonian winters: some threads of decayed cloth, and then a selection of curved bones covered in dirt.

"They're human bones," Thomas Doughty said.

"How d'you know that, then?" Tom asked.

"This one here, it's a collarbone; looks like an elongated 's'," Doughty said, running his finger along the length of the bone.

"If you say so, m'lord."

John Doughty uncovered what appeared like the top of a whitish ball. "Here, what's this?" he cried.

"That's a skull, as sure as I'm an Englishman," Thomas railed in triumph. "That's it, careful, John, hand it to me. Thanks. Oh, it's rotten."

Drake and his manservant watched the diggers. Thomas Doughty wiped off the surface dirt and held the tarnished skull in front of his own face. Perhaps awoken from its eternal slumber by its sudden emergence into the light of day, the eyeless skull seemed to stare back at him.

"There – told you so," Doughty said. "I reckon these are the last earthly remains of Gaspar de Quesada, an ally of Juan de Cartagena. Both captained vessels in Admiral Ferdinand Magellan's fleet."

"What happened?" Tom wanted to know.

"Juan de Cartagena was faithful to Spain and to his King, as I am to England and my Queen. He feared his admiral recklessly endangered his crew, and, in trying to save them from certain death, led a failed mutiny. He was marooned by Magellan for his troubles. Gaspar was hanged and gibbeted and this is all that's left of him."

"That's seditious," Drake said, thumping his fist in his hand. "Despite the mutiny of his trusted captains, Magellan succeeded in the end. Have no doubt, Master Doughty, that I will follow in his wake."

"Will you now?" Doughty spoke these words in anger. "You set sail with five ships, as did Magellan. I predict that your fleet will, like his, limp home with only one vessel manned by a few sick, weak men, with many hands lost, dead from scurvy or butchered by wild natives; drowned at sea or hanged for crimes."

"The Almighty will decide my fate, not a bunch of treasonous mutineers." Drake scowled. "And you, my lord, are no better than Juan de Cartagena. You're his English brother because you share his blood.

166

You're a conjuror and a seditious person. I arrest you for these crimes. You will sit before a jury of forty good men and true, who will decide your fate."

"So it's come to that?" Doughty nodded, pursing his lips.

"Aye, Thomas, it has. Now, Tom, lock him in chains. I'll convene a jury to try him by the laws of the sea, the laws of our Queen, and the laws of God."

Like some jaundiced orb, the low sun breached the horizon. It bore witness to the life and death of Master Thomas Doughty. Once a gentleman adventurer, he had fallen into the pit of mutiny and been sentenced to execution. His brother John escaped any punishment. With his hands tied behind his back, they bundled Thomas Doughty aboard a skiff, which bobbed up and down on the flow. He had missed the tide of his life and headed for the miseries of the shallows. As he sat on the skiff, he kept his own counsel. Perhaps he contemplated his great mistake, which it was now too late to rectify. There was a new game with new rules. He had played by the old rules and paid the price.

Nelan pulled on his oar as the launch cast off from the *Pelican* and headed for the Isle of Justice, or the Isle of Blood as the hands now called it. They led Doughty to his place of execution in the same spot where, nine days earlier, the gentleman adventurer had found de Cartagena's skull.

Drake assembled all the crews and said, "This great expedition is in the keen interests of England and its future empire. But you, Thomas Doughty, plotted to thwart Her Majesty's grand plans and cast evil spells against them. You have been found guilty by your peers of the onerous crime of mutiny. As is customary, you can make one last request before you are sent to meet St Peter."

"I wish to say a few last words," Doughty said, unbowed to the end. "I do not recognise this court, and claim the right to be tried by my true aristocratic peers in a court in England. And let it be known that, like *Capitán* Juan de Cartagena, I die here an honourable man, innocent of mutiny, free of treason, untainted by the practice of witchcraft. If I am guilty of any crime, my overriding desire is to protect England from arrogant and overambitious admirals." Pausing, he pegged back his shoulders, jutted out that chin of his, and stared right at Drake before uttering his last words on this earth. "As Ferdinand Magellan died at the hand of a native in the Philippines, so do I prophesy that you, Francis Drake, will never see the shores of Plymouth Hoe again."

Drake replied instantly with six words of defiance. They were French words, but had been emblazoned on the English royal throne for centuries. "*Honi soit qui mal y pense.*"

Nelan mouthed the translation to himself: *Evil be to he who thinks evil of me.*

Thomas Doughty said a last farewell to his brother, knelt down, laid his neck upon the block, and gave the signal to the executioner. Nelan covered his eyes, but not his ears. The executioner brought down the axe with a horrific crunch, spilling the gentleman adventurer's blood and mixing it with that of the Spanish mutineers.

Under sail once more, they approached Cape Virgenes, the south-eastern tip of the continent and the entry to the Strait of Magellan. On the 20th August 1578, Drake presided over an important ceremony: he changed the name of his ship from the *Pelican* to the *Golden Hind*. It was in honour of Sir Christopher Hatton, who bore the same animal on his coat of arms. Down in the forecastle, the men muttered about how this act had an ulterior motive: to appease Sir Christopher, whose personal secretary had been none other than Thomas Doughty. This was justice of sorts, but more like rough justice.

15

Mocha

20th August 1578

On that day, the forbidding Strait of Magellan hove into view: dark hills outlined against looming grey skies in an overwhelming vista. This was a turning point for the three remaining vessels, the *Elizabeth*, the *Marigold* and the *Golden Hind*. They were heading into the unknown and searching for the passage into the South Seas; the great Pacific Ocean.

They anchored for four days until the wind veered east-north-east and gave them entry into the Strait. They tacked the channel between the mainland to starboard and the isles to port. Tom delighted in telling everyone that the damn thing was as narrow as a maiden's foot, although Nelan wondered what kind of maidens Tom had encountered in his life. The channel was too deep to anchor, so when they found a sheltered cove in which to moor, the crew lashed the boats to the rocks and took to their hammocks and mattresses for the night.

Nelan checked the lanterns, made everything shipshape, and then joined Great Nelan on watch on the poop deck. Following his custom after serving the admiral's supper, Diego sauntered up for some fresh sea air. Nelan wondered if Drake's manservant ever slept, because he stared out into the deep blue yonder at all times of the day and night. Drake joined them, strolling about the deck like a man utterly in his element. That night, the four of them watched as a light sprang up on the shore, then another a little along the coast, perhaps in response to the first.

"You'll see," Diego said, pointing excitedly further along the coast.

Sure enough, moments later, the natives lit a third fire, almost equidistant from the first two, casting a pinpoint light onto the vast canvas of the dark, empty night. The fires rippled along the tops of the hills, glowing and flickering; a moving wave of red-and-yellow light. Soon, there appeared a string of them all along the coast, like a magical line of fire, pointing the way and offering guidance and safety to the sailors.

"*Sí*, it's called Tierra del Fuego for a good reason," Diego remarked.

"The Land of Fires, eh?"

"The Ona natives lit beacons when Magellan passed this way. It is how it got this name."

"Beacons, yes, of course," Nelan said. "I must remember that. Such a simple way to send a message!"

"The simplest is always the best. In Africa, my tribe gather in a circle and face each other with the drum between our legs. Then we beat the leather with all our strength. The noise, it is deafening, but it carries far away. It bounces off the cliffs and echoes down the valleys, and it follows the natural contours of the land. That is how the message is sent to the next tribe. At night, we light the beacons. The news, she travels faster than a man can run."

"I've never seen it done with such quicksilver speed. What message are the Ona sending?"

"They're warning their neighbours of our arrival. You heard the admiral speak of this. The natives don't trust us. You see what happened in St Julian's Bay."

Nelan furrowed his brow. "It's so strange. We're all humans. Yet there we are – the white people, Europeans. And there you are – the natives and the Africans. It's like oil and water, unable to mix or marry together."

Diego pursed his lips, then nodded.

"Can I ask you a question?" Nelan said, staring him fixedly in the eyes. "And I want an honest answer."

"What is it?"

"What's it like for you and your tribe in Africa?" Nelan asked. "You're living your lives as you've done for many a year, when from out of nowhere come these white men from Portugal and Spain; Christian kingdoms under the spiritual guidance of the Pope. They arrive on your shores wielding pike and arquebus, chain you in irons, and transport you across the ocean, far from your home. If you survive all that, they persecute you for being lesser than they." He shook his head in sorrow. "I'm appalled. If it were me, I'd extend the milk of human kindness to you and gently invite you into the Christian fold."

Diego nodded.

"We white people," Nelan went on, "should teach you – and the natives of Patagonia, Peru, Brazil and Mexico – about our religion, and then allow you free choice to accept it or not. Religion should never involve compulsion; yet we rape, pillage and plunder. I'm ashamed." It felt less like a question and more like a confession.

"I'm happy that you speak like this," Diego said, his chin trembling with emotion. "Long before the white man arrived on our land, my tribe heard his passage through the savannah. His heavy footsteps disturbed the spirits of the forest, the river and the mountain. They whispered to us, *Beware – the white man comes*. And if he's natural, he wouldn't annoy them. That's how we knew he brought trouble."

"We strive to be a kind and compassionate people – Samaritans, no less," Nelan said. "So, why have we perpetrated these terrible deeds upon your people?"

"Ah, this is difficult to explain," Diego said, scratching his head. "You see, I come from an ancient people who, like the elephant, have a long memory. The story begins even before Noah's flood. At that time, fewer people inhabited the earth than now. But they were full of reverence for the gifts of life. There was no war, no famine and no disease. No evil. No need for law, because hardly any crime. It was an idyllic time of harmony between the people and the angels of the land.

"Then the fallen angels came and spawned the hybrid Nephilim. They were giant beings with webbed feet and creatures with animal heads and human bodies. Then God, He send the flood to correct the evil they caused. Many perished, while some survived the killing waters. My tribe did. So did the Jewish people and the natives of America, and others too. The flood was a severe shock to the people of the world. Those who survived lost their knowledge of how to write, to build a house, to sow crops, or to do the most basic things. They regressed to living in caves, hunting for animals and gathering berries.

They had to rediscover everything and build civilisation again from the beginning. There was very little transference of knowledge from before the flood, but my people remembered some of our old ways. We followed the herds and the seasons, moved camps, and lived in tents and mud-brick houses.

"As the years went by, some grew restless of spirit, and there followed an exodus from the old ways. These people conceived new religions, built large nations and forged empires. They moved to fertile areas, farmed the land, and settled in villages which grew into towns and cities. Of these two different peoples, one followed the old ways of richness and roaming, like my tribe, and the other forged the new ways of settlement and city. For a while, the two peoples existed separately from one another. But one hundred years ago, they met through the voyages of the Dutch, the Dons and the Portuguese. My people, those of the old ways, hoped that those with the new ways would see that we are not lesser than them, but merely different. We sighed with disappointment when you called us primitive savages. And when you enslaved us, raped our women and trampled over our sacred lands, we feared for our lives. You *think* that we are the brutes. We *know* that you are. The two sets of people are like two poles, because you see, the people of the old ways – like the Jews, the Chinese, the native Americans and my people – have a different polarity from yours. It's as if we stand back to back, facing away from each other, not understanding the other, seeing life and living from different perspectives. That's why you – the white men – persecute us, the native peoples."

Nelan was lost for words. So many questions whirled around his head. How was it that this man, a so-called primitive, could relate such a clear, coherent narrative of the passage of ancient history? How could this travesty be put right? Who was Diego that he knew all this? Nelan scratched the white skin on his finger in the vain hope that it would come off. It didn't. It sat on him as a permanent source of shame.

Drake nodded gently and said, "I hear your words, Diego. Like you, I am a God-fearing man. You and I have often spoken of these matters. I have learned much from your ways of looking at the gifts of life. Although my participation in the slave trade at the beginning of my naval career was small, I deeply regret that involvement. I was blind to and ignorant of God's vision for humanity, and probably still am in many ways. But I see now that we are all human. There is no 'us' and 'them', for we are all God's people. The Creator is our benefactor, and we all live in awe of His wondrous universe."

Eye to eye, Diego and Drake shook hands with firmness and warmth.

Drake finished by saying, "Out of this small conversation, great things can arise."

They exited the Strait on the 7th September, making the passage in only sixteen days. The next day, a tempest unleashed by the Devil himself buffeted them, or so Fletcher would have had them believe. The rain was like icy spikes thudding against their skin and smarting with every hit. At the height of the storm, with wind lashing the three ships and the men cowering in the bitter cold, the crew of the *Golden Hind* heard cries rend the air. But whence they came, no one knew. Even the barrel man, rocked from side to side by the heaving ocean, couldn't see beyond the turbulence in the air. Nelan felt a chill down his spine. The other hands were just as convinced as he that the cries had been those not of birds, but of men; of dying sailors thrust into the watery depths. Though they searched the waves, they never saw the *Marigold* again; nor any of her crew.

To add to their woes, in mid-October they lost sight of their remaining companion vessel, the *Elizabeth*. But after they looked far and wide for Captain Wynter's boat, Drake called off the hunt. Perhaps he knew the fate of the two ships, but if he did, he never confided in anyone. From five to three and now to one. The *Golden Hind* sailed on alone.

While the ship battled the elements, the crew fought their inner demons, moping about the boat and moaning incessantly about missing their loved ones. Fletcher begged them to cease their cussing and say their prayers, because, as he put it:

If we be such terrible sinners,
It'll set them seafarin' spirits agin us.

The sea was a harsh mistress; unforgiving at one time and quiet as a babe in arms at another. She could be silent or raucous; shallow or deep; a tempestuous harlot, a stubborn vixen, or a calming mother. The Queen of the elements, though she came nowhere near Nelan's favourite: the enigmatic and quixotic element of fire. Life on the waves was hard and full of rigour. But the sea's many wonders offered easement. She was truly consolata to hardship. Nelan thought of Robert of Hull, the sailor he'd met in Marshalsea who had told him of his love of the sea; how she resembled a lady and so had to be wooed. Now Nelan shared Robert's mistress as his own.

As they sought their way between the isles of the Tierra del Fuego archipelago, Nelan enjoyed the periods of dawn and dusk the most. The natural buoyancy and mystery of those times stayed with him long after his eyes closed as he lay in his hammock.

It grew hot and torpid. His clothes stuck to him hard and fast. He saw things betwixt and between; the other world that Tom had mooted. St Elmo's fire and other magical things appeared in the ether, but when he looked again, they'd disappeared. He saw clumps of mist rising from the water. The tentacles seemed to follow the natural course of the winds and the tides. In the intense and suffocating heat, the sea boiled. The mists twisted in strange ways. Slowly, inevitably, they separated into three vertical wavy lines: the mark of the salamander. Nelan rubbed the lines beneath his middle finger. With his mind, he tried to manoeuvre the mists. Nothing worked anymore. One day, he promised himself, he'd master the mists, conjure the currents and raise the rains. The sea and her deep currents spoke to him, and he listened to her music. On that day she sang to him:

One day, I'll see,
Just how to be.
One day, in the lee,
I'll find the key,
Of how to be free,
Of me agin me.

By the end of October, they had made Cape Horn, a rocky headland surrounded by wild seas off the southern tip of South America where the Pacific met the Atlantic Ocean. By early November, they were tacking northwards up the Pacific coast of South America. They lost sight of land for a week, until one day, as Nelan was clearing away wine goblets from the table in the admiral's cabin, Drake and Nuño da Silva entered.

"Look," Drake snapped, "the waters around here are darker; the cats' paws more feral. That tells me we're not heading towards the coast, but out to sea."

"No, *Señor*," Nuño replied.

The admiral's hands trembled with fury as he laid out a chart in front of the Portuguese pilot. Nelan shuffled around quietly in the background, eager to hear the conversation.

"Look, we're supposed to be here!" Drake pointed to the chart.

"And?" Nuño answered.

"Then where's the blessed land off the starboard bow? Do you see it? Because I don't. And do you hear the barrel man crowing about it?" Drake cupped his ear in his hand and shook his head. "No, I don't either."

"*Señor*, what you sayin' to me?"

"Well, I'm saying to you, Master da Silva, that your chart is wrong."

"Is... not... wrong," Nuño stammered, clenching his fists and sticking out his chin.

"It's not only wrong; it's deliberately misleading," Drake said.

"Are you accusing me of false witness?"

"Yes, I am," Drake said, squaring up to the Portuguese. "You and your Spanish grandees want to prevent me from getting hold of the gold and silver from the South American mines. Oh, yes, I know all about their treasures. Why do you think I'm in these waters? And others will come after me. Just wait; soon, this coastline will resound to the raucous singing of English mariners."

Nuño hissed through gritted teeth.

"I don't trust you," Drake said. "I didn't take your advice last time, and I don't believe your rutters this time. I have acquired other charts of this coastline, and that's how I know yours are wrong."

"*Almirante* Draque, they say you have a magic mirror. With it, you see all there is to see about currents and oceans. Is this how you know my chart is wrong?"

"Master da Silva, you will not question my decision!" Then he turned to his pilot, and snapped, "Plot a course north by north-east. Now."

"As ordered, Admiral," his pilot replied.

Nuño stood open-mouthed. So did Nelan. He wondered how Drake had known. Did he, as Nuño suggested, have a magic mirror? Or was it simply supreme seamanship? Or both?

Some days later, the cry of "land ho!" echoed around the *Golden Hind*. The admiral stomped about the deck, hands behind his back, cajoling the crew to do their jobs for God, Queen and country.

On the 25th November, the *Golden Hind* anchored in a quiet cove near a wooded isle. With no sign of any Spanish ships or men, everything seemed peaceful. They needed food and fresh water, so, with his customary caution, Drake took a skiff. The natives greeted them and told them that the island was the Isle of Mocha, which lay off the coast of Chile. They directed the crew to a rendezvous in a small, confined creek fringed with high, thick reeds. Although the place smelled of rotting leaves, the natives welcomed them with gifts and – just as important – fresh water and food, including maize, root vegetables, a chicken and a couple of sheep. That night, the crew of the *Golden Hind* made merry and prepared to return for more fresh water and supplies on the morrow.

Following the night's feasting, everyone got up late, Nelan included.

Drake wanted to get ashore, saying, "Our native friends are waiting to meet us. Jump to it, lads."

Great Nelan looked worse for wear. One too many swigs of grog.

Diego shuffled towards them, his head drooped as if he'd just heard of a death in his family. "I'll not join you today," the *cimarrón* said.

"Why's that, then?" Drake asked.

"Bad feeling in the gut."

"You'll not have a gut if we don't get more food and fresh water," Drake said. "Come on, climb in."

Diego slid down the ropes into the skiff.

"God blesses us and protects us with His grace," Drake insisted.

But would their God look after Diego, Nelan wondered?

They headed to the meeting place the natives had shown them the day before. A couple of hands jumped overboard to pull the skiff ashore and make it fast. They got as far as the riverbank in peace before, raising a hue and cry, the natives raced out from behind the reeds and beat them with club and fist. Scores of them showered the crew with arrows, spears and rocks. There was no cover, and none was provided by Drake's God. They were all pierced with arrows. Drake took one to the cheek. Great Nelan lay slumped over his oar, his body covered with arrows. Nelan bent to shield his friend's head, only for his arm to be struck by an enemy arrow.

Drake barked orders. "Heave to!"

Quick as a flash, they pulled on their oars and headed back to the safety of the *Golden Hind*. Spears and arrows whizzed above them. Back on deck, they saw the full extent of the atrocity. Without Winterhay the surgeon, their only medical help was a boy whose goodwill far exceeded his skills. They patched up the wounded with rough handling and poor care. Great Nelan lay in a pool of his own blood, a great red smudge of a wound by his heart. The Viking warrior coughed a splurge of phlegm, his body arched in pain, and he slumped into Nelan's arms.

Nelan shook his limp body repeatedly. "No, no, no!" he cried. "You can't!"

But Great Nelan died in his arms. The only mercy – it wasn't a slow, prolonged death. Memories of their friendship came flooding back: their first meeting when Nelan had mistaken Great Nelan for his father. It marked a strange beginning to an enduring friendship. And they had both been pressed into the navy at the same time, bearing the same name. At one time, Nelan had hoped and prayed that they shared a twin destiny. The Fates clearly thought otherwise.

Through a veil of tears, Nelan made his testament. "May your soul rest in peace, Nelan Andersen. Great Nelan is no more. You called me Little Nelan. Now that you've departed this world to join your Viking warriors in Heaven, that name departs with you. From now on, I am simply Nelan, and much the lesser for it."

Fletcher pulled him away. "Lad, he's gone. Let me close his eyes and give him the Last Rites."

Diego also suffered injuries. Although he survived the attack, he no longer knew where he was and only ever spoke in his native African tongue; one that none could understand.

Nelan was alone. He mourned the loss of his close friend and confidant. Great Nelan had been like a father to him. Nelan had aspired to be like him: harsh but kind, uncompromising but merciful, firm but gentle, stubborn yet forgiving. Like his life, the manner of the Dane's ending had only enhanced that view. It was as if Nelan relived the death of his true father.

Diego never recovered from the attack. Over the months at sea, Nelan had drawn close to the *cimarrón*, both as a friend and companion and as a sage and worldly guide. He prayed for him, but no one knew how to cure him. It was sad to see him like that: a fine man reduced to a burned-out ember. Once Diego had strode across the decks, casting up the world and its mysteries and earning the respect of the admiral. Now he sat as if in a trance, and dribbled from his mouth. One side of his face drooped. He stared vacantly for hours on end, pointing now and again at the air, but there was nothing there; not even a ghost, a sprightly spirit, or a salamander. On that day by the reed bed, when the arrows had rained out of the sky, something precious had flown away from Diego, like a bird fleeing a nest under attack by a predator, never to return. Diego was a *cimarrón*; a runaway. Now he had run away for good, and he wasn't coming back.

On that day, too, Nelan had realised something about the natives. Before arriving at the Isle of Mocha, he'd become sympathetic to their plight; seeing them as a race unfairly treated and badly dominated by the Spaniards. They might live in a crude, basic way, but they still deserved consideration and kindness, not the brutality to which the Dons invariably subjected them. But the incident on Mocha had upset him and challenged that view. On the first day the *Golden Hind* had anchored off the isle, the natives had welcomed them and provided them with food and water. Yet the next day, without warning, they had lured them like rats into an ambush. Such planned deception was not only unacceptable; it was unforgivable. Nelan's compassion for them had dissolved in a puff of arquebus smoke, especially as their treachery had cost the life of his friend and companion Great Nelan, and snuffed out the candle in the eyes of his confidant, Diego. Now, he not only wanted revenge on the Spanish for his mother's execution; he vowed never to trust the natives again. After the night of doubt he'd experienced on the *Mary and John*, he remembered what he'd understood about bitterness and the soul and Dr Dee's biblical clue:

My soul is cut off though I live.
I will... speak in the bitterness of my soul.

The soul was a powerful and finely balanced instrument supplied by the Creator to assist a person in the basics of living on the planet and in finding their way in life. Its daily tasks ranged from digestion and breathing to providing abilities such as learning and memory, and all the other tasks it fulfilled to keep its host alive. Usually, the soul resided inside the body. It was not physical; it was a numinous entity. It could reside at a distance outside the body and still perform its many functions. When a person was bitter, or if they were cruel, barbaric, or committed any other conscious act of evil – any act that stood against the naturally gentle, kind human disposition – it drove the soul to live outside. In sweet moments, it would fly back into the body; these were moments of great well-being, exhilaration and joy. Yet the soul was cut off even while the person lived, because it resided at a distance. Dee had given Nelan that clue about the shoes that never wore out. Now he understood what they were.

Despite that revelation, he still felt bitter about the connivance and duplicity of the natives. Tom had already removed Oliver's empty hammock, but when the bosun ordered the removal of Great Nelan's, Nelan fought like a terrier to keep it in place; a treasured memento of his friend. Anger, suspicion and distrust of his mates filled the void of his friendships with Great Nelan and Diego.

As they ploughed their way up the South American coast, Drake reminded the crew that they'd encounter ships carrying the vast wealth of the Spanish Viceroyalty of Peru, plundered from the Potosí silver mines in the Andes Mountains. When Drake promised them all a share of the wealth, Nelan wallowed in the feeling of avarice coursing through his blood, shuffling off the numbness of his grief. Mocha had been a turning point in his life, as it had in the lives of his shipmates Great Nelan and Diego.

16

The Light of a Candle

29th January 1579

The ocean stretched out in front of them. Nelan had noticed that the colour of its waters changed from day to day and even from hour to hour. Why was it not always the same hue, and what made it differ? It was a mystery he wanted to solve. During the voyage, he talked to the other hands and spent hours staring at the waves, the fish, the birds, the clouds, the sky, the wind and the cats' paws. In the end, he realised that the variation depended on the speed of the current, the depth of the ocean, the nature of the earth beneath, and the wind speed and direction. Other times, it changed according to the moisture in the air, the texture of the light, the position of the sun in the sky, the cloud formation, the lunar cycle, or even the season.

That morning, off the Chilean island of Santa María, the colour of the waters was a glorious, sparkling aquamarine. Drake's pilot took readings from the astrolabe and informed them that they were crossing the Tropic of Capricorn. Now that the *Golden Hind* had returned to the Torrid Realm, the crew hoped it would bring about a long-awaited change of fortune.

What would Diego have said about the southern tropic? Nelan reckoned it must bear relation to its northern twin. If the Tropic of Cancer was the line of religious appearance, perhaps the Tropic of Capricorn was the line of divinity, consecrated to the practice, development and fulfilment of the religions that had appeared on its northern counterpart. The two comprised a dual destiny, like a man and a lady.

With Diego next to him, Nelan leaned on the gunwale, gazing at the water. Staring into the void, the *cimarrón* was as silent as a distant cloud. Nelan wished Diego could tell him more about the equator. He supposed it must do precisely that: equalise and balance the two adjacent influences. Another name for it was the Line of Libra; the astrological sign symbolised by the scales of justice.

They made good progress northwards until, towards the middle of February, they stood off Callao near Lima in Peru. The port lay about twelve and a half degrees south of the equator. This set Nelan's astrological mind aflame. The Tropic of Capricorn was twenty-three and a half degrees south of the equator. Between Libra and Capricorn were Scorpio and Sagittarius. In the same way, between the equator – the Line of Libra – and the Tropic of Capricorn, there had to be the Lines of Scorpio and Sagittarius. He reckoned that the Line of Libra lay in a band or ribbon three degrees to either side of the equator, the Line of Scorpio between three and six degrees, and the Line of Sagittarius between six and twelve degrees. Being a Sagittarian, he wondered if that was why he felt at home in this region; so much so that he had a strong premonition that their fortunes were about to change. And the three wavy lines on his palm – the mark of the salamander – itched like hell.

That morning, on the 13th February in the year of Our Lord 1579, the crew grew agitated because no ships left port. Then they spotted a ship sailing out of Callao on the late morning tide. Thomas Drake led the boarding party and sent a message back to the admiral that its hold contained no goods of value. Despite the disappointment, Thomas ferried the captured ship's captain across to the *Golden Hind*. On the poop deck, Francis Drake assembled a welcoming committee of England's finest thugs armed with a frightening array of cutlasses, knives, daggers, swords and plenty of menace to boot.

"Who are you?" Drake asked the captain.

"I am the *Capitán* of this vessel," the man said, his legs shaking visibly.

Drake asked, "Are you Spanish, sir?"

"No, *Capitán*, Corsican."

"Corsican, eh? Well, tell us what you know, else these lads'll hang you by the yardarm, quick as you can say, 'Jack Tar'!"

The man's eyes flashed from Drake to the yardarm to the ruffians. He trembled so much that Nelan thought he would wet his breeches. Through a thick brown beard he stammered, "No 'ang me, *Señor* Draque; me have two *bambini* in my *casa*. Listen, I tell you everything."

Drake folded his arms and said, "I'm waiting."

"Three week ago, big ship sail out of Callao. She heavy in water."

"What's her cargo? Come on, out with it!"

"She carry silver and gold."

"Good. That's better. Your *bambini* are safe. Now tell me, where's she heading?"

"Panama, *Señor*. Every year, she go there at the same time."

"And the name of this treasure ship?"

"The *Nuestra Señora de la Concepción*. Some call her the *Cacafuego*."

"The *Shitfire*?"

"I dunno this *Shitfire*, *Señor*. I call her the *Spitfire*."

"Why's that?"

"'Cause she carry boom-boom – you understand me? – guns."

"That's unusual," Thomas Drake piped up. "Because the Dons think they have no enemies in these waters, most merchantmen in the South Seas carry no armament."

"Until now, that is!" Francis Drake said. "The question to ask is this: can we catch the *Spitfire* before she docks at Panama?"

This was the premonition Nelan had received.

The wind dropped, and the *Golden Hind* lay outside Callao for the rest of the day. When night fell, Drake went to sleep in his cabin. Since Diego had been incapacitated, the quartermaster had asked Nelan to help the domestic staff serving Drake and the other gentlemen adventurers. With Drake asleep, Nelan snuffed out the candles in the admiral's cabin. He was just checking that the stern lantern was alight when he heard a mumbling sound. He looked around, but there was no one; not even one of the ship's gangly brown rats. Then he heard a voice, like an echo of someone hailing them from far away:

Cast the mast,
Away at last.

It sounded so numinous that he wondered if he was dreaming. Fearing he'd wake the admiral, he whispered, "Is someone there? What did you say?"

No answer. Perhaps the sea murmured. It wasn't uncommon. Nelan often mistook the creaking of the boat and the heaving of the wind in the sails for the voices of seamen talking, laughing and jesting amongst themselves.

Carrying a candle, he tiptoed past Drake. This time, he saw the admiral's lips move, saying:

Spit the fire,
Play the lyre.

The admiral was talking. But only he and Nelan were in the cabin. Then the thought struck Nelan: Drake was talking in his sleep. Nelan had heard of people doing that. He stopped to listen to what the admiral would say next.

Drake murmured:

The day a-score,
Not a day more.

Nelan waited to see if he'd say anything else, but he didn't. Nelan opened the cabin door to leave. As he did, the watch bell sounded and Drake woke up.

"Who are you?"

"Ordinary seaman Nelan, Admiral."

"What are you doing in my cabin?" Drake rose from his hammock in a flash.

"On duty, Admiral. Checking the stern lantern. And you..."

"And I what? Spit it out, lad." Drake stood nose to nose with Nelan while pulling on his jerkin. The light of Nelan's lantern flickered over his face, revealing his pointed beard and the lines of fiery passion etched across his seaman's face and forehead. "I must know. Did I say anything?"

"Yes, m'lord. You were speaking in your sleep."

"Tell me what I said. It's more important than you can imagine."

Nelan repeated the rhyme:

Cast the mast,
Away at last.
Spit the fire,
Play the lyre.
The day a-score,
Not a day more.

"That's it? The exact words? Nothing added or omitted or out of place?"

"No, m'lord."

Drake danced a jig of joy. "You've done well, lad; you've done excellent well. If I were king, I'd make you a knight of the realm!"

"Thank you, sire," Nelan said. "But what exactly *have* I done?"

"Oh," Drake said, turning back to him, "I talk in my sleep. I've done it for years. It gives me insight I could never have any other way. The Dons believe I possess a magic mirror through which I see and know everything about the oceans. But I don't. I do have a gift, though. I don't know what to call it, but it works and I trust it. It gives me premonitions. When Diego joined me as my manservant, he told me about it and explained the portent of the words I spoke while I slept. He told me that that is how my muse informs me of past and future events. You understand that *this* is my magic mirror. Now, you are the one to look into it for me. You must listen and then tell me what I say in my sleep. That's what Diego did for me. It's so sad that he's not up to the task anymore. But you've stepped into his shoes."

"I have?"

"It looks that way to me."

"What about the rhyme?"

"Oh, don't you see? It means we can catch the *Cacafuego*. In twenty days, we'll be rich beyond our wildest dreams! It'll be like plundering Neptune's treasure."

By the following day, all the hands had learned the rhyme, put it to the music of the lyre, and sung it with English gusto. A tangible frisson of excitement, the like of which Nelan had never felt, spread through the decks. The bugle blasted, and the whistle blew. The violin sang, and the lute was plucked. The tabor was struck, and hands clapped.

Winds spun the sails, and the vessel pitched. The men's spirits rose up to Heaven. The Holy Ghost had blessed them with a visitation.

After they rowed the *Golden Hind* out to sea to find a favourable wind, the chase began in earnest. On the 1st March 1579, they crossed the equator. The hue of the waters resembled the colour of the night sky; a deep, iridescent sapphire blue. Each man pulled his weight. The ropes were lighter to haul, the decks easier to scrub, and the days sweeter on the soul. They were the best ever on the ship. Even the winds pulled them along and guided them towards their target.

The portents improved tenfold when, with the sun at its zenith, a shout bellowed down from the crow's nest. "Sail ho!"

Drake's promise of a sizeable reward for the first man to spy the *Cacafuego* had already yielded several false alarms. Not this time. The ship boasted three masts and sailed four leagues (or twelve miles) ahead of them.

"Now we've caught the *Great Shitter*," Tom said, "how to board 'er without raising the alarm? What'll we do, Admiral? We need to take 'er in one piece. If we approach 'er now, they got guns. They'll fight us as sure as Bess is our Queen."

"The dark will be our angel," Drake said with an enigmatic grin. "We'll approach 'em under cover of dusk. Lads, hide the cannon. Change the flags. We'll show ourselves as a harmless merchantman."

"Yes! We're gonna do 'em!" the men whooped with joy.

"There's more," Drake said. "If we keep this sail, we'll catch her before nightfall."

"Lower the sail. Trim the sail!" Tom yelled.

"Bosun, don't do that!" Drake interjected. "We'll raise their suspicions. No, we need a ruse…"

Everyone knew the admiral had one up his sleeve.

"All hands to the cargo hold. Bring up the wine casks and barrels."

"And then what, Admiral?" Tom asked.

"Tie a length of rope to each of them. Attach one end to the gunwale, and drop 'em over the stern."

"Pulling all them casks'll slow the *Hind* right down."

Drake nodded. The men raised a huge cheer. With more vigour than Nelan had seen in months, they set the casks in place, slowing the *Hind* to a snail's pace.

"Now, we'll soon see who spits fire!" Drake cried.

The men rallied behind their leader, although he represented much more than that to them. Even the veteran mariners, the old soaks who had sailed with him to the Spanish Main and who had risked life and limb, were in awe of the man. He had a way of commanding them that called for instant respect and admiration.

As evening fell, Drake gave the order to raise a Spanish flag and haul the wine casks out of the water. Slowly the *Hind* caught up to the Spanish treasure ship. The men were as silent as lambs. The only noises were the squeak and rattle of the sails and the masts, and the flap of the sails in the light breeze. The stern lights of the *Cacafuego* grew brighter and twinkled in the dusk. Archers lined the stern; every bow and arrow at the ready. Musket men hid behind the barrels, guns cocked. They primed, then hid, the cannons. They dimmed the lanterns stern and aft.

Along with Tom and others, Nelan crouched behind the gunwale, waiting nervously for the order to board. Earlier in the voyage, before boarding a Spanish vessel, he'd be shoulder to shoulder with Great Nelan. But now the Dane protected him from his warrior's throne. Nelan missed his Viking companion. As he waited with his shipmates, the only time he'd been more excited and nervous was when he'd asked Eleanor for her hand. His instinct was up. This was the turning point in the voyage not only of his life, but of the lives of all those aboard. The tide in the affairs of these men, taken at the flood, could lead on to fortune – or be bound in shallows and in miseries.

As the *Hind* closed on the *Cacafuego*, every hand from the servants to the cooks, the able seamen to the officers, the aristocrats to the gentlemen adventurers, held their breath and mouthed a silent prayer to the Almighty. As directed by their admiral, they hid behind the shrouds and the masts, the sails and the gunwale. The ships drifted to within hailing distance. A vocal challenge – in Spanish – from the *Cacafuego*. Drake had told the crew not to respond. Angry shouts in Spanish. The challenge was repeated. Ready to pounce, the men of the *Hind* were coiled like springs. A third challenge: a musket ball across the bows of the *Hind*. Again, no response.

Once the ships were side by side, Drake ordered, "Fire!"

The men rushed out from their hiding places. A roar of English muskets fired almost simultaneously. The sound echoed in Nelan's ears. He could barely hear himself think. The smell of the gunpowder was noxious. A volley of arrows arced into the Spanish vessel, spreading mayhem amongst the Dons.

"For God, the Queen and England!" Drake cried as he led the boarding party.

Cutlass in hand, Nelan raced behind him. Raising a hue and cry, they leapt over the gunwale and swarmed like ants over every plank of the Spanish ship. Shouts and yells filled the night air. Shadows swept across the decks. Men grappled like bears. Sword and sabre flashed. Blood ran thick on the decks. Nelan dashed towards the stern castle, ducking and diving, avoiding arrow and musket ball. With John Brewer and Tom the bosun, he was to make fast the whipstaff. Nelan launched himself at the helmsman, who smashed him in the nose with his elbow, knocking him sideways. He leapt straight back onto his feet, helping his shipmates overpower the helmsman and lash him to the gunwale. The rudder was made safe. Nelan, John Brewer and Tom whooped with joy.

Taken by surprise, the Dons were overrun. When they realised the identity of their adversary, they laid down their arms with a whimper. With much pushing and shoving, the English rounded up the crew and shepherded them into the holds. Back on deck, the *Hind*'s crew leapt around like a pack of wild monkeys, climbing up the merchantman's shrouds, mainmast and high turret. The *Cacafuego* was theirs. The quarterdeck was awash with exuberance. The men punched the night air in raucous delight, their celebration rolling with the ocean waves, their faces drawn into broad smiles.

The admiral addressed them. "Boys!"

"Admiral!" they cried in return.

"We did 'em. We did 'em good," Drake yelled at the top of his voice. "And not a man lost!"

The crew raised the heavens.

"The ship's ours. Now for the treasure!" Drake's face was a picture of relief and joy.

With the *Cacafuego* lashed to the *Golden Hind*, Drake sailed westwards out to sea and away from the Spanish shipping lanes. The crew rested and slept, but not for long. Nelan nursed his nose, which had turned markedly red and swollen to twice its normal size. The crew needed no encouragement to call him 'Cauliflower'.

Early the following day, Nelan waited on Drake, who entertained the captain of the captured vessel at breakfast aboard the *Golden Hind*. The captain sat at one end of the table in Drake's cabin, while the admiral occupied the other. Eager to witness this clash of titans, English and Spanish officers and gentlemen adventurers crowded into the cabin.

"*Capitán*, you and your officers are welcome aboard my ship," Drake said, "where you will all be well treated. I am a friend of those who tell me the truth, but with those who do not, I quickly get out of humour."

The man nodded. He was tanned and fair-haired, with a pointed beard and 'tache, according to the fashion. He wore a silk jerkin and pantaloons, and carried himself with the air of a sophisticated gentleman.

"But you are to remain confined to my ship until my return," Drake said. "I apologise for this small but necessary inconvenience. And please don't try to escape. Help yourself to any delicacies. Here – I have some fine Spanish sack."

"Thank you, Admiral. My father-in-law is head of the Sarmiento family of Andalucía. The grape is almost certainly from his vineyard," the man said.

"From your accent, I would say you are English, *Capitán*," Drake said.

"Yes, I am. I lived in England but moved to Spain a while ago with my wife to join her Spanish family."

As the Protestant Reformation had taken hold across Europe, many Catholics from Ireland, France, the Netherlands and other countries had sought refuge in King Philip's Spain, and so an Englishman in a Spanish crew was not unusual. For a moment, Nelan thought he recognised the *capitán*. But what with the melee of people in the cabin, he couldn't get a good look at him.

"You are my honoured guest," Drake said. "Now, I must search the holds of the *Cacafuego* and verify that the cargo accords with your manifest." Turning to his brother, he said, "Thomas, keep these fine Spanish officers and gentlemen in the cabin, and do not open the door until I return. Guard it always. Understood?"

"M'lord," Thomas Drake replied.

All afternoon, the crew waited for news from the search of the holds. It was not a patient wait, like attending a church service – no, far from it. They were nervous wrecks, jumping at every noise. In the galley Nelan prepared food for the evening meal, all the while suffering jibes about his cauliflower nose. The cook proposed to cut it up and put it in the stew.

From the *Cacafuego* came whoops of joy. Was this the real thing? Had they found the treasure, or were the holds spitting *caca*? Praise the Lord if these cries heralded good fortune.

"All hands on deck!" the bosun ordered.

They raced out of the galley. The cook started up the ladder, then ran back, remembering that he needed to douse the fire. Everyone gathered on the quarterdeck, from carpenter to cooper and from able seaman to gentleman adventurer. A cheerful wave of expectant happiness greeted Admiral Drake as he strolled onto the deck carrying a scroll. Few could read, but everyone craned their necks to see what was on it. They all suffered from an intense bout of curiosity. Why? Because the scroll contained the cargo manifest of the *Cacafuego*. Drake's smile was as broad as the ocean as he waved it above his head. He nodded. The men ceased their banter, the gulls stopped squawking, and even the wind dropped. The threads of silence strained at the seams.

Drake crowed, "I tell you, lads, there's enough silver and gold to fill the caverns of Heaven!"

Men yelped and hugged each other like great bears. Mariners embraced gentlemen adventurers. Many of the crew knelt on the deck and raised their hands in prayer. Others broke down in tears and bawled like little children. Still more jumped into the air and punched the sky. They danced the jig and beat their chests. The drummer pounded a rhythm of glory. The piper piped a ballad of success. John Brewer blew three mighty blasts on his bugle. And why not? They had endured storms, mists, an execution, shipwrecks, the doldrums, drought, starvation and fear. With courage, grit and determination, they had survived them all and arrived at this point with clear resolve. Together, they had prevailed.

Despite his nasal predicament, Nelan felt joy aplenty. He wiped tears from his eyes as emotion welled up in him. This represented a great victory in his quest to right the terrible wrong of his mother's death. Capturing this vessel in the Pacific Ocean – in their own backyard – would hurt the Spanish and seriously dent their reputation as invincible.

Drake read from the manifest. "1,300 bars of silver!"

The crew raised a loud cheer.

"Fourteen chests of silver coins!"

And another.

"Jewels to enrich the Pharaohs of Egypt!"

And a third.

"And there are roof tiles, but no ordinary tiles. Gold is stuck to them like tar to the ribs of a ship!"

This last item intrigued Nelan, but he soon joined in celebrating with the rest of the crew. All hands cheered with such thunderous delight that he imagined the echoes could be heard across the way in Callao, across the ocean in Hampton Court, and as far away as El Escorial Monastery, King Philip's official residence. He had never seen such pure collective intoxication. From admiral, gentleman adventurer and officer to mariner and able seaman, they experienced it with the same intensity. It was a moment of transcendence and spiritual release. Nelan caught a glimpse of Drake. His face was a picture of fierce pride, relief and overwhelming satisfaction. This was the culmination of their voyage; its full and final justification. In finding this treasure, Drake had made himself a national treasure.

The admiral marshalled the men and spoke to them from the quarterdeck. He was like a giant amongst them; full of stature earned through self-discipline and incredible perseverance. His words resonated far beyond the gunwale of the little ship. "This is a turning point in history; not just for you and me, but for our country. England is no longer a small, isolated, misty isle on the western fringes of Europe. Now it is at the centre of the Atlantic Ocean; at the centre of the world. Today England is a player in a new game, a new era, in which she stands ready not to follow the old rules but to write new ones. Through this act, England has come of age. Britannia has broken the last chain of the gold shackles of Papist dogma and entered the silver age of exploration."

Laden with this glittering haul, Drake would surely hope that he'd have nothing to fear from the pro-Spanish Catholic sympathisers on the Privy Council. The Queen would take her massive share of the booty, and the admiral would not fear revenge from Sir Christopher Hatton over Thomas Doughty's execution.

The hands toasted their success with many a tot of ale, richly supplemented by Spanish sack poured from barrels found in the hold of the *Cacafuego*. The minstrels played drum and flute to accompany the dancing, the singing and the roaring. The men climbed up the shrouds and swung from the yardarm until one of them fell off into the sea. Then, yelping for joy, more of them jumped in and had to be hauled back onto the deck.

John Brewer blew his whistle and gave three great blasts on his bugle, calling the drunken celebrations to a halt. Despite their antics, the crew needed no other invitation. They staggered onto the poop deck, ready to receive their dues. As promised, Drake lined them up and handed each man his share of silver coins, gold bars and precious jewels. They made their mark on their claim and immediately handed it back to him for safekeeping, but that didn't stop some of them from settling into a heavy game of cards. The men danced and sang as each celebrated in his own unique way. It was a rare moment when not only a few combined to win a grand prize, but many did, and all at the same time. The hands invited the Spanish officers and men to share a drink of grog. There was dice and dance, music and mayhem, the sweet sound of violins and the plucking of the lute, all to the tune of joyous release.

Drake called Nelan to him. "I have a special gift for you," he said, handing him a small canvas pouch.

Nelan opened it and pulled out a richly decorated pendant. "It's like a golden lizard with small wings, legs, and a tail. And see these nine red stones – one set in its head, and then down its spine to its tail."

"Those are rich red rubies. Almost as red as your nose!"

"Yes, m'lord," Nelan said. "Very funny."

"Seriously, you notice it's heavy. It's made of gold."

"Admiral, I don't know how to thank you."

"You don't have to. This is a gift of thanks from me, because I won't forget your help in finding the *Cacafuego*."

"I will treasure this all my days."

"Good. And, of course, you know what kind of lizard this is?"

Nelan nodded. "Yes – it's a salamander."

"It's a good-luck charm, especially for a mariner, and even more so for one like you: a blacksmith who knows the ways of the furnace. As long as you have this pendant and are aboard the *Hind*, it'll protect us from fire."

"I'll remember that, m'lord," Nelan crowed.

Drake's success opened another door for Nelan. Perhaps, in due course, the admiral could use his growing influence in national affairs to protect Nelan from the arrest warrant back home. But Nelan had to choose his words carefully, so he merely hinted at the possibility by saying, "And one day you might be able to help me, m'lord."

"You never know," Drake said with a chuckle.

With all the treasure stored on the *Hind*, Drake invited the *Cacafuego*'s captain and a few of her officers to dine at his table with the English officers and gentlemen. Amidst the continuing air of celebration, he was the most generous and civil host imaginable. As the evening wore on, Nelan ran around serving them all and keeping their glasses topped up with the finest wine.

"Now, gentlemen of Spain," Drake said, "I have gifts for you all." He handed them unique coins, special keepsakes, and unusual trifles for them to take home to their ladies.

"We are honoured by your kindness and generosity, *Almirante* Draque," the *capitán* said on their behalf.

"It is my pleasure, *Capitán*," Drake said, his chest swollen by the fullness of the moment. "Because, after this meal, my men will row you back to the *Cacafuego*. *Capitán*, you may have your ship back and sail it wherever you wish."

"It is kind of you, Admiral. I thank you for returning my ship, and a small portion of its treasure to its rightful owner, the King of Spain. I trust that you will be a good custodian of the rest."

Amidst hoots of laughter, Drake concurred, "Well, yes, *Capitán*, I shall look after it with great pleasure and guard it with my life."

"You are most considerate," the *capitán* replied, to more gales of mirth.

"Before you go, would you tell me about the gold tiles?" Drake asked.

"With pleasure," the *capitán* said. "They are most unusual because normally gold is gilded, soldered or plated onto a surface, but in this case, as you have seen for yourself, it is fused to the tiles. We tried every way we could to separate it, but it was impossible."

"Where were the tiles found?"

"They were taken from the roof of an abandoned Aztec temple."

"Aztec?"

"We think they were an ancient civilisation."

"And why do the tiles have gold on one surface and not on the other?"

"It's a mystery. The natives told us that, because of the religious activities in the temple, flecks of gold manifested in the atmosphere above it, which then condensed onto the outer surface of the roof tiles."

"Do you believe that?" Drake asked, raising an eyebrow.

"No, I don't; it's superstitious nonsense," the *capitán* replied. "Look at the native people now; they're primitive savages. And the Aztecs lived here long before them, so they can only have been as primitive, if not more so."

After delicacies and sweets, Drake proposed a final toast. "To Kings and Queens and the sanctity of royalty."

They raised their glasses, and the Spanish officers stood up and took their leave. As Drake shook hands with the *capitán*, Nelan had the same inkling: that his path and the *capitán*'s had crossed before, but the man's appearance had changed unrecognisably since. Who was he? The question nagged him.

A gust of wind burst through the open window and blew out the candles, plunging the cabin into darkness. "*Fiat lux!* Let there be light!" Drake jested.

Nelan grabbed his char cloth, strike-a-light iron and flint. The spark danced in the ether and onto the char cloth. He blew on it to conjure a flame, which kissed the wick, bringing light back to the cabin. As he lit each candle, he felt uncomfortable because the *capitán* followed his every move with his eyes. As he finished, the *capitán*'s gaze burrowed into him.

"I would see that flint and iron," the *capitán* said. Before Nelan could stop him, he'd snatched them both from his hands. The *capitán* turned the iron and flint over in his hands and then held them up to a lantern.

"What is it, *Capitán*? Has the lad offended you?" Drake asked.

"*Offended* me?" the *capitán* scoffed.

Nelan had a bad feeling in his gut regarding the answer to come.

"Look here," the *capitán* said, pointing to a mark of provenance on the strike-a-light iron. "This is my family's coat of arms. My Southampton family quartered with my wife's, who is of the Sarmiento family of Andalucía."

"Your family name is Southampton?"

"Yes, Admiral. My name is St John of Hampton or, in full, St John of Southampton. In Spanish, it's San Juan de Antón."

The world stopped turning. Nelan gasped for breath. His mouth dropped open. Now he remembered where he'd seen the man before.

"I see," Drake said.

"This flint and iron," St John bristled. "Tell me, Nelan, how did you come by them?"

The atmosphere of suspicion deepened. Nelan didn't want to answer.

St John knew why. "Tongue-tied, lad?" he asked.

"Nelan, answer the man, will you?" Drake interrupted. "Tell the truth, now. I'll have no lies on my ship."

Nelan sucked in his breath. He couldn't answer, because…

"Here, I know," St John said, and he grabbed Nelan's right hand. Before Nelan could stop him, St John turned his hand over and examined his palm. "Yes – there they are!" he cried in triumph. "Three wavy lines beneath the middle finger. My stepson told me about them."

Nelan stood rooted to the spot. In that uncanny moment, the forces of the past caught up and mingled with those of the present, forming a blockage. He braced himself.

"I knew it," St John said through gritted teeth. "I thought I recognised you, but your scraggy beard and that bulbous nose threw me off the scent. Over the fifteen months since we last met, you've tanned and your face has filled out, but you're still a short-arse. Most of all, the stench of guilt hangs about you! I know who you are and what you did."

Nelan's mouth was as dry as the sands of the adjacent Atacama Desert. His stomach seemed to drag along the cabin floor.

"Will someone please explain what this is all about?" Drake asked.

"Admiral, this boy is a killer!"

"How do you know?"

"This iron and flint were gifts from me to one of my stepsons. His name was Guillermo."

Guillermo. How can I ever forget that name?

"And?"

"Four years ago, this boy murdered him."

"*Murdered?* Is this true, Nelan?"

Nelan was mute.

St John wasn't. "Yes, it is, Admiral. His surname is Michaels. Nelan Michaels."

"Is it, now? He's only ever presented himself as Nelan of Queenhithe," Drake said.

"His family lived in Mortlake on the Thames." St John was spitting blood.

"Oh, so that's how he knew Dr John Dee," Drake said.

"For sure," St John went on. "I lived nearby in the hamlet of Sneakenhall with my Spanish wife and her two sons from her previous marriage: Guillermo and Pedro."

The warmth slowly drained from Nelan's soul, and the colour from his face. The ghosts of the past refused to leave him alone. He could run away to the South Seas, but they still managed to find and haunt him. He turned to face the consequences of his actions.

"You're as white as a sheet, Nelan Michaels. You've a guilty look on your face. Say something," Drake said.

Nelan swallowed hard. "It's true that Guillermo died when we were at school. But, Admiral, believe me, I beg you: I was not responsible for his death. He brought it on himself. He tried to kill me."

"See, I told you," St John said. He wasn't listening to Nelan. "The boy's a liar and a murderer. Guillermo died of his burns; a horrible, agonising death. Then Nelan ran away. Fifteen months ago, he returned to Mortlake to put out a house fire. Guided by the hand of the Almighty, I spotted him and had him arrested. Last I heard, he was in prison. But here he is on your carrack, so obviously he escaped again. I demand justice for my stepson."

"That may be, St John, but the boy's served me well. So I will hear his testimony. Speak up, Nelan."

The memories of that dreadful incident spread their dark wings over Nelan's spirit. "I never liked Guillermo, or his brother Pedro. They were nasty to me, and I hate Catholics because they murdered my mother. Yes, we three boys shared a wherry to get to school, and the wherry master kept the peace between us. One day at school, Guillermo had this evil air about him, and I was sure he meant to harm me. I tried to avoid him, but he trapped me in the woodshed. He pulled out a wedge of gunpowder and ignited the fuse with this iron and flint. I had to stop him. I grabbed the iron and flint, but the spark had taken on the fuse. The gunpowder exploded and sent shards of wood everywhere, throwing me clear. But Guillermo suffered terrible burns and died during the night. Yes, I ran away and tried to clear my name, but St John had me arrested and imprisoned. Awaiting trial, I was working outside the prison when I was pressed into the navy, and here I am today. That's the whole truth, Admiral, so help me God."

"Bah! I don't believe it." St John scowled. "My wife suffered immensely after her son's death. Pedro has barely recovered from the shock and grief of losing his brother. I moved them back to Spain to be close to her family. Once we got there, my wife gave up the ghost, distraught at the murder of her son. In truth, this boy has wrecked my life and my family."

"That's a tragic story, *Capitán*," Drake said.

"And, Admiral, to add to my miseries, you've just stolen the treasure from my ship."

"That may be, but you stole it from the natives, so it wasn't yours in the first place!"

"Perhaps," St John said. "But can I ask a favour? This cur means nothing to you. I implore you; let me have him. I will see that he gets the justice he deserves before God!"

Nelan felt as heavy as lead. His stomach churned, his throat was dry, and his hands were moist. What would Drake say? After all that had happened – the smithy, the prison, and then the voyage – Nelan's fate rested in the hands of the son of a pastor; a man famed for privateering and adventure. He awaited the admiral's verdict.

Drake tugged on his beard. "It's complicated, St John. I'm his admiral. And it was only by dint of his initiative that we found the *Cacafuego* and you are standing here talking to me."

"That's ironic, but I still want him."

"If he has committed a crime, it falls under English, not Spanish, jurisdiction," Drake said. "And as *I* am the law on this vessel, he must explain his actions to me. So I can't allow you to take the lad."

"I respect your judgement, but I am bitterly disappointed," St John said. Clenching his fists, he brushed past Nelan and barged his shoulder.

When he'd left the cabin, Nelan murmured, "Thank you, Admiral."

"Don't thank me yet, Nelan."

"Why not, m'lord?"

"I may have refused to give you up to St John, but you are still a runaway. If we weren't short of able hands on deck, I'd clap you in irons. But you're confined to this ship until we return to England's shores, and during that time, you'd better behave yourself impeccably. On our return to Plymouth, I may hand you over to the constable to stand trial. Or I may not. I'll pray to the Lord for guidance."

Nelan slunk out of the cabin. His past had returned to haunt him but Drake had believed him, at least for the time being. Even a pyrrhic victory was nonetheless a victory.

As the crew of the *Golden Hind* watched the *Cacafuego* sail off into a muggy March night, lanterns blazing, Nelan couldn't help wondering whether his destiny was to hold the unfortunate title of the wealthiest man in Newgate or Marshalsea.

And all because of the light of a candle.

17

Walking on Water

13th March 1579

Skirting the Gulf of Panama, Drake steered the *Golden Hind* as near to the coast as he could without alerting the Spanish to their presence. To cover any unforeseen eventualities, he doubled the watch and kept all deckhands on high alert.

With the land basking in the rays of the setting sun, the admiral led the evening service. Pointing to a hill on the horizon, he said, "Many years ago, I stood on that spot. Look – can you see it? It may look like one more coastal mound, but that ridge is like a shrine for me."

Nelan was intrigued.

"At the time," Drake went on in his rolling West Country drawl, "I joined forces with John Oxenham. My *cimarrón* friends came too, and we followed them from Nombre de Dios on the Atlantic side of the Isthmus of Panama, through the jungle to the top of that ridge. Now, with a good eyeglass, you'd spy a wooden platform they erected on the crown of a tall tree. It's a vantage point like no other, for it offers the thrilling sight of not one ocean, but two. From there, looking north, I spied the familiar rolling waves of the Atlantic. But looking south, I witnessed the glistening emerald-green waters of the Pacific. That day, John and I were proud to be the first Englishmen to gaze upon that panorama.

"That moment was an epiphany for me. Because, right there on that wooden platform, I made a vow to return here and explore this ocean for my Queen, England and its angels, for have we not come out from the Island of Angels? And here I am. I have returned. It is a second coming. I have met my vow and fulfilled my dream, and for that, I give thanks to the Almighty."

"Praise the Lord," said Fletcher.

The crew responded in kind.

"What's next, Admiral?" Drake's brother asked.

"What's next? There is always a 'what's next?' God has planted the seed of discovery in us; the urge to seek more and find the next horizon. And that's what I'll do; what *we'll* do. You'll have stories to tell your grandchildren. Follow me, lads, and I'll bring you safely home, richer both in coin and in spirit."

"Amen to that," said Fletcher.

"Brother, you asked me, 'What's next?' I'll tell you," Drake said. "We have a great mission to fulfil here. So far, it's one the Dons have claimed as their own, but I vigorously dispute that. You've all seen the horrific cruelty the Dons have enacted upon the native peoples of this land. Soon, we'll sail along the coast of the Viceroyalty of New Spain, or Mexico as it's also known. I want to read you an extract from Foxe's *Book of Martyrs* that relates to this area of the world."

> In the space of twelve years from the first landing of the Spanish conquistador, Hernán Cortés, on the continent of America, the amazing number of 4,000,000 Mexicans perished through the unparalleled barbarity of the Spaniards. To come to particulars, the city of Cholula consisted of 30,000 houses, by which its great population may be imagined. The inhabitants refused to turn Roman Catholic, as they did not know the meaning of the religion they were ordered to embrace. So, the Spaniards put them all to death, cutting to pieces the lower sort of people and burning those of distinction.

The crew were stunned into silence.

After a pause, Drake said, "Like Reverend Foxe, I believe God commands the English to wrest back control of the Christian faith from the Dons. And, as Dr Dee himself has proclaimed, the way to achieve that is by building an empire, a British Empire, and with it a powerful navy. That is my answer to the question, 'What's next?'

"Be wary of the Dons. They see us as heathens, apostates and heretics. You saw how the *capitán* and the crew of the *Cacafuego* behaved with dignity in our presence. They feared for their lives, didn't they? If it had been the other way round, and they had captured us, they would have torn off our limbs, as they did to the poor people of Cholula. Or, at the very least, thrown us into a stinking prison, like they did John Oxenham. See how they've brutalised the natives of this great continent, who shudder at the mere sight of sail, armour or priestly vestments.

"We have also suffered at the hands of the Spaniards. Because of the fear they have instilled in the natives, the latter fought against us when we anchored in peace at St Julian's Bay and on the Isle of Mocha. There we lost friends, mariners and gentleman companions. I believe that the natives, dressed in skins and living in mud huts, thought we were Spanish. Why shouldn't they? Our skin is the same colour. Our ships, armour, crucifixes, and even weapons appear the same to an untrained eye. Do not fault the natives for their hatred of us. The responsibility for that rests squarely on the shoulders of the Dons."

Nelan felt the pangs of a guilty conscience. He'd blamed the natives for Diego's incapacity and the death of Great Nelan, but Drake's compassionate reading of the events touched the sentiment of Christian forgiveness.

That night, Nelan dreamed about sweet Eleanor. She walked in a meadow on a bright, sunny day, and stooped to pick a buttercup, yellow and gold. But then he noticed her body, and awoke with a start. She had cast no shadow. What was a body without a shadow? Had she shuffled off her mortal coil? Was she no longer of this earthly realm? The strange dream perturbed him, and he stayed in his hammock until they called for him to join his watch.

Four days later, they anchored off Isla del Caño, part of the Audiencia de Guatemala. They spent a week in a secluded bay, careening the ship before setting sail north by north-west. Unable to leave the *Hind*, Nelan felt trapped, although that wasn't much different to the normal state of things. He could hardly jump overboard and swim home, or even get ashore. He lay in his hammock, rolling with the waves, thinking about what he'd learned and wondering how much he still had to learn. Did he have an answer to that abiding question, 'What's next?'. Would he be tried in an English court for Guillermo's murder and end up back in Marshalsea or, worse still, swinging on the end of a hangman's noose? There was so much he yearned to know. How could a man conjure mist from the air? How could he guide and control the currents of the sea? How could he summon salamanders to work for him? What else was there to understand about bitterness and the soul? And what quirk of fate had led St John of Southampton to the *Golden Hind*, out in the middle of the ocean, fifteen months and thousands of leagues away from his and Nelan's last encounter? And what did it mean, if anything at all? Drake could have granted St John's request, but he hadn't. And for that, Nelan had to give thanks to the admiral.

They headed out into the ocean, searching for a route home and favourable winds, but none appeared. By early June they had been back at sea for fifty days and the men – notably Tom and his mates – were grumbling. There was too much sea fog, insufficient food and too little ale. Not to mention the proverbial ship's biscuits. Although frequent rainstorms had supplemented the water supplies, there wasn't enough. The gentlemen artists tired of painting cats' paws, flying fish and wispy clouds. Even the musicians grew bored playing sea shanties, madrigals, and 'Greensleeves'. Bent forwards, hands behind his back, the admiral stalked the poop deck like a hungry lion. On the horizon, another storm loomed; dark clouds beset them like an unwanted pest. It persisted for several days.

Amid the tempest, Fletcher called them together. With heavy rain beating against their tiny vessel, they prayed for salvation. "This is a reading from the Gospel of Matthew," the preacher said.

> *And the ship was now in the midst of the sea, and was tossed with waves: for it was a contrary wind.*
> *And in the fourth watch of the night, Jesus went unto them, walking on the sea.*
> *And when his disciples saw him walking on the sea, they were troubled, saying, It is a spirit, and cried out for fear.*
> *But straightway Jesus spake unto them, saying, Be of good comfort, It is I: be not afraid.*

Then Peter answered him, and said, Master, if it be thou, bid
me come unto thee on the water.
And he said, Come. And when Peter was come down out of the
ship, he walked on the water to go to Jesus.
But when he saw a mighty wind, he was afraid: and as he
began to sink, he cried, saying, Master, save me.
So immediately Jesus stretched forth his hand, and caught him,
and said to him, O thou of little faith, wherefore didst thou doubt.
And as soon as they were come into the ship, the wind ceased.

The crew of the *Hind* stood on deck in the driving rain, water dripping from their ears and noses. Then the storm abated as if following an edict from Heaven. Nelan even saw some men casting a wary glance out to sea as if to check whether the Lord walked by. But to Nelan, the Gospel reading was uncanny. It told him he had to have faith and believe that things could be done, and then they would happen. If he doubted, like Peter, then his desires would never happen. The rain became hazy and settled into a steady drizzle before it stopped altogether. A fresh wind blew away the clouds, leaving bright azure skies.

That night, Nelan dreamed that he glided out of his physical body. As this separate part of him, this astral body, drifted into the forecastle, it peered down on his hammock and he saw himself asleep like a babe. It surprised him. Were there more bodies inside him that had other extraordinary abilities? Bodies he'd never met nor encountered? He remembered a saying Dee had once told him of: *There are not many that you know, but many that know you.* Perhaps this was what the saying referred to. Nelan drifted through the decks and above the masts, and gazed down on the crow's nest. The vessel seemed far away, and he looked down on the ocean and the coastline, its lights flickering like stars. With an astral body of no substance, made of the warp and weft of dreams, what could be done in this new quicksilver mode of travel? Had the very first map-makers drawn their maps in this way? They must have known the art of astral travelling, and floated high above the land to get a panoramic view.

He willed himself back to the ship. It worked, which was a relief because it meant he could exercise some control over his errant spirit. The boat travelled north at a good clip, the bow parting the waves in two neat, equal streams. Hovering above the water, he followed the course of the vessel. The boat's lanterns were blazing. He wondered if anyone could see him in whatever realm he now inhabited. None of the members of the watch raised the alarm, and eight bells rang. He could see only the outline of the ship, and none of the intricate detail he would have seen in the physical realm. He wasn't walking alongside the vessel; he drifted. When his feet touched the waves, they didn't get wet. In the astral realm, there were no physical sensations such as thirst, hunger or cold. But he walked on water. Below the surface, the currents were as clear as day. There were channels within channels, some faster than others. Shoals of fish swam in those. It was as if some invisible force pulled them along, like a wind behind them.

Then he noticed that he had no shadow. But when he thought about it, if he weighed so little that he could walk on water, there was no substance to cast a shadow. Perhaps this was how he had perceived Eleanor in his dream. He occupied a body that walked on water, had no shadow, and gave him no physical sensations. How could it be? That thought triggered a memory of his meeting in Marshalsea with the Chinaman, Lao Long. The details of the conversation came back to him in a flash. Lao Long had said that people had two souls: one lower and one higher. The higher one had to be grown and nurtured like a flower in a garden. Perhaps the numinous body that walked on water was the higher soul.

That vision faded and a new one formed. Nelan saw a ship docking in a harbour; its sails flapping in a stiff breeze. He willed himself to explore it. At first, he didn't recognise the ship, or the port. The anchor clanged through the portal. The starboard bow crashed against the dockside. The gangplank thudded onto the quay. Ladies in their finery, gentlemen in their formal wear, mariners and bondsmen, ploughmen and stevedores, merchants and freemen, all lined the dock to greet the returning heroes. A man in a captain's uniform walked across the deck and stood by the gunwale.

Another man, wearing a mayoral chain of office and a long robe, marched up to the foot of the gangplank and shouted up to him, "Welcome to Ilfracombe, brave sailors! Queen and country are proud of you!"

As the captain strolled down the gangplank, the mayor led the crowd in vigorous applause and loud cheers.

The mayor shouted, "Welcome home, Admiral Drake!"

The man waved an acknowledgement and strolled onto the dock.

The mayor went to greet him, then hesitated and stammered, "Oh, wait. But… you're not Admiral Drake."

"No, sir. I be Captain John Wynter and this be my ship, the *Elizabeth*."

"I beg your pardon, Captain Wynter. I thought…"

"I know what you thought, but Admiral Drake isn't with me, and I don't know where he is or even if he still lives. But I do know that I was the first to cross the Strait of Magellan from west to east. The Lord did not favour our little fleet, and we were separated from Drake's vessel and the others. Despite searching high and low, we didn't find him. To salvage what we could from the disaster, I returned home, full sore against the will of my mariners."

The *Elizabeth*'s gentlemen adventurers and officers trooped down the gangplank to a frosty silence.

Then someone cried, "What have you done with our admiral?"

"Abandoned him, eh?" another yelled.

Nelan awoke bathed in sweat, and toppled out of his hammock. By Neptune's trident, Wynter lived! The *Elizabeth* had not only survived the storm, but had run away and gone home. He had to tell Drake.

18

And Tales of a Man Will Tell

17th June 1579

Nelan pulled on his breeches and climbed the ladder to the upper deck. The sea resembled a sheet of glass; a serene azure blue. He bumped into Tom. "It's Captain Wynter," he burbled.

"What about 'im? Got news, 'ave ya? Spit it out, then," the bosun replied, raising an eyebrow.

Some of the hands pricked an ear at the prospect of such news. It was life or death, like most matters at sea.

The admiral got wind of the new tidings and joined the melee on deck. His beard and 'tache were groomed to perfection; so much so that Nelan wondered how he kept them looking so prim. "Wynter? You have news of Captain Wynter?" he murmured.

"His rig's returned to England," Nelan said with bated breath.

"What? No, no, no. That's all wrong. He can't have. He's not far behind us. A week or two at the most."

"But, Admiral, I saw it myself. Just now, he's docked in Ilfracombe."

"You saw it? How's that possible?"

"In a dream vision, Admiral."

"Dreams, eh? After St John's accusations, I don't know whether to believe you or not."

"It's as true as I'm standing here."

"Nah, Wynter's no coward. He wouldn't turn back. He'd strive with all his might to keep abreast of the *Golden Hind*. I'll wager a small fortune he's harassing the Dons' shipping down south, all along the Chilean and Peruvian coasts, just like we did. Yup, that's where he is."

"I tell you it's true, Admiral. I saw him in a crowd on the quayside at Ilfracombe, waving and singing his greetings."

Drake frowned, curling his lips down to the deck.

Nelan had to convince him. He had an idea: he'd stroke the man's sense of importance. "Admiral," he said, "of the many folks gathered on the quay at Ilfracombe, none were expecting Captain Wynter to disembark."

"Who did they expect?"

Nelan paused and then said, "Why, you, Admiral."

"That so?"

"Yes, Admiral. As Wynter strolled down the gangplank, the crowd groaned in disappointment, because they only wanted to know where *you* were."

"They did?" Drake raised his eyebrows. "Well, we'll have to wait and see if what you're saying is true or not. In the meantime, Pilot, I want you to plot a course nor'-nor'-west, if you will. We're a long way from the Hoe. Before we set off across the vast ocean, we must make landfall and careen our golden beauty."

A few days later, they sailed into a broad bay with sandy beaches skirted by berry-laden bushes and verdant undergrowth. No sooner had they weighed anchor than the natives appeared on the beach. Desperate for food and water, Drake approached them with caution. This time, the Lord smiled on them, because the natives festooned them with gifts of exotic cockle shells and necklaces of coloured stones and beads. With the coast secure, the crew emptied the *Golden Hind* of all her cargo, sails and masts, lugged it all ashore, and then tilted her on her side and began the long and arduous task of careening the hull. Their every move inflamed the natives' curiosity, especially when the men built a stockade on the beach to secure their valuables. The more it appeared that the strangers intended to take up residence in their domain, the more the natives grew restless, perhaps fearing invasion.

With every man needed for the careening, Drake reluctantly granted Nelan special dispensation to work on the beach. One morning, he was scrubbing barnacles from the port underside of the vessel when a couple of dozen warriors, armed to the teeth with clubs, bows and arrows, emerged from the undergrowth. The crew took refuge in the stone-built stockade and watched in amazement as Drake strode along the beach to meet them with only his brother for reinforcement. A raucous bunch of natives approached them. Amongst them was a man who, from the colour of his skin, appeared to be a mix of native and European. With a red-and-white bandana tied around his forehead, and his skin painted with swirling patterns, he wore as little as the other warriors. Drake didn't twitch or shudder. Instead, he waited as if settled in the righteousness of his cause. Smart in his admiral's uniform, he stood with his back as straight as a tree trunk and his shoulders high; a proud Englishman and personification of the motto 'Honi soit qui mal y pense'. This occult wall, this portcullis of defiance, protected him.

The war party halted a stone's throw in front of him. They opened their mouths and stuck out their tongues at him. Despite the mockery and intimidation, Drake seemed for once to have left his ruddy, hot-headed Devon temperament in his cabin. He lifted his hands, showing his palms to the natives. He raised and lowered them slowly and repeatedly. The gesture sent waves of calm across the golden sands and imbued the fearsome natives with a quiet confidence in this stranger in their midst. After Drake made these conciliatory moves, the natives stopped thrusting their weapons in the air and stamping their feet. With Drake bowing in gratitude and respect, their frowns became smiles, and their mood turned as cool and quiescent as the azure skies above.

The man with the bandana introduced himself as Huyana. Because he was fluent in Spanish, he became a trusted intermediary with the Miwoks. His grandfather had deserted from Cortés's army in Mexico in the 1520s and, heading north, sought sanctuary with the Miwoks and married a native girl. Nelan felt a deep affinity for Huyana; they were of a similar age, and they were both the children of émigrés.

A month or so later, with the ship careened, and the planks caulked and tarred and embraced by the salt waters of the Pacific, Drake led a landing party ashore. Fletcher accompanied him, along with a painter, a musician and some gentlemen adventurers. Nelan, Tom and some other hands rowed them to the shore. The beach was so soft that Nelan felt his feet covered by the warm sand.

Drake said to his brother, "You're in charge while I'm gone."

"How long will that be?" Thomas asked, failing to hide a trace of anxiety in his voice.

"At most, a couple of days," the admiral replied. "The Miwok people revere us like gods. Before we leave, I want to learn more about them and their bountiful land."

He and his party set off inland. As Thomas and the other hands launched the skiff to return to the ship, Nelan heard a rustling in the bushes. Then he spotted a young woman with her back to him. She took a few steps and then seemed to faint, because she stumbled, fell over and disappeared from view.

"Nelan," Thomas Drake cried, "you can't be ashore on your own, remember?"

"But over there—" Nelan pointed to the bushes.

"Come! Now!" Thomas insisted.

Nelan wanted to abide by his agreement with Drake and return to the ship. But he also could not leave a damsel in distress. "Wait! I won't be long!" he cried, and ran into the bushes.

After searching the undergrowth and disturbing a small rodent and a bird, he found the woman lying on the ground, clutching her ankle. He'd seen her before, walking on the beach with Huyana. She glanced at Nelan, looked away, and tried to stand as if to get away from him, but then squealed in pain, spun around and fell again.

"I... I can help you," he murmured.

He didn't understand her language, but he did glean the sense of her words: *Leave me alone, or else!*

"Please, I won't harm you," he said, and held up his hands, showing her his palms.

She grimaced, although he suspected she was annoyed with herself for placing herself in this vulnerable position. Her skin was a silken brown, and she wore an animal skin to cover her body. Her furrowed brow spoiled the natural youthful beauty that shone from her eyes. He tried speaking in broken Spanish, but she stared at him, mute.

How can I put this frightened girl at her ease? "Me, Nelan," he said, pointing to himself.

"Knee-lan," she replied.

"Good, yes. You? Your name?" He pointed at her.

"Sanuye."

"Sun-ui?"

She smiled, politely accepting his pronunciation, then clutched her ankle, wincing in pain.

"Sanuye, need to get you back to Huyana," he said.

A glimmer of recognition flashed across her face at the mention of Huyana's name.

Nelan glanced at the *Golden Hind* and was shocked to see the skiff nestling against its hull. He was a poor swimmer, and some nasty predators cruised the deep Pacific waters. Had Thomas forgotten him? Or had he left him there deliberately and abandoned him to the natives? Late at night in the forecastle, he'd heard many a story of disgruntled ship captains marooning troublesome and rebellious mariners.

While he remained undecided what to do, Sanuye lay on the ground, writhing in agony.

"What am I going to do with you?"

She seemed to understand his question, because she raised her right arm and patted her armpit with her left hand. He noticed that she'd twisted her right ankle. Oh – she wanted a crutch. Why hadn't he thought of that? Was it because her luminous skin blinded him, or her silky black locks? And why did she stare at him with those soft, lustrous brown eyes? She pointed at a tree branch in the undergrowth. Using his knife, he cut it to her diminutive height and then carved one end to fit into the round of her armpit. She smiled as he gave it to her.

"Sanuye go home?" he asked.

She pointed in the direction of her camp. She stubbornly refused to let him help her, so their progress remained laboriously slow. The narrow, well-trodden path took them through woods and grassland. They struggled on until Sanuye collapsed. Nelan moved to pick her up, but she hissed at him like a snake. The day was hot and sweat fell from her brow. Then he heard a rustling in the bushes and the tremulous cries of birds in the trees. The forest seemed alive and full of unseen dangers. He knew what he had to do, but he didn't know if Sanuye would let him. He leaned down, moved close to her and slowly put his arms under her body. She tensed and stared at him, fire spitting from her eyes. Then he gently pulled her towards him and lifted her in one smooth movement. Her shoulders went taut as he adjusted his balance to hold her weight. Her light, slender, youthful body nestled in his arms. Probably out of sheer necessity, she reluctantly slung her arms around his neck.

He made good progress through a lush, verdant wood. Accustomed to the perpetual pitch and yaw of the boat, the sensation of walking on solid earth was odd. Sanuye relaxed in his arms. Her supple body smelled of a soft resin, and he loved her bright eyes when she occasionally stole a glance at him. As he walked on, she grew heavier, and so he rested.

A twig snapped nearby. A strong arm grabbed Nelan from behind. More hands snatched Sanuye from his grasp, but she fell awkwardly and hit her head on the roots of a large tree. Natives. Four of them. One held him in a headlock; two leaned over Sanuye. With a frightening roar, the fourth leapt into the air and landed in front of him. Huyana. Nose to nose, he glared at Nelan, then unleashed a torrent of abuse in a mix of Miwok and Spanish. Pointing a finger at Sanuye, he spat into Nelan's face.

Nelan felt dirty. *Oh, my God. He thinks I was kidnapping Sanuye! And that I hurt her!* "No! No!" he tried to cry, but the man behind him started throttling him. Nelan clung to one solace – that Sanuye would tell them the truth and endorse his story – but she was out cold. When she awoke, she'd tell them that he hadn't molested or abducted her. "I was trying to help her. I'd never hurt such a precious flower. You must believe me!"

They didn't, though. Huyana shook with anger. Sanuye's head flopped to one side.

Oh no! She can't be dead! Sanuye, please wake up, for God's sake!

They tied his hands and led him like a donkey, stumbling through the undergrowth like Thomas Doughty. Was this Nelan's Isle of Blood? They led him into their camp, arranged in a circle with about thirty wigwams. Mothers watched their children play in the bright sunlight. Children hurled stones and dirt at Nelan like he was a scarecrow. To one side of the camp sat a large pole with burned kindling at its base.

Oh, my Lord. That's for me. No, not a burning. Anything but a burning.

Huyana kneed him in the kidneys. Nelan doubled up in pain. In his weakened state, they lifted him like a sack of coal and lashed him to the pole. As word spread, soon the whole village danced and yelled around him like a bunch of demons. He felt ashamed and terrified. This was wrong. He prayed like never before that Sanuye would wake up. At least now he could speak.

"*¡Soy inocente!*" he said in garbled Spanish. "I'm innocent!"

Huyana looked up from tending to Sanuye and scoffed, "*¡Es usted un diablo!*"

"No! I'm not a devil."

A man dressed in a feathered array lumbered towards Nelan. He brandished a knife in one hand and a wand in the other. His face was painted in swirling greens, reds and blues. The medicine man prodded his finger at Nelan. Huyana urged him on and scowled at Nelan. The women joined the scuffle, throwing scorn at Nelan in waves. Led by the medicine man, they cavorted in a *danse macabre*, calling on the spirits to turn and rend Nelan. They wielded bows and arrows, clubs and knives. Daggers and axes rent the air. Children threw sticks and stones. Nelan stared death in the face, and death stared back at him, fearless, silent and uncompromising. This was the end of his days. His hourglass had turned for the last time. Yet he still had so much more to accomplish. He wanted to grow into a man. He wanted vengeance on the Spanish. He wanted a reprieve from his arrest warrant. And he wanted to discover his own destiny, as Dr Dee had suggested. Too late for all that now.

The medicine man cried to the sky, spouting a Miwok spell. The sun was setting; a great orb of gold descending in the west. Nelan would not see it again. The medicine man unsheathed a curved knife with a white bone handle. The crowd hushed in reverence. The medicine man turned to Nelan and lifted the knife. Nelan closed his eyes. The final stabbing blow to the heart would come quick. In the hiatus, he waited. The great powers invested in him waited, as did those who loved and cared for him, both alive and dead. His last breath drew near. His heart pounded. The blow was coming. Why did it take so long? He peeped out of one eye. The knife hovered over his heart, sparkling in the late-afternoon sun. The clouds parted. High in the sky, a tunnel pointed to his next port of call in his journey. This was his time to sail the tide on the flood; to surf a wave. He was as ready as he could ever be.

It only took a few words, a phrase, to save his life. He heard a girl's voice; Sanuye's. He didn't understand what she said, but the tribe did. The knife was sheathed.

Sanuye was awake. Huyana helped her stand. She spoke in Miwok. A hush spread over the tribe. Instead of cutting out Nelan's heart, the medicine man cut the knot around his hands. Nelan staggered forward, dropped to his knees, and raised his hands in a prayer of thanksgiving. God existed, and mercy was present as a silent witness. He hauled himself up to stand; to face the world, feel the earth beneath his feet, and take that unexpected but longed-for breath of clean air. Every breath was of pristine air; he knew that now. Life was more precious than a sunbeam and as soft as the whisper of an angel's wing in flight.

Huyana helped Sanuye hobble up to Nelan. He stood to greet them. The women shouted and wailed in a mix of relief and shame. The men howled in anguish like a pack of wolves at the full moon.

Huyana looked at Sanuye and said, "*Mi hermana quiere decir algo.*"

'*Hermana*' – *that means sister. Oh, so Sanuye is his sister. And now she wants to say something to me.*

Sanuye's rounded face was a battleground of intense pain, shame, and utter relief. She bent and kissed Nelan on the cheek; so gentle, so sweet, his knees almost gave way with joy. The crowd cheered their approval. Gone were the dark clouds of loathing, dispelled in a moment by a simple, heartfelt kiss. She glowed with a golden hue. She delved into a pocket, clenched her fists in front of him, and gazed longingly into his eyes.

"What are these?"

"*Un presente*," Huyana explained.

Nelan extended his palms beneath Sanuye's fists. She dropped a handful of conch shells into them. The moment seemed to hold a tremendous significance both for her and for those who witnessed it; a sense that was only enhanced when the men cheered and the woman cried hot tears of joy. Huyana patted Nelan on the back like a new-found family member.

"*Muchas gracias*," Nelan said to Sanuye.

She blushed and hid her face behind her long raven-black hair.

Huyana led him to a gurgling brook at the back of the camp.

"*Lávese*," Huyana said, pointing to the stream.

Nelan threw his clothes onto the verdant grass and sat down in the warm flow. The clean water removed all the dirt and debris from him. A simple baptism, it washed away the shame and the guilt. As dusk fell, he dressed; then Huyana led him up a steep hill to the entrance to a cave. Lights flickered inside. Wearing a frightening mask made from a coyote skull, the medicine man awaited them.

"Kaliska," Huyana said by way of introduction.

"Greetings, Kaliska," Nelan said.

Kaliska grabbed a lit torch from a cradle and beckoned them to follow him. Nelan had the nagging sense that what lay beyond would be momentous for his future. The tunnel got more stifling the deeper they penetrated the cave. Up ahead was the beat of drums. It rose softly, reached a crescendo, then fell to the murmur of a soft wingbeat. They entered a large cavern in which young men cavorted to the rhythm of the drums. Lanterns sprayed gentle light over the rising tumult. On the walls, the natives had painted strange animals with white tusks and huge midriffs; as ferocious as the wild boar in the forests and glades of old England. In the cavern were four large poles arranged in a circle. On top of the highest was a coyote skull, with three wavy lines etched on its forehead. On another sat the skull of a turkey vulture. On the other two were skulls of smaller birds; possibly a raven and a crow. A small fire burned near a tunnel, casting flickering shadows onto the walls. Next to it, Kaliska yelled, his cry echoing around the cave. Then he sprinkled a handful of green herbs onto the fire, sending up clouds of grey-white smoke. The smell was acrid and the taste bitter.

"What's this about?" Nelan asked. "*¿Qué hace?*"

"*Rito de paso,*" Huyana replied.

"Rite of passage? For me? But why?" Nelan asked.

Huyana nodded and replied, "*Mi hermana.*"

"Yes, your sister. What about Sanuye?"

"*La salvaste.*"

"I saved her?"

"*Sí, Señor* Nelan."

"I don't know what I'm letting myself in for, but if you're doing it, so am I."

The vibrant beat of the drums filled the hot, turgid air. The pulsating noise echoed around the walls. Nelan could taste the acrid bitterness of the smoke stinging his eyes. Spinning on the spot, he moved in time with the drumbeat. With delirious joy, he danced alongside the other young men. Sweat poured from his brow. The coyote skull with the three wavy lines stared at him. Along with the images of animals on the wall, it filled his mind with colourful visions of times past: of men with spears walking in a line through ancient forests, hunting buffalo and chasing them off a cliff edge, then using every single part of the corpses; not a hair wasted, nor a bone discarded, nor a piece of flesh left to rot. The buffalo, the men, the hunt, the earth, the sunbeams, the blue sky, the rain; all sacred because they were there. Existence itself was sacred.

He must have fallen asleep, because he was drenched in sweat when he awoke. The fire had gone out. The torches had burned low. The fumes reeked of bitter herbs. Young men stumbled about the cavern, intoxicated. Kaliska stalked the shadows, making soft whooping sounds and murmurs of appreciation as he summoned the spirits of his tribe's ancestors. The young men looked older and younger at the same time; older in the newly revealed knowledge of their destiny in life, and young in its fulfilment. Their eyes were keen, and a sense of purpose radiated from every pore.

They cheered as they led Nelan out of the cave. He felt he had reunited with his purpose, which had been there all along but had been buried by the injustices he'd suffered. The red cloud of dawn hung in the sky like a blazing lantern. They followed Kaliska to a grove of massive redwood trees; taller than a mountain and with trunks wider than a river. Writhing and spinning, the men circled Kaliska. Nelan bent his neck and howled like a coyote, filling the dawn air with yips and growls. As boys, they had left the camp, and as men, they returned. The air was charged with natural but irrevocable change. Sanuye waited for Nelan; a white flower in her hair. Friends and companions surrounded her.

Huyana said, "*Ella es tuya.*"

"She wants to be mine?"

"*La tendrás?*"

"Will I have her?" The question surprised Nelan. The tribe had been trying to pair him off with Sanuye but, stupidly, he'd missed the signs. First, he had saved her; then she'd given him a gift of conch shells. For the Miwoks, these symbolised matrimony. Then he'd been renewed and reborn, not once but twice: first in the baptismal cleansing and then in the dance. The rite of passage had been eased by bitter herbs cast upon a fire, sending his soul outside his body to reveal a vision of his future. As a man, he stood ready for a man's world and capable of committing to marriage. After he'd been suspected of abducting Sanuye, he'd been exonerated and then welcomed into the bosom of the Miwok tribe. Back in England, depending on the way in which the wind blew in Drake's mind, he could easily end up back in Marshalsea. *Dread the thought.* If he stayed here, he'd be an honoured member of the tribe with a beautiful bride. Yet he did not want to start a new life on strange shores. He had a role to play in the unfolding future of the Island of Angels. Dee had revealed that to him.

At this crossroads of his life, Nelan's eyes went misty, and a vision appeared before him. As clear as day, he saw Eleanor by their cross – Charing Cross – and he stood shoulder to shoulder with her. All those leagues had shrunk to inches. He breathed in the sweet smell of her. She whispered a verse from the Book of Ruth:

> *...For whither thou goest, I will go.*
> *And where thou dwellest, I will dwell.*
> *Thy people shall be my people.*
> *And thy God my God.*

Those words rekindled the sense of spiritual union he'd felt beside the Charing Cross when they'd promised to be man and wife. The moment was indelible and, like every indelible moment, it was etched rather than embossed on the scrolls of his life.

"*Señor* Nelan?"

Huyana's words jolted Nelan from his reverie. He knew three things about Eleanor: that she lived; that she had not abandoned him, and that she yet waited for him. Loyalty called for loyalty. He would not give up on her.

Huyana took Sanuye's hand, which held a string of beads in sea blues, verdant greens and shell whites. A gift for Nelan. Huyana offered it to him. Nelan looked at Sanuye, her pretty face glowing with the promise of youth. He glanced at Huyana, her expectant brother.

"No," Nelan said, and gently placed the conch shells back in Sanuye's hand. He bowed to her and added, "*Muchas gracias.*" To Huyana, he said, "*Debería irme a casa ahora.* I must go home now."

Amidst an air of disappointed acceptance, the natives trudged back with him to the beach for a final farewell. Nelan was mightily relieved to see his passage home, the *Golden Hind*, still anchored in the bay, gleaming in the morning sunlight. A skiff drew up on the beach. Francis Drake and his brother strolled onto the sand.

"Well, the English *cimarrón* returns," Drake said, sniffing the clear air.

"I never intended otherwise, Admiral."

"An uncertain fate awaits you in England. When I returned and you weren't on board, I thought you'd run away to join the Miwoks."

"I didn't, though, did I?"

"Actions define a man's character. Now I see what kind of man you are."

"What kind of man am I?"

"A man prepared to account for his actions. I admire that. And one who keeps his word. I admire that too."

"I'm here because I want to return to England, m'lord. The Miwok are a fine people, but they are not my people. This is not my place. My place is England. My wife-to-be waits for me there. I gave her my word, and my word is my bond. And I want to help defend the Island of Angels against the might of the Dons."

"Noble sentiments, young Nelan. I too gave my word – to St John. And I may yet hand you over to the constable in Plymouth. But your loyalty is commendable. I will see if there is a way that I can satisfy both you and St John."

"Thank you, m'lord."

As the admiral sauntered off to charm the natives for the last time, Thomas Drake pulled Nelan to one side and said, "I'm relieved you returned."

"Why's that?"

"The admiral was furious with me for letting you out of my sight. He sent me off to look for you and threatened to maroon me here if I returned empty-handed."

"I'm not a runaway."

Thomas whispered, "Thank God for that. And between you and me, I know he secretly wanted you to sail on the *Hind*."

"The admiral?"

Thomas nodded. "Remember the ruby charm? You still got it?"

"Here it is," Nelan said, and pulled out the salamander. "It's a part of me now."

"Good. For the admiral, and for all of us, you and that salamander are our safe passage home. It'll make sure there's no fire aboard ship."

As the *Hind* sailed out of the bay on a warm July morning, the natives gathered on the hilltops and waved goodbye. The crew provisioned on the Farallon Islands and headed into open waters three days later. The vast ocean of the South Seas stretched out before them.

Nelan's time with the Miwoks had been a turning point in his life. He'd arrived on their shores as an older boy seeking his way in life. He'd left them as a young man of one-and-twenty years, wiser and renewed in his purpose.

When he joined them in the forecastle, the crew belted out one of their favourite shanties:

The young one, no more a boy will be,
And tales of a man will tell, my girl,
And tales of a man will tell.

19

Home at Last

26th September 1580

It was midway through the afternoon watch. On a Monday. It wasn't any old Monday. It was a special Monday. Not because of an extra beer ration; nor because of the smell of fish emanating from the galley. No – it was because, on that autumn day, nearly all fifty-eight surviving crew members hung over the gunwale, their eyes dripping with expectation and glued to the horizon. On occasion, they glanced up at the topmast and the barrel man as if waiting for a message from the heavens. None came, even after they'd passed the Isles of Scilly. Nor did it come after they passed Wolf Rock. It surely wouldn't be long in coming.

As the creaking of the sails ceased, the *Golden Hind* glided serenely through the waters as if drawn forward by a divine wind. Even the gulls stopped squawking. A light rain shower washed the decks. The men gazed at the white flecks on the waves.

Amidst the quiet, a cry went out, and travelled down the mizzenmast, across the poop deck and into the soul of each crew member. "Land ho!"

Nelan stood next to Fletcher, who raised his hands like an Old Testament prophet and cried out, "Oh, my God!" Then he knelt on the deck, hands clasped in a prayer of thanksgiving.

The other hands – all long-haired, heavily bearded, and stinking of piss, ale and perspiration – planted their knees on the deck. To Nelan, that moment felt portentous. It was one of collective bliss in which men of all ranks, natures and ages shared a sublime experience and encountered, perhaps for a few seconds only, the most concentrated religious feeling in the world: that of belonging to each other and to a land. Perhaps they didn't know it fully, then. Maybe they had an inkling of it, as Nelan did. But at that moment, each of them knew that, through their voyage, their endeavours and their courage, they had unchained the shackles of the past, cut most of the remaining threads of the Gordian Knot of papal suppression, summoned the fresh, clean winds of the future, and set the people of England on a course towards the discovery of themselves and towards an exploration of the world and its peoples.

As the familiar jagged promontory of the Lizard hove into view, the hardy souls who'd survived unimaginable hardships together were stunned to silence. For once, their tongues stopped wagging. Where before they had been vocal in their japes and musical in their jaunts, now they were mute, stilled by the awe and wonder of seeing the distant contours of their land, their England, appear on the horizon. Their journey neared its end. They knew that another would begin as surely as God gave them the grace of another breath. They had not seen this land's green pastures and gentle slopes for over a thousand days; 1,018, the pilot told them. England. Home at last. They would greet friends they had not seen for two years and ten months. See children who'd grown from suckling babe to infant. Meet mothers who'd given birth in the interim. Comfort wives grown old from the worry, and embrace daughters who'd married during their long absence. They'd clasp hands with their brothers, fathers and sons, and hold them close. Such were the anticipated joys of homecoming. Since they'd set out twice from old Plymouth – once when storms had forced them to return to safe harbour, and later when they'd finally embarked on that fateful day in December 1577 – this was a second coming.

Nelan swallowed hard. He licked his parched lips. While he didn't expect anyone to meet him on the quay, he remained as excited as the native-born mariners to see old England. She was his home now. She had been a haven for Protestants from all over Europe fleeing the cruel persecution of the Inquisition. He couldn't go back to Sangatte or Leiden. The angels of the island coursed through his blood and enriched his soul. He belonged to them, and they belonged in him.

From within him there arose a poem of persuasion, a song of softness, a dance of deliberation.

One question hovered on the lips of the crew. But none dared speak it aloud. Not Nelan, and, for once, not even Tom. But it demanded to be asked. The answer would decide their fate; particularly that of the officers and gentlemen and, most of all, of the admiral. He had to be the one to ask it.

As they sailed by the familiar landmarks along the Cornish coast – Pendennis Castle, the Fowey Estuary and St George's Island – they reached the Looe Estuary. There, Nelan caught sight of odd things with his unique vision. He saw through the veil and peered into the strange, astral world; the one that was attached to the physical world but simultaneously separate from it. The ethereal things in it had no substance; they were the elementals, the salamander and the undine, the gnome and the sylph. The shapes, like puffs of smoke, moved like quicksilver. The colours were evanescent, pulsating; so alive in contrast to the dull hues of the physical world. In this realm, a man could walk on water if he wore the shoes that never wore out. These were the vast, undiscovered chambers of the astral world. With this vision he witnessed, suspended above the coastal valleys and moorlands, clusters of golden clouds which shrouded the hills and dales, the meadows and secret places of the gentle land of England. He blinked, wondering whether this vision was real or imagined.

He looked again. The vision didn't disappear back into the ether; instead, it grew clearer and more defined. The honeyed astral clouds pressed close against the trees and bushes. Their golden tentacles behaved like bindweed, creeping into every crevice and curtailing the growth of the meadow and the forest. The cloud suffocated the land, shrouding its natural beauty and gentle disposition like a heavy morning mist. To capture the vision, he borrowed a small brush from one of the painters and sketched the numinous scene as best he could. He wished he could ask Diego about how to rid the land of this unwanted cloak. With all his folk wisdom, the *cimarrón* would have divined the meaning of these golden clouds and known how to exorcise them. Alas, he had passed away in a cloud of madness as they had sailed by the Spice Islands on their way home in November 1579. There, they'd collected many herbs and spices previously unknown in

England. Then Drake had steered the *Hind* around the southern tip of Africa and up the west coast to home.

A cry of joy rose from the decks. The barrel man intoned the name like the opening of a solemn prayer: "Rame Head."

Home was so close. They could smell it in the air; feel its soft embrace in the wind. Yet the question hovered like the Sword of Damocles, waiting to thrust and splinter.

They pulled alongside a fishing boat. The crew waved excitedly at the fisherman.

"So, it's yourselves, now, is it?" the fisherman said.

"Aye, it's us. The *Golden Hind*; we've returned!" the bosun cried.

"I can see that with me own eyes, I can. Would the admiral be amongst you?"

A man marched up to the port side. His face seemed different. Battered and bruised, yet with an air of triumph, he had the stature of the first Englishman to sail around the world. Beneath one eye, he wore a small scar where an arrow had hit him on the Isle of Mocha. He cupped his hands around his mouth and yelled, "That be me!"

"Welcome home, m'lord!" shouted the fisherman.

The hands clustered around the admiral, waiting for him to pose *the* question.

"Is the Queen alive and well?"

"Aye, she is, and rules us all with a fair and gracious hand!" came the reply.

Drake raised his hands, puffed out his cheeks and let out a huge roar. "Then we'd better send her tidings of our return and incredible success!" he cried.

"'Tis said by many, m'lord, that she's already heard of it."

"How so? We've only just arrived."

"Aye, m'lord. But Captain Wynter brought news."

"Wynter, eh? He's back before us?"

"He is that."

"So, that is very interesting." Drake turned and glanced across the sea of faces, then nodded approvingly at Nelan. As the crags of St Nicholas Island rose from the slate-grey sea, the admiral bellowed, "Drop anchor! Get to it, lads."

They anchored on the north, seaward side of the isle; away from the prying eyes of landsmen, or so Nelan thought. For the rest of the afternoon, the crew made no preparations to go ashore. The ship's sails remained loosely furled. The hatches stayed shut tight, meaning no cargo would be unloaded. A gentleman requested an audience with the admiral. It was John Doughty, the brother of Thomas, the executed mutineer.

"Well, Master Francis Drake," he said with a snarl, "my brother was right."

"I doubt that," the admiral muttered.

"Remember his prophecy?" Doughty asked.

"I have a feeling you're going to remind me of it."

"That, like Magellan, having set sail with five ships, you'd limp home with only one. How many vessels do you see right now, Admiral?"

Drake folded his arms and said, "Well, unless my ears deceive me, we just heard that Wynter has returned. With the *Hind*, I make that *two* ships in harbour. And, my worthy adversary, if you recall, two of the others were scuttled. According to my tally, we only lost the *Marigold*, which means we lost only one, and that's better by far than Magellan."

Doughty glowered at the admiral. Gritting his teeth, he said, "My brother also predicted that you'd return home with many hands lost, drowned at sea, murdered by wild natives, dead from disease, or hanged for crimes. And here you are, with a paltry crew, sick as dogs and weak as chaff."

"The Doughty bile runs thick in your blood, as it did in your brother's," Drake said. "But you forgot one other prophecy that he made."

"What was that?"

"That, just as Ferdinand Magellan died at the hand of a native, I, Francis Drake, would never see the shores of Plymouth Hoe again."

Doughty frowned.

"Now, you know that over the other side of this isle is a certain port," Drake said, pointing in the direction of the Hoe. "And remind me, what's its name?"

John Doughty glared at him, turned and walked away.

"It's hard to be the brother of a doubting Thomas." Drake had the last word.

The crew desperately wanted to set foot on the soil of old England, to see their loved ones, to hold them in their arms, to down a tankard of English ale, to taste a morsel of English bread, to discover the news of everything that had happened during their prolonged absence from these shores. Instead, they were confined on board ship. Nelan had a forlorn hope that Eleanor would know of his return. How wonderful it would be to see her again, smell her scent, touch her soft cheek, and kiss her lips! Marshalsea prison was the last place where they'd physically been together. She'd promised to bring him food and money. But on the day she had been due to return, he'd been pressed into the navy, and missed her. Would she have discovered his fate? Would she have forgiven him? Would she still be his? The recent vision told him that she would.

Out of the green eye of envy, the crew watched as two men got into a launch and rowed ashore. If those two could clamber up Plymouth quay, why couldn't they?

Quick as the green flash, Tom climbed down the ladder into the forecastle and named names. "It's John Brewer and Thomas Drake. Brewer has been sent to trumpet our arrival to the Privy Council in London."

"And Drake?" Nelan asked.

"Ah, he's to fetch the admiral's wife," the bosun replied.

As dusk settled on that eventful day, a skiff rowed by Thomas Drake made its way across the Sound, approaching from Plymouth harbour. It carried two passengers: one a woman; the other a gentleman. The lady was Mary, Admiral Drake's wife, and fine and dandy she was too. Other than in his dreams, how long had it been since Nelan had clapped eyes on a fair English lass?

Tom wasted no time in spilling the gentleman's identity: he was the mayor of Plymouth. But there was a sting in the tail, for the man brought bad tidings. "The plague. It's all over Plymouth like a rash!" Tom said.

Three days later, John Brewer returned from London with news from the court.

Drake read the letter to the assembled crew. "Men, this letter's from Sir Christopher Hatton himself. He says we're most welcome in

England, and that the Queen longs to entertain us at court. But we're to wait until the plague abates, and when it does, some of you will be given your dues and allowed to disembark. The rest will make up a skeleton crew who'll transport the remaining treasure for safekeeping to Trematon Castle, on a small estuary off Plymouth's River Tamar."

Every moment felt weighed down by lead. After two weeks, the decks were scrubbed so clean they shone with the brightness of the Holy Ghost. The bowsprit, the boom, the rigging, the ropes, the shrouds and the sails were all primed as if the crew were about to set out on another circumnavigation.

While they waited, counting the bells, the turning of the hourglasses, and the ebb and flow of the tides, Nelan grew uncertain about his fate. Since the incident with the Miwoks, Drake had not revealed his intentions. Now that they were home, would he set Nelan free or call the constable? But Nelan's prophecy of Wynter's early return had proved correct, and would hopefully stand him in good stead with the admiral. Nelan gazed at the choppy grey waters of the Sound, wondering whether to swim for it or steal a skiff and row for the coast. But his conscience got the better of him, and he stayed put. He had been a runaway once. He wasn't going to run away again. Laurens Michaels would appreciate that sentiment. Nelan had given the admiral his word that he would stay aboard, and stay aboard he would.

As dawn broke on that Friday, the crew awoke to find themselves surrounded by a sea mist as thick as a Plymouth accent. It deadened every noise. The cold bit cheeks, earlobes and fingers. They barely heard a skiff pull up alongside, but they did hear John Brewer's bugle as they welcomed the mayor aboard again. This time, despite the fog, he wore a smile that shone as bright as his chain of office. Brewer accompanied him in the skiff; the mist dripping from his ears and nose. He stank of the road, and his cloak and riding boots were besmirched with mud. He'd returned from delivering another message.

Nelan told him, "We're blind here on the ship. We can't see the city, and they can't see us. You've just passed through the docks. Does anyone in Plymouth even know we're here?"

With a glint in his eye, Brewer said, "Aye; a few 'ave gathered on the quay."

The men sighed with disappointment because they, like Nelan, had anticipated a boisterous welcome. Still, nothing could take away that warm homecoming feeling. Even the chill of the south-westerly blowing off the ocean brought its own sense of belonging. And the feeling amongst the men was that they wouldn't have to wait much longer before being allowed ashore. Then they'd stir up a hornets' nest of a celebration.

As the mayor rowed back to Plymouth, Nelan and the rest of the crew wondered what had passed between him and the admiral.

Then Drake spoke to the bugler. "Give it me, John," he said, and Brewer handed him the latest message from the court. Silently and with a grim countenance, Drake read the first part of the scroll. But about halfway through, his shoulders relaxed and a thin smile spread across his bearded face. "Give us three long blasts on your bugle."

"That'll bring all hands on deck," Brewer said.

"Aye, it will that!" Drake said, and the bugler obliged.

With grins on their faces, the crew rushed onto the poop deck. There were tidings from Plymouth and London. It could be great news or not. They were soon to find out which way the wind blew. When the admiral sauntered onto the quarterdeck, their cheers rose to the top of the mainmast.

"Well, lads, today is a fine day," Drake said. "Because the plague's gone. I reckon your prayers have beaten it off. And, what with the recent news from London, you can loosen your shackles and... get ready to disembark!"

There was a huge roar, and then Drake said, "Now line up, you lucky lads, 'cause I'm going to give you all what you deserve after this voyage."

"Gis the treasure!" the cry rose from the hands.

"Good Queen Bess, our benefactor, has allocated me the princely sum of fourteen thousand pounds to share amongst you," Drake said with pride, and handed out every last morsel of treasure owed to each hand.

The men beamed with delight at the sight of riches aplenty. Nelan received his share and kept the ruby salamander. A few of the crew dragged their feet and moped around with slouched shoulders. Others stared forlornly at the decks. Nelan guessed that they had already gambled away their share of the takings in games of dice, cards and backgammon.

Crammed into the skiffs, the gentlemen adventurers and their legion of servants disembarked first. The officers and masters followed them, then the tradesmen, and lastly the mariners, leaving a skeleton crew. Each skiff disappeared into the swirling mist, overflowing with happy, laughing men.

Nelan fretted about Drake's decision. Every time a skiff returned from delivering seamen ashore, he wondered if it brought a constable to arrest him. A mariner on board ship lived in a cramped and stinking hole; conditions eerily similar to those he'd experienced in Marshalsea. He could already feel shackles heavy around his neck, feet and hands.

Drake summoned the bugler and said, "John Brewer, you've served me well. Thrice to London in a fortnight, but you've delivered your last message for me. Now, take that sore arse of yours home to your wife."

"Thank you, m'lord," Brewer said, giving a trill on his whistle.

Then the admiral turned to him and said, "Ah, Nelan, not going ashore with the others? What are you waiting for, lad?"

"For the constable, m'lord?"

"Aye, that's what I threatened. But I also said I'd ponder your fate. It's been a long voyage, and we've survived many a scrape. We're here by the grace of God, ready to set foot on old England's shore. Every man risked life and limb to keep us afloat. And you've helped to make this voyage a resounding success."

"I tried," Nelan said.

"Yes, lad. You did. You've done three things. Perhaps you did them as a penance; I don't know. Only Our Lord does. First, you told me my dreams when no one else could. Without you, we'd never have caught the *Cacafuego*. Second, you foretold Wynter's premature return to these shores. I didn't believe you at the time, but you were right. Third, when you had the opportunity to stay with the Miwoks, you voluntarily returned to the ship and, with good grace, accepted your fate – and you brought with you the good-luck token: the ruby salamander. These three things have convinced me that you are a man of your word."

Nelan's heart beat like a Miwok drum.

"Able Seaman Nelan Michaels, you strike me as an honest man, and so I believe your version of the events that unfolded at your school."

"Thank you, m'lord. You don't know what this means to me."

"I've had a scroll prepared for you."

Nelan took it and read it out loud:

In my capacity as Admiral of the Golden Hind, and by the powers endowed upon me, I hereby pardon Nelan Michaels of all charges relating to the tragic death by gunpowder explosion of Guillermo, the stepson of St John of Southampton, also known as San Juan de Antón.

Francis Drake

Nelan clutched the pardon to his heart like it was the key to Heaven. The shackles fell away, releasing him to a new future. He had so much to do. The Island of Angels was his spiritual home; he knew that deep in his soul. And he had a trial to endure for sacred England; one that would reveal his own destiny. Dr Dee had given him a vague idea of what it would entail, but it nagged at him like a terrier snapping at his heels. For the success of the voyage, and the taking of the treasure from the *Cacafuego*, his mother would have been proud of him. "M'lord, thank you kindly for showing me mercy."

"You can thank me by fulfilling your destiny. Be a God's man. Serve His needs. Do that by being true to the nature He gave you. Be kind to those whose nature is akin to your own. Avoid those who drive you into the shallows. Now, you're relieved of your duties aboard the *Golden Hind*. Get on with you, and God's speed, lad."

"I'm forever indebted to you, m'lord. If there's anything I can help you with, please let me know."

"Yes, there is, now you come to mention it. I need a messenger. Can you do that?"

"Yes, m'lord."

"John Brewer," Drake said, "show Nelan where to find his mount. It'll be in the stables next to The Sailors' Return."

"Willingly, m'lord," Brewer said.

"You're to deliver this message," Drake added, handing Nelan a scroll.

"Where and to whom?"

"To Francis Walsingham, at Barn Elms."

"Oh, I know the manor house."

"That's good."

Well, well, well; Barn Elms. What a small world! Nelan hadn't heard that name for many a year. He promised himself that, on the way there, he'd visit the little cemetery by the river at St Mary the Virgin at Mortlake. Since the days of Marshalsea and the *Mary and John*, he'd not seen his father's grave. He hoped the freemen of Mortlake had buried his remains there, so he could find peace in the arms of Our Lord. A diversion would also allow him to visit what little remained of his old house.

As the eight bells rang at the end of the forenoon watch, the admiral turned to his brother and the bosun. "Thomas, Tom, I have jobs for you both."

"M'lord," they answered.

"A few locals have gathered on the quay to welcome us home," Drake said. "Likely, some are relatives of hands who died during the expedition, such as those poor lads on the *Marigold*. It's our solemn duty to let them know what happened to their loved ones, so that mothers can grieve for their lost sons. Thomas, I want you to be the bearer of the sad news."

"Yes, m'lord," Thomas said.

"Take this scroll," Drake said. "It contains the names of all the unsung heroes of this expedition. It's a list of the dead and missing. Go to the quay and read it out."

"It'll be an honour," Thomas said.

"Tom, take this casket of jewels and precious stones from the *Cacafuego*. As Thomas reads out the names, see that the relatives receive their share of what's due to them."

"As ordered, m'lord," Tom said.

Just after midday, Nelan, Tom the bosun, John Brewer and Thomas Drake rowed to the quay with their meagre belongings but rich harvest. They could barely see their hands in front of their faces because of the mist. As the shore came into view, it disappeared again as the fog bound the quay in shrouds. Nelan thought he heard shouting and the banging of a drum, but the fog deadened the noise. The skiff in front of them moored by the quay, and the hands who'd travelled in it raced up the steps.

As Nelan's skiff moored next to it, he glanced up and saw a crowd cheering and clapping the crew as they stepped onto the dockside. "John," he said, "you told us there were only a few folks on the quay."

"Ah!" the bugler replied with a nod and a wink. "I wanted it to be a surprise for y'all."

"Well, it certainly is that," Nelan said, puffing out his cheeks.

Brewer waved his arms around like he wanted to fly, and said, "In truth, m'lad, word of our arrival's spread like a rolling wave round the streets and alleys o' the city and beyond. Be now, every yeoman, landsman an' ploughman in England knows we be moored in the harbour. You can see: there's more folks on the quay than live in the whole of the city, an' more excitement than Christ Mass, Plough Monday and Candle Mass all comin' on the same day. There's a big celebration a-brewin', that's for sure. Git up them steps, an' you'll see fa' yourself!"

Nelan grabbed his belongings, jumped out of the wherry and climbed up to the quay. A gust of wind blew a spiral of dried leaves across his path. On that October afternoon, the angels of the isle greeted him like that. It had been a long journey, but he was back in his adopted home. As he set foot on English soil, he felt a rush of warmth and well-being. The wind filled his sails, and he couldn't wait to launch the rest of his life. The clemency document proved that he was a free man; free of the shackles of past wrongs. It was more valuable to him than the fortune he'd earned, the experience he'd gained, and even the skills he'd acquired along the way. He was young and rich. He tapped his inner pocket to feel his reward: silver rings, a gold bracelet, precious stones, and the ruby salamander pendant. He smiled at the thought that he'd honoured the memory of his poor mother and wreaked vengeance on the Dons.

Dressed in his hat, chain and robe of office, the mayor of Plymouth waited for them on the quayside. "Men of the *Golden Hind*, welcome home to you, one and all!" he yelled.

Thousands of people lined the Hoe and crammed into the harbourside and nearby streets. A few enterprising youngsters hung precariously from the upper branches of nearby trees to get an elevated view of this unique event. Smiling eyes matched smiling faces. Family and friends mingled with the villeins and yeomen of Plymouth.

Hawkers touted for business, selling fishcakes, loaves of bread, tankards of ale, and flagons of wine. Cutpurses sniffed for opportunities. Scavengers and thieves squeezed in between the crowds, preying on the riches brought back by the sailors. Gentlemen adventurers embraced their wives. Able seamen kissed their lovers with passion aplenty. A more-than-healthy competition sprang up amongst the fair ladies of Plymouth to enjoy the seed of one (or even several) of the returning heroes. The dock brimmed with tears, laughter, kisses, and the joy of reunion. Folks had erected small huts of wood and bracken to sleep in overnight. Others had built tents and covered themselves in sailcloth to keep out the wind and rain.

Desperate for any news of his beloved, Nelan asked the mayor and his assistant if they'd seen a beautiful girl with green eyes and auburn hair. But they hadn't. Everywhere, he scanned the faces for his Eleanor.

Thomas Drake called for a semblance of quiet. With Tom by his side, he read out the names from the scroll. "Oliver, master gunner," he shouted. "Luke Adden, able seaman. Robert Winterhay, surgeon."

With each name, a small clump of people wailed bitter cries of grief. Then, as Tom gave them their jewels and precious stones, their grief mingled with tears of joy. To one side, a cluster of women comforted one another as they suddenly realised that they had entered the sad, lonely state of widowhood.

Thomas Drake asked for silence. The crowd hushed as he shouted, "Nelan!"

Nelan wondered if he called for him, but then realised that Drake's brother had read the name from the list. *No! It wasn't me. It was Great Nelan who died. If she's here and hears my name, she'll think I've perished.*

He was wondering how to correct Thomas when he heard a wail of sorrow that pierced his heart. It was a woman's cry, and one he recognised instantly.

20

The Island of Angels

10th October 1580

"Eleanor!" he shouted, so loud that they might have heard him at the gates of Heaven.

No reply. He pushed his way through the crowd towards the woman's cry. He was convinced it was her. It had to be. He ducked and dived between the taller folk and reached the area from which he'd heard the cry originate.

"Eleanor!" He turned this way and that in a desperate attempt to find her; to see her. But because of his size, he had to jump into the air and wave his arms. The crowd swayed in time to the music. Trumpets, flutes and drums raised a cacophony. Nelan could barely hear his own voice.

He pushed past people, and the crowd parted to let him through. A space opened up, and she stood there gazing at him. Wonder and mystery entwined the moment.

"But you're dead!" she murmured. "The sailor, he just called your name."

"No, no, sweet Eleanor, it was a mistake."

"No, it's not you. My eyes are playing tricks on me. You're a ghost." She took a step back.

"If I'm a ghost, can you feel this?" he said, and brushed the back of his hand against the softness of her cheek. "There, you felt that, didn't you?"

231

"*Is* it you?" She edged towards him. "You could be… someone else."

"No, I'm Nelan."

"How do I know?"

"Because… *It's you I adore, Eleanor, Eleanor.*"

"Oh, Nelan! That's our song. Is it really you?"

"Yes, look here," he said, showing her the three wavy lines on his palm.

"Oh my. The mark of the salamander! It *is* you. You're home at last."

They embraced. The folks around them cheered wildly.

"I feared you were dead," she whispered. "And when the man read out your name, my heart sank to the bottom of the ocean."

"Did you come here all on your own?" Nelan asked.

"No, Alexander the watchman came to keep me safe on the journey. He's drinking in The Sailors' Return."

"That's good. How did you know I'd be here?"

"After I found you at Marshalsea, I came the next day to see you, only to find that you'd gone. I eventually discovered that you'd been pressed into the navy. Then I asked old Christos, the stevedore, who told me you were aboard the *Mary and John* and bound for Plymouth. I guessed you'd end up sailing in Drake's wake. So when news of his return reached London, I had to be here."

"I missed you, I dreamed of you, and I love you," Nelan said with a beaming smile. "And I knew we'd meet again. And here you are, my wife-to-be!"

"Oh yes, we're going to get married before I lose you again!"

"Come here," he said, and pulled her to him and kissed her soft lips.

Around them was mayhem, the meeting of Heaven and Hell: Heaven for those returning and their relatives; Hell for the relatives of the dead. As they hugged, Nelan glanced across the crowded quay and spotted a hooded man approaching him. At first, he took no notice, but then he looked up again. The man closed in on him, pushing past people, his brow furrowed and his lips taut. In the next moment, he was peering down at Nelan. To protect her, Nelan pulled Eleanor behind him.

"What do you want?" he asked.

"I want you," the man replied.

"You found me. Now, who are you?"

The man fumbled in his purse and pulled out a strike-a-light iron. Instinctively, Nelan knew that it would bear the arms of the Southampton family quartered with the Sarmiento family of Andalucía.

"Pedro!"

"Yes, it's me."

"I haven't seen you since the fire at my house in Mortlake."

"I know."

"Your stepfather got me sent to prison."

"Because you killed my brother."

"I didn't. *He* tried to kill *me*."

"Bah. More Protestant lies! You must pay for your crime!"

"No, I don't have to now. I've been pardoned."

"What? How can that be?"

"I have a clemency document, signed by none other than Admiral Francis Drake."

"I-I don't believe it. You're lying."

"No, I'm not. See here," Nelan said, waving the paper in front of Pedro's face. When Pedro tried to snatch it, Nelan pulled it away and tucked it back into his purse.

A wild grimace spread across the Spaniard's face. Nelan had seen that look before: in the school woodshed, on the face of Guillermo.

Pedro said, through gritted teeth, "Your heinous sin will always bind you."

"You're as mad as your brother."

"Between you and me, Nelan, it's about the *fuego*. It's always about the *fuego*. It came back to haunt you."

"What fire? What haunting? What are you talking about?"

"I'm talking about an eye for an eye." Pedro spoke each word like a dirge.

"No, wait. On that day, you and your stepfather were at your house in Sneakenhall, packing your goods to leave for Spain."

"And?" Pedro sneered.

"And so… You started the fire. You killed my father!" Nelan turned to Eleanor and said, "Run, Eleanor!"

She hesitated.

"Get away! He's crazy!"

She turned and disappeared into the crowd, and Nelan launched himself at Pedro. Clutching him around the midriff, he grappled him to the ground. Pedro forced his way out from underneath him. Nelan punched the Spaniard and chinned him as hard as he could. Then he saw Pedro's fist coming fast towards his head. He tried to duck out of the way, but something hard and metallic smashed into his temple.

Nelan woke up. Before he could even lift himself off the stable floor, it struck him that his world had changed. It wasn't just the smell of horses, shit and straw. Not only was his father dead, he'd been murdered, slain by the brother of the boy who had tried to kill Nelan. Out of one injustice, a second had arisen. Pedro had set fire to Nelan's house with his father inside it. But in doing so he'd also set alight Nelan's sense of vengeance; his desire for retribution that would not be quenched until Pedro had paid for his heinous crime.

Nelan plucked the straw from his leggings and sat up. A man's shadow hovered by the stable door.

"Pedro?"

"Nah. It's me, John Brewer."

"John? What am I doing here?" Nelan touched the wound. It smarted. His head throbbed.

"You've taken a painful blow t' the 'ead."

"Yeah, I can feel it. And where's Pedro? And Eleanor?"

"Dunno those folks."

"You must have seen her. I can't lose her again. Oh, wait... I told her to run from that madman. But what happened to me?"

"Me and Tom found you out cold, laying on the ground."

"Yes, Pedro hit me."

"Didn't see no Pedro. But we brought you 'ere for your own good. Otherwise, you'd 'ave been crushed in the melee."

"Thanks, but I have to find her... and him," Nelan murmured. He staggered towards the stable door. The world was spinning, and he almost fell over. He put his hand to the wound on his temple; the same temple Tom the bosun had thwacked during the rite of passage as they crossed the equator. This new blow had opened up that old wound, and blood trickled down his cheek.

"Hold fast, lad. I got a cloth here. That's a nasty gash. Let me bandage it."

For once, Nelan did as he was told. John Brewer tied the makeshift bandage around his forehead, and Nelan pulled his hat down to cover it.

"Can you stand? Yeah, you can," Brewer said. "You look fit an' ready to ride to London now. You can't let the admiral down."

"I have to find Eleanor."

"You gotta go t' Barn Elms. The Admiral's message is more important than you and me. Besides, you promised."

"I know."

"You still got it?"

Nelan searched his purse and pulled out the scroll. "Yes, here it is." And he also had Drake's clemency document. Oh, the travails of divided loyalty!

"Then you knows what you gotta do, lad. See over there? That's your 'orse. He's all saddled up and ready to go. I gotta leave now. You'll see Master Walsingham gits the admiral's message, won't you?"

Nelan nodded, and John Brewer left.

Nelan couldn't stay in Plymouth; nor could he ride to London. Not yet, anyway. He opened the stable doors. Dusk drifted in with the onsetting tide. He had been out cold all afternoon. The harbourside was heaped with garbage. The crowd had moved into the local inns. The quay was stacked high with cargo stuffed in barrels and crates, alongside lifting gear and marine equipment. It was loaded with cast-offs, old sailcloth, ripped tents and broken barrels. Hungry seagulls swept the area for scraps. The lights of the tavern lanterns flickered on the choppy waters of the Sound. Nelan's life had split down the middle: he was half looking for vengeance and half seeking love.

He headed into The Sailors' Return. The crew and their friends and relatives were jammed into every corner like biscuits in a barrel. There were noisy disputes over card games, songs of celebration, fights over bets, drinking of tankards, and eating of beef. A man played the pipes while another plucked the lute. A group of sailors had their arms around each other's shoulders, dancing on the tabletops while singing

'A-Rovin', A-Rovin" at the tops of their voices. Well, they'd traversed the world; all the way round and back again. Who else could say that? What an achievement! They made merry. They boasted. They shouted down the rafters. They thumped the tables and bear-hugged one another. They fondled their lovers and kissed their almost-forgotten wives. They had stories to tell – tales of wonder, derring-do and treasure. Strange stories of strange peoples in strange lands; of mists, mutiny and the Miwok. It was a unique welcome party.

"Did you see my Eleanor? Or that cad Pedro?" Nelan pleaded with the crew.

Most were in no fit state to recall anything. He learned nothing about the Don or his Eleanor. Attracted by the sheer quantity of ale and sack, the crew's friends and relatives had crammed into the inn and a variety of local ruffians had joined the party: a man with a limp, another with one hand, a third with a scar down his cheek, a few shady-looking cutpurses, and a gaggle of cackling geese.

Nelan pushed his way back outside. The evening air was cool, and a light mist rose from the Sound. Gusts of wind blew across the quay, bringing the familiar smell of salt to his nostrils. He should have felt elated, but he was distraught. When his dreams had drawn so near, they had been snatched from his grasp. An unexpected squall had driven them away. Instead of a joyous homecoming that marked the beginning of a new journey, the events on the quayside had once again spun the threads of his life into a maelstrom. He stared out to sea, the dark waves rolling in mirroring the thoughts clouding his mind.

He walked across to the top of the quay steps, where Thomas Drake waited for a skiff to dock.

"What are you still doing here, lad?" Thomas asked.

"I got knocked out. Didn't Tom or John Brewer tell you?"

Thomas shook his head and said, "No. When you left me, I was reading out the names of those hands who'd died on the voyage."

"And you called out my name," Nelan said. "You should have called out 'Great Nelan' or 'Nelan Andersen'. Not just 'Nelan'."

"Oh, did I do that? Sorry, lad. It was crucifying for those poor women. The place was a vale of tears, and the emotion choked on me."

"I'm looking for my Eleanor. Did you see her?"

"A woman asked after you. She didn't say her name."

Hope at last. He'd found her. "That's wonderful. Where is she?"

"I don't know. I told her you were away to deliver a message."

"But why?"

"Because that's what you told the admiral you'd do. When you left me, I guessed you were heading for the stables before riding off."

"I *am* going to London, but I must find her first. Did you tell her I was going to Barn Elms?"

"No, not especially. I just told her you was off to London."

Nelan puffed out his cheeks. "I don't believe this. It's so cruel. She was with me. We were together."

"I didn't know, lad."

"Well, did you see a young man? He'd be my age, swarthy complexion and black hair. Name of Pedro?"

"No," Thomas said. "But listen, lad, you're late. You have to go and deliver the admiral's letter."

"The sun's set," Nelan protested. "I can't ride in the dark."

"That may be, but this delay will put the admiral in a bad humour."

"I'll set off at dawn," Nelan murmured.

He had the night to find her… and him. He had been looking forward to enjoying his new-found freedom and the riches that accompanied it, but instead he had three days of hard riding ahead. Before that, he had until dawn to find Eleanor, and not a moment to waste. She could still be in the vicinity, as could Pedro.

It rained through the night; at first a drizzle, and then a deluge. It didn't stop Nelan. He scoured the stables, the inns, the streets, the Hoe, the warehouses, the town square – everywhere he could think to look. He peered behind rubbish heaps and old barrels. He poked his nose in every church. He searched the quay again. Eleanor was nowhere to be found. Nor was Pedro. They had disappeared as quickly as they had appeared.

Nelan had an inkling that Eleanor would have set off back to London, so that was where he needed to go. He'd warned her about Pedro, and in a way he was glad she'd listened to him and run off. As long as she was safe. It broke his heart to think that he had been so near to and yet so far from reuniting with her. Without her, he was alone in the world with no one to share his silver and gold. Were those riches hollow trophies of material success?

237

And what of the unexpected appearance of Pedro de Antón? There was only one way he could have known that Nelan had crewed on the *Golden Hind*. St John of Southampton must have written to his stepson, and Pedro had sought out Nelan to gloat and for vengeance. The young Spaniard reminded Nelan of an untamed horse: feral and unpredictable; a lethal threat not only to Nelan's fortunes, but to England's. And he had the gall to confess to Nelan that he'd set the fire that had killed Laurens. Nelan gripped his anger in his fists. Pedro must be brought to justice for the murder of his father. Nelan would see that he was.

The night passed far quicker than he'd hoped. Soon, the first splash of dawn appeared on the horizon, and neither Eleanor nor Pedro had surfaced. Drenched to the bone, Nelan pushed wearily against the stable door. Through the wall, he heard singing, shouting and drumming. Those in The Sailors' Return had caroused through the night and into the dawn.

He adjusted the girth on the saddle of his horse. The mark of the salamander on his right palm itched, and he scratched it. Nothing happened, but he knew that the time would come for him to employ the arts he'd acquired. He had faith in Dee's prediction that he would have a part to play in the unfolding of England's future, and that it would somehow involve the angels of the island.

But for now he would head for Barn Elms. Many a time he'd passed the manor house on his way to and from Westminster School, but had never met its owner, Francis Walsingham, nor been inside it. Both those things were about to change. He led the stallion out of the stables, careful not to slip after the overnight rain. Nearly three years ago, he'd sailed out of Plymouth Sound, hiding his identity as a wanted man, and with a quiver of queries. Now, he'd returned as a free man armed with a fresh batch of unanswered questions. Across the waters of the Sound, he saw the silhouette of a ship; one he knew so well: the *Golden Hind*. Drake was sailing it up the River Tamar to store the treasure at Trematon Castle.

Nelan had wrapped up some of his unfinished business, but events had conspired to open up a lot more. After fulfilling his mission for the admiral, he resolved, he would find again and marry his beloved

Eleanor. Then he'd return to Mortlake, claim his father's land as his own, build a house, and start a family with her. All the while, he'd keep a wary eye on the Dons. Drake's exploits in the Pacific had wounded but not defeated them. No, not at all. The desire to avenge his mother's death burned in Nelan's heart as intensely as ever. What he'd seen over the past three years of the Spanish Empire and their terrible treatment of natives had only served to confirm that conviction. He had witnessed at first hand the spread of their power across the Americas. King Philip's motto was *Non Sufficit Orbis*: for the Don, the world was never enough. That alarming greed opposed John Dee's vision of a British Empire; a common wealth. Nelan would fight for that vision and keep England free from Spanish invasion. He trod the soil of the Island of Angels, and there he'd stay. He had no desire to sail again; at least not on such a long voyage. He loved England and wanted to engage with her angels – and his Eleanor was one of them. Her father had told Nelan that after the bakery fire.

And the mark of the salamander would help him to do that, alongside the skills and learning he'd acquired when wearing the shoes that never wore out. He realised that he was not a single body. Yes, he occupied a physical body, but it contained an ethereal or astral body. In the physical realm there was birth and death and coming and going, but in the astral realm there was only a continuum in which everything was permanent and nothing ever died or wore out. Travelling in the astral realm meant wearing the shoes that never wore out, and there he could summon the salamanders to defeat the Dons, right the terrible wrongs of his parents' murders, and bring about Dr Dee's vision of the limits of empire. In that realm, the astral body moved like quicksilver, yielding omens and prophecies of the future.

The rite of baptism was engraved on Nelan's thoughts. When performed at birth, it protected the infant's soul from evil throughout its days on earth. It provided a lifelong cocoon, allowing safe growth and development. Baptism was a sacred protection during a journey from one place to another; from birth to death. And what of circumnavigation? That had been another baptism of fire for Nelan and all the *Hind*'s hands. The admiral had hauled the mariners from the sealed confinement of an old era into the open seas of a new one. He had rediscovered discovery. His circumnavigation provided safe passage from one era into the next; in that sense, it had been a baptism for the Island of Angels too. Drake had led not only the crew, but all of England through a hellhole into the calm blue vista of a new permission for them as individuals and as a nation. He had sailed westwards around the world, not eastwards, and so had followed the course of the sun on its journey around the planet. Always with the rising sun at his back, he had passed through the gate of all 360 lines of longitude. In so doing, he had been washed in the sacred essences of the planet, just as, in baptism, a person was cleansed by the latest religious issue from the universe. So, the circumnavigation represented a different – and unique – kind of baptism.

The prospect of fighting the Dons again excited Nelan. According to Regiomontanus's prophecy, this would culminate in 1588 – in eight years' time. Leaving his drunken shipmates behind, he mounted the stallion and rode off on a new journey.

Acknowledgements

A novel is a curious mix of love and discipline, patience and impetuosity, clarity and obfuscation. This one is no different.

The initial idea for it came to me in September 2020, and was born out of a long-standing fascination with the significance of Tudor times in England's unfolding history. I applied the finishing touches to the novel in December 2022.

The Mark of the Salamander owes many things to many people, not least my nearest and dearest, Irene Jones, for her understanding and consideration.

Thanks too to my constant friends, whose ears were regularly bent by my procrastinations: Nick Deputowski, Jackie Carriera, Nick Calthrop and James Harries. Thanks too to Christine Pearce and Karni Zor for their considerable help with the astrological aspects of the story, and their enthusiasm for the project.

Beta readers are a special breed unto themselves. They selflessly read other people's manuscripts with a view to improving them. Hence, my sincere thanks go to Jennifer Pittam, Jonathan Posner, Jan Potts and Lilyan Arcier, with an especial mention for Carly Heilan and Nicole Hoepner, who both read two drafts of the novel.

Michael Turner and his In Drake's Wake website helped me correct many details of Francis Drake's circumnavigation.

A special thanks to the copy editor and proof reader whose eye for detail improved the manuscript, and to Paula López, who assisted in translating the Spanish. And to the Wolf family for their help in a final proofread.

Finally, I want to say a few kind words about Fiction Feedback, led by the inimitable Dea Parkin. Thanks to Matthew for his in-depth structural editing report, which helped strengthen the character arcs and plot line, and resolve many of the weaknesses in the earlier drafts of the novel.